THE PROMETHEUS DECEPTION

By Ivan Tritch

Novels

The Cain Connection
The Thought Network
The Reaper's Folly
The Woods
The Prometheus Deception
Final Shift
The Pilomotor Reaction

Collection

Dark Tapestries

Non-Fiction

WTF, Are You *Thinking?*
The Philosophies of an Ordinary Man

The Prometheus Deception

a novel

Ivan Tritch

The Prometheus Deception

Copyright © 2023 Ivan Tritch

All rights reserved. No part of this book may be reproduced
in any form, except for the inclusion of brief quotations
in a review, without permission in writing
from the author or publisher

Heartsbane Publications

*This book is for some good men,
who also happen to be my sons:*

Chance
Tyler
James
Lucas
Matthew
Ethan

*Guys, I used your names,
in this order, for some of the
characters in this story.*

I hope you don't mind.

*What an absurd thing it is to pass
over all the valuable parts of a man,
and fix our attention on his infirmities.*
—Addison

*There is nothing by which
men display their character
so much as in what they
consider ridiculous.*
—Goethe

*If we would read the secret
history of our enemies, we would
find in each man's life sorrow and
suffering enough to disarm all hostility.*
—Longfellow

*There is so much good in the worst of us
and so much bad in the best of us,
that it ill becomes any of us
to find fault with the rest of us.*
—Unknown

BEFORE

The screams of his wife and the hiss of the radiator blended together to create a terrible sound that increased the man's anxiety and fear. Her pains were quickening and, as if going into labor in the middle of a Nevada desert wasn't enough, the baby's head was beginning to crown.

The radiator had overheated a mile back with a sound like the tired breath of a dragon, and the car had stalled moments later. The man had been furious, but when his wife's labor pains began the anger dissipated, and he began to help with her breathing exercises. The heat in the car was fierce. Sweat rolled off his face, as though he were sharing her labor.

The man knew about breathing, but little about delivering a child. It appeared she would have it here on the side of the highway, and he knew they would need water.

As a contraction wracked the woman, she babbled something at the man.

"What?" he said.

She shook her head and pointed over his shoulder, out the rear glass.

Two vehicles were approaching from the east. The man could see, through the shimmering heat, men dressed in military fatigues. A man on the passenger side of the first vehicle was making some kind of gesture, flailing his hands and arms.

After a moment, the man realized he and his wife were being motioned to move...or get out the way...something. "I think we have to go."

"What?" she panted. "*Help* me."

He cast an anxious look at her, and then at the vehicles, which were Army jeeps in desert camouflage. The passenger in the first one was still waving, and seemed frantic. Both men wore listless, grim expressions.

The man's wife screamed as she was rocked by another contraction, and he got out of the car, turned toward the oncoming jeeps, and began waving his own arms. "Hey! *Help. Help us.*"

The lead jeep skidded to a halt beside the couple's vehicle. The second stopped behind it.

"Sir, you need to move this vehicle," said the soldier behind the wheel of the first jeep. "This is a restricted area."

"Restri—*What?*" the man said. "This happens to be highway—"

"*Now,*" the soldier barked.

The man noticed the apprehensive look on the face of the other soldier, whose eyes were skittish, as if some imaginary thing was chasing him.

"But our car broke down, and my wife's having a baby. *We need help.*"

"There's no time for that."

"But—"

"*Move!*"

And in the next instant, from the east, came a brilliant light. All-encompassing, without color, it engulfed everything in its path. It blinded the man and the woman, who had been able to do nothing but look into the intense flash.

The last thing the man saw was an image of the sand cooking into molten glass, and the thought that came with it followed him down into a silent, white void.

The sun. The sun.

*****

ONE

Ken and Valerie Malcolm were both nervous and excited as they drove in to town. The phone call from the adoption agency was more than a little responsible for their queasy stomachs, ceaseless pacing—this from Ken, while he waited for her to get ready—and nervous titters.

After eight long years they were going to be parents.

"Did you remember the video camera?" Valerie said. She prided herself on being organized, but today she felt scatter-brained. The thought of finally holding her own child created more delirium and joy than she could contain.

"I put it in the car while you were doing your hair," Ken told her. He possessed a sad, oblong face, as though the years of trying—and failing—to make a baby had left a physical mark. Now, his gray eyes were full of life, and when he smiled his face was transformed into that of the happy young man she had married.

They traveled down Woodsprings Road, which led to Highway 63 and downtown Jonesboro. Late morning sun sparkled off passing vehicles and transformed the trees on either side of the road into twinkling foliage that seemed almost magical.

It *felt* like a magical day. It was all too easy to remember the endless trips down this same road: trips to the doctor, to the fertility specialists, to the pharmacies, to the adoption agency itself. Their first trip to the agency had been more than four years ago.

"I'm so glad we're getting a boy," Ken said as they stopped at the intersection of Woodsprings and the 63 Bypass. "Not that it matters," he added.

"It doesn't," Valerie said. She could not quit smiling. The muscles in her face ached from maintaining that rare position.

"I would have been just as happy with a little girl," Ken said.

She leaned over the armrest and placed a delicate kiss on his cheek. "I know. I love you."

"I love you, too."

She leaned her head against his shoulder, thinking good thoughts. And still smiling.

Traffic was light in town, and they arrived at Smalley's Adoption Agency (*A Friend for Life* in small block letters on the sign, beneath the agency's name) a little after eleven.

Adoption was a big event for those involved, and Smalley's was known to be conscientious about the intimacy of the procedure. Therefore, the agency had made arrangements for not only the Malcolms to be at their offices this morning, but also their family physician, as well as the fertility specialist they had used. The agency would also provide a video record of the event, as a gift to Ken and Valerie (she had read of these personal touches a few years back, but they had seemed secondary to her, at the time—still were, truth be told).

Since Valerie could not conceal her excitement as they walked through the agency's doors for what seemed the hundredth time, she didn't try. Even watching another couple exit the building, somber-faced and unsmiling, did nothing to alleviate it, although she could sympathize with the couple. She and Ken had worn that same look for the past eight years, ever since they'd first realized they were having problems getting pregnant. It sometimes felt as though they had always worn the look—that it belonged solely to them. Thinking those thoughts now made Valerie's smile feel false, as though she were masquerading and would soon be caught.

Julia Mansfield met them at the receptionist desk. She was African-American, with attractive blue eyes and long black hair pulled back in a fluffy ponytail. Her eyes twinkled with a facsimile of the happiness the Malcolms felt. She shook Ken's hand and encircled both of Valerie's with her own elegant hands. "I know how excited you must be, so we won't waste time. Let's go back and see him."

Ken and Valerie looked at each other and grinned.

Julia led them down a corridor at the back of the office. From behind one of the doors came the sound of a baby crying.

Valerie reached for Ken's hand and squeezed it, and he put an arm around her shoulders.

His smile was radiant. Valerie could not remember the last time he had smiled that way. Ken laughed and smiled on occasion, but for a long time there had been something missing from those emotions. His new smile was refreshing. Valerie suspected that, in his eyes, she looked just as happy.

They came to the last door on the left and went inside. The first thing Valerie saw was a crib, at the eastern end of the room beside the only window, and a tiny pair of hands reaching up into the empty space above them, where sunlight fell at a slant into the room. The little pink fists shook as the baby cried.

Dr. Ricter, their family physician, and Dr. Caldwell, the fertility specialist, sat on a plush sofa on the opposite side of the room. They were conferring with each other (Valerie abhorred the fact that they both seemed to be ignoring the baby), and they looked up as Ken, Valerie, and Julia entered the room. A video camera sat atop a tripod across the room from the crib, taking in everything with a wide-angle lens.

The baby stopped crying when Ken and Valerie reached the crib, as though sensing its new parents. They had seen photos of him, of course, and as in the photos, the scars on the child's face were nearly invisible. The baby had survived a fire, which took his natural parents, and had required extensive surgery on his face and neck, but according to Julia Mansfield he'd had the best doctors.

To Valerie it didn't matter. She had fallen in love with the child in the photographs and now, looking down at the beautiful baby, she grew even more attached.

"Oh, Ken, he's so precious," she said.

And he was. His skin had a healthy pink complexion and was smooth, save for the faint traces of the scars that ran from his chin to beneath his ear on either side of his round face. His eyes twinkled like precious stones.

As they looked down at him, the baby smiled.

Valerie reached down and picked him up...and from that moment it felt so natural holding him that it didn't matter to her if he hadn't come from her own womb. She felt that, although exhaustive tests had shown there to be nothing wrong with her, or her husband's, reproductive system, she was meant to have only this baby.

Somehow it just felt right.

The room grew quiet as Valerie held her new son, and the silence was as golden as the sunlight filtering through the window above the crib.

Julia Mansfield broke it in a low voice. "Congratulations, Mr. and Mrs. Malcolm."

"Here, here," said Dr. Ricter in a loud baritone voice. He raised a glass of what could have been either sparkling water or white wine.

The baby ogled at his new parents.

Julia put a hand on Valerie's shoulders. "As I told you last week, his name is Chester. You do have the option of changing his name. That's up to you. And of course he will take the surname of Malcolm."

Valerie looked at her husband. "We do have a name picked out for him. His name will be Chance. A fine name, don't you think?"

Ken grinned. "Chance Malcolm. Yeah. A perfect name all the way around."

*****

For his part, Ken felt overwhelmed, and he experienced a surrealness that resembled a heightened state of awareness. It was like being in a waking dream. He had felt something similar to this for days, but it was enhanced a hundred-fold at his first look at the baby in the crib. Strangely, the feeling contained a large measure of relief; not because the adoption process was finally over but because when he first entered the room, he thought the crib was empty, in spite of the child's cries. A detached part of his mind knew he was simply seeing the crib at home that had waited, empty, for so long. However brief, it was for some reason disturbing. Then the indescribable joy when he saw the baby looking up at them. A new feeling, like a long circle completed; something never experienced.

He remembered their first trip to Dr. Ricter's office. They had been trying for about three months to get pregnant, without success, before deciding (with more than a little trepidation and anxiety) to see their doctor and determine whether anything was physically wrong with either of them. Ricter, a glass of sparkling water or wine on his desk, had pronounced them both fertile, and recommended that they keep trying. He told them to try not to think so much about getting pregnant, to just let nature take its course.

But it was hard not to think about it.

After two more months without conception, they had been almost heartbroken, sure that something *must* be wrong with one of them, or both. They saw Ricter again and he prescribed fertility pills at Ken's request, although the physician still insisted that measure was unnecessary. Four months later, appearing befuddled, he referred them to a fertility specialist.

Ken had begun to watch other parents and their children whenever he and Valerie were in town. Most parents with small children had a glow about them which Ken was certain only he could see. He was also sure that 'aura of happiness' was not visible on his own countenance. He often wondered if his dark aura—which is how he perceived it—was as visible to the parents he watched as their glow was to him. He came to the conclusion it must be, for more than once a mother with small children caught him watching her children, and gathered them protectively around her as she moved down a supermarket aisle, glancing back at Ken as though he were a child molester scouting out new victims.

Ken had, of course, felt envious of—and even a shameful, mild anger toward—those parents who doted around with their children in hand, unconscious of how lucky they were (he had once seen a young lady at a supermarket in town with *four* children in tow—how fair was *that?*). It seemed easy to take children for granted. Unless you had none, that is.

But now they had little Chance. After long months of searching for the right name, this one felt perfect and, yes, obvious.

They had applied for adoption a little over four years ago. Julia Mansfield had been their caseworker from the beginning, and she told them right up front how long the waiting list was and, perhaps more importantly, how long the wait could be on a mental level. On average, a couple wishing to adopt a baby less than a year old had to wait 2.5 years. The Malcolm's eager waiting period had been on the high side of the average, lasting eighteen months longer.

Ken felt it had been well worth the wait.

In fact, all that had been missing from their life together was a child to occupy the nursery in the upstairs bedroom of their home; a nursery which had been ready, but empty, for so long.

Now their life felt complete.

* * * * *

"When can we take him home?" Valerie said.

Julia smiled. "I just need a few more signatures on your way out, for the name change." She spread her arms, palms up. "After that, you're free to take him home. With our most sincere congratulations."

"Thank you."

"Are you going to let me hold him, Honey?" Ken said.

She handed the baby to him, and although Ken had only held a baby this small three times in his entire life (a cousin's daughter), Valerie thought he looked natural, as if he had always been a father, and for many years.

He's still not a father, she thought, *but he's a daddy, and somehow that's more important.*

They took pictures with everyone in the room before returning to the front office to sign the rest of the papers. Dr. Ricter wished them luck and happiness. "I'll want to see him in my office for a checkup in a couple of months," he said with a stern smile. He tossed back the last of his sparkling water or wine.

"You can count on it," Valerie said.

Outside, as Ken was unlocking the car doors, he looked across the roof of the vehicle at Valerie and she saw happiness emanating from his face. She couldn't remember him ever smiling for such a long stretch of time.

They left the agency, baby Chance now sound asleep in the new car seat, and Valerie thought how everything she and Ken had been through was worth this moment. It atoned for everything.

Everything.

* * * * *

As the Malcolms left Smalley's Adoption Agency, a man parked in a gray sedan across the street at a *Grizzly Adams* restaurant made a notation in a small, leather-bound notebook. When this was finished, he turned off the small recording device located under the ashtray and unhooked the wires from the portable receiver mounted on the dash. He removed the receiver and tossed it in the glove box.

He ran a finger through his mustache: his thinking mode. His name was John Milcheck, and he was ready to get back home. His eyes could not be seen through the dark glasses he wore, and he looked into the mirror over the dash and wiped a dab of barbecue sauce from his chin. Anyone who bothered to look at him twice would only see a man enjoying an early lunch in the comfort and convenience of his vehicle.

When he finished eating, he keyed the ignition. It would be good to get out of this town and back to Virginia, where another assignment would be waiting. He—or another agent—might still be required to monitor the Malcolm's periodically (so he had been told), but only when an occasion called for it. The agency was certain that there *would* be occasions, but John was not so sure. He didn't know much about this case—he was filling in on the assignment for an agent who had taken ill—but it looked and sounded to him as though nothing out the ordinary had happened today; a couple had adopted a baby.

He hoped his next assignment would be more exciting. He was a well-trained professional of the Central Intelligence Agency, and this appeared, to him, to be unimportant work. It had that particular feel about it (perhaps one, or both, of the parents, was in the Witness Protection Program, or something similar—who knew? Not John). But he reminded himself of some slow assignments in the past that had turned into the exciting work he preferred.

Maybe this would be one of them.

He pulled out of the parking lot and headed out of town.

* * * * *

Ken and Valerie arrived home thirty minutes later. The tree-lined street was quiet. Most of their neighbors were at work, and the stillness was peaceful. Birds twittered and cawed from the trees, instilling the late morning with a freshness which neither of them had noticed in a long time.

Their home was near the end of Cedar Lane, on the left side of the street. Set twenty yards back from the sidewalk, the two-story structure sat upon a well-manicured lawn. Flowers flanked the walk in neat, narrow beds; tulips, begonias, daisies, and Easter lilies. Ken and Valerie had both spent a lot of time in their yard, as if planting flowers and shrubs could make up for the one seed that could not get planted. Great oak and maple trees were sprinkled randomly across the large yard, the back of the property was bordered with an eight-foot-high cedar fence, and the lush green lawn dipped into a small, graceful valley to the rear. The homes in the neighborhood were for the most part older homes, similar to one another in size and acreage, with enough space between each to provide adequate privacy.

Ken smiled at her "Here we are."

Chance stirred in her arms. Apparently, the gentle movement of the

Volvo had kept him lulled. His small hands opened and closed, as though reaching for an unseen toy or face. As the three of them went inside the house, he began to cry.

Valerie had purchased bottles, diapers, bathing supplies, and other items for the baby just two weeks ago, and while Ken took Chance to the living room, she went out to the kitchen to prepare some cereal and a bottle of formula.

The kitchen was done in pastels; pink, light green, blue and orange. The cabinets were oak, and the necessities inside were all arranged meticulously, with thought, so that whatever was needed was within easy reach in an ordered place. Valerie grabbed a bottle from a cabinet and poured formula into it from a can she retrieved from the shelf above the plastic bottles.

Ken had the baby lifted high over his head when she entered the living room. She was startled at first, but as she watched he brought the baby down, face to face with him, and made a funny noise—"goody goody goo"—at Chance. The baby goggled merrily, and then Ken lifted him over his head again and repeated the game.

"I think he likes me," he said when he noticed her standing in the entryway. At the pause in the game, Chance began to cry.

"Okay," Ken said. He lifted the baby up. Brought him back down. "Goody goody goo!"

Chance giggled.

"You're going to spoil him," Valerie said, smiling. She went over and sat down beside him on the soft blue sofa.

"No more than I spoil you," Ken said, returning her smile. He lifted the baby. Brought him down. "Goody goody goo!"

"Oh, please," Valerie said. "Me? Spoiled? I don't know."

"You know it," he said.

"Well, we do have a baby now. I guess I'm a *little* spoiled."

"Anything for my dear wife."

"You're rotten," she said.

"No, just spoiled, like yourself."

"And Chance?"

"I'm working on spoiling him, too," he said.

"Well, it's time for that spoiled baby's lunch."

"Okay."

He handed Chance to her with obvious reluctance. She could tell Ken had already grown attached to the baby, and what did it matter that he had not fathered him? Before he'd held Chance in his arms for the first time, it somehow *had* mattered. Not anymore.

"I need to buy him a baseball glove," Ken said as she spooned cereal into Chance's mouth. The baby took the food without any dribbling down his chin.

Valerie said, "I think we should wean him from the bottle and let him grow up a little first."

"It's never too early to start him on baseball," Ken said with a playful smugness. "I can get him a glove and it will be here when he's big enough for it."

"Which is how long from now?" Valerie said.

"Oh, about three months, give or take."

"And how will you know which hand to buy for?"

"Easy. He's going to be a southpaw, just like his daddy.

"You think so?"

"Definitely, absolutely, and positively. Plus, he's using his left hand to reach for the spoon."

They both laughed, and the rest of the afternoon and evening of their first day with Chance rolled along in pretty much the same fashion. They took turns holding and playing with him, and when they laid him down for an afternoon nap, the two of them made love that was sweeter and more passionate than it had been in months, quite possibly years. No longer was the thought of failure on their minds, worrying about whether or not this would be the time that they succeeded at what had for so long been—for whatever unknown reason—out of reach. They explored lost passions while re-discovering the need for each other's warmth, something neither had experienced for ages. They felt like the luckiest parents in the world.

They lived a happy life in the months ahead as a family.

Together.

And it felt right.

They had no way of knowing that everything they said in their home was being monitored and closely scrutinized.

And it was eight months before the first strange thing happened.

* * * * *

TWO

Chance was fourteen months old.

A quiet child, who had slept almost every night straight through since the adoption, and rarely cried, he now sported a full head of fine blonde hair.

Ken and Valerie had celebrated his first birthday by inviting over a few friends, as well as each of their parents. Chance's adoptive grandparents were competitive, as if to see who could spoil him the quickest, and so far it was a close race. At least in Ken's opinion. "Oh, they're just showing him grandparents' affection," Valerie had countered when he voiced this concern to her. On that particular day, his father had brought two new stuffed animals for Chance; a puppy, and an E.T. doll. Chance's room was beginning to look like a game booth at the county fair. It seemed to Ken that Darrel Malcolm brought the baby a new toy every time he came to visit.

Valerie's parents were just as bad, if not worse. Beatrice Holman bought new clothes, toys, or both, for her grandson on a regular basis, and although it was obvious that she loved him, Ken thought he could see a look in her eyes at times: *Chance is nearly a perfect baby, but when you and Valerie make one of your own* it *will be a true family member, a real grandchild with Holman and Malcolm blood.*

For their own part, Ken and Valerie settled into the difficult yet gratifying job of parenting as though they were slipping into a pair of comfortable loafers, although there had also been some trial and error, when their inexperience shone through (when Chance began cutting teeth, Valerie had called her mother for advice on how to stop his pain and crying). But for the most part, things rolled along real well. Chance learned to walk rather early—at nine months—and they both looked forward to him eventually being potty-trained. And, like all babies, he got into things he shouldn't and had to be taught which things were 'no-no's' and which were 'okay'.

It was during the second week of April of that year when Chance disappeared for a short time. Later, after it happened, that was the only explanation Ken could give the unusual occurrence. Valerie had not really witnessed the event, and Ken himself would forget about it altogether until a few weeks later, when he was forced to take a different view.

* * * * *

It was a fine spring day. The winter had been a mild one for inclement weather, with only two major snowfalls in northeast Arkansas. What hadn't let up for months were the bitterly cold temperatures that bit into the area like sharp, jagged teeth. Today was the first temperate day of the year, and so the Malcolms decided to get outdoors for a while. It was a Saturday, about eleven o'clock. The sun was high in the late morning sky and a light, warm breeze blew through the trees. Birds frolicked in the branches overhead.

They had decided to have lunch outside on the picnic table at the rear of their property, where a stone grill was erected near the fence on the east side of the yard. Ken cleaned it out and then built a fire with new coals while Valerie set up Chance's playpen close to the table.

He tottered around the yard while his parents made preparations for lunch, and he made brief inquiries to them both; "Mommy?" Daddy?" Those were his two best-pronounced and most frequently used words in a growing vocabulary that included 'toys' (pronounced *toes*), 'eat', 'what', and 'water' (*wa-wa*).

Ken watched Valerie open the playpen and lay a blanket and some of Chance's favorite toys inside. She scooped him up and placed him on the padded bottom, where he grabbed a rattle and shook it vigorously. Then, her back to the toddler, she went about setting items on the table; buns, mustard, ketchup, pickles, paper plates, napkins, and mayonnaise.

When Ken had the grill hot, he went into the house to get the hamburger meat that Valerie had made into patties earlier, as well as two hotdogs for Chance, who had enough teeth now to do justice to what he ate.

The meat was on the kitchen counter, and Ken glanced out the window over the sink into the back yard as he picked up the plate of three patties. Valerie's back was to him as she arranged things on the table, but Chance was nowhere to be seen.

He squinted, looked harder.

No Chance.

Valerie had put him in his playpen. Ken himself had patted one of the youngster's cheeks on his way up to the house. Chance had hit his hand with the rattle in return and giggled up at him.

Now he was gone.

The window was open and Ken thought about calling through the screen to his wife and inquiring about the whereabouts of their young son. Then he realized that she had probably taken him out of the playpen and let him toddle around some more, and he had wandered out of Ken's field of vision. And he could hear the faint rattle of the child's toy.

Well, he would see when he went back out. It was nothing to be alarmed about.

He carried the burgers out the door, trying to determine which one was bigger, and thus his.

He stopped on the outside stoop.

The door banged shut behind him.

Chance was in his playpen. He was shaking the rattle back and forth. Ken could hear it over the moving branches of the wind-blown trees.

Now hold on a minute, here.

He took slow steps down the stone path which led to the table and grill, to his wife and son—his son, who was right where he should be, where he *had* been when Ken went into the house: where he *hadn't* been when Ken looked out the window less than a minute ago.

That can't be right, he thought. *It didn't take me fifteen seconds to reach the back door, open it, look.*

He rubbed his eyes with his free hand, as if he could bring back the image of the empty playpen.

She put him back in the pen when you were on your way out, he told himself. But he knew that couldn't have happened, either. Chance had been nowhere near Valerie when Ken had noticed he wasn't in his pen. There hadn't been sufficient time for Valerie to walk to wherever Chance had been, pick him up, set him back in the playpen, and walk back to the table and resume what she was doing. No *way* had there been time enough for that.

So, what?

So, your mind played a trick on you, he told himself.

Right.

He put the burgers on the stone ledge next to the grill and re-moved a spatula from the small assortment of utensils Valerie had placed on one end of the table.

"Those sure look good," she said.

He was slow to respond. "Uh-huh."

"What's wrong?"

"Nothing," Ken said. He smiled. "Did Chance enjoy his little trip around the yard?"

A puzzled look crossed Valerie's face. She pulled a lock of hair over her right ear. "What trip?"

Ken's stomach sank. *Here we go again,* he thought. Images flashed through his mind: a long low sofa, a white room, followed by a blinding, swirling light that he could almost hear—a sense of vertigo.

He pushed ahead anyway, in spite of both Valerie's obvious ignorance, and the fact that his mind might be opening a door he would rather keep closed. "Didn't you let him out of his playpen while I was inside?"

"No," Valerie said. "But I did think about taking that rattle away from him. He's been going non-stop since he picked it up."

As if on cue, the rattling stopped. Chance grinned up at them. "Mommy? Daddy?"

Ken smiled back and then said: "Did you see him while I was in the house?"

Valerie put down the plate she was holding and cocked her head sideways. Her eyes were penetrating (Ken felt his stomach flutter with that one probing look; it was a look he'd hoped he would never again see). "What do you mean, did I see him? He's right there." She pointed to the playpen.

"But did you turn around and *look* at him?"

A frown glided across her face like the shadow of a passing cloud. "Ken, what's wrong? You're not making any sense."

"Just tell me if you did," he pressed.

Valerie sighed. "Are you sure everything is okay?"

Now his face framed a frown of its own, as though it had interpreted the implication of that question. "Just tell me, Val."

"No, I didn't turn around and look at him. I heard him though. He had that rattle going ninety-to-nothing." Now concern laced her voice. "What's this all about?"

"Well, when I was inside, I could have sworn…"

"What?"

He told her about what had happened, what he had seen—or thought he'd seen, at any rate.

When he finished he saw the doubt in her eyes. It had been a long time since she had looked at him that way. "Honey, maybe you just *thought* he was out of his playpen. Maybe it was the light, the way the sun was shining or something."

"I know what I saw," he said with uncharacteristic annoyance. "Chance was gone."

"Sweetheart," Valerie said in a gentle voice.

Ken held up his hands. "Okay. Maybe it was the light. Or maybe it's my eyes. I've been having headaches an awful lot lately."

This wasn't exactly true, but he thought he detected suspicion on her face and in her eyes. There *had* been a few stress-headaches in the months before the adoption, but none since.

"That might be it," she said.

"I probably need to go in for an eye exam. I haven't had one since junior high school."

"You're kidding."

"No." He put the patties on the grill and turned back to her, smiled. "That's probably all it is."

"Do you think?"

He brushed barbecue sauce onto the meat. "I don't know. It has to be something…or maybe nothing. I mean, he's right there in his playpen."

She walked up and put her arms around his waist, and that made him feel comfortable, safe. "I have an idea," she said.

"What?"

"Let's just enjoy the day, and our little picnic lunch, and forget about it. At least wait and talk about it later, okay?"

"Okay," he said after a second or two of thought. The patronizing tone in her voice, however, did not escape him, and he knew what she must be thinking: *Ken's losing his marbles again. It's his brother, Jimmy, all over again, only it's Chance this time. And so let's just pacify him and try to forget anything even happened—because it most likely* didn't. He pushed these unjustified thoughts aside with some reluctance. Whatever had happened—if anything had—it wasn't her fault, and why open old wounds?

The three of them ate lunch and stayed outside for a couple of hours afterward. They had purchased a ball glove and, although it was still too big for him, Chance chased tirelessly after the baseball that Ken rolled to him across the soft grass. The warmth of the sun was refreshing.

They didn't talk again—that night—about what Ken thought he saw (or didn't see). He had his eyes examined the following week, and they tested normal.

A few days after that, Ken forgot about the incident.

At least for a while.

* * * * *

On the twentieth of April, agent John Milcheck entered the offices of the Central Intelligence Agency and wondered as he got on an elevator why he was being called in from the case on which he was currently working. It was an embezzlement investigation on a prominent senator, and the case demanded he and four other agents' expertise and attention almost around the clock.

But the director had called him off the case, even though it was known to be a top priority on the agency's agenda. At least according to John's limited knowledge (which didn't run deep, in part—he suspected—because he was still considered 'the new guy' in the agency).

Nine months ago, he had monitored an adoption in Jonesboro, Arkansas, and he had been even 'newer' then. He had since forgotten all about that slow case. Because of this, he was caught off guard when he entered the director's office and discovered the adoption case was the reason he'd been called in from the field.

The CIA director, William Calhoun, was a large man, but solidly built. At six-feet-seven inches he towered over John's five-ten frame like one of the Greek gods: Zeus, perhaps. He wore a white short-sleeved shirt that showcased his massive biceps, black twill slacks that might have passed for a pair of pup tents, and a red tie that was loosened around his neck as though he'd been tugging at it. His salt-and-pepper hair was close-cropped, little longer than an army cut, and his eyebrows were bushy and of the same color.

John entered the room and stood in front of the director's desk. Calhoun rarely invited his agents to sit while in his presence. He himself stood, his chair tucked beneath his desk. When he leaned over and braced both hands on the wood grain finish, it made John feel like a small child; as though he were receiving a lecture from his long-dead father.

"There's been a development in a case you were involved in nine months ago," Calhoun said briskly.

"That would be—"

"Project Lone Star."

"I see," John said, going through mental files until he matched the name with some of his recent work. "The parents who adopted a baby." He vaguely remembered thinking what a dull job that had been. "I'm, ah, not very familiar with the details surrounding Lone Star."

"You monitored the adoption."

"Yes, sir. I recorded the event with a long-range listening device," John said. "However, my involvement never went any further." He shifted his weight to his left foot, wishing he could remember everything about the case. Had his involvement been so minimal? He wasn't sure, and he didn't want Calhoun to think he'd forgotten. "What's happened?" he asked.

"Computer printouts of the Malcolm's conversations on April seventeenth and eighteenth suggest that something significant has occurred."

John said: "Everything is still being recorded after nine months?"

"Of course," Calhoun said, as though John had asked if his name was William. "Not only that. Each day a hard copy is printed and stored in a highly classified filing room. Top secret." He paused, cocking his head at an angle. "You should know that, Milcheck."

John cleared his throat. "With all due respect, sir, I was never fully briefed on Project Lone Star. I was sent to Jonesboro, Arkansas, in place of agent Mark Lomax, who was too ill to travel at the time. I set up a long-range listening device at an adoption agency and recorded conversations until the adoption was complete. I then transferred the data to headquarters and returned for reassignment." He shifted his weight back to his right foot, mentally cursing for repeating himself in front of the director.

Had he known the family would be monitored on a continuing basis? He thought he might have, and if that was the case then his memory had grown stale, which *never* happened—and which was frowned upon in his line of work.

Calhoun began pacing behind his desk. He rubbed his chin with one hand and then tugged at his tie. "I wasn't aware you knew so little about Lone Star."

John shifted to his left foot. "What do you need me to do, sir?"

Calhoun frowned. He stopped pacing. "You don't know the history of Project Lone Star." It was not a question.

"No sir, but if you'll fill me in, I'll be more than happy to assist any way I can."

Calhoun rubbed his chin some more. Then he resumed tugging his tie. "There's not a lot of time to fill you in, although I'll need to. Not today, though. What I need right now doesn't require you to know any more than you currently do. I called for you because you handled the adoption. When we requisitioned that done, we failed to foresee that we might also need devices in the Malcolms' vehicles."

He handed John a small folder of documents. "These are makes and models, as well as photographs, of the Malcolms' vehicles. There is also a schedule in here of what times they are in and out of the house. They're pretty regular. But that isn't always sure enough. Study them to decide when the best times would be to supplant the tracking units."

"Tracking units?" John said.

"Just a precaution, for now. If anything significant happens in the near future, we need to be able to locate Ken and Valerie Malcolm—and the child, of course—on the chance that they're away from the house and our surveillance."

John sensed that this case was, perhaps, shaping up into one that had potential for excitement and danger. Well, at least some excitement. While he didn't shy away from danger on the job or off, he always hoped to avoid it, if possible. He only wished that he knew more about this case.

Calhoun opened a desk drawer and laid a small brown box on the desktop. "We need it done as quickly as possible. The president is breathing down my neck as it is."

"The president?" John said with a raised eyebrow. He knew he shouldn't use this tone with the director—questioning everything he was told—but he couldn't help it. What could be so important about an adoption in a city a thousand miles away?

"Yes," Calhoun said. "Lone Star is a very important project, and because there have been weak security measures thus far, the chief is afraid we're going to botch the whole thing. And he's not the only one worried. Frankly, I am, too."

John felt more confused. "But it's been nine months."

"Yes, it has," Calhoun said. "but we only discovered our mistake after what happened on the seventeenth. Everything is being monitored by computer, and you have to allow for an element of human error when it comes to letting a damn computer handle work best performed by a real agent."

"In other words—"

"In other words, someone fucked up."

John knew the director carried an old-school mentality. Calhoun had been in the CIA over twenty-five years, and with the arrival each year of new computer technology—most not available to the general public—his beliefs in the old way of doing things seemed to erode only marginally. He often told his agents how computers had aided the agency in the past, and were still the most reliable way to obtain—and hide—information, but they couldn't reason and think as well as the human mind.

Calhoun handed John a manila envelope. "Here are your plane tickets, car rental, and hotel reservations. You shouldn't have to stay more than one night, but it's good for two in the event you need more time to complete the assignment. I had to do some serious negotiating to get approval for the air fare. The *computer* says that we are already over budget."

John put the envelope in his left breast pocket, thinking: *Of course we're over budget—this* is *an arm of the government.* "And the hardware?"

Calhoun pointed to the small brown box on his desk. "You're a good agent, John. I know the case you were working on is important, but so is this. When you return from Arkansas, if nothing new has developed in the meantime, you can resume your work. If something *does* develop, I will more than likely call you back in and give you the entire background of Lone Star. I want minimal agents involved in this case, and no computer errors when it comes to dishing out assignments."

John stood up straight, his weight equally balanced, his nervousness gone.

"Your plane leaves in forty-five minutes," Calhoun said. "Be careful, be alert, get it done and get back."

"I will, sir." John picked up the box and the file folder and left.

When he got to his car, a white standard-issue government model, he looked over the papers in the file folder, hoping to find a clue that would tell him more about this case. There was nothing but traveling papers and a list of times the Malcolms were away from home. He wondered what the hell Project Lone Star was all about. As far as he could tell, the Malcolms were ordinary people who, like any normal couple who had trouble reproducing, had adopted a baby.

So, what was so important that it required involvement from the CIA?

Something, of course. But what?

As he got on the expressway toward the airport, he figured he would know soon enough, but he hated to operate without knowing what he was dealing with, and why.

No matter. He would find out.

* * * * *

THREE

John picked up his rental car—a beige Ford Tempo—at Memphis International Airport in Tennessee, and made the hour drive to Jonesboro, Arkansas.

It was eight-thirty when he reached the city limits. Darkness held the night in a moonless grip. A few miles ahead, the lights of the city glowed against the bottom of the sky like a yellow dome.

As he got on a service ramp off Highway 63—and from there onto Caraway Road—he marveled at how a city with slightly more than fifty thousand inhabitants could stay so clean and at the same time sport virtually every convenience known to man.

He remembered the literature he'd read about the city before his first trip to the area, and could see how it would appeal to Arkansans, as well as immigrants from other states.

Nestled in the foothills of Crowley's Ridge, the city was sprawled like a thrown dishtowel; gently sloping hills here, land as flat as desert plains there, more hills and dips and valleys and flatland. And all green and neat and *clean*. Tonight, he could see the downtown section and surrounding areas in clusters of lights that dazzled the eyes.

John decided to eat something before going out to the Malcolm's address across town, and he knew from his last trip here that Caraway Road was the place. His hotel reservations were at the Holiday Inn on Caraway and Phillips Drive, and there was a *Grecian Steak House* directly across from it. After checking in, he left his small suitcase on the bed and walked across the street to the steak house.

As he ate, he thought about how he would go about planting the tracking devices on the Malcolms' two vehicles. He studied their 'schedule' carefully, trying to pinpoint the best time. It looked like either three to three-thirty p.m. or five to five-fifteen p.m.

Or after everyone's asleep, he thought. *Not on the list here, but it's always a good time for things like this.*

It was also the time frame that was closest to now.

He decided he would drive out to their neighborhood and scout it out before choosing a time. That would be safest.

When he'd finished dinner, he drove out to the Malcolm residence, consulting a map from the folder of documents. He parked a block down and walked the rest of the way. The house was dark, not a light on anywhere, and it was then that he decided to go ahead and start what he came here to do. But that wasn't all. He wanted to go inside the house, have a look around, and see if he could find out anything about this intriguing case.

For many years he had been a private investigator in Rockford, Illinois, and his instincts had not faded with the passage of only a few years. Always a firm believer in thinking things out in great detail instead of being spontaneous, he would never contemplate jumping right into something like this with his pants down. He usually had more facts to work with, but something about this case piqued his curiosity like no other had in years.

What was this adoption really about, with its covert details and government involvement? He couldn't stand the fact that he knew so little. He felt a need to know what was going on, and his instincts told him that he could find out easily enough if he put his mind to it.

His senses were sharp and he trusted them. He would just have to be careful.

A quick check of the property told him that the house was not equipped with a security system of any kind, and that one of the two vehicles was gone. It was only slightly past nine o'clock. The Malcolms might be out for a late dinner, or perhaps visiting friends. He had time to reflect that, if this were the twenty-first century instead of 1996, there would probably be technological gadgets at his disposal that would make this type of work obsolete. He, for one, would rue the day that happened. Technology was very handy—and the agency had the newest and best at its disposal—but it couldn't replicate the adrenaline and endorphins that saturated the body when the work was exciting, dangerous.

A light breeze whispered through the trees which overhung the driveway. The sound reminded John of cool nights in the deep woods behind his grandparents' house, where sometimes the soft sigh of rustling leaves was the only sound for miles.

He calculated that he had a little time, but not much. Small children were not kept out late by their parents—especially on a weeknight—and the Malcolms were probably no different. Spacious lawns and small patches of trees separated the homes in the neighborhood, and John was grateful for the adequate cover.

He would first take care of the vehicle that was in the driveway. Later, after the Malcolms had returned and retired for the evening, he would come back and install the device in the vehicle they were currently in, which according to his files was a 1995 Volvo. The vehicle in the driveway was its older, paint-faded twin; possibly a mid-80's model.

John tried the driver's side door. It was unlocked, but the click of the latch was loud, and he paused before pulling it open to see if the noise had aroused any neighbors. He knew it was irrational to think anyone had heard the latch but he was pumped up with adrenaline now; his body felt tight, as if bound with ropes.

He opened the door and got in. An air freshener dangled from the rearview mirror, and the cloying smell of wild strawberries hit his senses with almost the force of a physical punch. He left the door open to eradicate some of the odor, keeping the toe of his shoe against the small button on the inside of the door frame to prevent the dome light from coming on. Feeling beneath the dash with his right hand, he found a relatively bare spot to mount the sophisticated device. He peeled off the strip of thin waxy paper from the adhesive on the back of the one-inch diameter device and, leaning across the front seat, mounted it under the glove box. It would be out of sight from any angle inside the car, and could only be found if a person knew for what he or she was searching.

That done, he exited the vehicle and began using a hanky—as a precaution—to wipe over everything he had touched.

This transmitter ran on a small, powerful battery similar to that of a watch, and could be activated either from a remote switch that John left in his pocket, or from the CIA compound, by laser signals sent through satellite relays. In this case, a four-digit code activated the small tracking devices on the vehicles, thereby conserving battery power. With this technology, the transmitter could last for years.

John wondered, not for the first time, where the CIA came up with some of these gadgets. Since his employment with the agency, he had seen—even used—many technological marvels; remote control lifting devices, ran by magnetized hovering mechanisms, whereby large loads of freight could be moved by hand, super computers that made the latest publicly available processors sick and slow by comparison. He had even heard that, somewhere in the government, a teleportation device had been invented and was being tested on a growing scale. He thought that was most likely a rumor, but you could never tell—not with Uncle Sam.

When he had wiped everything down, he went around to the back of the house. The ground was soft under his feet, but not enough to leave lasting footprints. Had it been too soft he would have had to break into the front door, and even though no one was home, he knew that to gain entry through the front would be nothing less than foolish. He reached the back patio in less than a minute, and then, breathing evenly and with confidence, he reached into his pockets for the tools that would get him inside.

* * * * *

Inside the house, Ken was almost asleep. He sat in the den, in front of the television set, where an episode of *MacGyver* was nearing its conclusion. MacGyver had gotten out of a tough situation in this episode —he had made a bomb out of a vapor rub cream, a shoestring, and a hardcover novel—but since it was a rerun, Ken's lack of interest caused drowsiness to settle over him like a heavy gray mass. Valerie was at the mall, Chance was asleep upstairs, and Ken had decided to take advantage of the rare time alone to relax in front of the tube—something he hadn't done in a long time.

Relaxation came easy in the den that occupied the center of the house. The room was small, fifteen by twenty, and windowless, with two wood swinging doors set from floor to ceiling at the south end of the room. Because the hallway outside the den was also windowless, no light protruded to the outside of the house. The room might have been intended as a study when the house was built, and was as cozy a den as a person could ask for. A plush sectional was centered in the room in front of a big screen television set, a luxury for which they were in debt (Ken had to have his shows as close to live as he could get). Peach marble lamps sat on oak tables at either end of the sofa, and the forty-watt bulbs gave off soft ample light that complimented the room's atmosphere. Bracketed by bookshelves, a stone fireplace graced the east wall. The effect of the room was soothing.

Ken had just dozed off for good when a noise in the back part of the house snapped him awake. The noise was slight, muffled, a slick scraping sound, as though someone were dragging their feet across the floor out there.

He dismissed the sound. He was too comfortable to get up and investigate. Besides, it was probably just the house settling. The wind was blowing around the eaves (he could hear that muted sound even over the television set) and that always created other noises throughout the house.

Then he heard another sound, this time from the hallway, right outside the doors to the den: Something bumped against the wall. Using the remote, he muted the TV and cocked his head to one side, listening. Another light thump, then a squeak. There were two or three boards in the hallway that squeaked when walked upon.

Valerie must have come home. He hadn't heard a car door, but she would have tried to be quiet on her way in, assuming that he and Chance had already turned in for the night. On top of that, the doors were all locked and she was the only other person who had a key.

Smiling, he clicked the TV off and headed for the door. "Val?" As he neared the door, he heard several unmistakable thumps—someone running down the hallway. He paused with one hand on the door. "Val?" he said again, this time with some unease.

No response.

Now he was positive that someone was in the house.

His heart trip-hammered against his chest. Whoever was in the house didn't belong there. A prowler? A burglar?

He looked around and went to the fireplace and picked up the poker from the small wrack of tools mounted on a brass base. He owned a handgun, but it was unloaded—and upstairs in his underwear drawer.

It still might only be Valerie, he reasoned. *She might not have heard me call her name.*

But he knew better.

Instinct told him it wasn't his wife who had run down the hallway. He knew Valerie almost as well as he knew himself, and which floorboards creaked in the hall. Whoever had been out there—whoever was *still in the house*—was much heavier than his wife.

He gripped the poker in his right hand and slowly pushed open the left door of the den. Shallow light spilled out into the hallway. Because his eyes weren't yet adjusted to the darkness, he was unable to tell one shadow from the next. The light switch was to his left, at one end of the dark hallway. He would have to rely on his hearing until his eyes adjusted to the gloom.

He felt his way along the hall until he felt the light switch with his free hand. He flicked it on and raised the poker high, prepared to ward off—or strike—any intruder or attacker.

The hallway was deserted. Soft yellow light illuminated the emptiness.

Ken didn't feel relieved in the slightest. He suspected the intruder had merely moved out of the hallway and into another area of the house, and his belief was confirmed when he heard the back door snick shut with a hollow click.

Mustering all his courage, he ran into the kitchen, one hand catching the light switch on the way through the door, and then stopped in the middle of the brightly-lit room. He stood alone in the room, no intruders or burglars in sight. The only noise, other than his adrenaline-induced breathing, was the ticking of the small clock over the stove. He hurried to the back door. It was locked. After turning on the yard light, he looked out the window over the sink and into the back yard. Nothing moved in the thick tapestry of darkness.

Maybe I'm hearing things.

But was he? *Had* someone been in the house?

Leaving the outside light on, he moved across the kitchen and then almost bashed himself with the poker when a loud knock came from the living room, at the front door.

He did not put the poker away when he passed the den on his way to the front of the house. Instead, he gripped it tighter.

The knock came again: three quick bangs that echoed through the hallway as if through a tunnel. As he passed the stairs at the other end, he heard Chance begin to cry. He turned to ascend the stairs, and then there were two more knocks at the door. These weren't as loud or persistent, as though whoever was out there had given up hope of anyone answering.

Shaking only slightly, Ken reached for the door with his free hand.

* * * * *

When John Milcheck found the back door locked, he pulled a small set of tools from his jacket and in no time had jimmied the lock.

Confident the house was empty, he walked through the dark room, finding his way into the hallway by the small amount of moonlight sifting through the kitchen windows and door.

He'd made it halfway down the hall in his attempt to find the stairs to the second floor (where he assumed the bedrooms were—the child's included, of course), when a noise to his right, behind two large doors, caught his attention. He put one ear to the wood and listened.

A television.

Someone *was* home.

Feeling more like an intruder than ever, he turned to backtrack the way he'd come in and his right arm brushed against the wall. He cursed under his breath and maneuvered back down the hall. A board squeaked underfoot, and then another. He winced, then heard a voice: "Val?"

His heart beating hard, John dashed into the kitchen and out the back door. He knew he would probably be heard, but that was far better than being seen. He latched the door as he exited the house, and wanted to kick himself in the ass when he let the door bang shut.

Running around the house to the driveway and the relative safety of a large patch of darkness, John tried to figure what he should do next.

He had to get in that house somehow. *Had* to. His curiosity was piqued with this case and the feeling would not go away. He had been trained to 'think on his feet', and he did so now, taking seconds only. He could fake car trouble and ring the front doorbell, ask Mr. Malcolm—he was almost certain that's who was in the house—for help, or maybe to use his phone. That might give him a chance to get close to the child.

But what if the baby wasn't there? What if he was out with the woman, Valerie Malcolm? That was possible, with one of the vehicles gone, and John knew a large number of men didn't stay home with the kids unless they were virtually forced to by their wives, or by some unnatural circumstance.

He remembered his P.I. job in Rockford with loathsome feelings, instead of nostalgia, although he'd enjoyed it at the time. And because he was adept as a P.I., the job had helped him to land work in various government agencies, beginning with the Federal Bureau of Investigation. He had also worked a brief stint at the NSA before being placed in the CIA, but he still remembered how most men were. As a private investigator, he had been hired several times by wives who were worried their husbands were cheating on them, but more often than not it was husbands who did the hiring and, he soon learned, most of the cheating. In his line of work, most of the men he'd investigated were annoying, negligent, cruel, or downright abusive to their spouses. John had a hard time understanding this because he had been married once, and had been faithful, loyal, loving and compassionate to his own wife, Lily. But that had been years ago.

He hoped Kenneth Malcolm was not the 'virtual man' he had witnessed in those early years. He hoped he had the child with him.

The moon peeked out from behind a small cluster of clouds, illuminating the driveway in a pale glow. From his shadowy hiding place beneath a ficus tree, John took a deep breath, waited for his heart to slow down, and decided to go with his plan of a broken-down vehicle. It would be risky, but he was determined to get inside the house again, and he loathed the idea of going back to Virginia knowing so little about this case.

Approaching the front door, he smoothed the wrinkles out of his jacket and rapped on the door.

* * * * *

Ken turned on the porch light and opened the front door. He did this a little quicker than he would have under different circumstances, but he was still very much on edge.

Whoever is at the door now could be the prowler, he told himself.

But when he opened the door and saw the nervous-looking man in the sports coat and dark slacks, he dismissed the idea. He knew expensive clothes when he saw them, and most burglars did not wear such attire on the job.

"Hello," the man said.

Although he appeared innocent enough, Ken's grip on the poker tightened until his knuckles were white. "Yes?"

"I'm sorry for the bother, but my car broke down about a block from here, and I was wondering if I might use your phone." The man tugged at the collar of his shirt. "I'm sorry, but I promise I'll be out of your hair in only a minute or so."

Ken relaxed some. "What happened to it? Battery? Alternator?"

"I'm not sure. It acts like it wants to turn over, but it won't catch." The man paused for a moment. "Did I wake your baby?"

Chance was still crying, and Ken was amazed at—and irritated with—himself for forgetting about him. "No, you didn't wake him. I was just on my way up to get him when you knocked."

"If I caught you at a bad time, I'm sorry. There doesn't seem to be anyone else home around here. Or awake, anyway."

"That's okay," Ken said. "Tell you what; give me a minute and we'll go out and look at your car. I know a little about them. I might be able to save you a tow."

"Sure," the man said. "I really appreciate it."

"No trouble," Ken said. He closed the door without inviting the man in, partly because he didn't want him to see that he was holding the fireplace poker behind his back.

In a few minutes he opened the door again, Chance in one arm, a flashlight in his free hand. Chance had stopped crying when Ken picked him up out of his crib, and now he goggled merrily at the man. Then the three of them moved down the sidewalk toward the street.

*****

When they reached the car, John directed Mr. Malcolm behind the wheel. "Pop the hood latch and then try the ignition. I'll watch for anything wrong."

After the hood latch was released and John had the hood raised, he deftly backed one of the plug wires off the distributor. When Mr. Malcolm tried to turn the motor over it would catch.

"That's all it would do when it quit on me," John said with feigned resignation.

Kenneth Malcolm got out of the car and came around to the front. "Let me have a look." He held his child out to John. "Would you hold him? He's liable to take off if I set him down."

"Sure," John said. He lifted the child from Ken's arms. *Feels like a normal baby,* he thought. He looked at the youngster in the shallow light from a nearby street lamp. He could see nothing abnormal about the baby, except for some light, almost invisible scarring on each side of his face. He smiled at the child, who promptly honked his nose with two chubby fingers.

"I see the problem," Ken said from underneath the hood. "There." He raised up and smiled at John. "A plug wire came loose from the distributor. Try it now."

John handed the child back to Ken and then got behind the wheel and keyed the engine. It turned over easily. "I really appreciate it, Mr. Malcolm," he said as he got out of the car. "You saved me a small fortune in towing and repair. What do I owe you for your help?"

"Not a thing."

"Well, thanks. I'm in your debt."

"Tell you what, then. If you ever see me broke down by the side of the road, you can return the favor."

"I'll do that," John said. "Thanks again."

With that, he got into his car, turned around in the driveway nearest him, and drove away.

* * * * *

Ken watched until the car was out of sight, a good-Samaritan smile still on his face. It wasn't until he was back in the den watching television, this time with Chance dozing on his lap (one thumb tucked in his mouth) that his good feelings faded. A thought occurred to him; something the man had said: *"I really appreciate it, Mr. Malcolm."*

Ken and Valerie's mailbox had only the house number on the side of it, and Ken could not recall having told the man his name.

* * * * *

It was late, and when John reached his room at the Holiday Inn, he stretched out on the soft bed and thought about the Malcolms and their baby. Kenneth Malcolm hadn't acted like he suspected anything out of the ordinary, and for that John was thankful. He had come back to the neighborhood forty-five minutes later and planted the tracking device on the other vehicle when he saw that Valerie Malcolm had returned from town.

But what was it about the baby?

As far as he could tell, there hadn't been anything extraordinary about him. He was as plain as they came. With the exception of the scars, of course. About that, he could only wonder.

And he could also only wonder why the federal government was so insistent about keeping tabs on the youngster.

Not knowing the reason why ate at John Milcheck to no end.

* * * * *

Valerie returned from town thirty minutes after Ken came back in the house. After he put Chance back into his bed for the night, Ken told her about the night's events. He started with hearing what he thought to be a prowler in the hall outside the den, and progressed from there to the man's vehicle trouble. He left out the part about taking the fireplace poker to the door with him, but he told her about the man calling him by name.

Valerie was openly skeptical about that.

"You think I'm lying, making it up?" Ken said incredulously.

"I didn't say you were lying." There was a coolness in her voice. "I'm only saying that maybe you *thought* he called you Mr. Malcolm."

"I didn't think anything like that."

"*Maybe* you did. Is that better?"

"No, it isn't."

"At any rate," Valerie said, dismissal lacing her voice, "there was no harm done anywhere, or to anyone, right?"

Ken sighed. "I guess so. It's just really weird, that's all. I started thinking about Chance disappearing out in the yard." He held up one hand to silence Valerie before she could say what he knew was coming. "At least I *think* he did, anyway."

Valerie laughed a little. "That reminds me of our honeymoon, and how you tipped the bellboy at the hotel twice because you were certain you hadn't the first time. Do you remember that?"

"Of course," Ken said.

How could he forget? Not just that little incident, but the entire honeymoon. He and Valerie's marriage had been a big extravaganza, with over two-hundred guests from both sides of the family at the small Lutheran church in Paragould where Valerie had attended all her life. The honeymoon had been sweet and satisfying, an ecstasy just shy of heaven. They had stayed cooped up in their room for most of their stay, making love countless times, each time better than the previous one, and ordering up room service whenever they grew exhausted enough to think about eating. He seriously thought he had forgotten to tip the bellboy the first night of their stay, and although over-tipping would have set him at odds with himself on any other occasion, he had blown it off with a laugh and a smile when Valerie brought the gaff to his attention. He was too full of love and passion to care about the extra ten dollars. He probably wouldn't have minded if it had been a hundred.

He remembered that, sure, but so did Valerie.

He was a little upset how she seemed to doubt what he'd told her, but to drag the issue any farther would only cause an argument, and that wouldn't be worth it.

"Tell you what," he said. "I'll forget about it if you will. Deal?"

Valerie smiled. "Deal."

He leaned over and placed a kiss on her soft lips. The kiss became a lingering one, and then passionate. After a time, the two of them were in their bedroom making slow, tender love, as if they had years in which to finish.

It did end, though, and although Ken had made a small deal with his wife earlier in the evening, he did not immediately forget about the stranger. Or what he'd said.

*****

FOUR

John Milcheck arrived back in Virginia the next afternoon, a Tuesday, at two o'clock. He was due back at headquarters at three-thirty, to give William Calhoun his report—which usually consisted of going into his office and saying, "yeah, I got the job done."—and so he had time for a late lunch downstairs in the cafeteria. While he ate, his mind wandered (as it often did when he was idle and feeling somewhat lonely) to his late wife.

He had met Lily Burgess while a private investigator in Rockford. She had come into his small office one sunny afternoon, one hazel eye swollen shut and looking dull and out of place, the other one sparkling with vibrant life; intelligent, soft, and beautiful. It was her eyes that had captured John from the start. Even though one was bruised and hurt, Lily had still been as beautiful a woman as he had ever encountered; almond-colored hair, a thin petite nose that curved up to a small point, and full sensuous lips above the soft cleft of her chin.

He could see, without asking, that a husband or boyfriend had worked her over. He'd seen several such cases, and each time the woman hired him to trail her husband, to find something that would give the woman grounds for divorce. John sensed that each of these women wanted grounds other than spousal abuse because that would mean their abusive marriages would come out in the open, causing unwanted (and in his mind, unwarranted) embarrassment. In most of these cases, he had discovered that the abusive husband was also engaged in an extra-marital affair, and simple photographs and video satisfied his clients.

Lily Burgess had wanted something more than a divorce from her husband, Garret Burgess, who was a prominent power in local politics. She came that day to John's small firm hoping that John would kill him for her. John had been stunned speechless.

When he found his voice, he had said, "You've come to the wrong place, ma'am."

"But I don't know what else to do."

"Divorce him," John said. "Then move away to some place where he can't find you. I can tell you personally that it has worked for a lot of women."

"That won't work for me," she said stiffly, rising from the chair in front of John's desk. "He would kill me if I tried to divorce him. It wouldn't matter where I lived. Thank you for your time, Mr. Milcheck." She turned to leave.

All John could see, even while she told him this, was her lovely face; the sort of face he thought he'd never see in his lifetime—one of perfect beauty, regardless of the swelling. She was almost out the door before he caught himself calling out to her: "Wait, Mrs. Burgess."

She turned back to him, the bad eye seeming to look off to one side, the bright hazel one regarding him with so much hope and promise that John wasn't sure if he could refuse her. Later, he would entertain the idea that it was the moment he fell in love with her. His body broke into a cold tremble with the knowledge that he'd almost let her walk out of his life forever.

"Come and sit down. Please," he told her. "Tell me everything."

* * * * *

Forcing these thoughts from his mind, John finished his lunch and then drove the short distance to headquarters, where he used a secretary's office to type up his brief report for Calhoun. In it, he stated the fact he had planted the devices on the Malcolms vehicles, that there had been no problems, and that he had also tested the devices and found them to be in good working order.

At three-thirty he went to the director's office and gave him the report.

Calhoun paced behind his desk after reading the report, while John once again stood in front and shifted his weight from foot to foot.

"Your report looks in order," Calhoun said. "That's good, because the president wants to see it immediately."

John succeeded with only monumental effort to conceal his surprise. "Yes, sir."

"And you had no problems or complications, right?"

John shifted his weight from his right foot to his left. He had the uncanny feeling that the director knew about his brief excursion into the Malcolm household—that he could read it on John's face. He knew the thought was silly. This wasn't the first time Calhoun had asked him that question at the completion of an assignment. But the thought persisted at the back of his mind.

"No. No problems, sir." And then, because he thought he must cover the tracks he worried Calhoun had seen, he added, "I had a problem with the distributor on the rental, but it was minor and caused no complications."

Calhoun tittered; the first time John had ever heard him laugh. "The federal government seems to always get stuck with the clunkers from airport rental car companies. I guess we're hated by more people than just your normal blue-collar taxpayer."

John didn't laugh along with the director. He didn't dare. Calhoun was known throughout the agency for a temperament that flared unexpectedly, like an active volcano.

"It caused no additional problems," was all John could think of to say. He was repeating himself again. Why did he always do that in this office? He felt like kicking himself.

Calhoun's face fell slack, serious again. "No additional problems? Additional to what?" He placed his massive hands on either side of his desk and stared hard at John.

John's weight shifted back to his right foot. "In addition to the vehicle, sir. I guess I chose the wrong way to phrase that. The vehicle caused no problems, period."

Calhoun appeared more at ease and stood to his full height once again, seeming to tower over John as Goliath must have David. Although John was intimidated to a degree (or two) he took this chance to ask a question: "Have there been any new developments in Project Lone Star since my assignment?"

"No, none yet."

"Will you be filling me in on the project any time soon?" John said, failing to mask his curiosity.

Calhoun looked at him for a moment. "I forgot that you haven't been fully briefed on Lone Star." He ruffled through some of the papers on his desk, then looked at John. "I will brief you on the project before long. I've decided that I want to keep you on this case should any other developments arise, but right now I need you back on the Watson assignment. I believe you and your team are close to having enough evidence for an indictment, right?"

"Yes, sir."

"Good. I expect another week or ten days to finish up, then I plan to assign you, at least on a part-time basis, to Project Lone Star. Agent Lomax will be needing some help, and since you've had some hands-on in this case, I believe you'd be best suited for the job."

"Yes, sir," was all John could say. He had to fight to conceal his excitement at the prospect of knowing just what this case involved.

"I hope to see you here in about a week then. Get the Watson case wrapped up as soon as possible. The chief feels that Lone Star should be top priority, and what the president wants, he usually gets." The director's voice dripped with either sarcasm or scorn, perhaps both.

"Yes, sir," he said again.

"Then I'll see you in about a week."

John left the director's office and made the long walk to the room where a couple of agents on the Watson case were drinking coffee and talking idly while they monitored several computer screens, each showing different views of Senator Watson's offices.

"Look who's back," one of them said.

John shook hands with both men and then they filled him in on the past two day's work.

John found that, while he was excited about being put on Lone Star, he was still able to put it aside enough to immerse himself once again in the Watson case.

* * * * *

William Calhoun opened a drawer of his desk soon after agent Milcheck left his office and pulled out a hard-copy printout of conversation at the Malcolm residence from the previous night. He had only glanced through it, as he did first thing each morning, but now he remembered something John had told him.

He thumbed through the thirty-odd pages—the Malcolms were avid talkers, in his opinion, with as many as a hundred-twenty-three pages on their best day—until he came to what he was looking for: *"I'm sorry for the bother, but my car broke down about a block from here, and I was wondering if I might use your phone."*

Calhoun's forehead wrinkled. Milcheck said he'd had trouble with his rental car. Could it be...? *No,* he told himself. *John would have told me if he came into contact with Mr. or Mrs. Malcolm. It must have been a complete stranger.*

If agent Milcheck had come into direct contact, it might cause complications with Lone Star down the road. He would have to hear the recordings of the conversations for last night before he could be certain that John wasn't the man with the car trouble, and right now he didn't have time to walk over to the other side of the building to do so. His agenda was already full enough.

So thinking, he pulled on his jacket, and left his office for one of the many meetings he was required to attend each day, his thoughts and focus already on the details of the next one forthcoming.

* * * * *

On Friday of the same week, Ken was scheduled to make a business trip to Atlanta to attend a two-day seminar for work. He looked forward to the trip—knowing also that it would help future promotion possibilities—but he hated to leave Valerie and Chance. It would be his first time away from them since the adoption.

Although Ken knew they would get along fine, he had suggested they spend that time at her parent's house. Valerie balked at that idea, but had reassured him she would invite her mother over Saturday to spend the day with them. Her father was out of town, as usual, this time on an entomology excursion with a group of his students from Arkansas State University.

Ken tried one last time. "I just wish you would stay there."

"We'll be all right," she said. "When you went to Philadelphia last year, you were gone three days and I was fine."

"But we didn't have Chance, then."

"So, that will make it easier this time," Valerie said. "I'll have someone here to keep me company...and busy. Go on and enjoy your trip. We'll be fine."

Ken had kissed her then. "I love you."

"And I love you. Now, let's get to the airport before you miss your flight."

That had been two days ago.

It was now early Sunday morning, and as the plane circled Memphis

International Airport, Ken found himself impatient to see his family. The seminar had been informative and interesting, but when he went over his notes on the plane, he hadn't been able to make sense of them. His mind kept returning to Valerie and Chance. *Not long now,* he told himself. *Not long now.*

But when he stepped off the plane thirty minutes later, Valerie and Chance weren't there.

He walked through the terminal, looking for them. People bustled down the concourse, pulling or carrying luggage. The PA system announced that this was a non-smoking facility. The smell of fried onions scented the air from a nearby deli.

He had reminded Valerie of his arrival time last night on the phone, and the flight had been on time, so where was she?

His stomach fluttered. In his mind, he imagined her stranded on the shoulder of Interstate 55 with a flat tire, or engine trouble. He saw someone stopping for them—someone who did not intend to lend a hand.

He shook his head. Thoughts like that would not help his frame of mind.

After a few minutes, he realized he should call her cell phone. They had only gotten the phones a few months back, and for purposes just such as this. His own phone was dead (after a lifetime of landlines, he just could not get into the habit of charging a telephone), but there was a bank of pay phones ahead near an airport lounge, and a drink would be a start toward relieving his anxiety.

He was heading for the pay phones when he noticed two men in dark suits standing near the entrance of the lounge, watching him.

They're not watching you, he told himself. *They're probably waiting for someone who just arrived off a plane.*

That was plausible enough, but when he looked again, the men were still there, standing idly. One of them spoke to the other, but both men kept their eyes on him. Or at least appeared to. Feeling slick with unease, Ken decided to claim his baggage before calling home. Bad enough that Valerie wasn't there. Now he was becoming paranoid.

But it wasn't just those things, and he knew it. It was the thought of what Valerie might think if she knew he had acted on those feelings by rushing to the nearest phone in a blind panic.

As he rode the horizontal escalator, he thought about the two men and tried to convince himself he was over reacting. One had been dark headed, the other blonde, and both in dark suits with matching ties. He was halfway through the short trip on the conveyor when he glanced behind him and saw the two men step onto the moving walkway.

They are *following me. They're probably going to come up to me and say that something terrible has happened to Val and Chance.*

But that was ridiculous, wasn't it? Besides, these two men looked more like special agents in a James Bond movie than they did police officers or deputies, from whose hands bad news would be delivered.

When Ken got to the baggage claim area and spotted his luggage, he grabbed it (one suitcase and a small duffel that he'd chosen not to carry on) and looked around, searching for the two men.

They were gone.

People moved in an untidy wave around him. Though it would be difficult to spot a particular person in that mass, he knew it wouldn't be a problem sighting the two men.

Breathing a sigh of relief, he realized he *was* just being paranoid. Now he could concentrate on the task at hand, which was finding out where his wife was, if she and Chance were okay, and why she was late.

There was a bank of pay phones near the exit to the short-term parking garage. He used his calling card to call Valerie's cell phone and hung up after the tenth ring.

Okay, so she's late and not answering her phone. Or, most likely, she's let her battery run down, same as me, or is in an area where no signal is available. He imagined, again, her and Chance on the side of the road, changing a flat tire—he refused to think anything worse than that—and this time the thought carried more weight.

Now he tried Valerie's parents' home—with the same result. He hung up, resigned to the possibilities being showcased in his mind's eye: Valerie and Chance murdered on the side of the highway; Valerie's parents' house being ravaged by fire with the four of them inside; Valerie and Chance getting hit by a motorist with a high level of alcohol in his blood and not enough sense to stay away from the wheel; Valerie and Chance caught in the grip of a destructive tornado—which was odd, because the weather was nice. And more. Much more.

These visions traipsed through his mind so fast he was only able to stifle their onslaught with the utmost force of will.

He was trembling when he finally regained control and calmed down, and that is when the two men grabbed him.

One gripped his arm and the other nudged something hard into his back. Ken felt like a rabbit caught in a snare. They pinned him against the bank of phones so he couldn't see their faces. Any other time, he would have had to stand in line for a phone, but most people in the area had flittered away to their destinations.

The man who held his arm leaned close and whispered in his ear. "Do not yell or try to run. We don't mean to harm you." Ken turned his head to the left and caught a glimpse of dark hair. He smelled bubble gum. "Do you believe me?" the man said.

Ken was frightened, but at the same time wanted to believe the man. In his mind, the only thought now was that Valerie and Chance had been kidnapped and these two were here to demand a ransom. He knew that it was a ludicrous thought, but there it was. He turned around to face them, and they allowed the movement, but both men still pressed close. "My wife. Where is she?"

The man holding Ken resembled the actor, Nicolas Cage, but had a harder face. Except for his eyes, which were…nervous? Yes. Ken thought the blue eyes looked hurried. "I don't know anything about your wife," the man said in a low conversational tone, "but I know about your child."

Ken reacted violently then, pushing and pulling against the men until the one with the gun pushed it so hard against his ribs that Ken subsided. He was panting. "Where is he? *Where*, you bastards."

The Cage look-alike laughed, a soft, papery sound. "With your wife, I suppose. I don't know."

"Then what do you want?" Ken said. Perplexity laced the edges of his voice.

"Your child," the man said, "is not what he appears to be."

"What? What do you mean?"

"He is—"

A hand shot out and grabbed the man's shoulder. The hand belonged to the guy with the gun. His dusty blonde hair was thin, his forehead high, and he sported a very light mustache and beard. He shook his head in a quick left to right movement. "Not yet."

"What do you mean?" Ken said again.

The man who resembled the actor was visibly irritated. He glanced at the partner who had stopped him, appeared to think about saying something, and then said to Ken: "If you want a normal child, keep him out of the sun. They won't know, then. If something happens, they'll hear you, so don't make a fuss if something does happen. They can hear you now, in fact."

"Sun? Who?"

But the man let go of his arm, and he and his partner abruptly walked away. They merged with a crowd of passengers who had just deplaned, and then they were gone.

Ken wanted to chase them, but he couldn't move. His legs felt like two giant icicles. He looked around. If anyone saw what had just transpired, he couldn't tell. The diminishing crowd seemed to have the same single-minded purpose common to all travelers; getting to their destinations as fast as possible.

After a few minutes he walked on shaky legs back to the terminal where Valerie was supposed to have met him. There, he sat in one of the lounge chairs, luggage at his feet, trying to make sense of what had happened. But he couldn't. His tired mind could only think of his family, and wonder if these two men posed a danger to them. Maybe the men had mistaken him for someone else. Ken knew he had a common, plain look.

Incredibly, after about ten minutes, he was nodding off, and a few minutes later he was asleep, his chin resting on his chest.

He was awakened a short time later, although it felt as though hours had passed. In his groggy, sleepy mind he was again being confronted by the guys in the suits, and when the hand shook him, he sat up straight, prepared to fight his adversaries, who had done something to his wife and child.

But the men weren't there.

It was Valerie.

"Honey? Are you okay?" She shook him again.

"Val? Where have you been?"

She told him the car had stalled three blocks from home.

"Where's Chance?" Ken's eyes darted around the terminal.

"He's with Mother. The car finally started, but I didn't trust it. I borrowed her car. She wanted to watch Chance, and I really didn't want to bring him with me, anyway. He's cutting another tooth and he's fussy."

Ken was relieved. They were okay after all. He mentally gave thanks for her car stalling only three blocks from home instead of fifty miles. He kissed her and said he was ready to go home.

When they got to the car, he put his bags in the back seat and told her he didn't feel like driving.

"Is anything wrong?" she said.

"No. Just tired."

Yet, on the way home he thought about what *was* wrong: the two men, and what they had said. He knew he should tell Valerie about it, but remembered how she'd reacted to his belief that Chance had disappeared, and that the man with the car trouble had called him by name. What would she think about this? Besides, the whole incident had a dreamlike patina to it now, as though it hadn't really happened.

He would give it time—time for him to think about it, and what it all might mean—and only then would he decide whether or not to tell her.

* * * * *

FIVE

The underground compound was a complex tangle, with tunnels linking offices, laboratories, and living quarters, as well as two massive hangers. For half a century, this installation had resided beneath a large mountain at the edge of a Nevada desert. In the late forties it had been a single large bunker used for munitions storage, but in the decades hence had branched outward in all directions except up, as though it was a spider weaving a wide, sluggish web.

The compound served the United States government in various capacities, each of which was classified top secret. Indeed, the location of the installation, as well as the knowledge it existed at all, was available to certain government branches on a need-to-know basis, and only to certain members of those branches. The men and women who worked at the compound also lived within its confines, with no chance of ever returning to civilian life. In fact, all but a handful of employees did not even exist to the outside world. Many of the men and women had been beneath the mountain for four decades or longer. They were toilers in the vineyards of progress and technology, and not one of them would trade his or her secluded life for that of the richest civilian. Too much of the future lay buried beneath this hill.

That's what most of the residents claimed, anyway, like a mantra against civility.

Quartered in the center of the complex, near the most important and highest classified chambers, Duke Tarkington would claim different, if he could. To him, the giant complex was a mountain of anxiety in which detached and unemotional people ran the computers and machinery with the monotony of programmed robots on some futuristic planet in a science fiction novel; a place where, if you let your mouth overload your asshole, you could get your tongue eviscerated from your mouth. At the tender age of twenty-two, Duke knew about *that*, also. Occasionally he bungled things, but at least his mouth no longer got him in trouble.

He was one of several third-generation children born in the cool rooms on the central level, where the most important work was conducted. His grandfather had been one of the early pioneers here, and Duke's father, Derek Tarkington, was currently the top man in charge. Duke would follow in *his* footsteps only when he thought the steps worthy of being filled.

On a Saturday morning in April, Duke scanned his ID card, and then the palm of one hand, on a bio-scan computer located to the right of the thick door that led into the main laboratory chamber. The seal loosened with a hiss of air, and the door moved inward and to the side on well-oiled bearings, revealing the heart of the complex.

Because it was a weekend, the immense room was dark and shrouded in silence. Banks of computers and other sophisticated equipment occupied almost every available space along each wall, their lights providing a dim, eerie illumination with the overheads turned off. Ranks of filing cabinets, work stations, and small projects at various stages of completion took up the remainder of the room, and were arranged in a circular pattern.

Duke glanced at his watch. Although only a minimal amount of security was required throughout the remote installation, this area was of sufficient importance to warrant the need of video cameras for around-the-clock monitoring, as well as a physical check each hour by the floor security officer on duty. Duke wasn't worried about the video cameras, for he had disabled them beforehand, and no one occupied the observation room on a Saturday unless an important task necessitated weekend work. But the security guard would make his rounds in another forty-five minutes, so he would have to be mindful of the time.

If someone higher up discovered that 'feeble' Duke Tarkington knew how to regulate the security cameras—as well as some of the other equipment in this room—he would probably lose more than just his tongue, regardless of his father's rank.

As he did each time he came down here, Duke looked, with endless fascination and wonder, at the 'subject'. In the gloomy light, the 'subject' sat on a chair in the center of the room. He waved a hand at Duke and formed a ghostly facsimile of a smile upon his face. As always, Duke smiled in return and saluted his friend with a quick outward flick of his wrist, and they both laughed. It was a private joke, a parody of all the saluting that went on in this place.

The 'subject'.

That name had been attached to his friend decades ago—shortly after the subject's imprisonment—by one of the nameless morons who'd worked under Duke's grandfather. Duke hated that name, and the 'subject' did, as well. In his short life, Duke had learned that this underground world (where brief respites out into the desert sun were anticipatory occasions—at least for him) was infested with uncompassionate men and women whose personalities resembled those of the robots down in Substation F. The man in front of him wasn't the 'subject'. He was Prometheus, which Duke initially thought a funny name when, four years ago, the two had first become friends of sorts. Prometheus had told Duke that it wasn't his real name, only a Greek name he'd adopted for himself since his capture.

That was fine with Duke. A name was only a name. The person behind the name was important, and he hadn't needed the almighty Derek Tarkington to teach him that. What he didn't learn from Prometheus, Duke learned from the books in the library on Level Four. He retrieved a chair from a corner of the room and sat down, careful not to touch the bars of the hydrabeams that kept his friend imprisoned.

In the two years since Duke's tongue had been removed, Prometheus had taught him sign language. Duke's hearing was normal, so he used the silent language only to speak to his friend. He also employed facial expressions, which portrayed a wide array of emotions more accurately than any language signed with a pair of hands, or movement of lips.

"Not much time today," Duke signed. "Garrison's on duty. He's not as regular as the others."

"Garrison is paranoid," Prometheus said in a soft voice, although there was no danger of being overheard. In addition to the video cameras, Duke had shut down the audio reels.

Duke nodded and for the umpteenth time he signed: "I wish I knew how to deactivate the hydrabeams."

Prometheus gave him a paternal smile—or perhaps one of a brother. "Duke, it's very admirable of you to reiterate those sentiments, and I'll tell you as I always do, that I wish you could, also."

Duke looked at his shuffling feet, and then back at his friend. "It isn't fair."

"Maybe not, but remember what I've told you—"

"I know. With patience, any possibility is attainable, any mystery comprehended."

The wide smile on Prometheus' face was enough to send Duke's pessimism into remission.

The computer terminals and other machines beeped and blinked around them in soft conversation. The room sounded like an intensive care ward in a hospital.

In Duke's eyes, Prometheus was a better teacher than any of the men and women who educated small classes of children in the dormitory on Level Four. All he knew about one-room schools was gleaned from history books and historical novels, but he felt the educational atmosphere of the compound resembled one.

"Ready to play?" Duke signed.

Prometheus' smile widened, revealing a neat row of small, straight teeth. "I think I'll have you in two more moves, three at the most."

"Yeah, right." Duke opened the plastic bag that was between his feet and extracted a chess board and pieces, which he placed upon a small table that he put between himself and the orange and brown swirls of the hydrabeams. He took a folded piece of paper from a pocket of his jeans and smoothed it out on the flat surface. Consulting his crudely drawn diagram, he placed the chess pieces in the proper places, until the black and red board contained remnants of a game in progress.

"I can't believe you got it all written down from the last time," Prometheus said.

"I didn't, exactly. A lot of it I memorized before Flaugherty made it into the room.

Tim Flaugherty had been on security duty last Saturday morning and had made his ten o'clock rounds at nine-fifty-five. If it wasn't for a warning device placed discreetly fifty feet down the exterior hallway—a clever contraption which Prometheus had taught Duke to make out of a few simple electronic components—Flaugherty would have caught the cameras off and the two of them conversing. He would then have wasted no time reporting the incident to Duke's father, and four years of a carefully nurtured friendship would have been lost. Duke could handle anything—even the loss of his speech—but not losing his best and only friend.

"Bishop to knight-three," Prometheus said.

Duke moved the piece and studied the board for the near-invisible attack on his king that he knew the move preceded. Prometheus was not a liar. He *would* have Duke in checkmate in two or three moves, and although that knowledge could have been frustrating, it wasn't. His friend was open, honest, and best of all he made Duke use his mind, which was more beneficial than capturing an opponent's king. He paused from his study of the board and signed: "Is the child okay?"

"For now," Prometheus said, and was quiet.

Duke knew from experience not to press this topic, but he was also aware that Prometheus spent long, lonely hours dwelling on this very thing. So he pressed on. "What do you mean?"

Prometheus sighed and waved a dismissive hand. "There will come a time in the near future when the answer to that question may be a painful one."

"When?"

"I'll know when the time comes."

"Do you think my father knows that you are aware of what has happened?"

"No," Prometheus said, and a smile turned the thoughtful look on his face into sunshine. "And always remember that, Duke. Secret knowledge is power, strong power. And so is feigning ignorance in the eyes of those in authority in this…this place. The men in charge of this labyrinth, including your father, who would have the tongue cut from the mouth of his own son, believe they possess secret knowledge because of the work they do here, but they do not. Not really. Someday soon, enlightenment will rain down upon men who believe they have the answers to every question, the solution to all problems, and the sole right to free will." He held up one pale finger. "The knowledge will escape. The only question may be whether or not it survives…but it *will* escape."

Prometheus looked into Duke's dark eyes a moment longer, and then at the board. "Do you plan on countering my move?"

Duke nodded and moved a pawn one square forward, so one of his own bishops would be free to move on his next move. But his mind was troubled now—as it usually was whenever Prometheus spoke of things he should have no way of knowing—and his move probably wasn't the most strategic one he could have made. Duke didn't care.

His mind continued to probe at Prometheus' words; to bend, shape, and mold them, in an effort to work them into some shadow of comprehension. He knew his friend would stand for no more questions today, so he was at least able to resist that temptation.

"Checkmate," Prometheus said, and smiled.

Duke grinned. If you didn't pay attention and keep your mind clear of things other than the task at hand, you lost more quickly than you otherwise might have, and any chance of victory became nonexistent. Another bit of his friend's insight and wisdom.

"How?" Duke signed.

Prometheus explained his moves and the strategy behind them, and then Duke put the board and pieces in the box. The two spent the rest of the hour in amiable conversation which, had it been recorded, would have sounded one-sided, conducted by a captive with a voice full of wisdom, compassion, and loss.

At five minutes before the hour Duke put away the box containing the chess game and moved the chair and table. He reactivated the video surveillance, as well as the audio sensors, and as he stood in the open doorway on his way out of the room, he looked back at his imprisoned friend with a sad look that conveyed more than could any spoken words.

As the door slid shut behind him with a soft hiss of air, Duke thought the same thing he always did at his departure: next Saturday would be forever getting here.

In that moment, he believed he could feel some of his friend's profound loneliness.

* * * * *

On a warm day in late April, almost a week after Kenneth Malcolm's incident at the airport, John Milcheck sat in the easy chair that, along with a beige sofa, occupied the front room of his small house in the suburbs of D.C. The house had been he and Lily's first and only home, and although he knew if he moved out he might better cope with his wife's death, he just couldn't bear the thought of losing that last link with her.

The house was a two-bedroom brick home decorated in a sparse rococo; beige carpets throughout, plain white walls adorned with lots of artwork—some of them originals she'd picked up god-knew-where—and plenty of end tables and coffee tables which looked antique but weren't. When Lily was alive the house had been full of live plants that gave the sparse furnishings verisimilitude, but John had neglected the yuccas and ferns, and they'd died slow, miserable deaths.

He was never home enough. Work kept him busy, and he gladly let it.

He and his small team of agents had finally brought an indictment down on Senator Watson in the embezzlement case, and with the help of a criminal lawyer and prosecutor from New York—the senator's home state—the CIA's involvement had not been splashed in any newspaper in the country. Not one.

Tonight, his thoughts were on Project Lone star, his usual brooding about Lily taking a rare backseat to his confused thoughts about the project. Yesterday, William Calhoun had briefed him on Lone Star—if you could call it a briefing. Although John knew much more about the project than he had prior to the meeting, he was still puzzled by certain aspects of the case.

He had met with Calhoun in the director's office, and this time there had been a chair both in front of, and behind, the desk, and John had been invited to sit. He did so, trying not to let his anxiety show.

"Project Lone Star is the result of a series of covert operations that took place in the Nevada Desert eighteen months ago," Calhoun began.

What kind of covert operations? John had wondered but knew better than to ask. The director seemed irritable and brisk.

"There was some trouble on the last day of the operation," Calhoun said. "A man and a woman got by security, somehow—I suppose one of the men on watch was gone to the bathroom, or something. This would have been okay had the couple driven straight to the temporary camp a few miles up the road from the project's boundaries, but a different set of complications arose when their vehicle broke down. Two soldiers were dispatched to either make the couple turn back or, if necessary, bring them to the camp.

"The covert operation going on out there was named Project Lone Star, and the child is all that is left of it."

"I don't follow you, sir," John said.

"You see," Calhoun supplied, "the woman was pregnant and she had come to term while she and her husband's vehicle was stalled on the side of the highway. The two soldiers apparently got mixed up on their orders and shot the couple. The woman was in the last stages of labor by then, and the soldiers didn't realize what they'd done until they dragged the woman from the car and saw the infant's head poking out from between her legs (John winced at the director's bluntness). They got scared and raced the two miles back to camp, where they reported what had happened. A medical team was dispatched, and when they arrived, the baby's head was still out, laying on the hot tarmac, but alive when they pulled the caul from over his face."

"A caul?" John said.

"Yes. The child was born with part of the embryonic sac covering its face, and it was this that saved his life. Part of the tissue had been eroded by the pavement and sand, and the child's face was burned, but the caul protected the vital areas—eyes, nose, and mouth."

"But the baby lived? That's incredible."

"Yes, it is," Calhoun said. "It wasn't breathing when our medical team arrived, but they did CPR on the trip back to camp. The infant required major surgery on both sides of his face to replace the burnt tissue. We rushed him to D.C., where some of the best surgeons are located, and they did a decent job."

John had a lot of questions, but asked the one that was most important on his list: "Why the surveillance? Why the bugs and tracking devices, and recordings?"

Calhoun, still sitting his chair, leaned across the desk, a smile playing at the corners of his mouth. "I knew you would be wondering about that, and it's a good question. That," he said, "was a decision made by the commander in chief."

"The president?"

"The president. He wanted the baby put up for adoption so that it could live a normal life. President Clayton is a family man, a firm believer in the family structure. That creed is part of what got him elected." Calhoun appeared to scowl.

"But why would the president be notified in the first place?" John asked.

"Well," the director said with a sigh, "it seems that there was a newspaper reporter who was traveling on the same highway as the child's parents, and..."

A soft knock on the door stopped Calhoun in mid-sentence, and a young woman John recognized as Calhoun's secretary poked her head in. "Sir? I have the Tarkington report, when you're ready."

"Thank you, Susan. I'll only be a few minutes more."

The woman nodded and closed the door behind her, with an apologetic smile to John.

"Anyway," Calhoun continued, "Clayton wanted the child monitored for the first year or so to make sure he was placed in a proper family—one whose love for the child would be sincere regardless of the light scars, and the fact that he wasn't genetically their own. I think it's Mr. Clayton's pet project, although his approval ratings would plummet if the average taxpayer knew how much this project was costing them."

John was confused, but at the same time knew better than to ask too many questions. He would have to take what Calhoun said, and figure out what the director *meant*, on his own. "Why *is* so much time and effort being spent on the child? After all, children are adopted every day."

"Not sure," Calhoun said crisply. "There are some in the know who think Clayton plans to use the project as a tool to get re-elected next autumn. The compassionate president who took a dying baby under his wing and placed him with the average American family, although that family must, of course, remain a closely guarded secret. The spin would still work. Others feel he can't do that, because of the slip-up with the child's parents. They were killed by U.S. soldiers, remember, and it wouldn't do him any good if his public knew that."

"Of course not," John said, for some reason disturbed. Again, he had dismissed it.

That conversation had taken place yesterday, and the more he thought about it, the more he thought Calhoun had left out a large chunk of information about Project Lone Star. Perhaps *several* chunks.

Two things in particular stood out in John's mind: First, how did this couple get so lost as to end up in the middle of a federal covert operation? Did they make a wrong turn, lose their map? The second thing puzzled John the most. It was, perhaps, what he wanted more than anything else to understand: Calhoun said the covert operation was named Project Lone Star…and that the baby was all that was left of it. Now, unless John was mistaken, Calhoun wanted him to believe this—to take it at face value—when what he had said implied that the baby was *already* a part of Lone Star.

Once again, how did his parents just happen to drive up on this operation, of which their unborn child was a part, and not know it?

John sighed. The truth here, as he saw it, was that the scenarios given to him by the director did not make sense. If anything, he felt he knew no more about Project Lone Star than he had when he'd been called in to Calhoun's office. He'd been expecting much more than what he'd gotten, and the director hadn't delivered. That was the bottom line.

Is it? John asked himself. *If he wants me on this case so badly, why didn't he come clean with me about the details? Why couldn't he come clean?*

These questions trooped through his mind like toy soldiers, and it irritated him that he had no satisfactory answers.

He hated being lied to, but he sensed that is exactly what Calhoun had done.

Why? And for what purpose?

He would have to be cautious on this case, which was turning into the type of assignment he had hoped it might become. Even more intriguing was the fact that he was going to have to delve deeper to find out what Lone Star was *really* about.

John found himself anxious for the task.

* * * * *

SIX

Valerie was acting peculiar—although Ken hated to use that broad term—and when he asked her what was wrong, she told him it was 'that time of the month', and she was having unusually bad cramps. He tried to console her by saying in an encouraging voice which sounded condescending instead, that it would get better. "Easy for you to say," she snapped at him.

Ken had brooded for almost a week now about the two men at Memphis International, and he reasoned that Valerie seemed irritable because he himself had felt that way of late. It wasn't something he'd consciously set out to do, but there it was. Hiding something from his wife never failed to send the synchronicity of their marriage slightly out of orbit.

The three of them were going to visit Ken's father. Darrel Malcolm lived in Bono, six miles northwest of Jonesboro, and Ken didn't visit him as often as he knew he should. Darrel had invited them over for a barbecue—hamburgers, hotdogs, and trimmings.

Bono was a nice town and small, with a population of just under twelve hundred. Ken had yet to come across anyone who lived there who wasn't hospitable. As they neared his father's house, he said: "Listen, Val, I'm sorry."

"Sowwy," Chance cooed from the back seat, where he was securely strapped in his *Big Boy* safety seat, and playing with a Happy Meal toy.

"Sorry that I'm on my period?" Icy, but he supposed he deserved the lowered temperature.

"No. Sorry that I've been so short with you lately. I've had a lot on my mind, I guess." *Oh, good one.* he told himself. *You sound like every*

man in every movie there ever was where 'something is bothering him'.
But something *had* been, hadn't it?

Yes. Certainly.

It wasn't every day that a guy was held at gunpoint by two thugs while they told him that his child wasn't what he appeared to be.

Some of the sarcasm left Valerie's voice. In its place was the first trace of concern. "Well, honey, what is it? What's bothering you? You haven't been talking to me. Maybe I can help."

Ken considered telling her about the two men—had, in fact, been struggling for days with the question of whether to or not—but again decided not to. It wasn't only that it was not the right time or place, he just couldn't make himself do it. "Nothing," he said.

"Nonsense. You just told me that you've had a lot on your mind."

"Yeah."

"So, what is it?"

He took one hand off the steering wheel and waved it around dramatically. "I don't know. Work, I guess. Going to see Dad. Worrying that something's bothering *you*."

"Bothering me?"

"Yes."

"Like what?"

"I don't know. You've seemed a little distant this week."

"No," Valerie said. "You're the one who's been distant. Don't try turning this into my problem. You know that doesn't work. Or help things."

Ken couldn't argue that. In the past, he'd dealt with problems in that very way, by imagining or believing that another person—be it Valerie, his father, his doctor…whoever—had the same problem. It was his mind's way of trying to cope, by mirroring what the other person believed or felt, instead of dealing with an issue on his own. His doctor had a name for it, but he couldn't recall it.

"What about work?" Valerie said.

"Ken sighed. "Just added pressure with the job. Nothing that wasn't expected, though." This was actually another fib. There was certainly pressure in the job of finance, but no more lately than normal. He looked at her and managed a wink. "I'll adjust to it. Just give it a little time."

Valerie returned his smile with a confident one of her own, as if she knew that, of *course* he would adjust. He had adjusted to a lot of things in his life.

Ken's father lived on a quiet street, in a squat brick home, two blocks down from the Bono City Park. Darrel Malcolm had been living here for almost two years now, having moved from the house in the country that Ken had grown up in. The house was small, but seemed to be all his father needed since the passing of his wife and younger son.

Darrel came out of the house as they pulled into the driveway. He was a small man who resembled a stereotypical college professor; thin hair, bald on top with hair curving over his ears around the side of his head, the hair a mixture of gray and black. There was a fleck of what might have been food on his goatee. "Hi there, gang," he said as Ken and Valerie got out of the car.

"Hey, Dad," Ken said.

"Dad," Valerie said and smiled. She got Chance out of his car seat and put him down on the ground, where he promptly ran up to Darrel and hugged his leg. "Hi, Pa Pa," he said.

"Ho, ho," Darrel said. "It's about time you learned how to say my name."

"Yep," Chance agreed in his childish voice. "'Bout time."

Ken and Valerie looked at each other with their mouths open and eyes wide. Chance had never attempted to say *any* of those words before, and they had rolled out of his little mouth as if he spoke them every day.

The senior Malcolm took Chance's small hand and led him into the house, out of the hot sun.

"Did you hear that?" Ken said.

"Yeah," Valerie stumbled. "B-but I'm not sure I believe it."

Chance's vocabulary had increased only marginally in the past month, although he could now say 'mamma' and 'daddy' very plainly, as well as a few other words. This was the first time, though, that they had heard him speak in a complete sentence. *Two* of them, in this case, even though they had been short ones.

As Ken and Valerie walked up to the side door, Ken's forehead frowned in thought. He was thinking once again about the men at the airport: *Your child is not what he appears to be.*

Just what had the man meant by that? Ken tried to tie the words with what had just happened, and didn't know if he could do it. Aside from that, it was also silly. Babies were known to talk a lot earlier than fifteen months. Ken knew that from all the books on babies and child rearing he and Valerie had read while they were trying to get pregnant. Chance's words had just caught him off guard. It was reasonable to assume if

Chance could speak in a complete sentence he would have done so before now; first with incomprehensible sounds, and then with articulated words.

Gradual. Not all at once.

But it *had* been all at once. That was what bothered Ken now.

When they got into the house, Darrel picked up Chance, who had been trying without success to climb into the recliner in a corner of the living room. The kitchen, into which they entered through a side doorway, was roomy and filled with sunlight that slanted through a large window over the sink. A small table and four chairs occupied the corner closest to the living room, and Darrel removed stacks of pamphlets and books from the seats so they could all sit. "Sorry about the mess."

He handed Chance to Ken and then began to prepare the hamburger meat and hot dogs, working the ground beef into patties with the practiced ease of a seasoned veteran.

The three of them talked about various things while he did this. This included the weather, which threatened to become an all-out heat spell, but also about Chance, with whom Darrel had taken to as much as he would if Chance had been his paternal grandson. "Chance is a real corker," Darrel said. "I wish your mother could see him."

Ken agreed that his mother would have been elated to have a grandson. She had passed away three years ago. Three-plus packs of cigarettes daily for twenty years had given her lung cancer, and she had suffered the last eighteen months of her life. Ken himself had quit smoking shortly after her diagnosis, and it sometimes irritated him that his father couldn't give them up.

"Jimmy would have like him, also," Ken said. Jimmy had been his brother.

Darrel paused in his work only for a moment and looked up. "Yes, I suppose he would have."

He finished the patties and was getting a pack of hot dogs and a bottle of barbecue sauce out of the refrigerator, when Chance startled them all by saying, "Pa Pa? Can I go outside?"

Darrel turned from the refrigerator and looked and Ken and Valerie with a stern expression. "You didn't tell me he could talk so well. I saw him less than two weeks ago, and he couldn't even say 'pa pa'."

Trying to keep a straight face to conceal his surprise, Ken said, "Well, lately he's been talking a lot better, I guess." Which was not a lie. Ken just hadn't known it.

Valerie was staring out the kitchen window. She looked in deep thought, as though she was not looking *through* the window, but past whatever lay beyond it. Ken wasn't even sure she'd heard Chance's newest prattling.

"Can I?" Chance repeated in his small, piping voice.

Darrel laughed. "Sure can, big fella. Just let Pa Pa get his burgers and utensils and we'll go out back."

Chance clapped three or four times and grinned. A light string of drool ran from one corner of his small mouth.

"I guess we're ready to go out," Darrel announced, and the four of them went out the side door and around to the back patio.

"My God, Ken," Valerie said in a whisper on their way out. "How did he learn those words?"

Ken shrugged his shoulders, offered a baffled grin, and wondered why he felt guilty.

The back yard was roomy, not quite as large as Ken and Valerie's. A twelve by eighteen-foot concrete patio was against the back of the house, and on it was a barbecue grill, a picnic table and benches, and a light blue baroque lounger with an ashtray stand next to it. Ken knew it was in this chair that his father sat, smoking and drinking beer, while he thought about his lost wife and son, supernatural realms and, possibly, what it all meant. He felt a stab of pity in his heart for his father.

That's just life, I guess, he told himself. *Sooner or later, something like this happens and there's no way to properly prepare for it.*

The rest of the backyard was lushly green, with three or four planted trees peppering the lawn at irregular intervals. The lawn was freshly cut.

He always keeps it short. He stays busy.

There was a five-gallon bucket at one corner of the patio. In it were toys for Chance, and Darrel removed the lid and dumped the toys out onto the lawn at the edge of the concrete, for easy access. Chance laughed and giggled as he played with first a plastic truck and then some colorful rubber blocks in the shapes of the alphabet.

Valerie had brought a potato salad, and she excused herself to go get it.

"Would you get Ken and me a beer while you're in there?" Darrel said.

"Sure." She glanced at Ken and then went inside. Ken knew she didn't approve of drinking, but they were past argument on the issue. He didn't approve of shopping, and his argument to her was that he did a lot less of the former than she did of the latter. Besides, he rarely drank, and what was a beer or two with his father? The two of them had not been close during Ken's childhood, but for the last six or seven years they had begun to foster a growing relationship that was more like friends than father-son.

Ken helped put the hamburgers on, spreading the barbecue sauce on them after Darrel laid them one at a time atop the hot grill, commenting on how good the beer was going to taste.

"Where's Chance?" Valerie said, coming back out and putting the potato salad and beer on the table.

"What?" Ken said, turning around quickly and scanning the back yard at the same time.

"Chance," Valerie repeated, this time with alarm in her voice. "Where is he?"

Now concern showed on both Ken and Darrel's face as they looked around.

Chance was gone.

"Maybe he walked around the side of the house," Darrel offered.

The three of them dashed toward the front yard, hoping to catch the baby before he toddled out into the street.

But Chance was nowhere in sight.

"Oh, God," Valerie said. "Where *is* he?"

Ken was breathing hard now, and fighting the first stirrings of adrenaline-induced panic. "Calm down, Honey. I'm sure he's around here close. He couldn't have gone far."

"*Don't tell me to calm down,*" she screamed. "I wasn't gone three minutes. Can't you watch him that long?"

Ken looked into his wife's eyes and repeated slowly, "He can't have gotten very far."

Darrel had gone to look along the side of the house opposite the door, an area that was nothing more than bushes and shrubs planted close to the house. He reported that Chance wasn't there.

"He might have gone into the neighbor's yard at the back of the property," he said. "Let's check there."

The three of them returned in a run to the back yard...and stopped in their tracks when they reached the corner of the house.

Chance was back where he had been, playing with his toys on the edge of the patio. Sunlight bounced off his toys and his light head of hair. He was rolling the plastic truck back and forth across the tops of some rubber blocks that were laid out in front of him on the grassy lawn.

Valerie ran to him and scooped him up in her arms. "Oh, Chance. You scared Mommy. You scared her." She hugged him close and then wiped a tear from the corner of her eye. "Don't do that anymore."

"Do what, Mommy?" Chance said in an innocent voice. He shook the plastic truck he still held in one small hand.

While Valerie consoled the baby, Ken happened to glance down at the blocks, and he inhaled sharply, his heart stuttering-thumping in his chest.

He looked over his shoulder. His father was pinching Chance's cheek playfully, making him giggle. Valerie was still trying to calm Chance—and probably herself, as well—by rocking him back and forth despite this. She had apparently been so scared, and glad to see Chance, that she hadn't noticed the toys on the lawn, or what Chance had done with them.

But Ken had.

He stood there for a couple of seconds, to be sure that what he was seeing was real, and then he bent and scattered the toys, his forehead and back breaking out in a thin sheen of cold sweat.

I didn't really see what I think I saw, he told himself. *Not really.*

But he'd found out long ago that lying to himself never altered things: it never changed reality.

Before he'd scattered them, the rubber alphabet blocks had been arranged in a jagged line, forming three words that stood out in colorful and eerie contrast against the bright green of the lawn:

CHANCE DADDY PAPA

* * * * *

The curtains over the kitchen sink fluttered and flapped, pushing along a warm breeze. It was four o'clock. In the windowless den the atmosphere was comfortable, with the door propped open upon the breezy hallway. Chance was fussy, and Valerie had finally gotten him to take a late nap. Ken was grateful for his wife's infinite patience.

Ken, Darrel, and Valerie had talked a little about what had happened earlier in the afternoon. Ken had not mentioned the toy blocks, or what they had spelled. He didn't want his father—or, especially, Valerie—to know something was odd about their child, and he had steered the conversation toward Chance's brief disappearance, and how quickly he was learning to talk.

Darrel laid out a scenario that put Chance on the right side of the house while the three adults were on the left and in front. Chance simply toddled back to his toys moments before they returned to the back yard. This seemed as good an explanation as any, but Darrel's voice shook as he proposed it. At one point Valerie had taken Chance inside to change him and get him a cookie—this was after he'd finished his hotdog and handful of chips—and the senior Malcolm had confided to Ken that he had another idea about the strange occurrence (it was this idea that Ken believed had caused the tremor in his father's voice). Darrel told him that Chance might have actually disappeared—might have flipped over into a plane of existence invisible to the naked eye—and that a supernatural force was at work.

Darrel appeared excited about this prospect, and he reminded Ken—not for the first time—about the afterlife and how, one dark night, his dead wife had come to him as he sat in his recliner and told him that she was waiting patiently for him, and not to worry about her because she was fine.

Ken grew tense and fidgety whenever his father brought up this subject, because he didn't believe it had happened. He'd heard this story many times in the two years since it had supposedly occurred, and he always marveled at the apparent joy and excitement in his father's voice over an incident that had most likely been nothing but a vivid dream. Or wishful thinking.

Ken's tension had only grown when Darrel stated his belief that his beloved wife might have taken Chance through the 'plane', over to her side, to visit him, look at the grandson she'd never seen—Chance's guardian angel, so to speak. Jimmy had quite possibly been there, as well.

Ken was glad his father knew not to speak of 'the other world' in front of Valerie. She believed Darrel's ramblings even less than Ken, but was more vocal on the subject.

And Ken *didn't* believe it. He'd loved his mother much more than his father, although it was often difficult to admit that, even to himself. But if he believed that his mother was sending messages from 'beyond', it would tarnish the memory of her.

He also knew that, had Darrel not had four or five beers circulating through his system, he would have been just as baffled by Chance's disappearance as were Ken and Valerie, and might not have deferred to that explanation. He wondered how his father would react to what had *really* happened—the part with the blocks—but he guessed he already knew the answer to that question; Darrel would undoubtedly see it as a message from his dead wife, dead son, or some other entity.

Now, as Valerie flipped through the channels on the television, Ken recalled how he'd felt when he saw the words in the grass. A chill had stretched almost sensuously up his back, from his tailbone to the place in his neck where spinal cord met brain. From there, it had spread down his arms, to the tips of his fingers, as though it were an electrical impulse triggered at a low amperage in his lower back, and then throttled up to a full two-twenty by the time it completed its course through his paralyzed body.

Then he had scattered the blocks, and he wondered now if the message had ever really been there.

It was there, all right. You know it, so don't kid yourself.

It *had* been.

So, tell Val, then. Tell her.

But he couldn't. It was too easy to imagine what she would say, or at least think—*Oh boy, here we go again*—and he knew he couldn't handle that reaction.

While Valerie finally found a station she could live with, and Ken stared at the books lining the shelves in the den—not to find a particular tome, but because they were in a direct line with his field of vision—he thought about something else: Chance had returned to his toys in exactly the same spot where he'd been before Valerie went inside after the beer. Ken was certain of it. He had even been turned in the same direction; back at an angle to the patio, his small body facing the back right corner of the open lawn. And what about this: what if Ken hadn't scattered the rubber letters? *That* could have led to some interesting possibilities. At the very least, Valerie would have either fainted, run screaming down the street pulling her hair, or—most likely—would have accused Ken of arranging the blocks. She would then proceed to ask him why he had left out her name. Forget that she would *know* he didn't have time to sort the blocks and spell those three words; it would be the only rational explanation—and she would grasp at it.

Her actual input to the conversation—after she'd finished crooning over him—was about how well Chance had talked. The toddler had not spoken in the hours since his disappearance, other than normal baby gibberish. This oddity seemed to amaze her, and as they'd discussed it over lunch—during which she tried to coerce Chance into talking more, which he wouldn't do—the topic seemed to help calm her further.

Valerie thought Chance had spoken three times, but Ken had counted four. "Hi, Pa Pa," as soon as he was out of the car. Chance had spoken his first complete sentence: a salutary—and voiced as though he spoke these two words every day. The second time, if he remembered correctly, had been after his father remarked that it was "about time you learned to say my name," and Chance had voice an agreement that included something Ken was sure even two-year-olds didn't pick up on very quickly—slang: "Yep, 'bout time." Ken never used 'yep' as a substitute for 'yes', and he'd never heard Valerie use it, either. Where had Chance learned *that*? Chance's third complete sentence—and Ken was sure of this, although he didn't remember it until later, when his mind had time to go back and pick over details of the trip to his father's house—had been a directed question: "Pa Pa, can I go outside?" And the fourth time had been when they returned from hunting for Chance in the yard. It was this last one that Valerie had apparently failed to remember, and with good reason; she'd been upset. She had told him, "You scared Mommy. You *scared* her. Don't do that anymore." And little Chance's reply: "Do what, Mommy?" Another question, although this one was threaded with the innocent doubt of a small child; Chance hadn't realized he'd done anything wrong.

Four complete sentences, and each of them suggesting possibilities that were, to Ken, incomprehensible.

Unless he was totally in left field somewhere, a fifteen-month-old baby could not talk in complete sentences without stumbling over at least a few vowels, syllables, or consonants. There would be at least *some* mispronunciation.

Ken had been his daddy for a little over nine months now, and in that span of time he had heard Chance pronounce words in much the same way as other infants might; through hearing the word repeatedly—such as 'mommy' and 'daddy'—and through many attempts at articulating the word. Ken believed—or at least *wanted* to believe, as most parents do—that his son was a quick and capable child, and would learn and do things in the normal time frame it took other infants.

But this...

What had happened today wasn't right. It wasn't 'ordinary' in any sense of the word. His son had gone from using slow, infantile speech (through normal trial and error) to articulating concise words and sentences—while at the same time appearing to know into which context and tone of voice to phrase the sentences.

He was sure there were other children in the world who learned to talk at a much younger age than Chance—he accepted that with a resignation similar to what he'd felt when he finally realized he couldn't father a child—but it was different when the sentences came from a mouth which had never spoken in such a way.

Ken shook his head and glanced at Valerie, who was lying at the other end of the sofa, engrossed in a movie. He wished he could, like his wife and father, come up with a plausible—if not completely sane, in his father's case—explanation for his son's...what? Spontaneous intelligence? If he could do that, he could be enjoying a quiet evening in front of the television, or perhaps with his nose in a book, oblivious to the possibility that something was not right. Things he was afraid to contemplate, missing links on a heavy chain of mystery where there should *be* no mystery.

There was the adoption. Ken and Valerie knew nothing of their son's background, with the exception of his medical records, including the fire. By law, Smalley's could not disclose names, or detailed histories. And wasn't there something else? Something about that day at the agency when the adoption was finalized? Something tugged fleetingly at Ken's mind, and then disappeared just as quickly.

Then, of course, was the weird chain of events since then: Chance's brief disappearance four weeks ago from his playpen, the man with the car trouble who had somehow known Ken's name, and then the two men at the airport who had held him at gunpoint. At *gunpoint*.

Did that really happen? he asked himself for what seemed like the thousandth time. *You might have dreamed that, you know.*

Right.

Inside, Ken didn't believe he had dreamed *any* of it, yet at the same time he felt as though he was living in one—that it was all one big dream. Soon he would wake up and rejoin the real world; a world where he and his wife were trying unsuccessfully to make a baby, and seeing doctors and specialists about their problem, and secretly wondering who was at fault. A world where such strange, recent events didn't occur, and a man could hold his sanity in a firm, secure grip.

But *that*, he was coming to believe, was only wishful thinking. What had happened was real, no matter how outrageous, and he was going to have to find out how and why.

Because the more he thought about everything, the more he felt the firm hold on his sanity slipping. He wouldn't—couldn't—let that happen again.

* * * * *

SEVEN

John awoke at two o'clock in the morning, drenched in perspiration, his chest heaving beneath the sweat-dampened sheets. Tears trickled from the corners of his eyes, though he was unaware of them.

He dreamed of Lily most nights, although those dreams were not as vivid as this one had been, and therefore less painful. This one had been a virtual replay of Lily's first visit to John's old PI offices in Rockford, with a menagerie of visions toward the end that did not quite reflect reality as it had played out. Because her first visit had been a momentous day, the memory was painful to John only in retrospect.

And in dreams.

John led Lily Burgess back into his small office and before he knew he was going to, he told her that he would help her, but it wouldn't be easy, and many precautions would have to be taken first.

On this initial visit, he wanted only to hear her story, find out as much as he could about Garret Burgess' routines and habits, and look into Lily's one good eye and one swollen-yet-beautiful eye until he became lost. Her countenance deterred his concentration more than once, and he repeated some questions because of it, apologizing constantly and assuring her that he wasn't missing anything. But in fact, he had been.

Midway through the visit, looking at that damaged hazel eye while hearing a heart-wrenching tale of a brutal and abusive marriage, John felt anger rising within him, gaining in intensity to the point where it seemed it could not be contained by the mere skin, tissue, and bones of his body. He felt he *could* kill Garret Burgess. And he could do so with a smile on his face and very little guilt on his conscience.

Although he didn't know it then, John Milcheck, son of an Illinois factory worker, and a PI who rarely did enough business most months to pay the bills, was head over heels in love. He would understand later that deep, true love was the only thing that could have even remotely led him to consider the murder of another human being. Later still, when the hardest of the pain was past, he would realize it was this same kind of love which had gotten his lovely wife killed.

He blamed himself for that, and always would.

Garret Burgess had been a local boy in Rockford, who became a reputable dentist. He'd later gotten involved in local politics, first as a Justice of the Peace, and then working his way up to president of the Rockford Chamber of Commerce. A strong and commanding man when it came to city politics, few people knew he was also a demanding husband who struck his wife with the quickness of a cobra if she so much as strayed an inch from the rules by which their marriage was governed. It was his way or none at all.

Lily told John that first day about some of the things Garret did to her: the chastising, the beatings for no good reason, the strange sexual demands. For some reason, these were harder for John to listen to than any of the beatings, although he'd only known Lily for less than an hour, but in John's mind all these events took place before him, as though he were watching two characters act out the violence and betrayal she had undergone. In his mind, he watched as a ruthless man struck a beautiful woman time and time again; watched as he forced her to her knees to orally accept his maleness against her will, made her keep it there until he was done; watched as he sodomized her brutally—according to Lily, this happened only when Garret had drunk too much—with no regard to how much pain or humiliation it caused her; listened as he degraded her like an animal while he did these, and other, terrible things to her.

There had been plenty of tears that first day. John kept a box of tissues on his desk, and Lily Burgess went through quite a few before she finished talking. Although John admired the way she'd gathered the strength and courage to even come to his office and talk about her innermost feelings and fears—a first step—he realized after listening to her story that this one act of courage was the only one in her. She was nearly a defeated woman.

"I used to love him," she said. "Believe it or not, I did."

John nodded and handed her another Kleenex.

"He wasn't this way at first. Never. Not once. Until we were married."

John asked her how she felt about that.

"I feel a lot of things. I've been an idiot, a fool, but most of all I feel betrayed."

John thought she would say no more, but she'd plunged ahead with her story. Apparently, she had kept everything bottled up inside all these years, and now that she'd let some of it escape, the rest was pushing with so much pressure that to hold it back would do more damage than continued concealment.

Later, while John was at home taking a long hot bath, drinking a cold beer, and seeing nothing but Lily Burgess' face in his mind, he would think she had told him every detail about her marriage because she felt she had to justify murder—in her own mind if not in his.

But she'd gotten to John that first day, and by the time she left he had been willing to do anything to help get her out of the mess her marriage had become.

John would have asked her to stay with him, but Garret was due home at six—and Lily said he arrived like clockwork—and things had to go along as they always had, in order to allay any suspicions. John told Lily this with some reluctance. He gave her a list of items to bring to his office on her next visit, scheduled for the following day, and with a slight tug of regret watched her walk out of his office to once again face the world that had thus far been so cruel to her.

John already cared for this woman. In the past, there had been women in the same predicament—albeit without murder on their minds—who had come to him much the same way Lily had, but none had affected him the way she had.

In his dream just past—his very *vivid* dream—he watched as Garret and Lily partook of dangerous games in a marriage that seemed destined to end in death.

And, in his dream, it did. Garret struck Lily across the face with so much force that the bridge of her nose was simultaneously broken and driven upward into her brain.

That is when John awakened from the dream, feeling overwhelmed with anger, fear, and loss. Loss of the woman he had grown to love ever more over a period of weeks and months.

He lay in bed, gasping and sweating, the dream already beginning to fragment in his mind like a mirror that has been struck with a stone. The only thing which didn't fade was the feeling of loss; a feeling so viable and huge it threatened to swallow him.

He didn't return to sleep. Instead, he sat on the edge of the bed, drinking water from the glass he kept on his bedside table, and smoking one cigarette after another. Eventually the cloud of grief that had escaped into this world from his dream began to dissipate, and by the time the faint light of dawn crested the horizon, John felt he could function well enough to face another day—one of the many that lay ahead—without his lovely Lily.

He wondered, as he always did, how he would be able to cope.

* * * * *

EIGHT

Ken watched Chance toddle around the den.

Valerie and her mother had left for town less than fifteen minutes ago to shop for the youngster, who was steadily outgrowing his clothes, as children will do in the narrow land between infant and toddler.

It was a quarter past six o'clock, Monday, and the weather segment had just finished running on the KAIT news. The weather was the only news for which Ken had an interest. The other news—violence at home, war in the Middle East, death—was too depressing, as if the world existed under a gloomy cloud of pessimism and despair. Keeping up with the weather was something supplanted in Ken like an inner watch; an endearing yet troubling habit that was integrated so deeply in his adult life that nothing could deter his compulsion to know what nature had in store. That included the strange events that had so recently focused around his adopted son.

Strike that. The weather *had* been one of the most important factors in his day-to-day life. Until now.

Ken looked at Chance, thinking.

"Hi, Chance," he said.

Chance raised his head in recognition of his name, but looked innocently at Ken and giggled. Ken detected no more intelligence in his son than he had before, or since, the incident at his father's house.

Chance grabbed a rattle that lay in the floor—along with various teething toys and a variety of plastic trucks—and shook it vigorously. Then he giggled again.

"Who am I, buddy?" Ken said. The words sounded strange, sort of like talking to himself when alone, but his mind would not rest until he pursued this.

Chance ogled up at him, and a thread of saliva drooled from a corner of his mouth, like liquid mist. It formed a small and tidy puddle on the blanket Ken had spread for him to play on.

"You can say my name, I know you can," Ken tried. His voice was encouraging now, but again Chance said nothing.

Ken was at odds. He felt somehow detached from his son. He had done nothing but loved Chance unconditionally—as if he were biologically his—and now he found himself in an uncomfortable position; he was trying to coax the child into showing some of the intelligence he had previously displayed, and he felt like a fool and a stranger for doing so.

Chance looked at him for a moment, as though he expected Ken to continue talking, and then shook the rattle.

Ken decided he would have to either think of a different way to do this, or just stop trying.

The television was turned low, the house quiet.

"Chance?" Ken said.

Chance looked up and grinned, shaking the rattle with his right hand in small jerky motions. The toy was then directed into his mouth, and he removed it quickly, giving it a look of distaste. Ken would have found this extremely funny under other circumstances, but not today.

"Chance?"

"Dada," the baby said.

Da-da, Ken thought. *He used complete coherent sentences on Dad, and I just get Da-da. Not to mention he has called me Daddy for at least a month.*

"It's *daddy*," Ken said. "Say da-a-addy."

"Dada?" The voice was small and sweet.

Ken felt the first stirrings of agitation, even though he knew it was a senseless reaction.

"How about pa pa? Ken said. "Can you say pa pa?"

"Pa pa," Chance said amiably.

"Where *is* Pa pa?" Ken couldn't quite believe he was actually sitting here in his den attempting to converse with a fifteen-month-old child. That, in itself, wasn't abnormal—a child learned to talk by listening to repetitive sounds. What *was* abnormal was the fact that he was expecting Chance to hold up the other end of the conversation. It was almost funny.

"Where's Pa pa?" Ken said again.

Chance looked at him, and for a moment Ken thought he glimpsed, in his son's eyes, a fierce intelligence that was foreign, raw, and totally out of place. It flickered for a second, and then was gone. Chance shook his head, as if saying 'no', then he looked at the lamp that was perched on an end table at the far side of the sofa, to Ken's left.

"Pa pa?" Ken mimicked, in an effort to get his son to repeat him.

Chance looked at him and again shook his head. Then he looked at the lamp.

Ken got a strange feeling, and he wished suddenly that Valerie was here. Chance was trying to tell him something.

But what?

And why did he feel so uneasy about it?"

To top it off, why didn't Chance just come right out and say it, if he possessed the ability to do so?

He was clearly trying to tell him *something*.

A shake of his head, a glance at the lamp.

What could Chance be signaling 'no' about?

Something about the lamp?

He could see nothing wrong with it. It was a plain old, garden-variety lamp; green glass base with a yellowing shade over the bulb. The shade had been white when they bought it, but had faded over time and was only in the den because a new one had taken its place in the front room of the house when they'd changed color schemes a few years back. It was an ordinary lamp, although small, and it put out a good deal of light—

Ken suddenly thought he understood.

The bulb beneath the lampshade was a low-watt brand, but because he was in the floor it was probably shining right in Chance's eyes.

He got up and switched off the lamp. The soft light from the television set would be adequate enough for Chance to see and play.

He had been trying to read something into nothing. All along, there had been too much light shining in Chance's eyes, and if he could talk he probably would have said so. Chance was showing him, instead of telling him, and because Ken was still somewhat new at parenting, he had not seen it for what it was.

"That better?" he said, sitting down. "Did that old light bother your eyes? Huh, sport?"

Chance shook his rattle and grinned up at him.

Ken leaned back on the sofa. *Maybe the light was diverting his attention. Maybe he'll talk to me now.*

Oh, please. That makes a hell of a lot of sense.

Feeling a little foolish, and doing it only because they were alone, Ken said: "Chance? Can you talk to me like you talked to Pa pa at his house?"

Chance stopped shaking the rattle, and again Ken thought he caught a glimmer of something behind his eyes. But it might have only been a reflection of the television. Then Chance shook his head again, harder, and this time *nodded* his head toward the lamp, cutting his eyes toward it briefly and then looking again at Ken. Then again; eyes moving to look at the lamp, a nod of his head, and then an innocent look back to him.

This startled Ken, although part of him was not surprised at all; a part of him which suspected, with a shadowy knowledge, that the shake of Chance's head and the glances at the lamp had meant something more. Now, he was *certain* that it did.

Chance was trying to tell him something. Maybe not with words, but with the next best thing: signs.

Ken wasn't sure how to proceed.

Just forget about it, then, he told himself. *Maybe you are reading something into this. The same way you did Jimmy's death. You let that shit drive you half-crazy, so why should this be any different?*

He forced the voice from his mind. It *was* different.

"The lamp?" he said.

Now, instead of shaking his head 'no', Chance nodded: 'yes'.

He understands me and knows what the word 'lamp' signifies, Ken thought. *Okay, that's a start.*

"Can you say lamp?" Ken said. What Chance did next was disturbing, but something for which Ken would later be grateful. He would look back in the days ahead and recognize this moment as when his life—and way of thinking—changed almost completely.

Chance looked at Ken, shook his head 'no' again…and then raised one tiny index finger to his lips, in a mimicry of a mother telling her child to shush; be quiet.

To Ken's knowledge, Chance had never before seen this particular gesture—not even from TV, and Ken realized only now that Chance had never developed a child's affinity for the idiot box, even when children's programs played—and watching him do it caused a chill to walk its icy fingers up his back to his neck, where the small hairs stood on end as if stimulated by static electricity.

Valerie, Ken thought. *Valerie needs to be here to see this.*

And it occurred to him that she was never around when something happened for which Ken had no explanation: Chance's disappearance in the back yard (she was there, but professed to see nothing), the stranger with the broken-down vehicle, the two men at the airport. Now this. The only exception had been three days ago, at his father's house, when she had witnessed Chance's brief mastery of speech. Still, she hadn't seen the blocks.

Instinct now told Ken to do what his son had pantomimed. He obeyed that inner voice, and instead of talking, he pointed to the lamp and raised his eyebrows.

Chance nodded more vigorously, and then got up and walked over to the lamp. There, he pointed to the top of it and looked at Ken, then back to the lamp, then to Ken again.

Ken was reminded of the *Lassie* shows he had watched as a youngster. Lassie always did that when she wanted to show something to Timmy. Only Lassie would bark instead of point. Ken thought—crazily—that if Chance were to start barking, it would drive him completely out of his mind.

Chance didn't bark, of course, and although Ken felt some absurd relief at that, he still wondered why he didn't just come right out and say what he wanted him to know.

Yet he was smart enough to comprehend that Chance wasn't talking for a reason, and it was more than likely the same reason he wanted Ken to refrain from speaking. So, what *was* the reason?

Ken trusted his instincts and followed his son's lead.

Chance pointed again to the lamp and Ken stood. He picked up his son, setting him in the crook of his right arm, and he whispered, "What is it? What's wrong?"

Because something *was* wrong.

He moved closer to the lamp, and Chance reached out and laid one small finger on the top of it. Then he looked at Ken, leaned over, and whispered in his ear. "Right there."

Ken's heart thumped. Chance's vocal cords had produced those two words as capably as could his own.

He turned the little black knob beneath the lampshade, and the room was once again filled with soft amber light.

Chance blinked his eyes at the change in lighting, and then reached over again to touch the top of the lamp.

Before his little finger made it there, Ken saw, and his heart raced faster. His chest now felt tight, compressed.

The lamp was a typical one, and the nut holding the shade onto the fixture looked like a short top hat, similar to one in a *Monopoly* game.

At least it had been.

It had always been there. Ken had removed the shade from this lamp perhaps a dozen times in the past, whenever he and Valerie had moved from rent-house to rent-house. Since they had purchased this home—almost five years ago, now—he had never had a reason to remove the lampshade.

Where the hat-shaped nut should have been was a small device that he did not at first recognize. It was round, a little larger than the hat-shaped nut had been, and had tiny silver holes in the top like the recording speakers on most small cassette recorders. The area containing these holes was perhaps half an inch in diameter. On one side Ken could see—barely—minute letters and numbers inscribed into the dull metal. Holding his hand above the bulb to shield his eyes, he saw a hair-sized wire running from the bottom of the device down to the base of the bulb socket.

A loose cramp stroked his stomach.

He reached down (his hand warming from the searing heat of the bulb—it was amazing how much heat they produced) and plucked the wire loose from the base of the light socket. That done, he tried unscrewing the gadget from the top side of the shade, and was surprised that it turned as easily as the hat-shaped nut always had.

When he'd removed it, he could see why.

The bottom of the device was hollow halfway through, and was threaded as neatly as a nut right out of a machine shop. There was even a dab of oil on the thin threads. That detail brought the truth home to him like nothing else could have: someone had bugged his house, and they had wanted to make sure it didn't rust onto the lamp fixture. Great, tedious care must have gone into the design of this high-tech listening device.

Ken felt the cold grip of fear. He'd watched plenty of movies where someone—usually the FBI or the bad guys (or both, in the same role)—planted bugs in a character's home, and every time he saw one of these movies, he would cringe at the thought of that happening to him; of someone knowing everything he said, hearing every sound he made, invading his privacy. Invading the privacy of his *family*.

He wondered for a moment how long the bug had been there, and pushed the thought away before his mind could stop to examine it.

"It's a bug," he said in an awed voice.

He held it between his thumb and index finger above the light, and turned it this way and that in front of Chance's face.

"Bug," Chance agreed softly, and Ken, in spite of the implication of the listening device, nevertheless marveled at the clarity in that small voice.

He thought of the men at the airport. What was it one of them had said? *Your son is not what he appears to be.* Ken shuddered.

As he stood there looking at the device, he wondered if they were responsible for planting it here. After a moment's thought, however, he came to the conclusion that it was an improbability. If the two men wanted to eavesdrop on his family, they would have continued to be discrete; they wouldn't have confronted Ken in a public place, with nothing to disguise their faces. No, it couldn't have been those two. If anything, the confrontation at the airport had been an effort to warn him. Of what, he wasn't certain, but he had not felt hostility from the men—as he should have, considering one of them had put a gun to his ribs. And hadn't they said someone could hear?

But you dreamed that, remember? his mind screamed at him.

Did I? If I dreamed that, am I also dreaming this?

If those two men—

A light tapping on his shoulder dragged him from his thoughts.

It was Chance.

He looked right into Ken's eyes, and now there was no mistaking the gulf of intelligence there. He leaned close.

Chance whispered: "There's more."

* * * * *

William Calhoun was sitting behind his desk, filing his nails with quick jerky motions, when his phone rang, although no sound emanated from the phone on his desk. Instead, it was the phone in the bottom left drawer. This phone was only used in emergencies, and he was only alerted to it by a flashing red light that glowed from a paperweight on the desk next to the normal phone. The paperweight was a small piece of granite in the shape of the 'rock' in the *Prudential Insurance* commercials. Calhoun was a friend of that company's current CEO, and the 'rock' had been a gift. He'd had the red warning light installed later.

The light flashed again, and as he opened the bottom drawer he wondered what was up.

"Calhoun," he snapped when he put the phone to his ear. *This better be important,* he thought to himself.

And, of course, it was. This encrypted line was never utilized for anything but the most serious situations, and this time was no different.

He listened to the voice on the other end for about thirty seconds, scraping bits and pieces of clippings into the middle drawer of his desk. Adrenaline coursed through his body like the upward sweep of a kite.

When he hung up, he used the phone on top of his desk to call his secretary. He wanted agent Milcheck to report as soon as possible to his office. Milcheck was to be told it was extremely urgent, and no more. Then he made a few more calls.

That done, he put the phone into its cradle, moved his chair from behind his desk, and began pacing back and forth. He did this without thinking; he would be standing when John arrived.

While he waited and paced, he thought about the call. One of the listening devices at the Malcolm residence had been deactivated. The technician who had called him could only speculate as to whether the device had been found, or accidentally disabled.

A few minutes later the red light on the paperweight began blinking again, and when Calhoun got off the line this time, he was able to rule out an accident; another bug had been deactivated. The devices had recorded no activity for the past twenty minutes, and that was another sign that something had gone wrong in Jonesboro, Arkansas.

As the director awaited the arrival of his agents, he paced the floor behind his desk, unable to keep his eyes off the 'rock'.

After a while, the red light began to blink.

* * * * *

NINE

Ken and Chance discovered four more listening devices.

To be precise, Chance found them. The toddler pointed the way, not saying much, his baby instincts apparently taking over and causing him to believe that what the two of them were doing was a pretty fun game. He seemed disappointed when it was over.

As Ken held him—switching him often from arm to arm—Chance led him with one small index finger held out, like a beacon, from the den into the kitchen. There, he pointed to the four-slice toaster on the countertop to the right of the sink. Ken walked over to it, and Chance leaned down and put his outstretched finger on the left side of the toaster, on the level that triggered the heating elements.

Ken looked at it closely, and could see no difference between this lever and the one next to it, which controlled the other two slots. Then he saw another hair-sized wire leading from the handle to the inside of the toaster. He pulled the lever loose and turned it over. Underneath was another smooth piece of dull silver metal dotted with tiny holes; another listening device, and a clever one at that. He also checked the lever on the right, but it was clean. He put the device inside his shirt pocket, where he'd put the one from the den. Chance pointed to the short hallway, and then to Ken and Valerie's bedroom door. Anger clouded Ken's mind for the first time since finding the bug in the den, and it took the edge off the fear. *Our bedroom,* he thought. *Rotten bastards!*

When they were inside, Chance pointed to the bedside lamp that sat on a small stand to the left of the bed. Ken walked to it on stiff legs, turned it on, and immediately saw a replica of the bug from the den. He twisted it off the fixture and jerked it—and the minute wire—loose in one swift movement. The lampshade teetered against the light bulb.

Have to get some nuts to hold the lampshades on when I'm done, he thought. It was funny what your mind thought of when it was over-stimulated and knocked out of kilter.

"Any more in here?" he whispered.

Chance shook his head.

Ken was infuriated that someone had planted the device right beside the bed. His and Valerie's lovemaking had always been good, but since the adoption it had been intense, incredibly satisfying, and more passionate than ever. There was no more thinking about the act itself, wondering if this time would be the magical, enchanted moment when conception took place and all their fears and doubts diminished like the wind. Instead, the sex had been at times over-powering, their glistening bodies seeming to flow and fuse together into one gasping, shuddering climax that felt endless. They were seldom quiet, and someone, somewhere, had been listening to every grunt, moan and giggle.

He put Chance on the dark green comforter and ran a hand through his hair.

How much had been heard coming from this room?

How long had this particular bug been here?

Never mind about the others. Forget about them. At the moment, this one was all that mattered; this small gizmo with its threaded middle and its tiny recording speakers, and even smaller wire. How long had it been here, recording all of Ken and Valerie's most intimate conversations, and even more intimate lovemaking?

How long?

Ken felt his anger bubbling higher, getting close to his tolerance level. But what could he do then? Throw a tantrum? Grab something and chuck it across the room? He had a small child with him, for crying out loud. Now wasn't the time to lose his cool.

He took a big breath, held it, released it in a long sigh, and was surprised to find that old trick worked; he felt calmer, like he could actually think again.

Okay. They'd found three bugs thus far—den, kitchen, and bedroom. There was bound to be more, wasn't there?

Ken looked at his son. "Do you know where any more are?"

Chance nodded, then leaned over and whispered in his ear. "In the living room. In my room."

"Good boy," Ken said, and walked out into the hallway. Because his mind was preoccupied with other things—the listening devices in general, and what they might mean—he seemed to take Chance's speech as a matter of course.

They went down the hall, into the living room.

This room was sparsely furnished with Victorian era pieces that they had purchased a piece at a time over the last four years; maroon cushioned sofa and sitting chair, sculpted wood end tables with glossy surfaces, and elegant lamps with colorful cloth shades in the same soft tones as the upholstered furniture. The family rarely ventured into this room.

A beautiful stone and marble fireplace faced the room from the east wall, and Chance led Ken to it with one small index finger. Ken was reminded of a song he had learned in Sunday School as a child. The song was called *This Little Light*, and they would all stand or sit in a circle and hold up one index finger—much the way Chance was—and sing: 'This little light of mine, I'm gonna let it shine'.

And that's what my son's doing, Ken thought. *He's showing the way, letting his little light shine.*

But what was leading Chance? How could he know where these bugs were, when he wasn't even three feet tall? Ken cast those questions aside for later examination. Right now, he had another bug to get rid of.

This one was on the fireplace mantel, between a framed photo of Valerie's parents and one of Ken and Valerie on their wedding day. It was a round cylindrical device that resembled a miniature soda can. It was a dull white color, and blended in with the white marble of the mantel. The end of it had a thin metal mesh on it with tiny holes that, by now, were easily recognizable to Ken. This one, how-ever, did not have a wire connected to it, so he smashed the device against the marble.

He stuck the bug in his shirt pocket. He was acquiring quite a collection.

He shifted Chance to his left arm.

"Where to, Buddy?" he said in a low voice, but of course he knew the answer to that one: upstairs to the nursery, to Chance's room.

The upstairs was a loft of sorts. At the top of the stairs a five-foot long hallway led to the nursery, which Ken and Valerie had remodeled to their tastes. They'd replaced the blue and white wallpaper with a fresh coat of off-white paint and a twelve-inch border with brown, gray and dark green carrousels. The crib, changing table, and rocking table were a lustrous oak, and a musical carrousel adorned a set of drawers that were built into the nook beneath one of the room's two windows. A wooden, hand-sculpted carrousel stood in a corner near the crib, and many painted ones rode the walls on all sides of the room. Valerie had drawn these exquisitely detailed horses from tracing-patterns she ordered from a magazine, and had slowly and meticulously painted them in the long months when they had tried to conceive the child who would enjoy the beautiful nursery.

When he and his son entered the room, Ken was reminded once again of how close he and Valerie had come to not being able to adopt a baby. Forget that they couldn't have one of their own. Ken had learned to accept and live with that in his own way, but if they hadn't been able to adopt Chance, his outlook on life would have been severely diminished. Every time he came into this room—which was often, though not as frequently as he had when Chance was smaller and in need of more attention—he was thankful for his son. Thankful that he was here at all.

And he was now, as well.

During the short trip down the hall and up the stairs, he had time to realize that, if it wasn't for Chance, he wouldn't know about the bugs. In fact, he was pretty sure that he would never have stumbled across any of them on accident. They were hidden that well.

And if it wasn't for Chance, those bugs wouldn't be here in the first place.

Now *there* was something to think about.

He actually paused on the fourth riser before pushing that thought to the back of his mind. Right now, his son was still the sweet and innocent child with whom he and Valerie had fallen in love—not the stranger at which his mind hinted.

They went into the room. Ken looked at Chance and raised his eyebrows inquisitively.

Chance looked at him and smiled his best baby smile, and then his eyes...changed. It was only for a moment, and subtle, but Ken was certain he'd seen it. They became narrower somehow, and in them Ken saw an unfathomable sea of knowledge. Chance pointed to his crib. "There."

Ken looked at him again, a strange and thoughtful look on his face.

Then he moved to the crib. When he got there, Chance pointed to the Black Beauty nightlight that hung from the end of his mobile. The mobile was—to make things unanimous—also a carrousel, with five horses on painted poles beneath a striped canopy. Ken had argued with Valerie against a night light in the room. He believed that if Chance was to ever become afraid of the dark—and he figured the child would go through that stage at some point—*that* would be the time to put a nightlight in his room. Until then, there was no sense in getting him use to having that small glow every evening, only to cause a fear of the dark to surface if he ever had to sleep without it. In the end, Valerie had won that argument. That had come during the first week or so after the adoption, and Ken had been too happy to put much fight into *any* argument (not that there were many—there was not).

Yet, here he was now, with Valerie gone and he and his son—his intelligent, *talking* son, no less—on an adventurous quest through the house to locate and deactivate listening devices that some unknown person, or persons, had planted. Once again, he felt the insane urge to laugh out loud. It was like some crappy spy novel.

Oh, if Valerie could see us now.

The urge to laugh passed and he thumbed Black Beauty's tail to the up position, which turned on the small light. He studied the horse and didn't see anything. Then he peered upward, to the top of the carrousel, and there it was. This bug was a little larger than the other four; square, black, with tiny holes covering most of the exposed surface. By the light coming from Black Beauty and what came through the windows, Ken made out the tiny, hair-like wire leading from the device downward, into the back of Black Beauty, where it connected to the small electrical innards of the horse.

Ken traced the wire with his finger and was fixing to yank it loose when Chance tapped him on the shoulder.

He stayed his hand and looked at his son.

Chance shook his head. His eyes were stern, somehow.

Ken leaned close and whispered in to Chance's ear: "Why not?"

Chance leaned back and looked at him, his small baby's face never more innocent and beautiful, and pointed toward the floor with one finger. Then he silently mouthed: *Downstairs.*

Of course. No talking. The listening device was still functioning.

That fact alone gnawed at Ken, because he wanted to yank it loose, destroy it as he had the others. But he didn't, of course. Chance's advice had so far proven to be good, so why question it now?

Once downstairs, they went into the den.

He put Chance on the sofa and then sat across from him, on the glossy surface of the coffee table.

"Is it okay to talk in here now?" Ken whispered, and Chance nodded.

"Good," he said in his normal voice. He glanced at his watch. A quarter of seven. *Is that all?* It felt like hours since Chance had begun their great expedition by pointing to the lamp in this room, but less than thirty minutes had passed.

He shifted his weight on the hard surface of the table and heard the bugs in his shirt pocket rattle and click against each other like hollow teeth.

"Now that we can talk," Ken said, slightly uncomfortable, "I've got a few questions, okay?"

Chance smiled, clapped his hands together, and said in his best baby voice, "Okay."

* * * * *

TEN

Night had fallen outside the subterranean government compound, cloaking the foothills in a dark shroud. The evening was almost preternaturally silent.

Deep inside the complex, Duke Tarkington was trying to get lost in a book, but not having much luck.

A blank-faced librarian manned the library on Level Four until eight o'clock each weeknight. This librarian was also a night-duty sentry on the east end of the compound. Most of the employees here fulfilled more than one function each day, and this man would work fifteen hours by the time his guard duty ended.

Right now, the man seemed anxious, and as Duke watched him with discreet glances over the top of his book, he guessed the librarian probably liked his second job better and couldn't wait to get to it.

It was almost eight o'clock, at which time a part-time librarian would come in and sort and shelve the day's return of books (usually heavy—reading was by far the biggest hobby inside the compound), after which he would lock the doors to the library promptly at ten.

The full-time librarian/sentry on duty now was Blake Henry, and Duke cared as little for him as he did most of the other inhabitants of the complex. The part-time librarian, on the other hand, was a nice fellow by the name of Tyler James, and Duke liked him. Tyler didn't compare to Prometheus—Duke figured no one alive could—but he was the only other person here that seemed to genuinely like books. Many people in the compound were academics and read because it was the most accessible form of entertainment.

Duke spent a lot of his free time in the library, and had passed many evenings conversing with Tyler about various books each of them had read. Although Tyler could sometimes seem distant, like most people relegated to living below ground, Duke found him friendly enough.

He would be in soon.

The book Duke held open in front of him was a novel by Dean Koontz, and although the story, *Cold Fire*, was good, Duke's mind was focused primarily on watching Blake and waiting for Tyler's shift to begin. Another book lay unopened to Duke's left. It was a book about the game of chess, called *Moves of the Champions*.

Duke's first visit to this library, when he was only five, had enthralled him—and it still did. Never had he known that so many books existed. His mother, before her death twelve years ago, always read to him at bedtime—and occasionally during idle hours of the day—and Duke had loved the fictional stories and adventures of which she told him. But he had been stunned into silence at the mountainous shelves of books in the library. Two stories of shelves graced all sides of the cavernous rooms, and the rows stretched as far as Duke could see; thousands upon thousands of books. Years later he would learn, from a future friend known only to him at that time as the 'subject', that this, and one other library here, held a copy of every book copyrighted in the United States, along with many other, foreign editions. It was like a replica of the Library of Congress.

And the 'subject' was the reason Duke was here tonight, instead of in his living quarters. Tomorrow was Saturday, and Prometheus had asked Duke to bring *Moves of the Champions* for their hour together. He wasn't sure why his friend wanted the book. As far as he was concerned, Prometheus didn't need any pointers on playing Chess.

He pretended to read while he watched Blake Henry look at his watch and put on a light jacket, and Duke guessed that maybe he should peruse the book himself. *He* could sure use some helpful moves and strategies.

And then Tyler walked through the wide double doors near the front desk, and Blake was brushing by him—on his way to his sentry-duty, Duke supposed.

Tyler turned and watched him leave, and then offered Duke an amusing smile. "Talkative guy, sir Henry. I *guess* everything's okay here, thanks for filling me in. How are you, Duke?"

Duke gave a quick thumbs-up, and then reached for the pen and pad of paper on the table to his right. He scribbled on the top sheet, gathered up his two books, and walked over and handed Tyler the note. Tyler read it out loud, as he always did, although he was not a slow reader and was quick of mind. Duke supposed he was one of those readers who preferred to *hear* the words they read.

"Hi, Tyler. Doing okay? (Tyler paused and returned a thumbs-up) I would like to check out these books. Thanks."

"You got it, man," Tyler said. He had carried in two books of his own. "Just let me put these down and I'll fix you right up."

Duke smiled and raised an eyebrow at Tyler's books. Both had been written by scientists who were housed here at the compound. They were books for the research teams only (Tyler's primary job), and would never see publication outside the mountain complex. There was a complete section in the library containing over three hundred such books, and most of them spawned from research done on the 'subject'. These books were kept under close lock and key in a back room.

Tyler probably guessed that Duke's inquiring look meant something other than "you're actually reading this stuff?" He shook his head and told Duke: "Sorry, man. Nothing today."

Duke hadn't thought there would be—not this close to the weekend—but it never hurt to check. Sometimes Tyler brought a message to Duke from Prometheus. There were always requests for books, and fetching the 'subject's' reading material fell within the realms of Duke's own job—a gofer, mainly, although he also could have served as a computer technician had someone higher up (his father, for instance) known, or paid attention to, how intelligent he was.

Tyler was one of only a few that *did* have an inkling of how smart Duke was. He was a thin man, pale of skin like most who lived here, with sandy hair the color of the outside desert. He scanned Duke's books and handed them to him, eyeing the cover of *Cold Fire* with a raised eyebrow. "Big plans for the weekend?"

Duke shook his head and then scratched on his pad: "Not really. Same 'ol same 'ol."

"I hear you," Tyler said, and laughed, after reading the note aloud.

Duke went back to his table and sat down to read more of the Koontz novel. He'd only read twenty pages thus far, and the action in the story had yet to subside. He loved it when he found a novel that kept his attention and made him anxious to turn the pages. This one was going to be good.

It was when he reached page forty-six sometime later that he found the note tucked between the pages.

As his fingers played over its smooth surface, Duke briefly entertained the idea that someone before him had left the paper in there as a bookmark. So, it wouldn't hurt anything to unfold the small scrap...except...except a feeling had come over him by some premonitory sense, which Prometheus had told him all human beings possessed—though few knew how to use.

It wasn't a *bad* feeling, so much as that, if he read the note (for it *was* a note; he *knew* that, as well as who it had come from), some chain of events would be set in motion that would change everything he had come to know during his life beneath these mountains.

And would the change be for the better, or worse? He read newspapers from time to time (most were from either New York or Los Angeles), and it seemed that violence, hatred, and greed ran rampant in the world, and that made him almost grateful to live this comparably sheltered and isolated life.

He looked up at Tyler, who was busy thumbing through a magazine that had been left on the counter. With trembling hands, Duke unfolded the paper, and when he saw his name scrawled in the salutation in black ink, he was not surprised. Neither was he relieved.

He read the letter:

Duke,
  The time has come for a favor, my friend. You may
be surprised at the arrival of this letter, but please do not
let that affect your thinking. A preoccupied mind does not
see the other things it contains.
  The child is in jeopardy. Therefore, I need your help.
Duke, the risk on your end for your help will be great.
I will not lie about that. I only wish it could be different.
There is something that I need for you to do before you
visit me in the morning, and you must be extremely careful...

Duke read the instructions given him by his friend, then he reread the last two sentences of the note over again, although the ones preceding them were the ones which troubled him.

If all goes well, the child will be safe, and I will be free at last. I hope you understand, and that you will help.

>Your Friend Always,
>Prometheus

Duke folded the note and marked his page with it before closing the book. He tapped on the counter lightly and Tyler looked up from his magazine. Duke jerked a thumb toward the door: *I'm leaving.*

"Okay, man," Tyler said. "You take it easy."

Duke gave a thumbs-up and a smile that felt forced, sad, depressed. He left the library and walked slowly down the hall toward the dormitory.

Take it easy, Tyler had said.

Yeah, right. Take it easy.

That was the problem.

What he had to do before being able to sleep in the comfort of his bed (if indeed sleep would put in an appearance at all) was not going to be an easy task.

Duke shivered.

* * * * *

ELEVEN

John Milcheck arrived at the CIA offices shortly after four o'clock, and he immediately sensed something important when he walked into Calhoun's office. Aides and secretaries bustled here and there, in and out of the room, and Calhoun himself was in the left corner of the office, conferring with a man John recognized as agent Mark Lomax. Lomax had blond hair, a red mole on his pale square chin, and blue eyes that sparkled like new coins. He noticed John first, nodded his head, and looked at the director.

Calhoun turned around. "Good afternoon, John," he said. "Glad you could get here so fast."

"Schooner told me it was urgent," John said. Jake Schooner was the agent who'd called and told him to get his ass over to headquarters ASAP.

"It is, it is," Calhoun said. He went to his desk, where he began pacing. John thought about standing on his toes, peering over the desk, and checking the condition of the carpet back there, but of course he didn't (he could imagine a hole worn through the fabric, or perhaps even a long, rugged gash in the floor itself).

"Is it Project Lone Star?" John said tentatively.

"Yes, it is."

John was both surprised and excited about this.

He was surprised because, in his tenure at the agency, he had never witnessed the urgency that was on display in this particular office. And he was excited, of course, because something had evidently happened; something important.

On his trip to Jonesboro to plant the tracking devices he'd noticed nothing unusual about the Malcolm's child. Now, however, it was obvious that his perceptions that evening had been wrong. He felt he could contribute that to the fact that, on the night he'd met Kenneth Malcolm and his son, he had been more concerned with devising his 'broken-down vehicle' story.

Perhaps he hadn't paid enough attention to the boy.

He *had* held the baby, however, and he'd noticed nothing out of the ordinary. He had slobbered a little on John's jacket, but wasn't that to be expected from a child his age?

So, what was it about the child that had everyone in this office in a tizzy?

"—there right now."

John fidgeted. "Excuse me, sir?"

Calhoun stopped pacing long enough to look at John. The director looked irritated, but did not orally convey that feeling. Instead, he began pacing again. "I said, I wish we had an agent there right now. In Jonesboro."

"Yes, sir," John said. "Sorry, sir."

Calhoun flapped a hand at him, as if John's inattentiveness were no longer of any consequence.

"What about the FBI offices in Jonesboro?" John said. "Could they be utilized?" Providing input or offering suggestions to the director was always iffy, but the words were out of his mouth before he could stop them.

"Too risky," Calhoun said. "This project is top-secret."

"Right, sir." Again, he wondered what the hell this case was about.

The director finally quit pacing. He braced his arms on either side of his wide desk and looked at John. "The listening devices in the Malcolm household have been deactivated. All of them but one, at any rate, and we've got to get some agents out there to find out why."

"Do you think they found them?" John said.

"We have to assume they have. Our technicians ran a check on the satellite and all the other electronic components, and everything checked out to be in working order. No malfunctions anywhere except for four of the voice-activated devices inside the Malcolm residence."

John knew—if he could believe what he'd been told thus far—that everything the Malcolms said in their home was recorded and then transferred to hard copy somewhere in this building. "Was there any indication on the recordings that they suspected the devices were in their home?"

"That's just it," Calhoun said. "We have very little recorded from this afternoon. Mr. and Mrs. Malcolm talking about the clothes she was going to shop for—mostly for the baby—and a few snippets of conversation by her mother, herself, and Mr. Malcolm. There was nothing that might prove they were suspicious of anything."

John wanted to inform the director that the Malcolm's silence would be a purposeful one if they suspected eavesdroppers, but he kept his mouth shut. Calhoun was on pins and needles here, and a part of John was glad at the fact the director had overlooked an obvious detail. Calhoun should have been more honest with him about the history of the project. Perhaps a little petty, he knew, but John decided now to listen to what the director had to say, sort out the bullshit, and draw his own conclusions.

"Could it have been an accident?" John said. "A short circuit somewhere in the equipment that the computers might have overlooked?"

"No," Calhoun said briskly. "I don't think so, although a computer can't always be trusted. I do, however, trust the men controlling them, so I've pretty much ruled out the possibility of malfunction. We used state-of-the-art equipment in that home."

He ceased pacing long enough to open his top desk drawer and extract a cigar from a leather case. He lit it with a silver Zippo from the same drawer, then exhaled sweet-smelling smoke in a long cloud. "We don't keep an agent in Jonesboro around the clock because this technology makes it unnecessary. Or at least it should. Damn the President, anyway. If he'd let me do this my way, none of this would be happening. The child would still be in the compound under less expensive surveillance, and the Malcolms would have some other child. *Damn.*"

Although John was relieved the director's fury was concentrated on someone other than himself, he was still a little shocked and surprised that William Calhoun had lost his focus.

Even as a private investigator John had understood the importance of keeping focused. He had even, he thought, done an admirable job of it, save for the one incident concerning Garret Burgess.

"What do you need me to do?" he said now.

Calhoun stopped pacing and again gripped the sides of his desktop. His cigar smoldered in an ashtray and formed a cloud around the director's head. "You and Lomax are to go to Jonesboro. If the Malcolms *have* found the equipment in their house, they may have decided to run, although I doubt it. You and Lomax are to drive to Arkansas—no flying this time. If they *are* running, they will be heading east. It will be easier for you to reach them if you're in a vehicle. Both of their family relatives who aren't in Arkansas are east of the Mississippi, so that would be the obvious assumption. We'll be able to track them with satellite uplinks through the devices on their vehicle, and we'll keep you and Lomax informed by the equipment in your car."

A private line with a scrambler was one of the newest luxuries with which all agency vehicles were equipped. All conversations were scrambled during transmission and could only be deciphered if the phone on the other end had similar technology. It lessened the ease with which someone could monitor or trace calls. Without a scrambler, keeping a conversation private on a cellular phone was a gamble at best.

"I've already given Lomax the paperwork," Calhoun continued. "You're to leave ASAP and if the Malcolms decide to run you will be notified, and when you catch up to them you are to apprehend the entire family. If that becomes an impossibility, then get the boy regardless. You will then give a detailed report via modem from the laptop in your vehicle." Calhoun's stare was even more intense when he said, "Don't let anything or anyone get in your way if you have to apprehend the child."

John knew what he meant by that: he would be required to go to Jonesboro fully armed.

Calhoun was quiet for a moment.

Agent Lomax had been in the corner talking to a secretary, and now he came and stood beside John in front of Calhoun's desk. Mark Lomax was six-three, slightly taller than John, but about fifty pounds lighter. Because he'd been briefed earlier, he was already dressed in street clothes; tan twill slacks, black leather belt, and a striped gray and maroon shirt that hung loosely from his bony frame. John guessed Lomax would go about one-forty soaking wet. He glanced at John as he came up beside him, and smiled almost smugly, like a child who has gotten his way. The blueness of his eyes was deep, penetrating.

"Is there anything else?" John said.

"Yes," Calhoun said. "Be careful. We don't know exactly what's happened, and although we don't know the child's full potential, we have to assume he's a threat, that he's dangerous."

Dangerous? John's mind spun. *We're talking about a child here—a baby.*

He briefly entertained the idea that the director had this case mixed up with some other one, but reluctantly decided he didn't. Again, he said nothing. He was finding out there was more than a little he didn't know about Project Lone Star. When the director of the CIA calls a fifteen-month-old child dangerous, then there undoubtedly must be a good reason for it. John had no idea what the reason could be, but that was okay. It would be a long drive to Arkansas with Lomax, who apparently knew all about the project.

John was envious of him because of this. Sure, the man had been the initial agent chosen for this project, but he'd taken ill at the onset and since then what had he done? John had been assigned all the dirty work—all but planting the listening devices in the Malcolm residence; that had been done by a faceless team of operators known to very few in the agency—but Lomax knew more about the case. It should have made John want to laugh.

Instead, he felt the creeping tentacles of anger, and he made an effort to hold it in check. He shifted his weight to his right foot, away from Mark Lomax.

When he focused his attention once again on Calhoun, he found that the director was talking and he had again missed a portion of what the man had said. He began to feel edgy, and managed to push that grainy feeling aside. He wouldn't ask Calhoun to repeat himself. Besides, for all John knew, it could be more lies about the project. That much *wouldn't* surprise him.

Calhoun finished giving his instruction, and within an hour John and Lomax were on their way to Arkansas.

As they left Virginia, John driving the late model Ford Taurus and Lomax not saying much, John wondered what they would find when they got to Jonesboro. The child he'd seen and held on his last trip there had seemed no more threatening than a newborn puppy. He still found it difficult to believe that the director had called the boy dangerous.

But John also knew that appearances were often deceiving. All he had to do was think about the situation with Lily, and primarily with her ex-husband.

It was going to be a long drive, and so he focused his attention on the most important task at hand: getting all the information he could from Mark Lomax about Project Lone Star.

* * * * *

TWELVE

Ken looked at Chance and struggled to keep his emotions from becoming complete turmoil.

He felt strange, sitting here in front of his young son, preparing to converse with him on a level he had not anticipated having to do until Chance was much older. Ken had envisioned, in the months following the adoption, sitting down with Chance one day and explaining things about life; sticking up for himself when being picked on at school, the 'birds and the bees', responsibilities on driving a car—and countless other things that would help him grow and develop into a man.

He wondered, as he sat upon the coffee table in the den, if all of that would now be lost. How much of the future would be forever changed in light of Chance's apparent intelligence? It was difficult to say.

He looked at his son, these thoughts rocketing through his mind, along with disquieting thoughts about the listening devices that had been discovered and dismantled. Where in hell had they come from? Who had put them there?

Chance stared back at him, an innocent smile on his round face.

"I guess the first thing I'd like to know," Ken said with a shaking voice, "is how you are able to talk so well. You've lived with us the majority of your life, and until recently we had no idea you could talk this…this well. Why is that?" He had included Valerie in what he'd said, but he knew he could only speak for himself. To the best of his knowledge, he was the only person who'd witnessed Chance's intelligence to this extent. Ken was uncomfortable, but he nonetheless awaited his son's response in the same manner in which he would expect an answer from an adult.

Chance continued to smile, and then his eyes changed again. It was subtle, same as before, but Ken could not deny it happened. His hazel peepers went from the innocent eyes of a child to a pair of eyes that seemed to contain infinite intelligence and wisdom. Their color took on a darker hue of green and looked like the faded emerald eyes of an older person. Perhaps, even, one much older than Ken himself.

Then Chance spoke: "I learned my language from you and Mommy, of course." He spoke in a slightly deeper, matter-of-fact voice which was much different from the babblings that had issued forth from his little mouth in months past. His voice sounded more like a kindergarten-aged child than a fifteen-month-old.

"That's natural enough," Ken said, his body tingling. "In fact, that's how *all* children learn to talk, I guess. It just so happens that you've appeared to learn more quickly than an average child."

"Yes," Chance said.

Ken rested his elbows on his knees and tented his fingers beneath his chin. "How is that possible?"

Chance squirmed a little on the vastness of the sofa. He looked tiny against that backdrop. "My…other…parent gave me that ability."

"Your birth parents?"

"My birth mother is dead." There was a lack of emotion in his voice that Ken ignored.

"I know she is. The house fire."

"Not a house fire," Chance said, and now there was something else to wonder about.

"The people at the adoption agency said you were injured in a house fire."

"They were not informed well."

"What about the scars?"

"I was burned badly," Chance said, "but not in a house fire."

"Then how?"

Chance squirmed again. "I can't say."

"Why not?"

"I'm not allowed to."

"Who says?"

"My father."

Ken bristled some. He couldn't help it. "And who is he?"

Another squirm. "I can't say."

"*Why?*" Ken said again. He was getting frustrated now, regardless of

101

how uncomfortable he felt. There was a certain innocence between himself and his son that was lost now—maybe forever—and some of the frustration stemmed from that alone. According to some of the books he'd read, that feeling of loss was usually experienced at some point during the teenage years. It wasn't fair that he was sitting here with a fifteen-month-old whom he loved more than anything, talking in a way nature had never intended. Chance shouldn't be able to talk like this, to say these things.

But he was.

Somehow, he *could*.

"What about the bugs?" Ken reached into his shirt pocket and withdrew the collection of listening devices. He put them all in the palm of one hand and held them out between himself and Chance. "How did you find these?"

"I could hear them."

"You could *hear* them?"

"Yes. When they came on. Whenever you or Mommy talked."

"So, they are voice activated?"

"Yes. But...I hear more from the one in my room."

Is that how he 'communicates' with...whoever? Ken cast that aside. He thought again of the bug they'd found in he and Valerie's bedroom, and felt the anger begin to resurface. He pushed it back with some effort and rubbed his eyes with the thumb and fingers of one hand.

"So, someone has been listening to everything that has been said in this house." It wasn't a question.

"Yes."

"Jeez. For how long?" Ken whispered to himself.

"Since I came here," Chance said.

Ken looked up sharply. "You heard me say that, just now?"

"Yes."

Ken had entertained doubts that Chance had 'heard' the listening devices, but now he found himself believing it. No matter how insane it sounded, he believed it. If he could believe that his young son could talk as intelligently as any adult, then he figured the boy ought to be able to hear as well as a dog. Perhaps better. Why not? Curiously, he was once again on the verge of laughter. He felt a vertigo sense of surrealism pick him up and swirl about his mind in hurricane fashion. No, in *tornadic* fashion.

When that feeling faded to some degree, he asked another question to which he needed an answer: "The listening devices. What do they mean?"

"That someone is listening," Chance said, and his eyes—those somehow old and wise eyes—gleamed playfully.

"I figured out that much," Ken said with a small chuckle. He couldn't help it. "But *who* has been listening?"

Chance seemed to hunt for his words for the first time since their conversation had begun. "People in a higher place."

"Higher place," Ken said, thinking. "Like the FBI, the government?"

"Yes," Chance said. "The gov-ern-ment." He said it slowly, and Ken wondered if it was the first time that he'd ever heard the word.

"Like that man," Chance said.

Ken sat up straight. "What man?"

"The man who came inside the house. The man with the broke car."

"*He* planted the bugs? That man?"

"No," Chance said. "He's in the government." This time he spoke the word without the slightest pause.

"But why would the government plant listening devices in our house?" But he guessed he knew the answer to that one. He even felt foolish for asking it.

Chance confirmed it. "Because of me, of course."

"But why would they even let us adopt you if they wanted to keep an eye on you so badly?"

"That decision was not theirs."

"Not the government's?"

"Yes, the government's. But not the people who planted the bugs."

"Someone higher than them?"

"Yes."

Ken sat back a little. Who could have planted the bugs in his home? Chance apparently didn't know, not specifically. There were many more questions he wanted to ask his son, but where to begin?

He would like to ask him about the two men at the airport, for instance. But Chance hadn't been in Memphis that day, so he probably wouldn't be able to tell him anything in that regard. Besides, that incident was still secondary to recent events.

"What happened at my father's house? How did you learn to spell?"

"I don't know," Chance said. "I just can." His eyes seemed to penetrate Ken's. "How did *you* learn to spell?"

"I was taught," Ken said, and then let his mouth snap shut when he saw the knowing smile on Chance's face. "You were also taught? By whom?"

"I don't know," Chance said, but he let his eyes drift sideways, and Ken sensed a lie. It also brought to mind the bug in the crib upstairs. Perhaps that bug was not merely a one-way device. He shook the thought away.

"Where did you go at Pa Pa's house? We couldn't find you before you made the message with the blocks."

"I was hiding," Chance said.

"But where did you go? Where did you hide?"

"Nowhere."

"You didn't walk or crawl out of the yard?"

"No."

"You didn't go *anywhere*?"

"No," Chance repeated.

"Well, you disappeared *somewhere*," Ken said.

"Yes, but I went nowhere."

Now Ken was thoroughly confused. But he also felt a bristling chill on his neck that might have been fear. "Are you saying that you turned invisible or something?"

"What is in-vis-ible?"

"Transparent, unable to be seen by the eye."

"Yes," Chance said after a slight pause. "Invisible."

* * * * *

John Milcheck and Mark Lomax were heading west, into West Virginia now. Lomax had taken over driving duties a few miles back, when the two of them stopped at a truck stop for a light supper of steaks, home fries, and toast. The sun was on its descent in the west, casting long shadows behind them like dark shapes through spun gold.

Lomax had been talkative thus far, speaking mostly about himself and the many cases and projects he'd been involved in during his eight years in the CIA. He talked endlessly about his numerous escapades in various parts of the country, as well as some foreign ones, making himself out the hero in almost every case, and highlighting his wits and courage *every* time.

It didn't take John long to figure out that Lomax was an egotistical shmuck. What was odd is that he had *liked* Mark the first time he'd met him, a year ago; no particular reason, other than instinct. John usually tried to see good in people. It was his experience that every person possessed at least at little. Now he hoped that Lomax would, as well, although John had thus far not seen a hint of any. Worse, was thinking that his initial read of the blonde agent might have been glowingly wrong.

Lomax talked less when he was driving—thank goodness—and John took the opportunity to manage the conversation and ask a few questions. During the course of his earlier ramblings, Lomax had stated that he was excited to be involved in Project Lone Star. He had elaborated no further, perhaps because he'd done little or no fieldwork on the case (to John's knowledge), and thus had no heroics of which to speak.

"So," John said, taking a big breath and trying to sound casual. "What do you think of this child, this boy?"

A smile spread across Lomax's face, and John felt his heart sink. Lomax was going to tell him the information was classified, and he couldn't talk about it with him—that Calhoun had given that order himself. Instead, Lomax assumed his 'talkative' pose, which is the way John perceived it; head held up, and a smirky look on his face reminiscent of Barney Fife on the old *Andy Griffith Show*. His red mole stood out with prominence from his chin, and in profile looked like the tired thumb of a hitchhiker.

"I think it's amazing that they were able to save him," Lomax said. "It's even more amazing that his appearance wasn't altered much. Aside from a few minor scars, he's healed nicely. At least from the photos I've seen," he added, and there was something missing in his voice when he said it.

Ah, John thought. *He doesn't know as much as he would like me to think he does. Probably hard for you to admit that all you've seen are photographs, huh Lomax? Hell, I've held the child in my arms.*

But he couldn't come right out and say that.

He shifted in his seat. Lomax might only have seen photographs of the child, but John still felt certain the high-strung agent knew more than he about Project Lone Star.

He wondered if Lomax knew who 'they' were. The 'they' who'd saved the child from something. He thought about asking, but he couldn't think of a way to do it without divulging his general ignorance about the project.

He remembered when Calhoun briefed him—*briefed me, yeah right, that's funny*—on Project Lone Star. The director had mentioned how it was President Clayton's idea to have the child raised by a normal family. He wondered if Lomax knew that little tidbit of information, and when he asked him, John was surprised at the answer he received.

"Oh, yeah," Lomax said, smiling and staring out at the highway. "That's the President's ace in the hole. A little political security, I guess."

The sun was sinking on the horizon, piercing the windshield and turning both men's faces a brazen gold color. From a shirt pocket, Lomax pulled a pair of *Oakley* sunglasses.

"I overheard Calhoun on the phone one day, just before the adoption, while I was in his office reporting on an assignment. I think it was the crisis with the Cuban who was spying for the old Soviet Union."

John smiled flatly. That case was one of the several Lomax had described, at length, at the onset of this trip. If Mark could be believed, he had captured the spy single-handedly after the man had killed two assisting agents.

"Anyway," Lomax continued, "it didn't take long for me to figure out two things. The first was that the boss was upset, and the second was that he was talking to the President."

"How did you know it was the President on the phone?" John said.

"Because he kept calling the guy on the other end 'sir', and I think we both know that Calhoun calls no one 'sir' *except* the President of the United States."

John nodded. He'd heard that legend.

Calhoun, as far as anyone knew, answered in most matters only to the commander-in-chief. It made John wonder sometimes just how many top-secret projects and covert operations the director was privy to, or involved in. He imagined it was quite a few.

It also made stronger his conviction that Calhoun had fed him some false information about Project Lone Star and the Malcolm child.

There was something going on, sure, and although he realized that the director couldn't tell every agent every detail about each top-secret assignment, he was still angered at the fact that his boss had out and out lied to him. According to Calhoun himself, after all, John was now the primary agent on Project Lone Star. Unless he had lied about that, as well.

A service station came up on the right and John asked Lomax to stop because nature was calling.

"I'd better go myself," Lomax said. "I don't feel the urge, but if I don't go I'll probably have to as soon as we get five miles down the highway."

He laughed a little and John surprised himself by chuckling along with him. He couldn't help it. Mark was for some reason likeable, in spite of his obvious flaws.

Lomax signaled and took the exit off the interstate. Moments later the two were in the service station's men's room, relieving themselves. The bathroom was small, with a porcelain sink, off-white commode, and a single urinal, all dingy and corroded. The place had a musty smell; sweat, urine and feces, mingled with stale body odor. Lomax entered the small room first—John wondered what his hurry was, since he didn't have to go very badly—and so John got stuck with the commode. Someone had forgotten to flush it—by the smell it had been two or three days ago.

"God, it stinks in here," he said.

"I wonder if the Malcolms have kept the child out of the sunlight," Lomax said. He had a thoughtful look on his face as he emptied his bladder. "I sure hope so. But they aren't privy to anything, so it's doubtful."

They aren't the only ones not privy to everything, John thought. *But the sun? What does that have to do with anything?* He was now beyond letting on how little he actually knew about the case. He zipped his fly and looked at Lomax. "Just what the hell does the sun have to do with anything?"

Lomax, still standing in front of the urinal, looked at him and John saw mistrust in the agent's eyes. He wore a guarded, curious look; as though he was looking at some rare specimen of animal that had just jumped up and bit him in the ass. John's stomach roiled noisily, and he wondered with a sense of dread if he was going to have to drop his pants and turn around in front of this near-stranger.

"You haven't been fully briefed on Lone Star, have you?" Lomax said stonily. He continued to stare at John.

Those eyes. Stop looking at me that way.

Before John could answer, the door to the restroom opened and a well-dressed business man came in. At least that's what he looked like. He wore a dark three-piece suit that was wrinkle free and he had an upper-class air about him. His nose was the only thing that wrinkled as he came in.

John had finished urinating, and he walked over to the sink and began washing his hands. Lomax remained in front of the urinal, eyes now staring at the wall in front of him, as the man relieved himself in the commode.

The man nodded at John. "Ripe in here, isn't it?"

"You got that right," John said.

Lomax remained silent.

The man finished, flushed (John winced when he realized that *he* had forgotten that simple necessity), and left.

When he was gone, John looked at Lomax. "Well?" he said. "What does the sun have to do with the Malcolm child?"

Lomax zipped his fly and flushed the urinal. It made a hollow, gurgling sound. "You answer my question first." There was a hint of anger in the agent's voice.

John sighed heavily, thinking what the hell. "No, I was never fully briefed on Lone Star," he said. "Calhoun said he was briefing me, but what he actually did was feed me a pack of lies. I'm sure most of it was, anyway, because with what *he* told me and what little *you've* said about the project, I am thoroughly confused about this kid." As he spoke his voice, by degrees, increased in volume. "In fact, I'm about ready for a little truth here, because when we get to Arkansas, I'm not going to have a clue what we're up against, and I'm not going to feel safe until I do. I've got a loaded gun in my shoulder holster and I have no idea where, when, or why I may have to use it. So, I guess you'll just have to overlook the idea that I seem a little unfamiliar with the case, because the fact is, I *am*, and it's beginning to *piss* me off.

"Now," he said in a more moderated tone, "if you've got a problem with that, it's your problem." John paused for a few long breaths and then added what he hoped was the final touch: "The other problem you have is that *you* are *also* going in to an unsafe environment—if it's really unsafe, and I guess if we're having to carry then it must be—because the man you're going in with, *me*, doesn't know what the hell to expect."

John looked at the agent and waited.

"What, exactly, did Calhoun tell you?" Lomax said. His words were clipped, though not as sharp as they had been moments ago.

In a few sentences, John told Lomax everything the director had told him about the project.

It was Lomax's turn to sigh. He rubbed absently at his chin. When he moved his hand, the small mole looked red and irritated.

John was surprised at what came out of the agent's mouth next: "You know, that sort of pisses *me* off."

John raised his eyebrows.

"I mean, I know you haven't been in the agency as long as I have, but there are procedures and precautions which have to be taken with a case like this. Hell, with *any* case." Lomax stopped long enough to dry his hands with a crinkled paper towel from the roll that was on the toilet tank.

"I've been involved in a lot of top-secret assignments over the years, and you're right about one thing: an agent can't work or function properly in a potentially dangerous situation without first knowing and understanding what is involved."

He looked at John and his eyes weren't hard like they'd been before. They were once again soft—the color of a blue sea—and they hinted at the good person that John felt was beneath the surface of Mark's cool exterior. John felt a surge of relief, yet he would not feel total relief until he knew what he wanted—needed—to know."

"I don't understand why Calhoun would send you out on this assignment without a full briefing. Has he ever done that to you before?"

"No," John said. The fact that Lomax implied that this was the director's fault made him feel much better. The rest of that relief was still out of sight, but a corner was protruding from the murky mud that this case had so far been. "Calhoun has always laid all the cards on the table," he told Lomax, then added: "At least the ones I needed to see."

Lomax nodded. "That makes sense. That's his job." Another thoughtful look crossed his face. He looked up at the bare florescent light. John followed his gaze. There was nothing up there but dusty spider webs and crud.

"I don't mean to toot my horn or anything," Lomax said, "and I hope you don't think that's what I'm trying to do, but I know a little bit about how Calhoun thinks."

John mentally rolled his eyes. He was paying close attention to what Lomax said, however, and knew he would have to be patient with the agent's natural inclination to talk about himself. At least the man recognized that his ego was, indeed, a little inflated.

"Yeah," Lomax said. "Calhoun knows damn well what the procedures are for a case of this magnitude, and I don't think he would skip them on purpose."

John thought about the attempts Calhoun had made—only hours ago—to lay blame on someone, and forced himself to keep quiet. Lomax had been in there, as well.

"But what if," Lomax said. He began pacing back and forth in the small bathroom, as though he were actually trying to *be* the director, although John didn't think he did it consciously. "What if Calhoun *did* intentionally feed you false information about Lone Star? He would more than likely have a good reason for *that*, also, and from what I know I would have to guess that his decision probably stemmed from the fact that he was against the infant living a civilian life in the first place. Remember when I told you I overheard him and President Clayton talking on the phone and that Calhoun was upset?"

"Sure," John said.

"Well, after he hung up, he started pacing around the room, raving about the way Clayton handled things, and saying things like how his eight-year-old grandson could make a better decision than that bastard."

John interrupted. "He actually called the President of the United States a bastard?"

"Not to his face or anything, but yeah, he did. At first, I thought he'd forgotten I was in the room. He was ranting and raving even worse than he did this afternoon."

John made a mental note: Lomax *had* observed that little tantrum.

"Anyway, the director has been against the baby living with a normal family from the beginning, and he told me as much. 'It's a mistake,' he kept saying over and over. 'The reporter was the first mistake, of course, but we need to keep the child in our custody, to study him, protect him, and possibly...' He left the sentence unfinished because I think he realized it was only one of his field agents standing in front of his desk and not his mother. He composed himself rather quickly then, and only added in what I thought was a pouting voice that 'Clayton will see what a bad mistake he's made. He's getting his re-election hopes jumbled up with what's right for this country. The boy should *not* become a civilian. It's too risky'."

Lomax stopped pacing and looked at John.

John unconsciously shifted his weight to his right foot, as though standing in the director's office, in front of the chair-less desk.

"I think that Calhoun has sent you to Arkansas—on purpose—without the full knowledge of your mission." Lomax began pacing once again, and John shifted his weight to his left foot (he had no idea he was doing this, and would never remember it). "I think he did this knowing damn well what would happen, and I think he's put himself in a league right up there with Clayton—putting himself before the good of the country." A disgusted look crossed Lomax's face. "That makes me sick."

John was both confused and curious, but he asked the question he needed an answer to in spite of the fact that he knew without a doubt what the answer would be. He was beginning to feel sick himself. "Why?" he asked. "Tell me why he would do that."

Lomax stopped pacing and stared into John's eyes. "Because if there was an accident and an agent was killed—if *you* were killed—then President Clayton would have to reconsider his decision, bring the child back in, and place him in the custody of a government agency. Which is what Calhoun has wanted all along. You see?"

John nodded and ran a finger through his mustache. "Yeah, I think I'm beginning to." A little more of the truth was sticking up from the mud, but there was much more buried beneath what had protruded and was beginning to dry. "Tell me more," he said. "What I need to know. I'm not ready to die just yet, accident or no. I would gladly die for my country, of course, but not for some bullshit political reason like this. Tell me."

"In the car," Lomax said. "We still have a long drive before we get to Jonesboro." He started for the door and then paused in front of it. "That son of a bitch."

"Who?"

"Calhoun." The hard look was back on Lomax's face. "Who's to say *you* would be the one to have an accident? Who's to say it would be you?"

* * * * *

THIRTEEN

The skies over Jonesboro began to cloud over around four o'clock. At five-thirty, Chance was sitting in the floor of the den, playing with some of his toys, and Ken was looking through the living room window, just down the hall, as rain pelted the house. He hoped Valerie and her mother had taken an umbrella with them.

He glanced at his watch. They should be back soon.

He had already checked the forecast for the evening, turning on the television set long enough to catch it on *The Weather Channel*. The skies were supposed to clear by darkfall, and there were no thunderstorm or tornado watches or warnings, so he didn't have to worry about his wife and mother-in-law getting caught out in bad weather.

What he worried about was what he was, or wasn't, going to tell them when they returned from their shopping trip. A lot had happened in the few hours they'd been away.

Ken's mind was in constant turmoil now, and the cloudy sky didn't help things. That only got him thinking about Jimmy, and that was no good, either. What he tried to think about mostly were things more recent.

He would start to think about one aspect—the listening devices, for instance—and he would almost physically feel his mind spiraling up and up, higher and higher. It was like riding the world's biggest roller coaster, up the steepest part of the track, at three times the normal speed. If his mind continued at this pace, what would happen when the car reached the summit? Would it make a sharp, jerking and pulling turn in to equally uncharted territory? The dips and curves of madness, perhaps? Or would the car simply jump the rail, lose all connections with the track, and reach the fabled land of insanity in one giant free fall?

Ken didn't want to find out and so, whenever he felt that spiraling sensation near its peak, he made a conscious effort to divert his mind to something else. Like how Chance could talk, or how he knew where the bugs were, or how he'd stated so innocently that, yes, he had made himself invisible. And so on and so on, in one large loop. It was a hell of a roller coaster ride, alright, but there was still one spot where coherent thinking was possible (the roller coaster terminal?), and he was currently there, although he didn't know for how long. The time spent here in his mind had been very brief at first but was slowly expanding to longer intervals, the looping circles of the roller coaster ride coming less frequently.

Just what would he tell Valerie when she returned from town?

What would he tell her mother?

Nothing, that's what. I'll have to wait until she leaves.

But what if Beatris didn't want to leave, or there were signs that she was planning one of her 'super-long' stays? After all, her husband was off chasing insects on yet another field trip.

Then I'll make *her leave, somehow.*

His mother-in-law wouldn't be staying forever, so there was really no need worrying as much about that as about how he could tell Valerie about the abilities their son had displayed this afternoon.

What would she say?

What would she *think*?

That one was easy.

She wouldn't believe it, of course, and she might even go as far as voicing an opinion that Ken was in need of psychiatric help. Already she was doubtful about the other events of which Ken had told her: Chance's disappearance from his playpen in the back yard, the stranger who'd called Ken by name. If she didn't believe any of that, was there any reason for her to believe that Chance had found some high-tech listening devices and could carry on an intelligent conversation?

Of course, he could show her the bugs, and then she might believe him. Now *there* was something to think about. What would the two of them do, and how would they handle the situation?

Everything aside, Ken loved his wife and he didn't want to frighten her. Because he knew that, with belief, fright would be her initial reaction. Yet to have her with him in this, by his side, was a comforting idea. The two of them against the world, just as it had been so many years ago, when they were both young and—tell the truth—scared.

He was shaken from that thought when he saw her car pull into the driveway. The rain had tapered off to a light drizzle, and through the gray light Ken could see the white faces of his wife and mother-in-law. His heart galloped and he felt his mind pull out of the terminal, preparing for another run at increasing speed around the loop.

He looked into the den at Chance, who was alternately rolling a plastic truck across the carpet and glancing at a cartoon on the television, and he was able to change gears.

Ask Chance what you should say, a voice in his mind whispered. *He might know.*

Yeah, right.

If he could find those listening devices that he says have been here since he has, and you *overlooked them all these months, then who's to say he won't know how Valerie will react?*

Ken tried to ignore that thought. It was stupid, anyway. He would feel like a total fool asking his son for advice. That was something Chance was supposed to one day ask from him: 'Dad, I really have something to tell this girl at school, because I like her. How do I handle it? What do I say?'

That's the way it was supposed to be. *That* way.

Comfortable with the fact that the issue was laid to rest, Ken picked his son up and asked him what he should tell Valerie.

"She's not going to believe me. She's going to go completely off the deep end, and so is your grandma," Ken babbled. He paced about the den much like another man was doing in a dirty restroom eight hundred miles away at almost the same moment. "What am I going to do? What?"

"Nothing," Chance said. He held his favorite rattle in his hand, and he shook it playfully, then put it in his mouth, slobbering down the side of the toy. He looked like any other teething baby in the world.

Ken pulled the toy away and looked closely into Chance's eyes. "What do you mean, nothing? She's here. She's getting out of her car as we speak. Now, just what do you mean?"

Chance's eyes once again changed slightly, shifted somehow, as if he was sifting through information that only he could see, examining and discarding each piece. He looked at Ken. "We can't tell Mommy anything."

"Why not?"

"Because she might tell."

"Tell who?"

"Someone."

"She might tell someone?"

"Yes."

Ken hadn't thought about that. Sally Parker from up the street came by for a cup of coffee with Valerie at least once a week, and sometimes two. He had voiced his opinion to Valerie once that Sally was one of those nosy neighborhood gossips—a nosey-parker, pun intended—and Valerie had laughed and told him not to worry, because a gossip couldn't dig up much dirt from a person who wasn't one herself.

But that could mean anything, couldn't it? Ken knew his wife as well as he could, he supposed, but he was also aware that there were holes in his knowledge of her, some of them quite large. He knew quite a bit about her childhood—near perfect, if you believed Beatrice, who had filled him in on most of Valerie's days at home—but he didn't know a lot of real meaningful, *personal* details of Val's years in her early twenties, when she *hadn't* lived with her parents. He supposed it was because those days were before the two of them. He also knew she was about the most honest, caring, loving person he'd ever met, and most days that was enough.

But you've heard her gossiping with Sally on occasion, despite what she says about gossips. Chalk it up to human nature.

Still holding Chance, Ken walked to the kitchen and met Valerie and her mother as they came through the door, their arms full of packages. He put Chance down and removed the load from his wife's arms.

"Mommy," Chance exclaimed and toddled to her.

She grabbed him up, hugged him, and kissed one of his round cheeks. "There he is," she said. "Were you a good boy while Mommy was gone?"

Boy, was he ever, Ken thought.

Chance grinned. "Goo," he said, not pronouncing the 'd' sound. Some slobber ran down his chin and Valerie wiped it absently with one hand.

"When are you going to be through cutting teeth?"

"Teef." Chance smiled proudly, showing the five white nubs in his small mouth.

There was laughter around the room, as was always the case when Chance pronounced his words wrong. It was all part of the learning process, but it was so *cute.* The four of them settled around the kitchen table, Chance in his high chair, while Valerie and her mother showed off the clothes and other items they'd purchased at Turtle Creek Mall and other retail stores.

Beatrice was short, with reddish-orange hair styled in a sensible old-woman's bun. Today, she wore a shirt with flower patterns of copper, red and brown, and a maroon skirt that floated to the top of her calves. She appeared to be in a good mood—Ken had noticed that since the adoption she had grown increasingly affectionate to he, Valerie, and Chance—and she didn't even light a cigarette until after the purchases were put away. She went onto the patio to smoke it, and Ken followed her.

"Beatrice, you know you didn't have to buy all of those clothes," he said after he'd closed the sliding door.

"Bah," she said. "I know that, don't I? I did it—I *do* it—because I want to, not because I have to." Perhaps sensing why he had fol-owed her out here in the first place, she said: "I know you can take care of your family, Ken. I *know* that." She took a drag off the cigarette, inhaled deeply, and exhaled in a long white plume. Droplets of rain dripped from the trees and bushes in the back yard, made plopping sounds that were lonesome and hollow.

"You and Valerie tried so hard," Beatrice said. "and now that the two of you have Chance, I finally have a grandson to spoil." She tossed her cigarette onto the wet ground, where it extinguished with a hiss. "I don't mean to go overboard or anything. I just want him to be happy, to have things."

"He will be, and he does," Ken said, "and we appreciate all that you do for him. Just don't feel like you have to do these things for him to love you. Or for *us* to love you. It's not necessary."

Beatrice took another cigarette from her purse and lit it with a hand that trembled slightly. "You're a good boy, Ken."

Boy, he thought, amused.

"I've always thought that, always known it, and I'm glad Valerie hung in there like she did."

Ken grew uncomfortable. He knew she was referring to his 'bad time', and not implying that he had been a low-grade bum who had pulled himself out of the gutter in order to win the fair lady—although the whole thing with Jimmy *had*, initially, taken a toll on their marriage. "Thank you, Beatrice," he said.

Although Ken and Valerie had been in their mid-twenties when they married, Beatrice had tried vainly—and then with some success—to help them out financially in nearly all aspects of their new life together. She'd finally convinced Ken to let her make the down payment on their home after their succession of rental houses and apartments. He had only allowed this to keep her from bugging the shit out of him about it. At least that's what he told himself. When she and Earl had offered to furnish the house as well, Ken had drawn the line, allowing them to buy one item as a house-warming gift. That gift had been a six-chair dinette set made of a dark maple that became the centerpiece of the formal dining room. Already Beatrice must have been thinking ahead into the future, and a house full of grandchildren. It was rather ironic that the dinette set was seldom used. Ken and Valerie, and now Chance, usually took their meals in the kitchen. The table was smaller, but in many ways made them feel closer than they would be sitting at a large table in a spacious dining room.

Valerie's mother—and, to a lesser extent, her father—had helped out during his 'bad time', as well, mainly by offering moral support to Valerie. Something of which Ken had been incapable. And if he wanted to be really honest, they had helped him, also, treating him as they always had—as if he were their son.

Beatrice took a drag on the cigarette and then flicked it out onto the grass near the other one. Ken reminded himself that he would have to come out tomorrow and pick them up. Valerie didn't like cigarette butts lying around, and neither did he, really…

…and how did he even get to thinking about *that*?

It was funny the way the mind worked. Just a mere twenty minutes ago he had been thinking darker, more complicated thoughts. Now the roller coaster in his mind had stopped. He didn't want to guess how long it would remain that way. Probably not long.

They went back inside, where Valerie was preparing dinner and Chance sat in his high chair, shaking his rattle vigorously before inserting it into his mouth and then taking it out to look at it, before taking another whack at it with his small teeth.

Beatrice offered to help and Valerie declined. She invited her mother to dinner and Beatrice begged off, sighting the fact that she had to get home and prepare supper herself. "Earl is getting back early from his trip, thank God, and he acts close to starvation when he gets home, you know." She kissed Valerie and Chance, and left.

When she was gone, Chance looked at Ken and held his arms up. "Da-Da." Ken sensed something about the motion and word, something that was at once dreadful and exciting. He wasn't sure why he should feel either way, but in light of what had happened this afternoon, he did.

"We're going to watch some TV," Ken said as he lifted Chance from the chair. "Call us when it's ready."

"Okay."

They went into the den. Ken turned on the television and, as he was walking to the sofa, Chance leaned close to his ear and spoke in a low voice.

"I have to tell you something, Daddy. About the bugs."

* * * * *

FOURTEEN

John Milcheck and Mark Lomax were already a third of the way to Jonesboro, Arkansas, although neither of them was aware of this. The urgency they had felt on the onset of this trip was something else of which they were no longer aware, although it still lurked somewhere in the back of the minds of both men. They had just passed through the city of Huntington, West Virginia.

Although the two men planned to sleep and drive in shifts, with no unnecessary stops in the night, John knew that when his shift for rest came up at eight, he would not be able to sleep.

"Tell me about the child," he said, trying to concentrate on the road. "Start with his conception and birth."

"The child was conceived artificially," Lomax began. "His mother, a woman by the name of Miriam Logan, could bear children, but her husband, Steven Logan, couldn't do the job at his end, so they chose to receive donor sperm. Everything went without a hitch as far as the impregnation goes, and the Logans were given a biography of the sperm donor. They were told he was an accountant from the Memphis area, happily married with four healthy children of his own. He had artificially fathered many others. The Logans were shown a photo of him, and of his children, and they agreed on him as a donor."

"What's so odd about that?" John said. "These days, people have children like that all the time."

"Nothing odd about the procedure, no," Lomax said. "But what the Logans didn't know was that the biography they were given on the sperm donor was a false one. They were misled by the government."

"How? And why would the government be involved in the first place?"

"I'm getting to that," Lomax said. He seemed to relish keeping John in suspense. "You see, Mrs. Logan's egg was fertilized by someone in the upper circles of government, and not by some accountant from Memphis."

"Who?"

Lomax paused only briefly. "I don't know. I was never told the identity of the real sperm donor, and I never found out, although I did some snooping. I was able to get a little information from a former colleague who was privy to some of the inside story, but I didn't get much."

"Former colleague?" John looked quickly at Lomax and then back at the highway. He was well aware that there was no such thing as 'former' anything when it came to federal agencies.

Lomax's voice resonated with a nervous undertone that jarred with his normal confident tone of voice. "Yes, former," he said. "That's why I don't know more than I do. I won't mention the agent's name, but on the day he was going to meet me with the donor's name, he had a...an accident."

John nodded but said nothing.

"He had already told me that the actual donor was top secret, and that he was one of the most intelligent minds in the world, if not *the* most intelligent. Needless to say, I really wanted to know his identity, but this colleague was killed before I had a chance to get that info, and I've never spoken of him, or this whole project, with anyone since. Until now. It just seemed too dangerous."

John remained quiet, thinking. Who had he ever heard of that could be classified as the 'most intelligent person in the world'? Answer: no one.

"At any rate," Lomax said, "Mr. and Mrs. Logan were invited to the home of the donor when she was in her ninth month. They never made it there."

"The accident," John said.

"Yes, the accident. An accident had been waiting for the Logans, but not one like you might be thinking. Their vehicle broke down before they could reach the destination they were given. At about the same time, another breakdown was occurring, this one at a top-secret government facility less than five miles away. It was something that was unforeseen, yet seemed inevitable."

Lomax paused again and took a sip from the can of *Pepsi* he'd purchased miles back at the gas station with the dingy men's room.

John took a sip of his own soda and then said, a bit impatiently, "What was it?"

"Well, the Logans were from Phoenix, and the drive to the alleged donor's house was well over six hours away, across a leg of the Nevada Desert. There was, however, no donor's home anywhere on the other side of Oasis, Nevada, which is where the Logans were told to go. What *was* out there was—and still is—a top-secret installation. In a way, I suppose the Logans *were* going to meet the sperm donor, because from what I've been able to gather over the last six months, I think the government owns the donor, and consequently, the child."

"But what kind of accident was it?" John demanded. "What *was* it?" What he also wanted to ask, but didn't, was: *and just what do you mean by the government owning the donor?*

"I'm getting to that," Lomax said, almost sourly. John sighed and resigned himself to the fact that Mark talked only at the speed he desired. "On the same day that the Logans were to meet the donor, another top-secret organization was testing weapons at an underground installation less than two miles away. It may seem odd that the government would have two bases so close to one another, but to any civilian on the outside there only appeared to be one facility—a small airstrip with two or three single-engine planes sitting around the tarmac for show.

"There are underground tunnels connecting the two bases, and in fact you could say that both bases were by all intents and purposes entirely underground. There are probably more facilities under the desert and nearby mountains, but those two are the only ones I've become aware of. Stan Arkham from the Lab has told me that *no one* knows for sure just how many are down there. The two bases are used for different purposes. You know that agency money is always tight, but a portion is still funneled into the budgets of these operations."

John nodded. He was pretty familiar with how the CIA, as well as the NSA, DSA, and other agencies received some of their funding. Much of it came from the private sector, from the pockets of current and past politicians who, through a complicated series of lobbyists' kickbacks, were looking to make history—and if not that, then a quick buck—on new advances in technology in virtually every aspect imaginable. The remaining funding for covert operations not made known to the public was channeled to the agencies through programs that were vastly overfunded and utilized alarmingly less than the public realized, or was told. NASA was a good example.

Lomax finished off his soda and smashed the can with one hand as though he'd just killed a beer in a brute contest. He tossed it over his shoulder, where it bounced off the seat and clanked off a couple other cans that littered the floorboard.

"I can't say for sure exactly what kind of weapon was being tested on the day Lone Star was born, but I keep my ear to the ground, and I've heard from a few people who circulate in some respectable circles that it was a compact nuclear warhead."

"Testing nuclear weapons is common out there," John said.

"Yes," Lomax said, "but this weapon was not your garden variety warhead. This bomb was so small it could be designed to incredible specifications, from the size of a legal pad down to that of a pack of cigarettes. It could be carried in a person's pocket or briefcase. The cigarette-sized weapon held enough power in its small casing to annihilate twelve square blocks of a city the size of Los Angeles. At one point, this bomb was the military's most well-guarded secret, and with good reason. Who knows what could happen? The possibilities would be endless. What if these technologies were to fall into the hands of terrorist groups? Or to a communist country like China? What then?"

John shook his head. He didn't know, but he could imagine, oh yes, he could imagine it. He could have used something like that in the past, when it had come time to deal with Garret Burgess. Maybe not something *nuclear*, but he could...

He pushed the thought away. Now was not the time for that. What Lomax had to say was important. The thought about Garret and Lily lingered at the peripherals of his mind, and then exited stage right. It would be waiting patiently backstage for another chance to steal the show, watching, envious, as other thoughts played their parts under the lights. It would bide its time, looking for the smallest slip, at which point it could enter center stage when John least expected it.

"Something went wrong with the experiment on this compact bomb," Lomax continued. "I'm not certain exactly what happened, but to tell it in a nutshell, the bomb detonated before the NSA could get it to the underground test site."

"The National Security Agency did this?"

"Yeah. It was their project. When the bomb went off it took out some bunkers that were just a couple of stories underground, and consequently most of the data on the weapon was destroyed at detonation. The data was stored on computers in one of these bunkers, and hard copies were also stored there."

"Not a smart move for the NSA, storing all of its nuts in one hole."

"Right," Lomax said. "And unfortunate for them to have not made any backup copies of the vital data."

"So that project is history now? That's actually comforting."

"Yes," Lomax said. "but from what I hear there are efforts being made to duplicate the technology. Of course, it will likely take months, if not years, to reach the point it was at before the accident."

It was totally dark now, and the men's faces were occasionally bathed in white splashes of light from vehicles in the eastbound lanes of the interstate.

John moved in his seat to a more comfortable position. He hated sitting in cars for long periods. "What does all of this have to do with the Malcolm's child? I hate to ask, but unless I missed something I haven't made the connection yet."

Lomax sighed, perhaps resigned to the fact that he wasn't going to get to tell the story exactly how he wanted.

"Like I said, the Logans were on their way to meet the donor, and when they were close to the rendezvous point, the accident with the compact nuclear warhead occurred."

"Calhoun told me that they had car trouble or something," John said.

"Yes, they did. That much is true, and apparently Miriam Logan went into labor while they were stranded at the side of the road. The blast from the bomb killed the Logans, but the baby survived."

"How?"

"The child was still in the birth canal when the explosion happened. At least most of his body was. The head was out, and that was the only part that was injured." Lomax pulled a battered pack of cigarettes out of the inside pocket of his jacket and lit one. He took a long drag on the cigarette and then cracked the window on his side of the car and blew smoke out into the night. He coughed once, then took another drag.

"I didn't know you smoked," John said.

"I don't, normally," Lomax said, "but I keep a pack around in case I feel under too much stress or pressure. I guess I've been on this same pack for the last three months. The damn things are getting downright stale."

"I bet," John said, chuckling. He had personally been trying to quit for years. "Now, you were saying...?"

"The baby was saved." According to who I got my information from."

"The agent who had the accident, I presume," John said flatly.

"You got it. According to him, the child's donor father was the one who saved the baby. After a few weeks spent in one of the government's compounds, the child was recovering nicely, and President Clayton was notified and asked for his advice. There was also a reporter from a local paper in a small town nearby who stumbled over the accident. I guess you wouldn't be able to help but notice the detonation of a nuclear warhead, if you were anywhere close, and the ensuing cover-up did not actually cover everything up as planned. So, the reporter had to be isolated, of course."

John thought about asking him more about the reporter and decided against it. What was information about some reporter compared to info about the commander-in-chief of the United States? Besides, it was simple to put together what he knew: the guy got the story out, then he got scrubbed out—he had an 'accident'.

"Eventually, President Clayton decided to do what has happened; place the child with adoptive parents who were civilians, and let the child live a normal life. It quieted John Q public, who were enthralled for a few weeks by the child's survival.

"What Clayton didn't know, at first, was who the child's donor father was, and by the time he knew he was already standing firm in his decision, primarily because of the press coverage. I guess the director called it right when he said that the president was thinking only of politics, and I have to agree with Calhoun that something like this should never have happened. But he only made that decision because of the reporter's breaking story about the explosion and the unusual birth."

"So, who was the child's father?" John asked. He'd slowly begun to believe that this was what he now wanted to know more than anything else. Maybe it would clear up some things. "Who was he?"

Lomax looked across at him, visibly frustrated. "I already told you. I don't know. Before I could get that information from my source..."

"...he had an accident."

"Yeah," Lomax said, almost sadly. "He had an accident."

*****

FIFTEEN

"They're coming now," Chance said.

Ken leaned back on the sofa and rubbed his eyes with both hands. Maybe this was all a dream; like the two men at the airport were dreams. But he was beginning to believe he could no longer deceive himself about that. It had been real. He could hear Valerie out in the kitchen, and he felt envy creep over him: it must be nice to be oblivious to what was going on.

He put his hands in his lap and looked at his son. "Who is?"

"Men."

"What kind of men?" But, of course, he knew the answer to that, didn't he?

"From the government," Chance said. He was standing on the floor in front of the sofa, looking at Ken with eyes that were once again foreign, intelligent. And scared? Yes, that too.

Ken's mind clicked along with gaining speed. The roller coaster was threatening to leave the terminal again, and he had to make a gallant effort to keep it idling there, although he couldn't turn the damn thing off.

"Yes," he said, more to himself than to his son. "I guess they would know by now that their bugs have been tampered with."

"Yes," Chance agreed.

"How far away do you think they are?"

"I don't know. How far *is* the government?"

"Not far enough," Ken said softly. "Never very far away, in fact."

"I can sense them sometimes."

Ken almost jumped, and at the same time felt the tendrils of fear close around him again. "How?"

"I don't know."

"You don't know?"

"No. I just can. I can't explain it better."

Ken felt that Chance was telling the truth. He didn't know how he knew—instincts, he guessed. Now his mind was whirling again, but this time there was only one thought: *What are we going to do? What are we going to do?*

As if reading his mind, Chance said, "We have to leave."

"Leave?"

"Yes. Go somewhere. Hide."

"But...but *why*?" Ken fumbled. "Why do we have to leave?" In a far part of his mind, he had held out a faint hope that everything could be dealt with logically, that it wasn't the end of the world, that somehow they would come through this okay—scratched and bruised mentally, perhaps, but okay. But if they had to leave it took away all points of security and safety. This was their home. How could they just up and leave?

"We need to leave pretty soon," Chance said. His head was canted slightly, as though contemplating something.

"What are they going to do? Kill us?"

"They are going to come and take me away," Chance said. "Kill you, if necessary."

The flat, perfunctory way he said this stunned Ken. "*Kill* me?"

"Yes."

"Why?"

"Because they want me now. And they won't stop."

Ken was struck speechless; someone from some faceless government agency was going to kill him in order to kidnap his son. He wasn't sure if he was frightened more for himself, for Chance, or for the possibility of losing something he and Valerie had tried for in vain, and had finally gotten—a family. If they were to lose that, what else was there?

After a moment he found his voice long enough to ask a question that nagged at his mind in spite of his fear: "How do you know all of this? How could you *possibly* know?"

"My father told me."

"Your father?"

"Yes. I can hear him sometimes, too. He also told me, when I was younger, that he would be back for me some day, that he was only pleasing a friend. Someone who had helped him once."

When I was younger, Ken thought with a wry smile on his face. *The ride just goes on and on, doesn't it?*

That was it. The roller coaster pulled out of the terminal. Ken could almost hear the bearings and gears clicking on the cars as it jerked up the first steep rise in the track. His mind swam with ideas and possibilities about what Chance was implying, but luckily no particular one stayed at the front of his mind.

Before the roller coaster reached the summit of the hill, Valerie called from the kitchen that supper was ready. That one familiarity was just enough to turn Ken's mind onto a track that was easier to handle, and he felt the roller coaster come—grudgingly—to a halt.

"Are you ready to eat?" he asked Chance.

"Yes." Then, in a slightly lower voice: "But we should hurry."

Ken sighed and said in resignation, "Because we need to leave."

Chance nodded and Ken began thinking about how he was going to break that news to Valerie.

* * * * *

A pleasant aroma permeated from the kitchen, and he could tell what Valerie had prepared even before he and Chance entered the kitchen: Cheeseburger Macaroni *Hamburger Helper.* It was one of Chance's favorites. Not that he had told them as much, but they knew the foods he seemed to enjoy more than others—like most parents did, they assumed—and this was one of them.

Along with the *Hamburger Helper,* Valerie had tossed a garden salad packed with chopped vegetables and spicy dressings, and a bowl of fruit that she placed between the three of them: apple and orange slices, grapes, and a small saucer of salted peanuts. Being somewhat finicky about her weight, she wouldn't eat the Cheeseburger Macaroni.

The three of them ate in relative silence, Ken and Valerie watching Chance make the usual mess in his high chair. He did manage to get at least two out of every three forkfuls in his mouth without spilling its contents. That was an area on which he had been improving during recent months.

Ken watched his son, not really tasting the food despite its rich flavors, and the thought suddenly struck him that Chance could be faking a lot of things. Eating, for instance. As Ken watched him struggle with the fork, he began to believe that it *was* a put-on, and that Chance could probably eat as efficiently as he or Valerie. In his mind, he could picture Chance finishing his meal, dabbing his mouth with a napkin, and saying, "That was delicious, Mother."

Wouldn't Valerie die if he did that? Ken mused to himself. *Wouldn't she just* shit?

But of course Chance wasn't going to do any such thing, although Ken was firm in his conviction that he *could*. For some reason, Chance hadn't really shown his intelligence in front of Valerie. If Ken didn't know better, he could look at his son right now and see an ordinary fifteen-month-old *behaving* like an ordinary fifteen-month-old. His movements, sounds, and prattling betrayed nothing odd. Even his eyes reflected only childish good humor.

Ken finished his meal and then watched Valerie clean Chance's face with a wet washcloth after he'd stopped playing in his food long enough—a signal that he was through. He turned his head to the left, then to the right, his mouth tightly closed, his eyes squinted, as the washcloth roamed his messy face.

Ken had to wonder at this, also. The child he saw before him was not the same one who had carried on a conversation with him thirty minutes ago, not the same one who'd pointed out the listening devices with uncanny accuracy. He couldn't be. The child in the high chair at this moment was the charming, beautiful baby he and Valerie had adopted when their lives had been at their bleakest. He was the child who had given their life back. Ken thought that if he could keep the 'two' separated in his mind he would be better able to deal with this, because at the moment, with his son behaving normally, he didn't feel the pull and tug of the invisible roller coaster straining to roam the contours of his mind.

If Valerie knew that the 'other' Chance had talked of things that threatened to take away this wonderful existence, she would not be able to handle it, and with good reason. Ken still wasn't sure *he* could. He already worried that Valerie would think he was relapsing into the mental state he'd found himself in four years ago, after the tornado that had ripped his life apart.

Was Chance aware of that somehow? Is that why he faked this innocence while around her?

Ken didn't know, and it did no good to torture himself with those questions. Right now, he had to think about the last thing Chance had told him: *"We need to hurry."*

As Valerie cleared the dishes and utensils from the table, Ken told her he was going outside to see if it was clearing up yet, and he also told her he would take Chance with him. She smiled as he picked up Chance. "Thanks. That will make cleaning this up a lot easier."

Outside, Ken looked up at the sky. It was nearing twilight, but enough of the day lingered for him to see that the clouds were dispersing. Shallow orange and violet rays from the sinking sun poked between tufts of clouds at irregular intervals, forming a fragmented panorama of color. Ken sighed. It looked to be a clear night, but he would check the forecast later, just to be sure.

He sat Chance on one of the lounge chairs, righting it for him—Ken habitually turned all lawn furniture upside down when not in use—and now he looked at his son. "I think I know what I'm going to tell your mother."

Chance looked at him, saying nothing.

"I'm going to try and get her to go with us."

Chance started to say something, but Ken held up one finger. "I'm going to try that first. I'll tell her that I want all of us to take a short vacation, get away for a while."

"You can't tell her why," Chance warned.

Although he wasn't certain, Ken thought he detected a measure of sternness in those words. He felt anger flush his face. "Well, I can't just leave her here—I won't. They might hurt her, might try to get her to tell them where we went."

"She will be okay," Chance said in a low voice. "She will."

"And how do you know that?"

"They want me, not her."

Ken ran a hand through his hair and reminded himself that he was dealing with a child here. "Don't you think they will do something to her if they think she knows where we went? Don't you think that's a possibility?"

"No."

No. Of course not, Ken thought. *How can I expect a fifteen-month-old kid to understand the logistics of this? Small children don't think with that much complexity.* What bothered him the most, though, is that he wanted to believe Chance was right, that they *wouldn't* come here and perhaps torture Valerie for the information they wanted. And considering she didn't have any information to give—freely or otherwise—the torture would in all probability be of a long duration.

Those sorts of thoughts made Ken fear for his wife in a way he never had before; a helpless feeling that was unlike anything he'd ever experienced. Valerie was so much a part of him, so important to his very *existence,* that the thought of dealing with all of this without her by his side scared him. Scared him bad.

And yet…he felt compelled to believe his son. After all, Chance apparently knew more than he did about what was going on, and that had to count for something. Besides, he had already been dealing with all of this *without* Valerie's knowledge or support.

A vague uneasiness crept over him for a brief moment; was he preparing to put his life, as well as Valerie's, into the hands of a small child simply because that child had displayed some astounding abilities? The only answer was just as brief; yes, he was. Logic had to fit in somewhere, and to Ken it was *very* logical—once he got past the fog of panic and fear that had initially clogged his mind—that whoever owned the listening devices (which still rolled and bumped against each other in his shirt pocket) had planted them for a reason, and might very well come after he and his family if those devices were removed.

Which they had been, of course.

The flip side of the same coin of logic was that he didn't want to frighten Valerie.

If he went into the house and told her they had to leave, that someone was coming after them, she would doubt his stability and sanity, even without him telling her that their son was a genius, could articulate with logic and reason, and was the target of some as yet invisible government agency. She would be frightened, yes, but only because she would believe she was witnessing her husband's mental deterioration.

She would think he was crazy.

That's still a possibility, too, he told himself. *It* does *sound crazy, so maybe I* am. *That's still a good possibility, so don't rule it out.*

But he couldn't believe that. Couldn't *think* that. Right now, denial could only lead to disaster. He had to concentrate on getting his son away from here.

"Let's go back in," he told Chance. "Mommy should have the dishes done by now."

He picked Chance up and carried him inside. Valerie was wiping her hands on a dishtowel, the sink gurgling as the water drained. They owned a dishwasher, but it was rare that one meal resulted in a full load.

"What was so interesting out there?" Valerie said as she hung the dishtowel on a drawer handle by the stove.

"What do you mean?"

"Well, I could see you through the window, and you were talking to Chance about something. Must have been important." She smiled warmly and laughed.

Ken hadn't even considered that Valerie might have witnessed he and Chance's conversation. He felt a little relief that the kid's back had been to the window over the sink.

"I was just telling him about the weather, and what it looked like it may or may not do. It's definitely not going to rain any more tonight." Then, because he felt as though he should add something else, he said: "Not that Chance really understood anything I said." He laughed a little shakily.

"Of course not," Valerie said, gentle sarcasm lacing her words. "It just looked like you were really into the conversation. Very animated."

"I guess I was," Ken said after a slight pause. "He's got to learn to talk better sometime, and I'm sure not going to baby-talk him."

"I know you aren't," Valerie said. "You just tickle me sometimes, that's all."

"Now *there's* an idea." He smiled and then leaned over and kissed her lips. They were warm and soft. "I love you. You know that, don't you?"

"Yes, and I love you." She looked at the wall clock, a green and orange eye sore that had been a wedding gift. "It's almost time for my shows. Why don't you and Chance come into the den and play while I watch television?"

Sudden inspiration struck Ken, and he said: "No. I think I'm going to take Chance with me up to the bank. I've got a few papers to pick up that I forgot to bring home, and I need to have them finished within a couple of days."

"Why don't you leave Chance here with me? It's getting dark, and it's going to be his bedtime pretty soon, anyway. Plus, I was going to give him a bath. You won't be gone that long, will you?"

"No," Ken said. "I suppose not."

"Well, there's no need for you to drag him in to town with you. He'll be fine here." Now Ken could detect something strange in his wife's voice; a firmness and a...what? Coldness? Yes, a coldness. Ever so slight, but there. Or maybe he was just being paranoid. He had never once entertained the idea that Valerie might be jealous of he and Chance's admittedly close relationship.

"What about your shows?" Ken said, summoning up a smile he suddenly didn't feel like wearing. "Won't it be kind of hard to concentrate on them with Chance babbling and crawling all over you?"

Valerie locked eyes with his. She was no longer smiling. "I think I can manage to do both. I didn't want a baby so I could try to keep it out of my way when I wanted to do something."

Back off, man, before you really get her wind up, he told himself. *Tell her that you want all of us to go on a short vacation. Remember the plan?* He remembered, all right. The trouble was, he no longer thought that was the best plan. After all, how do you plan for a vacation for which you had to leave within the next half-hour or so.

Have to think of something else.

Yeah, but what?

He knew he would have to come up with something, because Chance had said that they needed to hurry.

He had to get Chance away from the house. He was beginning to believe that, above all else, he had to do that.

* * * * *

SIXTEEN

Ken drove down the quiet street, away from his house, with Chance in the child safety seat beside him. Yellow light from periodic sodium vapor street lamps cast a soft luminescence onto the dark street.

He drove out of the neighborhood, past quiet homes where lights glowed softly in windows. He thought about how nice it would be to be at home himself, watching television or reading a book in the comfort of his den, not having to worry about the complications that had so recently entered his heretofore organized life. At the back of his mind was a nagging, heart-wrenching feeling that he would never again see his wife, or his home.

"Chance didn't have a nap this afternoon," he'd told Valerie, just before he could reach the point where he knew he would give in to her request that the baby stay home. "He'll fall asleep in the car, you know that. Just let him ride along with me and he'll be asleep by the time I get back."

Valerie had seemed to relax some then, and waved a hand at him. "Oh, go ahead, I guess. I'll be watching my shows when you get home."

"Why don't you go to your mother's and watch them with her?" Ken had said in a spurt of creative thinking. "Chance and I will meet you over there later."

"No thanks. I just spent the entire afternoon with her. Besides, Dad's coming in this evening, remember? She hasn't seen him in ten days. I don't want to be in the way, and I can talk to her on the phone while we both watch the same show."

"Oh, come on," Ken said. "You know she loves you to visit. And we'll be there before you know it."

Valerie had sighed—a potential victory shaping up—and Ken had eventually persuaded her to go to her mother's house until they returned. He had hurriedly prepared a diaper bag, and he and Chance had left.

Now Ken felt guilty about the fact that he wasn't going to be returning home. Not soon, at any rate. More importantly, neither would Valerie. As soon as he'd had some time to think, and to sort some of the recent events, he would give her a call, making a point to advise her that staying at the Holman residence would be the safest thing she could do. Because he had—according to Chance—a short time frame within which to take some type of action, he would have to work out all the details as he went along, improvising when circumstances demanded it of him.

If what Chance had told him was any indication, there was no way to know *when* they would be able to return.

But one thing helped eased his mind: Chance said that Valerie would be safe, and Ken felt compelled to believe him. Regardless of how his son could know these things—and Ken was reluctant to even think about that right now—he had no reason to believe that what the child said was anything but the truth.

He turned off Dan Avenue, which dissected the city near its center, onto Hasbrook Road. The headlights picked up trees and shrubbery on either side of the road, along with expansive lawns fronting occasional homes. Insects ticked against the windshield like dry pellets of grain. Lights from a car behind them reflected a pale glow on the back on Ken's neck, and in the dim light he looked at his son. "I didn't think we were ever going to get away." Then: "Where are we going, anyway?"

Chance spoke, and Ken was thankful that he couldn't see his son's eyes. He remembered all too well how they had changed earlier. "I should be asking you. You are driving."

Right, Ken thought, then said: "Will we be safe?"

"Safer than if we had not left."

"But Mommy...Valerie—"

"Mommy will be fine," Chance said again. "She will be at Grandma and Grandpa's, so she will be fine."

"Right." Ken found himself once again reluctantly taking some comfort in that.

The road curved to the right and Ken eased the car into the bend. As he did so, he noticed that the vehicle behind him had moved closer. So close, in fact, that its headlights reflected in both rear view mirrors bright enough to be uncomfortable.

"Jesus," he muttered to himself. "Back off, buddy."

The vehicle continued to tailgate him, and as Ken hit a straightaway, it flashed its high beams twice in rapid succession.

There was no oncoming traffic, so Ken slowed some to let the vehicle pass.

But it did not attempt to pass.

"What's wrong?" Chance said.

Ken adjusted the rearview mirror so the glare wouldn't be as fierce. "I guess someone needs to pass us. I gave them plenty of opportunity, but they wouldn't go around."

They were approaching another curve, so now the vehicle *couldn't* pass. Nevertheless, it flashed its high beams twice more.

Ken grew irritated. He tried to think of what else could be wrong, mentally going over what a signal like that from another motorist might indicate. Other than a desire to pass, it could either be a signal to Ken that he had a tail light out, that his car's running lights or brake lights weren't working properly, or perhaps a distress signal.

Ken decided that he was going to have to pull over to find out which it was, because he had no idea. He only knew that, if there was a malfunction with his vehicle, he needed to be aware of it. He couldn't risk being pulled over by a law officer for *any* reason. After all, if some government agency was really after them, would it not stand to reason that city and county law officers in the area might also be utilized in the search? He didn't know, *couldn't* know. But it was best not to take any chances.

At the back of his mind another thought presented itself; what if the person behind him wanted to pull him over for the purpose of robbing him, or something worse? Wouldn't *that* be something.

The houses on this stretch of road were sparsely scattered, but a streetlight and a well-lit house were just up ahead on the right, and he slowed the car to a stop to one side of the mailbox, at edge of the property. The vehicle behind him also pulled over, and Ken's heart picked up speed.

Stay calm, he told himself.

"They are okay," Chance said. "But what do they want?"

They? Ken thought. *It could be just a single person, couldn't it?* "I don't know. I've probably got a tail light out or something." *And how do you know they're okay?*

"I don't think so," Chance said. His curiosity had been replaced with what sounded like relief. "It will be okay, Daddy."

Ken felt adrenaline spread through his system like an electric charge. He remembered the way Chance had somehow known who was after them, and why. Now it was okay?

Car doors thumped shut behind him, first one and then a second.

They, Ken thought again.

He resisted the urge to tromp the gas pedal and speed away from there. What if these people were those Chance had said were coming after him?

Almost simultaneously, he realized that if it were, it would do no good to run from them. They could probably catch him. On top of that, even though Chance had shown unusual intelligence and abilities, he was still a child, and Ken would not jeopardize his safety by involving him in a high-speed car chase. Besides, he didn't possess the driving skills to maintain a pursuit without ultimately crashing his vehicle at some point.

So, when he heard gravel crunch beside his car, he activated the power locks and cracked his window just enough to communicate with the person now standing beside him. He could see the man from the neck down. The guy was wearing casual dress—a teal-colored shirt and blue jeans. Probably not a police officer, at any rate.

"What's wrong?" Ken asked, tilting his head up toward the opening at the top of the window. Through his peripheral vision he saw that another man stood outside the passenger-side door. "Have I got a tail light out or…?"

The man outside his own door bent over to answer and Ken recoiled against his seat. It was one of the men from the airport. The tall, lanky one who resembled Nicolas Cage. The other man was in all likelihood the one who had put a gun to his ribs near the bank of phone booths that day.

"Oh, *shit*," Ken said. His fingers fumbled for the power window button. The window closed.

Apparently not perturbed in the least, the man pecked on the window with his knuckles, a sound that was similar to how Ken imagined a knock on a closed casket might sound from within that confined space.

*****

Valerie had no intention of going to her mother's house.

She stood outside the front door and waved at her husband and son as the car backed out of the driveway and moved up the quiet street. She saw Ken raise a hand in return, and she fancied that she saw Chance raise one small hand, as well. He had learned to wave 'hello' and 'goodbye' several months ago.

When the car was out of sight, when the sound of its droning motor could no longer be heard, she went back inside the house.

A frown had formed on her face, turning that smooth landscape into an unfamiliar and rare terrain. Something was wrong. Call it mother's or wife's instinct, but she sensed that Ken was hiding something.

What, she didn't know.

Tonight was not the first time she had noticed Ken's preoccupation, his reluctance to converse with her about what was eating at him. She knew what some of it stemmed from—or at least thought she did, at any rate: the stranger he had told her about the other night.

She had expressed doubt and disbelief when she first heard his story, and that bothered her. She was well aware that, when it came to Ken's unsubstantiated word, it was best not to let her first reaction be disbelief or any of its cousins—doubt and skepticism chief among them. Reactions like that stung him. She *knew* that. Yet sometimes she couldn't help herself.

On occasion, Ken could be annoying, whiney (especially during the spring storm season), and seemingly devoid of common sense. The rest of the time he was the kindest, most loving man she'd ever known, and she would wonder what she would do without him. She knew his history— God, did she; his brother, the storm, his seemingly unending guilt, the slow healing of psychiatric therapy—and loved him despite, and because of, what he'd been through. But when he was in one of his moods, when it seemed that at any moment he might revert back several years to his 'bad time', she generally left him alone. She knew he preferred selfanalysis when possible, and would not disclose what was bothering him until he felt the time was right.

Tonight, however, she could not leave it alone. Something was going on with him—and, perhaps, with Chance as well—that was different from his usual mood swings, when he would sometimes brood for hours about a gathering storm, or about how, if he'd been a little slower, Jimmy would still be alive. And she had noticed the subtle difference in he and Chance's relationship. Oh, Ken was still a wonderful daddy—she'd always known he would be—but lately, today especially, she had noticed him looking at Chance with a peculiar look that seemed one part curiosity and two parts confusion. Valerie had first chalked it up as a 'dreamy' look. She had worn the same look on her face for almost a year now, and it had been nearly constant in the months following the adoption. That look was filled with love and pride; it was great being parents.

Over the last week or so, Ken had seemed more absorbed in his thoughts, and his time of self-analysis should already have passed. Curiously, it hadn't, and that is why her thoughts dwelled on him now.

She went into the den and tried to get involved in an episode of *Friends*, but couldn't focus on the sitcom. Her mind kept turning relentlessly back to her husband and son. His mood tonight had been decidedly strange. He had never—not once, ever—taken Chance for a car ride to get him to sleep. Oh sure, the baby would sometimes fall asleep on family outings, but never had she or Ken taken him for a ride with the express purpose of lulling him to sleep. That was one thing. The animated way he'd talked to Chance earlier outside on the patio was another. Something was up with that. She hadn't wanted him to take the baby, because she worried Ken might be experiencing episodes of delusion. His therapist had said he might have those on occasion, but for three years he had not had one—to her knowledge, anyway—and so she had nothing with which to compare his current behavior.

Quit it, she told herself. *Don't do this. Not right now. Give him some more time. He'll eventually talk to you about whatever it is—he always does.*

That brought some comfort, but it was only marginal. She was getting an increasingly strong feeling that something else was wrong with Ken, and it was frustrating to not know what.

And why had he wanted her to go to her mother's house? His insistence troubled Valerie. What was wrong? Did he maybe have a girlfriend or something, whom he wanted to bring to the house while she was away?

No, that was *really* silly thinking, and she knew it. It was something else.

She wouldn't be going to her mother's house, that was for sure. She would stay here until they returned, and she would just ask him point-blank what the hell was going on. He would tell her then. She would demand it.

She turned back to the television and began to wait.

* * * * *

Ken held his finger forward on the power windows, as if removing it might somehow cause the window to descend on its own. He could not pull the car forward, onto the road, without running over a mailbox, and could not back up without hitting the vehicle parked behind him.

Were these men government agents? They had been wearing suits at the airport, and had certainly looked that type. Now, their clothing did not cause the words 'government agents' to come to mind. He removed his finger, and after a moment's thought put it back down and lowered the window. "I know you," he said.

The man outside his window looked in both directions up and down the road, almost nervously. "You might." He had a semi-deep voice that was nonetheless clear and strong.

What was it he had said to him? *Your son is not what he appears to be.* Yes. It had been that and something else. Something about keeping Chance out of the sun. Something. And in a flash, it came to him: *If you want a normal child, keep him out of the sun. They won't know then.*

They.

Ken shivered. He had been so caught up with Chance's new intelligence, and by association his ability to find the listening devices and ascertain their meaning, that he had almost forgot what these two men had told him.

"The airport. In Memphis. It was the airport, wasn't it?"

Instead of answering, the man said: "Mr. Malcolm—"

"How do you know my name?" Ken snapped.

Again, the man ignored his question. "Mr. Malcolm, I'm going to be as brief and to the point as possible, because we need to get off this highway as soon as we can."

Ken started to speak and then stopped. The two men didn't appear to be adversarial. He could see no weapons in either of their hands.

"Do you remember what we told you about your son?" After he asked this, the man leaned down and looked into the car at Chance. "How you doing there, big guy?"

Chance smiled and slobbered like the small child he was, but said nothing. However, his smile eased Ken's mind more than any words could have. He relaxed some.

"I remember," he said evenly.

"Good. And has anyone been watching you? Following you?"

Ken uttered a short laugh devoid of humor. "Well, other than you and your friend here, I would have to say no."

"Are you sure?" Once again, the man glanced around. No traffic, and apparently they were being quiet enough that they weren't disturbing the people in front of whose home they had stopped. Or maybe those people were on the phone right now, giving the county sheriff a yell.

What's he *nervous about?* Ken thought. I'm *the one who should be scared here.*

"I'm sure," he said.

"Good, then maybe we've still got time."

"Time for what?"

After a last look up and down the road, the man said, "Mr. Malcolm, you and your son are in danger, and we need you to follow us to a safe place. Could you do that?"

"Why?" Ken said, growing both angry and apprehensive. "What kind of danger?"

"Mr. Malcolm, we know about the listening devices."

"The—"

"We know they've been disarmed."

Chance had said that people from the government were coming after him, but Ken never thought they would get here *this* fast. Besides, he felt that these two men were not the people to which his son had been referring. They had a hurried manner about them, but they still had not produced so much as a single handgun or pair of handcuffs.

Yet, they knew about the bugs.

His anger continued to fester. He rolled window down another inch. "Hell, yes, they've been disarmed. You have no business coming into my home and planting—"

"They're going to be coming now," the man said, a ghostly imitation of words spoken by Chance a mere hour ago. "If they haven't already arrived. Now, *please* follow us, Mr. Malcolm."

They, again. Not these two men, but *they.*

Ken looked down at Chance, and he alone saw the child's slight nod.

Ken sighed. "All right. We'll follow you, but you have to promise two things first. Otherwise, forget it. We'll sit here all night."

"I'll try," the man said. "What are they?"

"Don't harm us, and when we get to a safe place, you tell me what this is all about."

The man seemed reluctant, but he said, "You have my word."

He and the other man ran to their vehicle and pulled back onto the road.

Ken put the car in gear and followed them, wondering as he did so what they wanted from him, who was after Chance, and what they —he and his son—were getting involved in.

*****

SEVENTEEN

Duke Tarkington stood outside his room, nervous and scared.

Level Four was dark and silent, with most of the compound shut down for the night. The residents were either asleep in their quarters or entertaining themselves with books or classical music—the only music deemed worth listening to by those in charge.

Duke's father was one of those in command (had, in fact, been the one to select which music was most suitable to the residents) and Duke had never been more thankful for something his father had done. The sad thing was that it was probably the *only* thing about him for which Duke felt gratitude. The music. Classical scores from Beethoven and Bach, to the Philadelphia Symphony Orchestra. The PSO was Duke's personal favorite. He had read about the City of Brotherly Love in books and on compact discs on computer, and the harmonious anthems flooded his mind with images that teased his imagination and filled him with wonder that such a place existed. He loved books above all else—raw knowledge could be gained from them, while what one learned from musical scores was more sublime and below the surface—but it was music that helped him slip off to sleep each night, and it was by music that he woke each morning.

He had read somewhere that 'music soothes the heart of the savage beast', and though he didn't know whether or not that was true (although he suspected it was), the music drifting through his small living quarters tonight had done even more. Tonight, the music had masked his departure from his room.

It was Duke's hope that the music might also save his life.

Because if he was caught out of his room at this hour...

He braced sweaty palms flat against the wall behind him as he sidled down the darkened hallway. The only illumination came from a recessed light at the end of the hall near two elevators that looked like a pair of pale square eyes. The distance from his room to the elevators was only thirty yards, but right now it looked to be *at least* half a mile. Perhaps more.

There were also eight other doors between here and there, rooms occupied by other residents of Level Four. Tim Flaugherty, the weekend security man on Substation D, where Prometheus was kept, occupied the second from the end on the left. It was the door to this room that worried Duke the most.

Or rather, to be honest, who was behind it.

He inched another ten yards down the hall. Behind him, to his left, came the sound of the PSO, muffled by the thickness of his walls, yet still there. He had turned the volume up, as he sometimes did at night, but not *too* loud. He didn't want to wake anyone. Especially Flaugherty.

Tim Flaugherty was lanky and only semi-tall, but he was as quick-tempered as Duke's father, whose anger was legendary around the compound. Duke was smart enough to know *why* he feared Flaugherty to such an extent. That was easy: the man had worked the knife that took his tongue. That had been two years ago, of course, but not nearly long enough for Duke to forget the fear and terror of that day.

He shook his head in brisk jerks. It would do him no good to relive—or even think about—that right now, when time was imperative to the task Prometheus had given him. To Duke's knowledge, no one in the compound knew how much of the computer system he actually knew (no one but Prometheus, anyway), and that fact alone would free him of any suspicion once the task was completed.

If he wasn't caught away from his quarters.

When he was only thirty feet from the elevators, he noticed soft light spilling across the hallway from beneath Flaugherty's door. His heart began beating harder, his breath quickened, and he was unable to proceed. The light, and fear, held him like a deer to a spotlight. *Move,* he told himself.

As he watched the bottom of the door, a shadow passed through the light.

Perhaps Flaugherty had sensed him out here, prowling down the hallway at an hour when he should have been asleep, or at least in his quarters.

He could be on the phone right now, calling security, telling them that Duke was out of his room, and that apparently something *else* was going to have to be cut off for him to learn his lesson. Maybe his *legs* this time. Duke shivered. He knew better, of course: Tim Flaugherty *was* in security, and it was doubtful that he would require help in dealing with Duke. What fun would there be in that?

A thud-crunch from near the elevators made Duke jump. He would have hollered out, had he possessed the equipment to do so. As it was, his mouth opened in a silent scream of surprise and fear and his body thrummed as though it had received a jolt of electricity.

Then he realized that it was only the small ice machine across from the elevator. A fresh batch of ice had dropped down inside the machine.

Duke let out his breath in a tight hiss. A thin sheen of sweat glistened on his forehead. It felt as though he had been out of his room for hours, although it couldn't have been more than a couple of minutes. He should have already been to the elevators and on his way down to Substation C.

You have to be quick, stupid, he scolded himself.

He sidled down the hall, his back pressed against the wall as though he wanted to melt into it, and watched the bottom of Flaugherty's door. The shadow passed by on the other side once again, and seemed to pause for an eternity. Duke held his breath and pushed on, and he finally made it to the elevators.

The thudding of his heart did not slow. Instead, it accelerated.

Now came the hard part: getting onto the elevator without drawing anyone's attention. Now is when the music would—hopefully—mask some of the noise he would make.

Two orange buttons were set into the wall to the right of the sliding doors. One showed a black arrow pointing up, the other one down. Duke pushed the down button with a held breath, and the clicks and clangs from inside the shaft, though muffled somewhat by the thick walls, sounded to Duke like a dozen church bells going off. He was thankful that the elevators did not chime when coming to a stop at each floor.

When the car arrived, the door slid back smoothly, and Duke exhaled with relief when he was inside and the doors were closed. With a shaking hand, he pushed the button marked 'c', which would take him down seven stories to the Communications Center on Substation C.

As the elevator descended, the downward motion brought back memories of his childhood, when the elevator (including this very one) was a pleasant and exciting experience; what riding a thrill ride at an amusement park must feel like—or at least what he *imagined* it must feel like. The out-of-control sensation caused by the cabled carriage remained, Duke found, years after he had been 'Daddy's little buddy', and Derek Tarkington was still more father than tyrant.

The elevator came to an abrupt, cushioned stop, and the doors slid open, revealing another ice machine in a small patch of light. Outside the dim illumination, the darkness was as impenetrable as that on Level Four, but with an added bonus: no Flaugherty. Duke almost snickered out loud when he realized that he had pulled one over on 'nosey-rosey' Flaugherty, who seemed to always have a hundred or so questions to ask Duke whenever their paths crossed, as if he took pleasure in watching Duke struggle to communicate. It was funny to think of him upstairs on Four, completely oblivious to the fact that Duke was someplace that was off-limits at this time of night.

What if he decides to check on me, tell me to turn my music off because he is ready to go to sleep?

The smile fell from Duke's face. What *would* he do? That was a good question. There had been occasions in the past where that very thing had happened, and not only to Duke. Tim Flaugherty pushed his weight around with the other residents of Level Four, as well.

Think about Prometheus. Only of him. Stay focused.

He tried, but his apprehension did not fade as he stepped off the elevator and into the deserted hallway. There were no dormitories down here, nor any security guards. The thought of intruders was preposterous, after all, with security devoted almost entirely to the outside perimeters of the compound and the upper levels.

There were, however, plenty of cameras to worry about.

With a deep breath to help calm his nerves (although it didn't seem to help a whole lot), Duke reached into his right front pocket and strode casually over to the numeric keypad set into the wall to the left of the ice machine. When he removed his hand, he held in it the note that Prometheus had left for him between the pages of *Cold Fire*. He unfolded it, smoothed it against the wall, and then punched the five-digit code on the keypad to his right: 64234.

A green light appeared on the lower left corner of the keypad, blinking like the steady beat of an alien heart.

Now Duke *could* relax some. He had just deactivated the security cameras in the Communications Center, which was at the end of the hall to his left.

Almost there, Prometheus, he thought. He walked quickly to the doors at the end of the hall and inserted his plastic ID card into an electronic lock. Another green light flashed, and the door clicked open. From where he stood, just outside the entrance, he could almost feel his friend, who was directly below him on Substation D. He could envision Prometheus, looking up toward the ceiling and wondering if Duke would fail at the task he'd given him. With his acute hearing, might he not be, even now, listening to Duke's feet walk across the floor of the Communications Center to do what he himself could not?

What would it feel like to know that something so important balanced on the shoulders of one young man?

No one is down here, Duke soothed himself. *Everyone but topside security is either asleep or in their rooms.*

Yet he knew it wasn't that simple. Couldn't be.

He would, in all likelihood, be caught before the night was over—he *knew* that—but the fact remained that he felt obligated to his friend. It was an acceptable risk. Not only that, either. He also felt an inner feeling —perhaps some of that ESP stuff Prometheus sometimes talked about— that this went beyond the normal boundaries of an obligation or favor. It felt, instead, as though it was an obligation toward many people—and not just those in the compound.

The child.

Yes, the child. As he prepared to breach the entrance to Communications, Duke told himself that what he was doing had little to do with Prometheus, and much to do with the child that Prometheus seemed compelled to protect.

A shuffling noise just ahead of him, on his left, broke him from his thoughts, and Duke's heart began a rhythmic thumping that caused his ribs to ache.

The Communications Center was mostly dark, but not totally silent. Banks of monitors and computers cast a glow like blue moon-light across the tiled floor, complimenting that eerie illumination with soft blips and bleeps. Duke was not afforded a view of the entire room from his vantagepoint. The monitors directly ahead of him were visible, of course. Banks of screens and monitors lined the walls to the left and right, as well, and only about half of this equipment was in his field of vision. Whatever had caused the noise was out of sight. If there had been anything there at all.

The sound came again, and from this slightly closer distance Duke could tell where the noise was coming from, and guess its source. It was not a shuffling, scraping sound, as he'd first thought. Instead, it was a thumping sound, and it was coming from the floor to his left. But not *on* the floor: from *beneath* the floor.

Prometheus.

Telling him to hurry.

As a not-too-subtle reminder that time was an important factor, his friend's attempt at getting his attention worked like a charm. Duke went to the general vicinity where the thumps had originated and jumped up and down twice—as hard as he could—on the floor.

The compound itself was not made of mountains and rock, but was built inside an extremely large series of holes that had been blasted into the pile of rock and limestone. The floors were merely thin slabs of cement supported by steel girders, and sound carried through them as easily as they would have had the structure been any other building above ground.

The silence beneath him told Duke that Prometheus had gotten his message. He turned his attention to the computers on the far-left end of the room and stood facing them, his back to the door.

Again consulting the note, Duke began tapping keys on the keyboard.

The monitors to either side of the computer terminal would normally have shown dark images of deserted hallways and other rooms at this time of night. Now, they watched over Duke like dead, blank eyes. On the screen in front of him, a three-dimensional diagram of a satellite turned slowly toward Duke. At his direction, with the attached mouse, the computer-generated image was halted. With another click and a series of taps on the keyboard, the image zoomed to one hundred percent magnification over the part of the craft Duke had carved out with the mouse and series of keystrokes.

It was the control panel for the craft.

Cool sweat beaded on Duke's forehead. *Almost there.* Consulting the note, and using the mouse as an extension of his hands, he typed in a series of codes on the control panel, hitting the *enter* key after each series of numbers. That done, he clicked the *enter* key a final time, let out a long breath, and wiped a forearm across his brow.

Nothing happened. On the screen, the satellite control panel remained as it had before. Duke was disheartened. He must have miss-keyed one of the numbers or letters when he was putting in the code.

Must have. Following this let down was a feeling that touched him even deeper: he had failed Prometheus. He had screwed up what might be his one and only chance to help his friend. The note had cautioned that the code could only be keyed once. If he messed up, he could not try again for thirty minutes without setting off alarms throughout the compound.

Duke hung his head in defeat and shame…and then jerked it up quickly when the computer bleeped. On the satellite control panel a red light began blinking, and a message appeared on the screen in front of him, flashing like a heaven-sent bolt of lightning:

SATELLITE DEACTIVATED

Duke breathed a sigh of relief. It had worked.

Yeah, and you're probably going to get caught any time. Hurry up and finish it.

He fumbled the note, folded it over until he could read the last few lines of print, and began typing in the series of codes that, according to the note, would automatically bring the satellite back on-line after a certain length of time. That done, he folded the note, put it in his pocket for later disposal, and turned off the monitor. If anybody were to come into the room, the screen would be blank like the others.

He walked over to the same spot in which he had thumped acknowledgement to his friend, and jumped up once, as hard as he could.

He was answered with two quick thumps: *thank you.*

Duke smiled.

All that was left to do now was to make it safely back to his room.

He left the Communications Center, reactivated the security monitors, and then pushed the button for the elevator. He stepped inside and the doors whispered shut behind him. He punched the button for his floor and the elevator began its ascent. When it reached Level Four, the doors slid open and he got out.

The hallway lay in shadows, dark and forbidding. He could not see more than eight or ten feet past the point where the light and darkness met, but he knew his way from here. As he neared his room, he fumbled the key from a front pocket of his jeans.

He was almost there. The relief he felt was tremendous, pumping his body full of adrenaline and a sweet feeling of accomplishment. He had helped his friend do something important. He wasn't sure what that something was, but Duke trusted Prometheus more than he trusted anyone, and he knew his friend would tell him, in time, what he had helped accomplish.

He reached out into the darkness for his door, and at the moment when he realized the hallway was silent, that the music in his room was no longer playing, a hand grabbed his wrist in a firm grip.

He gasped.

"Well, well, Duke," Tim Flaugherty said. "Where have *you* been?"

* * * * *

EIGHTEEN

Ken grew worried when the car in front of him turned right onto Culberhouse, at the end of Hasbrook Road. They were being led further away from the familiarity of the city. He still knew where they were, but that didn't help his uneasiness.

Forty-five minutes later—with Chance asleep in his car seat and a peaceful look on his small face—the two men pulled onto a secondary road on the southern outskirts of the city of Paragould. Ken followed close behind. At least they were staying off the main highways. On occasion, his headlights splashed across the vehicle in front of him, affording him a look at the back of the men's heads as the cars topped gently rolling slopes.

Ken still knew where he was. He had an aunt in the Paragould area, and had spent many weekends during his childhood on Sunday visits to her house. And Paragould itself was only about twenty miles or so from the northern side of Jonesboro.

With the cover of darkness not much was visible, other than some trees or mailboxes on either side of the road. Ken mentally kicked himself for leaving his cell phone at home on the charger. He was tempted several times to hit his brakes, turn around, and go back into Paragould and call the police.

Irrational thinking, that was. He knew if he did that, he would be making himself—as well as Chance—a marker for the people who were pursuing them.

A short while later, the car ahead of him slowed and turned into a driveway on the left. Ken parked his car to the right of the other one. A small house stood at the end of a sidewalk that led from the chat-covered driveway. Flanked by side yards full of trees, the house itself showed little character, as if it were designed for indifference.

Ken let Chance sleep. He got out of the car and closed the door softly. The two men got out also, and the driver—the one who resembled Nicolas Cage—jiggled his keys as he walked down the sidewalk, his back to Ken.

The other man remained near the car, looking out toward the road. "I don't think we were followed, Steve," he said.

The first man stopped on the sidewalk and turned around. "Steve? Did you actually just call me *Steve?* What the hell?"

The other man, who had thinning hair and a light beard, fumbled some. "I don't know—I just thought—you know, that you wouldn't want Mr. Malcolm to know our real names."

The Cage lookalike sighed. "And why not? Have we got anything to hide? No. We don't. Good grief, Bobby, we're not in the agency any more, remember?"

'Bobby' cringed a little. Apparently, *he* was averse to using his real name. "I know that," he said, "but I still think we should have used different names. I could have been—"

"Excuse me," Ken interjected. "No offense, guys, but I really don't care *what* you call each other as long as you tell me what the hell is going on here, and who is after me and my son."

"I understand your concern," Cage said, glancing at Bobby and bugging his eyes out briefly, as though challenging the man to say something else. He unlocked the door and opened it. "Mr. Malcolm, we will explain everything to you. I gave you my word, remember. Why don't you go and get Chance and bring him inside? There's a bed to lay him on. I'll make some coffee, and *Bobby* here," he said, glaring at the man again, "will keep an eye out for any unwanted visitors."

Ken looked from one man to the other, started to say something, then shrugged. Normally he would hate to wake Chance when it was this far past his bedtime, but tonight he didn't think about that at all, nor did he have to worry about it. He moved him from the car to the house without waking him, and the youngster was soon asleep in a bedroom at the back of the house.

The house was an older one, and the inside walls were of dark wood paneling that reminded Ken of his grandparents' home. A ceiling fan turned lazily from the high ceiling and a light burned from a globe beneath it, bathing the room in a low light that reflected dimly off several computers, a printer, and fax machine that sat atop a long table against one wall. A table cluttered with stacks of paper and printouts fronted another wall, which made the room look like an office instead of a living area.

"Who *are* you guys?" Ken said. He was standing near the hallway that led to the room where he'd laid his son. Although he was still a little uneasy, Chance apparently wasn't, and that helped more than anything to calm him. Chance's instincts seemed to be very reliable.

The Nicolas Cage lookalike spoke. "I'm sorry we haven't introduced ourselves yet, Mr. Malcolm. I apologize." He walked forward, extending his hand. "I'm Adrian O'Donnell." He took Ken's hand and shook it lightly. "And this," O'Donnell said, pointing to the other man, "is Bobby Templeton."

Bobby shook his hand, then went back to the computer monitor he'd been watching. "Nice to meet you."

Ken nodded, then looked back at Adrian. "So, his name is really Bobby?"

"Oh, yeah. It's Bobby, all right," he said, chuckling. "We were in the safe zone when I mentioned that. Get me out in the street and it might be a different story."

"Safe zone?"

"The house," Adrian said. "It's clean."

"Oh," Ken looked again around the room. "I guess you two already know my name," he said, "and you know something else. I think I'm ready to hear *that*."

Adrian looked from Bobby to Ken. "Okay," he said. "Let's sit down. I'll get us some coffee and then we'll talk. How do you like yours?"

"Black," Ken said. "But—"

"It won't take but a minute," Bobby interjected in a soft voice. I made some while you were putting Chance to bed. All Adrian has to do is pour."

"Oh," Ken said. He looked at the cluttered workstations. "What are those computers for?"

"Tracking operations," Bobby said.

"What, exactly, are you tracking?"

Bobby's answer was succinct. "You…and them."

Them again, Ken thought. *Oh, boy.*

Adrian returned from the small kitchen with three steaming mugs of coffee. The aroma was pleasant. "Sit over there, Mr. Malcolm," Bobby said, pointing to the sofa. There was just enough space on one end, next to a scattering of papers. He and Adrian sat on a sturdy coffee table in front of the sofa.

For a few minutes the men sipped their coffee, and the only other sounds in the room were the beeps and whines of the computers.

"Where should we start?" Adrian asked Bobby.

"How about at the beginning," Ken offered.

"I have a better idea," Bobby said. "How about you ask us what you want to know, Mr. Malcolm, and we'll go from there. Sound fair?"

"Sounds okay to me." That was Adrian.

"I guess," Ken sighed. "There's just so many things I would like to know, I don't know where to start." He thought for a minute, and the two men didn't rush him. "Okay," he said at last. "I guess the main thing I would like to know right now is who put the bugs in my house."

"First off," Adrian said, "it wasn't us. Let me clear that up right now, before we go any further. We are on your side, Mr. Malcolm. It may not seem that way to you at the moment, but I can assure you that if we weren't, we would have eliminated you a long time ago. Isn't that right, Bobby?"

"Oh, absolutely," Bobby said. "Right as rain."

"Then who...?"

"The government," Adrian said. "They planted the listening devices."

"I know that much already," Ken said. *Eliminated? Surely I didn't hear that right.*

"How did you come by that information?"

"Chance told me."

"He did?" Bobby Templeton jumped up and ran over to a computer, where he began punching keys. After a moment he said: "I see no record of where he told you any such thing. In fact, I see no record of him talking to you at all." He walked back to the coffee table and sat down.

Adrian looked at Ken. "Chance *talked* to you? Are you sure?"

"Yes," Ken said. "I figured you guys knew that already."

"No," Adrian said. "We know your child is an extraordinary little guy, but we had no idea he could talk."

"Wait a minute, Ade," Bobby said. "The child is fifteen-months old. A lot of children talk at that age, don't they?"

"I can guarantee you," Ken said, "that no fifteen-month-old ever talked as well as Chance can. When he wants to, anyway."

Adrian still looked confused. "Hold on here. We have nothing that indicates the child talking, other than normal childish words, half-phrases, and other gibberish. Perhaps an equipment malfunction...an auditory hallucination on Mr. Malcolm's part." He appeared to be talking more to himself.

"Now just a damn minute," Ken said, growing increasingly uncomfortable with what was happening. Adrian O'Donnell's reaction mirrored Valerie's when Ken had told her about Chance disappearing from his playpen, and about the stranger with car trouble. "Just how in the hell can you guys claim innocence about the bugs, yet claim you have knowledge of what was picked up by them?"

Bobby glanced at Adrian—*oh, oh*, his eyes said—and then back at Ken. "Well, you see, Mr. Malcolm, what was picked up..."

"Okay, that's it," Ken said, throwing up his hands. "I'm getting my son and we are getting the hell out of here." In his mind he could see these two men sitting in this very room, listening as he and Valerie made love. They probably ate popcorn and drank beer while they did it, too, and that image alone made him ache with fury. He jumped off the sofa and started down the hall to the bedroom where Chance was sleeping.

He was stopped by Adrian's voice, and by the snick of what could only be a handgun being chambered with a live round. "Hold it right there, Mr. Malcolm."

Ken froze, his back to them, his mind swirling with madhouse thoughts. How could this be happening? How did he ever let these two men talk him into following them here? The floor seemed to sway beneath his feet.

"I said we wouldn't harm you," Adrian said. "and I meant it. This is not what it looks like."

Ken turned around slowly and looked at him. "Then I guess you'd better explain yourself a little better, because to me it sounds as though you guys are the ones who have been eavesdropping on my life. I mean, come on, I'm looking down the barrel of a *gun* here. What would *you* think?"

Adrian lowered the gun but he did not put it away. Bobby was in the corner by the bank of computers, watching with interest. His dark eyes stood out from his square face like two coals in a snow bank. Ken interpreted the look as nervousness. "Mr. Malcolm, we *haven't* been spying on you, regardless of how it might look."

"Then what would you call it?"

"I can sum it up in one word," Adrian said as he snapped the handgun into a shoulder holster.

"Then please do."

"Espionage," Adrian O'Donnell said. "We've been spying on the people who have been spying on *you*."

Espionage.

* * * * *

John Milcheck and Mark Lomax arrived at Cedar Lane in Jonesboro, Arkansas, at a little after seven the following morning. As they drove slowly down the quiet street they saw only one person—a man with a steaming cup of coffee in his hand, dressed in a bathrobe, picking up his morning paper. He was the Malcolm's neighbor two doors down. The man took the paper into his home without a glance at the agents' vehicle as it passed.

"Looks like they're home," John said as they cruised past the Malcolm residence. A vehicle was visible at the rear of the driveway. They couldn't tell if there was another one parked behind the house, or in the garage. Hedges and shrubs flanked the outside perimeters of the lawn like dark green sentries.

"What's our next step?" John said.

As if in answer, the cell phone on the console between them blurted its shrill cry, and the two men looked at each other.

"That would have to be Virginia," Lomax said as he reached for the phone. "No one else has this number." He picked it up. "Lomax here."

John listened to the only side of the conversation he could hear:

"We've just arrived in their neighborhood," Lomax said into the phone. "It looks as though at least one of them is home." Then Lomax seemed to fumble. "I—we didn't know they weren't here. With all due respect, sir, we just arrived—"

"What's wrong?" John said when he saw concern and anxiety cross the agent's pinched face.

Lomax held a finger up to him as he listened. "Just a minute," he mouthed to John.

"What about tracking devices?" Lomax said. A pause. "I see. Yes, sir, we will."

He hung up, sighed heavily, and looked at John. "The Malcolms and the child have disappeared."

"You're joking."

"Do I look like I'm joking?"

"No," John said, "I guess not." In fact, the agent looked kind of

155

'yellow around the gills', as John's mother would have said. "Where are they?"

"No one knows right now. The agency lost track of them at the end of a…" he looked at a piece of scrap paper he'd used to jot down a few notes. "…a Hasbrook Road, over on the south side of town. We've been told to go there and see if we can pick up any sign of them, or which direction they might have gone."

"Going to be tough," John said.

"Tell me about it. But it's what Calhoun wants."

Something entered John's mind now; something that didn't quite sound right. "How did the agency lose them? They have tracking devices on both their vehicles. I installed them myself. I even tested them. They worked fine."

Lomax looked ahead, grim-faced as he spoke. "Calhoun said that the satellite network used to track the vehicles went offline last night, and still hasn't come back online."

"Inside job?"

"Calhoun didn't say, but it would just about have to be. The satellites that Uncle Sam controls are more secure from outside hackers than any secure site on the Internet could dream of. He thinks that, by going to where they last picked up a signal, we can at least better our chances of locating them. You ask me, we should be waiting right here, but I guess orders are orders."

"How long has it been since the agency lost track of them?"

"It was late last night when the last signals came through."

"Jesus." Then another thought struck John. "When the satellite is back online, won't they be able to locate the vehicle by the signal from the tracking device?"

"I'm sure they will," Lomax said, "but for the time being Calhoun says they are preparing to conduct satellite video grids with a different satellite uplink, in an expanding circle, beginning with the last place the signal was received. They'll have the location within twelve hours or so—he claims—so he wants us out to Hasbrook as soon as possible, in case they haven't gone far. We'll have a better starting point, at any rate. And if the satellite comes back online before then, we'll have an even better shot."

John nodded, and they pulled away from the curb and headed toward the edge of town, Lomax consulting a map and looking for Hasbrook Road.

NINETEEN

Ken was anxious to hear what Adrian O'Donnell and Bobby Templeton had to say, yet he also felt a faint tug of regret that it would be quite some time before he would be able to lay next to his son and get some sleep. At present, the long light of dawn was still hours away.

Sitting once again on the sofa, sipping hot coffee, Ken listened as Adrian talked, and he spoke only when he needed to ask the man something or to clarify what he had said. "So you call it espionage, but you guys aren't foreign agents or anything like that."

"Right," Adrian said. It was apparent that he was going to do most of the talking. Bobby had his back to them, attending the computers and occasionally jotting down notes on a yellow legal pad.

"At least you're Americans, then," Ken said lightly, and with some relief. In the last few minutes, he had begun to entertain the not-so-pleasant idea that the two men were foreign agents, despite the fact that neither carried an accent.

"Yes. We're as American as you are."

"Treason, then?" Ken said, but he was smiling. He didn't believe that, either.

"Not likely," Adrian said. He sipped his coffee and grimaced. "We like to think of ourselves as government defectors instead of government outlaws. Isn't that right, Bobby? Bobby?"

"Uh-huh," Templeton muttered. His attention was focused on the screen in front of him.

"We were with the CIA at one time," Adrian continued, "and though we now do basically the same type of work, we are more like... freelancers, I guess. Independent contractors who work for themselves and pick and choose their jobs." His laugh was deep and pleasant.

"And I suppose one of the jobs you chose has something to do with my son?" Ken said curtly, his lips a thin line on his face.

"Actually," Adrian said, "keeping up with your son is the only job we've been on since we left the agency."

"The only one?"

"Yes."

"But why?" Ken said. "Why is keeping up with my son so important to you?"

Adrian looked at him squarely, and Ken noticed Bobby pause in his work at the computers. "Mr. Malcolm, your son is the reason we left the CIA. The *only* reason. And he's our only job. I was kidding about the freelance stuff."

Ken was perplexed. To think that two agents from the Central Intelligence Agency of the United States of America had quit their jobs—and in all probability any future career in the government—for a fifteen-month-old child was ludicrous, wasn't it?

And the real question was, *why?*

Ken found he wanted that answer more than any other. If these two men could tell him what their interest was in his son, then perhaps he could finally begin to understand how and why Chance could talk like he had been lately; why he was so intelligent.

And he also thought that, because someone else knew about Chance, he—Ken—could stop worrying so much about his own sanity, and whether or not the things he had witnessed the last few days were real. The roller coaster in his head would finally come to a complete stop, the motor that pulled it along its track would falter and die, and the track and car might corrode and rust in quiet idleness.

Just the thought of that occurring was a great weight lifted from his mind, but there was still a mountain of things lurking in there; wonders, worries, and questions about the young child asleep in the room down the hall. He had looked at Chance as his *son,* for crying out loud, and he was suddenly amazed to discover another interesting fact, as well—he still did. He found that his fatherly instincts—his protectiveness—toward his son remained. Sure, he had been Chance's parent for only ten months, but that length of time was sufficient enough to learn what being a father meant. It was enough, and it was something that he didn't want to lose.

Outside, night pressed against the windows.

"So, why did you guys leave the CIA? You said it was because of Chance, but what happened?"

The two men looked briefly at each other and then Adrian spoke. "Mr. Malcolm, the CIA is a very powerful agency. A lot happens within the realms of that bureau that the public knows nothing of. In fact, there is quite a bit that goes on there that most government officials know little of, if any at all."

"Okay," Ken said slowly. "I follow you." He was wanting the man to get to the gist of the situation, and he had figured out that much information through books and television.

Adrian continued. "One of the things that only a few people in the agency knows about is your son, Chance."

Ken sat up straighter on the sofa.

"Chance's mother died giving birth to him," Bobby said, turning briefly away from his computers. "That's one of the reasons he was put up for adoption."

"The other reason was a mistake on someone else's part," Adrian said. "They didn't know who his father was. I'm sure the president didn't, at any rate."

"President?"

"Yeah."

"President...Clayton?"

"Yeah."

"Wow." Ken's head swam with this new information. "So, who *is* Chance's natural father? Are you telling me that his father is the President of the United States?"

Adrian chuckled softly. "No, not the president. But his father *is* one of the most influential figures in the nation, and probably the world. Only no one really knows it."

"And that is also part of our job," Bobby said.

"Eventually," Adrian added.

Now Ken was really confused. "You mean—"

"That your son's father is a powerful force of the U.S. government, and that the CIA believes it was a mistake to put the child up for adoption. President Clayton wanted the child, once rescued from the accident that killed his mother, to live a normal life. What he failed to realize, of course, was just who this child was."

"And the reporter complicated the whole thing, of course," Bobby said.

"Yeah, that too," said Adrian absently. He sighed and finished off the coffee in his mug. "So, the CIA has been keeping tabs on the youngster ever since the adoption and President Clayton knows no-thing about it because he remains ignorant as to the identity of the child's father. There is a faction inside Central Intelligence that is overseeing this project, and all involved oppose the president's decision to let the child live a civilian life."

"How about the two of you?" Ken said. "Do you oppose the president's decision, as well?"

"Oh, absolutely," Adrian said. "But then again, Bobby and I know more than most other people involved."

Ken sipped his coffee and tried to make some sense of what Adrian was telling him. It all sounded like something that could only happen in a movie or a book; CIA, the President, secret agents, covert operatives who'd defected from one of the alphabet-soup agencies of the government, listening devices and intelligent children. What would be next? Anything else could not possibly surprise Ken further.

But he was wrong about *that,* also.

"How did Chance's mother die?"

Bobby turned away from his computer long enough to answer him. His voice was more melodic than Adrian's, like a honey bee full of nectar. "There was an accident. The child's birth mother and her husband were on their way to meet the sperm donor for the child she was carrying. They had never met him, but both wanted to, although she was at the end of her term and might have the baby at any time. The meeting was set up to take place at a secret military installation in Nevada, and this was by design. So-called 'doctors' at this facility would remove the child from its mother's womb and then terminate both she and her husband."

"Terminate?"

"Yes. Both his parents believed that they were going to the donor's home. I guess it never occurred to them to wonder why he lived in the middle of the desert."

"But then came the accident," Adrian said, picking up the con-versation from Bobby as though the two men had rehearsed it. The latter went back to his computers as though the topic was of no further interest to him. "The accident is something that *nobody* expected, although since then we've been able to put together a theory that perhaps the child's natural father might have known, or perhaps even caused it." Before Ken could ask about *that*, Adrian waved a hand at him. "But that's putting the cart before the horse, I guess."

"And there was the reporter, of course," Bobby said. "He was the reason the president learned of the child in the first place."

"Go on," Ken prompted.

"The accident was caused by a malfunctioning compact nuclear warhead about the size of an attaché case. The reporter was about eight miles behind Chance's parents on the highway, and he reported the explosion over his cellular phone. Central Intelligence intercepted, but only about midway through the call. The child's mother, a woman by the name of Miriam Logan, was in the final stages of labor when the bomb detonated. Chance was in the birth canal when both parents were incinerated by the after-blast. The reporter came upon the three of them, and while he was on the phone, reporting the situation, he was exterminated. Chance's head had by now exited the birth canal."

"His scars," Ken said softly.

"Yes," Adrian said. "Your son was worked on by a team of the finest physicians in the world, and I would even go so far as to say that he's lucky to even be alive. In fact, he—"

"I think his father had a lot to do with that," Bobby interjected, and he shot Adrian a stern glance. *Careful,* was the message those eyes seemed to convey.

The look did not go unnoticed by Ken. But something else occurred to him at the same time; something that he needed to know, that he hadn't thought much about, perhaps because he'd initially thought these two men were figments of some warped dream.

"When we were at the airport in Memphis," Ken said, directing his words toward Adrian. "You guys mentioned something about my son. You said that if I wanted a normal child, I should keep him out of the sun. You said he wasn't what he appeared to be."

"And do you agree with that?" Adrian said.

"Of course, I do. Now, anyway. But at the time I had no idea what you were talking about, and you scared the hell out of me. Now, I know that he *is* different. I don't know *why*, of course, and I still don't know what you meant about keeping him out of the sun. So, if you could shed a little light on that for me..." Ken forced a smile and impatiently blinked his eyes a couple of times.

Adrian looked at Bobby, who only shrugged his shoulders and returned his attention to the bank of computers. "Okay," he said. "I guess that's part of the reason you agreed to follow us here in the first place."

"Yes, it is."

Adrian ran a hand through his hair. "I don't know how to say this delicately, Mr. Malcolm, so I'll just say it. Your...son, Chance... well, there's a good possibility that if he's exposed to sunlight long enough he might...his molecular structure...he might be able to..."

"Become invisible?" Ken supplied.

The look on Adrian's face was worth going into a photo album. Bobby left his computers and returned to the sofa. "You *know* this already?"

Ken recalled the cookout in the back yard. He remembered Chance not being in his playpen when he should have been (and inside he winced when he also recalled the look Valerie had given him when he told her of it). On top of that memory came the incident at his father's house in Bono; Chance's unexplained disappearance and the message that had been spelled out with toy blocks when he reappeared near the back patio. The sun had been shining brightly on both occasions. It had.

And on the day of the adoption there was something else, wasn't there. Ken felt a tug again, as though on the brink of remembrance, and this time the memory came through in a sudden bout of clarity and understanding: When they had entered the room, the crib where Chance lay (*Chester. He had been Chester, then*) had been beneath a window, where sunlight splashed across the crib and onto the small arms and hands that stretched, shaking with his cries, up into the sunlight. Chance's hands and arms were all Ken had seen initially... but for a brief moment it had looked as though the small limbs were made of fine, fast moving dust motes, and hadn't Ken fancied that he could almost see the wall behind—no, *through*—them? He had. He had.

"I've been able to put a few things together," Ken said with a calmness he really didn't feel. Inside, he was beginning to feel the first threads of excitement.

"Have you actually seen him disappear?" Bobby asked. His voice carried his own level of excitement.

"Well, in a way," Ken said. "I've seen him not be where he was a moment earlier, and then be there when I looked again. I've never actually witnessed it, you know...actually happening."

"Amazing," Bobby said. He looked at Adrian. "Do you know what this means?"

Adrian nodded. Ken could almost hear gears and ratchets grinding and clinking together as the man thought.

"What?" Ken said. "What does it mean? What are you talking about?"

"If the child…Chance…can become invisible, then that means that he is exhibiting at least some of the molecular and genetic traits possessed by his natural father," Adrian said.

"And if that's the case," Bobby added excitedly, "then there's hope yet."

"Hope?"

"Yes. Hope for everyone, everywhere."

A stab of anxiety pierced Ken's heart. The word 'hope' should not have caused such a reaction, but it had.

Adrian got up and began pacing, in an unconscious imitation of a boss for whom he no longer worked.

"I don't get it," Ken said. "I don't understand."

Adrian quit pacing and stood in front of Ken, looking down at him. "Hope, Mr. Malcolm. For all humanity."

Ken was awestruck for a moment as the words sank in. "For some reason I feel this uneasy excitement," he told them. "As though something important is happening, or about to happen. But at the same time, I'm scared shitless."

Ignoring him, Adrian rushed over to the computers and conferred with Bobby. Ken eased closer to that corner and caught some of what they were saying.

Adrian: "Go to the Lone Star file, then the satellite and check on whether or not it…"

Bobby: "Already working on that." And in a softer voice in spite of which Ken could hear: "Do you think he's telling the truth about the transparency?"

Adrian: "I don't know, but I think so."

Bobby: "Yeah, why would he lie?"

"I *am* telling the truth," Ken told them, not caring that the two men probably thought him intruding on their conversation.

"Of course, Mr. Malcolm," Adrian said.

Ken sighed, letting out pent up breath. "Call me Ken or Kenneth, okay? I mean, you two have had a gun pointed at me twice now, so I think we're intimate enough to go on a first-name basis here."

"Okay...Ken. I think you're telling the truth. In fact, I'm almost positive." Adrian smiled, and in that gesture his face was transformed from a somber Nicolas-Cage-look to that of a schoolboy on the brink of summer. His eyes were twin sparkles of shimmering glass filled with hope and wonder.

"Then what—?"

"Mr. Mal—Ken?"

"What."

"I need you to do something for us." Adrian nodded toward Bobby, who had stopped his work on one of the computers and turned toward the two of them. "Something very important. In fact, I can't *stress* how important this is."

Ken looked from one to the other. "You're not going to finish telling me everything, are you?"

"Ken—"

"I knew it," Ken said. He threw his hands up and let them fall against his thighs. "I'm right, aren't I?"

Adrian sighed, and then talked in an increasingly rapid monologue. "I think we've given you quite a bit of information. We've held up our end of the agreement." Ken started to protest, but Adrian held up one hand. "Hear me out. Hear me out. We just need some time on the computers, and time to run a few errands. You're safe here, Ken, you *and* Chance, but I need you to put some faith in Bobby and myself while we look into some things. It's going to take some time, but trust me when I say this: Bobby and I are the only protection you have against the agency. This house is safe, nothing to worry about, but we need some time, so what I'm going to suggest is this..." he glanced at his watch, "We all get some rest tonight, including Bobby and myself after we've run a few preliminary queries on the system, because tomorrow is going to be a busy day for me and Bobby. We'll need you to stay here, have to *trust* you to stay here, but we have no other choice. And if you'll cooperate with us here, Ken, if you'll trust us for the next day or so, then we will explain more of what we know to you. We won't leave you in the dark. I promise you that much." He looked at Ken with the somber Nicolas Cage face. "We both want something here, Ken. You want more information, and we want you and Chance to stay here, to stay *safe*. We're willing to hold up our end. So, what do you say?"

Ken looked from him, to Bobby, and back again. "Okay, we'll

wait, but I have to call home first, or my in-law's place, check on my wife, make sure she's okay."

Adrian's face fell, and he shook his head. "I'm sorry, but we can't do that."

"Why not?"

"Because by now the agency knows that you've skipped out, so we can't take a chance of them finding our location."

"But my wife…"

Adrian held up a hand in a calming gesture. "Bobby and I will scout around tomorrow while we're out and see if we can locate her. We were sort of counting on her being with you tonight, but we had to act when we did. I'm sure she's all right, though. You said she doesn't know where you and Chance went?"

"That's right," Ken said, "but by now she's probably already called the police."

"The agency will intercept any outgoing calls right now," Bobby said. He paused and said thoughtfully. "That is, they will when their satellite system is back online."

Adrian jerked his head around. "It's down? No kidding?"

"No kidding," Bobby said softly, shaking his head and then returning to the task on the screen in front of him.

"The point is, we will look after your wife tomorrow," Adrian said, facing Ken again. "I promise you that, as well. Now. Do we have a deal?"

Knowing that he had little real choice, Ken said: "I guess we do."

Both Adrian and Bobby relaxed visibly at his acquiesence, and Adrian said: "How about you get some rest now?"

Ken went down the short hallway, to the room where his son lay sleeping. Chance was curled under a light blue sheet, one small thumb tucked securely in his mouth. He was overwhelmed with love for this child, and felt a protectiveness toward him that was almost primal in its intensity. He would let nothing happen to Chance. Nothing. And god help anyone who tried to harm him.

Weary from the events of the day past, Ken fell into a fitful sleep that was full of dreams of government agents, children who weren't really children, and an overall sense of futility that was akin to a cyclonic tornado on the dry and dusty plains of his mind. He woke briefly from these dreams around three in the morning, and when he was at last able to sleep again, he slept without dreams.

* * * * *

Ken and Chance woke the next morning to an empty house. The computer equipment in the corner sat silent, sentinel, as though awaiting its owner's return. There was a note on the counter in the small kitchen, next to the coffee maker. It was signed by Adrian and contained brief, cursory instructions: stay inside, keep away from the windows if possible, help yourself to food, we'll be back sometime this evening. There was also a short sentence thrown in beneath the man's slanted signature, and it was to these few words that Ken's eyes kept returning: *We're trusting you, Mr. Malcolm, so please trust us.*

So, Ken did as the note said.

He and Chance watched cartoons in the morning while eating eggs and toast, and passed the afternoon building card-houses from a deck of playing cards Ken found near one of the computers (he was tempted to look at what was on one of the systems, but his mind kept returning to the last sentence of Adrian's note and he resisted the urge). The day was a pleasant respite from recent events, and was layered in an atmosphere similar to the way things had been shortly after the adoption, when Chance's innocence and childlike mannerisms were nothing to be scrutinized. And he hadn't acted like anything *but* a child during the lazy course of the day.

For a while, Ken was able to forget about everything—the CIA, what they were going to do, whether Adrian and Bobby would be able to locate Valerie—and enjoyed his son in a way he had begun to fear he would never experience again.

If it wasn't for what happened later that night, the near-perfect day might have been satisfyingly complete.

* * * * *

TWENTY

Later that same evening, shortly past midnight, a phone rang.

John Milcheck and Mark Lomax both jerked in their seats, startled. They were parked near the intersection of Hasbrook Road and Culberhouse, a four-way stop outside the city limits. They had spent the day holed up at a small motel on the outskirts of the inner city after Calhoun himself had called to report that their satellites were going to be delayed being brought back online, and that the video grid was progressing much too slowly. The agents could sense the mounting frustration in the director's voice. They were instructed to wait at the *Colonial Inn* until further notice. The room was pleasant, and they needed the rest after driving all night, with a clean décor and the comforts of a major chain, but it was still idle time when they woke from much needed naps. Especially for John, who was consequently subjected to more tales of Lomax's field heroics. Thirty minutes ago, they had finally received orders to return to Hasbrook Road: the satellites were almost operational.

Now the real orders were coming. The ringing phone told them that much.

Both agents stared at the phone on the console between them as though it were a foreign object planted by an equally foreign nation or entity.

Lomax was on the driver's side, and after a quick check to ensure they were alone at the intersection, he answered the phone.

"Lomax."

Again, John got to hear only one side of the conversation. Normally this would have annoyed him, but the surprised and excited look on

Lomax's face as he listened to the caller on the other end piqued his curiosity. The same look had periodically surfaced on the agent's face at the hotel, when he'd been relaying (or possibly, re-living) his array of field experiences.

"I see," Lomax was saying. "Yes, uh-huh. No, we're at Hasbrook and Culberhouse now." He motioned for John to give him something to write on, and John supplied a notepad and pen from his pocket.

Lomax began jotting on the pad. "About twenty-five miles north? Okay…yes. I guess we can make it in about thirty-five to forty minutes. Yes. I see. Roger that."

He put the phone back on the console, tore out the piece of paper, and handed the pad back to John. "The satellite is back online and we've got the Malcolm's location."

"Where?"

"About thirty minutes from here. In the city of Paragould."

"Which way are they traveling?"

"They aren't," Lomax said. He turned right and accelerated down the two-lane road. "They've stopped somewhere. Probably to rest for the night, a relative's house or something, but if they move before we get there, we'll be alerted."

"So why are we in such a hurry?" John said, holding onto the handle above the door on his side of the vehicle.

Lomax wore a grim look. "That was the orders. We've been directed to treat Kenneth Malcolm as armed and dangerous, and take all precautions in capturing the child."

"They want *us* to bring the child in?"

"You got it."

"Mr. Malcolm might not like that," John said, remembering the tight physical build of the man, and how his first reaction to the man was a feeling that the guy was ready to pounce on him. "It might be more difficult than we think."

"I know," Lomax said, "but we have orders for that situation, also."

"And what might they be?" Although John thought he could guess.

Lomax was thin-lipped, lines of concentration on his forehead and a gleam in his eyes that John didn't like, one he privately hoped he was misreading. "If he gives us any trouble, if he won't give up the child, then we are to terminate both he and his wife."

John let out a long sigh and leaned back in his seat. He pulled his handgun from its holster beneath his jacket and checked the chamber, loaded, and the magazine—full. He stuck the gun back into the holster. *Oh, boy,* he thought. *This isn't going to be fun. Not at all.*

* * * * *

Adrian and Bobby returned to the house in Paragould around ten-thirty that evening, just as Ken was beginning to worry that the two men might have fallen victim to his and Chance's pursuers. He and his son had eaten a light supper around seven o'clock, and Chance had fallen asleep in front of the television during an episode of *MacGyver* (in this episode, MacGyver had caught the bad guy in a foolproof trap made of a ball of yarn, an empty paint can, and a stick of butter). Ken put him in the back bedroom, tucking the blankets gently around him and thinking about the wonderful day just past.

"Food?" Bobby said, holding out a waxed container of Chinese cuisine.

"No, thanks. We ate earlier."

"Find everything you needed?"

"Yes, fine. I was beginning to wonder about you guys, though." And he *had*. He had even entertained the idea, during a bad fifteen minutes or so after Chance was asleep, that Adrian and Bobby had set them up in an escape-free trap, only feigning the role of protector, and that their colleagues from the CIA would swoop in for the capture at any moment. He had not completely lost the feelings of doubt until he'd noticed the relieved faces of the two men when they came through the front door. Clearly, they had not expected he and Chance to still be here.

"We're okay," Adrian said as he sat on the sofa and spread his food on the coffee table in front of him. Bobby took his take-out over to the corner of the room and turned on the computer monitors. "Where's Chance? I got him something." He held up a teddy bear.

"Sleeping."

"I kind of figured that." There was a trace of disappointment in the man's voice. He put the stuffed toy beside him.

"What about Valerie?" Ken said. He had been afraid to ask about his wife when she didn't return with the two men. It felt like there was a rock sitting inside his stomach, pulling him down.

Adrian looked at him with compassion in his eyes.

Stop! Ken wanted to shout. *Don't say it. Forget I asked, because I don't think I can handle what you're going to tell me, so stop!* Instead, he turned his head and motioned with one raised hand for Adrian to stop.

"It's not like that, Ken."

"Where is she then?"

"We don't know. She's not at your home, that's for certain."

"What about her parents?"

"We checked that out, as well, but didn't see any sign of her. Your parents were home, but she wasn't with them."

"But…"

"She could have been out, or something," Adrian said. "Just because she wasn't there doesn't mean that something has happened to her."

Ken sighed. "I know. I was just…you know…hoping you found her. I miss her," he said simply. "She belongs with me and Chance."

"I understand that, I really do," Adrian said. "And Bobby and I both feel bad for not locating her today. Personally, I feel like we failed you. But we *did* look the best we could. There were other things for us to do, as well. Mainly covering our back trail by creating some false trails."

Bobby turned away from the computers for a brief moment. "We're hoping we've misled them enough today so that we'll be safe here a little longer. If it's any consolation, I believe we at least succeeded with that part."

"Well, *that's* encouraging, I guess," Ken said, but inside he thought: *Yeah, I bet you covered your ass on securing this house, because my wife really isn't your chief concern, is it?*

Bobby said: "We'll be able to tell more, even about your wife, when the government satellites are back online. I can't believe they aren't yet. We need their eyes to see where they are. When it's up, we'll tap into their system and see if there has been any activity in your neighborhood in the last eighteen hours or so, then we'll go from there. Odds are, there will be some information that will help us locate her."

"Okay," Ken said, but he still felt uneasy.

The two men finished their supper while Ken used the remote to surf the channels on the TV. He wasn't seeing anything on the screen, but in his mind he was imagining all sorts of bad things that might have happened to Valerie: torture, murder; perhaps rape, depending on the personalities of whichever thugs captured her. He knew he shouldn't do this to himself, but he couldn't help it.

He got a break from his thoughts when, just before midnight, Bobby hollered, "*Yes*" from his corner. "They're up and running again."

Adrian, who had been dozing off at his end of the sofa, jumped up and hurried over to the computers.

Ken watched the two men fuss over one of the monitors, Adrian telling Bobby to do this or that, and Bobby say, "I am, I am." After twenty minutes of this the men had seemed to relax some and were likely now more efficient at whatever task they were performing. *As long as one of those tasks is finding Val.* He got up and hovered behind the two men. "Have you found—?"

"They're coming now."

The three men turned toward the new voice.

It was Chance. He was standing at the end of the hallway, one small arm rubbing sleep from his eyes. His hair was in disarray.

"Chance," Ken said. "What—?"

Before he could finish, an alarm went off on the bank of computers, soft but shrill.

"Shit," Bobby muttered. Both men had been staring open-mouthed at the youngster, but now Bobby looked at one of the computer screens.

"Damn. Damn, damn, *damn*." He began rapidly punching keys.

"What?" Adrian said. "What is it?"

"They've found us. They're locked on." He slammed a fist onto the table.

"Shit. How? We've covered everything, haven't we?"

"I don't know." Bobby continued punching keys, and then he paused. "Maybe I *do* know. It must be Ken's vehicle. The only thing it *could* be. We've been here for months now and they haven't been able to make us. I can't believe we didn't sweep the car. Totally forgot. Shit."

Chance had come over to the sofa, and now Ken picked him up, sitting him in his lap and putting a protective arm around him.

An unasked question hung in the air. Ken could feel it: *how had Chance known?*

Adrian ran a hand through his hair. "All right. We've got to go. There's about a thirty-minute delay in the satellite feed, so we need to hurry."

Bobby was already unplugging a couple of laptop computers from their docking stations and checking their batteries. He threw them into carrying cases and put extra nicad batteries into side pockets. "This is all the equipment we're going to be able to carry with us," he told Adrian.

"Okay. Get them out to the car. I'll grab us some clothes and stuff. Ken, grab whatever you need for Chance and take him to our vehicle."

"But—"

"We don't have time right now!" Adrian hollered, and Ken flinched. "They want your son. Don't you understand that? They want him, and they will stop at *nothing* to get him. So *move* it."

Ken went to the spare bedroom and grabbed the diaper bag, changed Chance in record time, and then they started for the door. Before he exited the house, he noticed Adrian placing large metallic objects toward the rear of each of the three PC's left on the tables. Then he was out the door.

By the yellow glare of the porch light, he saw Bobby close the back door on the driver's side of the two men's car. "You two ride with me in this vehicle," Bobby told him.

"What about my car?"

Adrian came out the door then, carrying two duffel bags and a holstered handgun. He threw the bags into the trunk of the same vehicle, nodded at Bobby, and said to Ken, "I'm taking your car."

"Taking it where?"

"The opposite direction from where you three are going."

"Why?"

Adrian took the car seat from Ken's car and brought it to the other vehicle, wiping a thin sheen of sweat from his brow. "There is a tracking device somewhere on your vehicle. That's how the agency located us. We don't know how close they are right now, or how far away, but they are coming, and this is no longer a safe place for any of us. Especially you and Chance."

Before Ken could comment further, a surge of adrenaline rushed through his body as he realized the implications Adrian had just made. The man's earlier words echoed in Ken's head like a far-away scream: *They want your son. Don't you understand that? They want him, and they will stop at* nothing *to get him.*

Okay. Okay.

He took a deep breath and then picked Chance up and locked him into his car seat. "It's okay," he said. "Don't worry, little buddy. I'm not going to let anything happen to you, all right?"

Chance nodded and managed a light smile, but he didn't say anything. Ken knew that what the child had said in the house a few moments ago was all that needed to be said about the situation.

"Ready?" Bobby said.

"Yeah, I guess," Ken said. He handed Chance the stuffed toy Adrian had put in the vehicle.

"All set, Bobby," Adrian said. "All I need is some keys."

Ken fumbled his keyring from his pocket, removed the key to the car, and tossed it to Adrian, who thanked him as he plucked it from the air.

"I'm going to try to put some distance between myself and whoever they have on our tail," Adrian told Bobby. "When I think it's safe enough, I'll wash the vehicle for the tracking device, and when I find it I'll meet you at rendezvous point A in our little contingency plan. Once you're there, wait two hours, and if I'm not there go on without me. You know where. Okay?"

"Okay," Bobby said. "Be careful, Ade."

"You got it, man." He looked at Ken, who was fastening his seatbelt. "You have a special little guy there. I hope I'm able to see him again."

"So do I," Ken said, and found that he meant it. Although he and Adrian O'Donnell hadn't known each other long, they were no longer complete strangers, and Ken didn't want anything bad to befall the man. Especially because of him or his child.

"All right, let's go," Bobby said.

Ken shut his door and the car backed out of the driveway, onto the paved road.

* * * * *

As soon as Bobby, Ken and Chance were gone, Adrian shut off the motor, got out of the car, and began searching for the tracking device.

This was not part of the plan he'd relayed to Bobby, but it would save valuable time if he could locate the device and leave it out here in the yard. This place was no longer safe, regardless, and if they tracked the device here, the agency wouldn't be able to tell how long they'd been gone. He'd taken care of the remaining computers inside the house. Now he just needed to find the 'squealer', which was shoptalk for the tracking device.

He heard the whine of the car Bobby was driving fade until it was gone, and the ensuing quiet in the front yard was pierced only by an occasional locust or cricket. Onion and clover scented the early morning air.

"Shit," he muttered under his breath.

This operation had been going so well, for so long, that the rapidity with which it had fallen apart was almost shocking.

At least the child is safe.

True. For now, anyway. But the thought brought little comfort.

Adrian ran his hand along the front bumper, feeling for the squealer. Monitoring the child had always been a priority for he and Bobby, but protecting him was the *number one* priority. If the boy was to fall into the wrong hands—and the CIA, and other agencies, *were* the wrong hands, as far as he was concerned—then everything would be lost. He and Bobby believed that with a passion that could rival any religion. Adrian realized, not for the first time, or the hundredth, that he would die for the child if need be. The thought brought no remorse or self-pity. It was just a simple fact.

The front bumper yielded nothing, and he worked his hand along the undercarriage on the passenger side.

A vehicle was approaching. He heard the whine of the engine coming up the small hill just down the road. A look over his shoulder revealed the beams of headlights probing the darkness. He ran around to the front of the car and crouched low as the vehicle approached.

A pickup truck. It passed the house without slowing.

Adrian breathed again and returned to the passenger side, checking under the wheel wells and beneath the frame with nimble fingers, frantically searching for the small betrayer. But there was nothing to be found on that side, either.

Crickets and locusts scolded him from the surrounding trees in the darkness.

He felt along the back bumper. "Come on," he muttered. He could feel time slipping away from him like grease. "Where are you?"

He finally found it beneath the glove box. The squealer. It was a small metallic object with a sticky strip on one end, and it fit easily into the palm of Adrian's hand.

"There you are, you little sucker."

He looked around the yard, thinking. It would probably be best to just leave the damn thing right here in the yard and then get the hell out of here; get a jump on whoever was coming. If he was quick enough, he could be a couple miles from the house before they arrived.

He tossed the squealer over his shoulder, got into the car, and started the engine.

He was backing out into the road when a vehicle approached from his left, seemingly out of nowhere, tires screeching on the macadam, blocking his exit.

"Well, shit," he said.

*****

The sedan turned off Highway 49, which ran through Jonesboro, Paragould, and other points north. Behind the wheel, Mark Lomax was grim faced, and looked to be concentrating on both his driving and the task ahead.

In the passenger seat, John Milcheck sat tense, his hand holding the panic bar above the window in a sweaty grip. "You're sure this is the right way?"

"Positive," Lomax said. "It should be right over this next hill." John could imagine an anticipatory grin on the agent's face.

The car reached the summit of the small hill, and on its descent the headlights reflected off a vehicle on the left of the road, backing out of a driveway. Lomax gunned the engine, closing the gap between it and themselves. "Here we go," he said. "Hold on."

"I am," John said.

Lomax slammed the brakes, tires squealing, and managed in one expert attempt to effectively block the other car.

*****

Adrian pulled the car forward, one hand holding the handgun he'd pulled from its concealment beneath his light jacket.

Going forward did no good, of course. There was only one way off the property, and that was the driveway. Trees dotted the yard on either side, and although they weren't very dense, it would be difficult to maneuver through them, and even if he *could*, without crashing into one of them, the embankment up to the road was progressively steeper on either side of the yard. A small creek that was little more than a large, overgrown ditch flanked the back of the property.

He thought about throwing the car into reverse and ramming the other vehicle, but he saw through his rearview mirror that two men were already getting out of the car and making their way cautiously down the drive, guns drawn. If he tried to run them over, they would only have to step to either side of his car as he passed and shoot him through the window.

Adrian did the only thing he could do. He got out of the car and ran as hard as he could toward the back yard.

* * * * *

"Come on!" Lomax said. He and John ran after the man, their guns out. They stopped at the rear of the house, pressing their backs against the white siding.

"Alive," Lomax said in a soft voice that was filtered through heavy breaths.

"What?"

"We want the child alive. Don't shoot unless you're sure the child is not in the line of fire. I don't think Malcolm is carrying, because if he is, he would have shot at us by now."

John nodded but said nothing. He would operate under the assumption the man *was* packing. Lomax would be wise to do the same.

The sound of crunching leaves came from their left, around the corner of the house. Running footsteps. John wished they had thought to bring a flashlight. His stomach rumbled with anxiety.

"Let's go," Lomax said. He started around the corner of the house, and John followed close behind.

* * * * *

At the back of the property, Adrian moved from the cover of one tree to the next, anticipating shots fired at any time. He knew the contours of the yard, and at the moment this familiarity with the terrain was his best advantage. The men by the house—for he was working on the assumption that there were at least two, possibly more—would not be able to see well into the thick tree-shrouded darkness at the rear of the property. They had probably split up already, one on either side of the house, waiting for him to give himself away.

Crouched low, he moved to the tree closest to the house, and from there he scampered around to the front side of the house, his gun aimed in front of him.

Pausing at the front left edge of the house, he heard leaves crunching underfoot to his right and behind him and he knew that he'd been spotted. He moved, cat-quick, away from the house and toward the car, and just as quickly the night air was filled with the sharp report of gunfire. A sizable piece of wood blew away from the corner of the house in fragments, inches from where his head had been.

He immediately turned and dropped to the ground, his handgun out in front of him, and squeezed off two quick shots in the general direction of that corner. He heard a man yell, "He's packing!" and another man's sarcastic reply: "No shit?"

Adrian fired blindly again. Maybe that would stop their advance long enough for him to escape.

He stumbled through the front yard, toward his car. Another shot exploded in the night and the driver's side window beside him blew in with a muffled thump of burst glass. He rolled on the ground and squeezed off three rapid shots.

"Shit," one of the men yelled.

"You all right?" The other man, so there were only two, then.

"Yeah, just a graze I think, but burns like hell. Where's the kid?"

"Not here, unless he's in the house."

"Great."

Adrian knew the men would not leave just because what they were after wasn't here. No. They would finish this job first—or at least try. There was no way he was going to let them get away from here and continue to pursue the child if he could help it. He would die first, or be killed. He thought the latter was the most likely, but he was ready to do what he had to do.

He moved around Kenneth Malcolm's car, putting it between himself and the two men. Then he took a shot in the general direction of the house and heard the bullet whine off the side of a tree. "The child isn't here!" he yelled into the darkness. "Go away!"

Go away? he thought. *That's real good, Adrian.*

Where's the kid?"

Off to the right. Apparently the two men were still behind the cover of the house, at the corner.

Adrian started out of his crouch to look in that direction, but before he could move three quick shots were fired, two zipping over his head and the other thunking into a tire on the other side. The vehicle sagged with a hiss.

What the hell? he wondered. *They can't even see me.*

True. But they were probably aiming in the direction his voice had come from. Why had he even opened his mouth?

Stupidity, he guessed.

Then he realized what the three shots had meant. They had been cover-shots; one man shooting in quick succession while the other maneuvered into a better position.

And all caused by Adrian letting his stupid mouth pinpoint his location.

"Where's the boy?" The same voice again, from the corner of the house this time.

Not falling for that one again, chump, Adrian thought. He knew what they were doing. Had he himself not done this type of work before? Of course. One man was trying to get him to open his mouth again so that the one who had repositioned himself could draw a more accurate shot from a closer range.

Shit, why couldn't I have had just two more minutes?

He ran to his left, up the incline of the driveway, toward the car that belonged to the two agents, and which was still parked halfway on the road. He made as little noise as possible, but his feet crunched on the chat driveway despite his precautions.

Belatedly, he heard more feet on the rocks, closer to the house and coming his way, and he knew that he wasn't going to get out of this. He slipped against the front bumper of the car, and then lurched forward with an adrenaline-fueled effort and grabbed the driver's side door handle.

"Hold it!" From behind him. Commanding. "Don't move, and put down your weapon."

Adrian froze. He was within accurate range of one of the men, and with the fire play that had transpired thus far, the nameless figure would not hesitate to pull the trigger. He would be as pumped up as Adrian was himself.

His shoulders slumping in apparent defeat, Adrian lowered the hand that held the gun toward the ground. His heart thudded in his chest. *All or nothing here, man. Shit.*

"That's it," the voice behind him said, and Adrian marked it.

With one fluid movement, he tucked his head low and rolled to his left, bringing the gun up and firing. The noise reverberated off the car and echoed loudly in his ears, but something else registered there, as well; the stunned yelp of the man as the bullet struck its mark.

A streak of hot lead zipped over the top of his head. Adrian didn't know if the shot was purposeful or caused by reflex, but neither did he care. He opened the car door and climbed inside, slamming it shut behind him.

The keys were in the ignition. As he started the engine a bullet slammed into the rear door on his side, less than a foot away. Another whined off the top of the roof panel. Adrian threw the car into reverse and tromped the gas pedal, spinning up small bits of rock and dirt from the soft shoulder of the road, then roaring onto the macadam. He heard another shot, muffled by the racing of the car's engine, but the vehicle was not hit.

He turned on the headlights, so that tail lights would allow him at least a small view of the road behind him, and when he glanced forward he saw a man standing at the head of the driveway, legs spread, hands raised in a shooter's stance. He heard small pops, like cap guns, but none found their target. He was almost two hundred yards away by now, out of accuracy range of most handguns, and he slowed the vehicle to a stop. He backed into a small drive that was an entrance to a dark hayfield, and then he headed east, toward Paragould and the many highways which led away from that city.

When he had made a mile or so, he began to breathe easier. He knew he had not yet fully escaped. The two men would not be following him any time soon—not with one of them wounded, and a flat tire on Kenneth Malcolm's vehicle—but those two agents weren't the only people after the child.

Adrian knew that, before long—if it hadn't happened already—federal agencies would release more men and resources to find the missing child of Project Lone Star.

For now, anyway, he and Bobby had bought the boy a little time.

* * * * *

TWENTY-ONE

In the darkened corridor on Level Four, Duke Tarkington trembled outside his room while Tim Flaugherty prodded and interrogated him. The light at the end of the hall, near the elevators, was just sufficient enough to cast the man's face in shadows, making it blessedly difficult for Duke to see the sinister gleam in his eyes. But he knew from past experience that it was there, so the lack of illumination was only partially effective.

"Well, where have you been?" Flaugherty repeated.

Denied his voice but not his mind, Duke pantomimed getting a drink of water.

Flaugherty's face, though full of menace and cunning, relaxed some. His grip on Duke's arm lightened a little. Just a little. "I didn't see you getting a drink from the fountain. I saw you get off the elevators."

Duke's nerves tightened, but he somehow managed to keep calm. He had to think. He pulled his arms up and hugged himself, then shook as though chilled. The chills were not entirely faked. Then he pointed at the floor. He repeated the motion and shrugged his shoulders, even though he knew that gesture might be interpreted as being 'smart-ass'.

He would have to hope his real message got through to the man. Flaugherty would take any sign of nervousness or fear as a sign of guilt, and there was no telling how he would then react.

The grip on Duke's arm fell away. His pantomime had worked. Everyone on Level Four, including Tim Flaugherty, knew that the water fountain on Level Three dispensed the coldest water in the compound. The water on this floor was lukewarm, at best.

"Went for some cold water, huh?" Flaugherty was clearly stalling, trying to think of something with which he could pin Duke down.

Duke nodded. He figured that all the man really wanted was to frighten him (and so far, had done a formidable job of it). Flaugherty seemed the type who gained a perverse nourishment from other people's fear, and Duke knew if he showed any the man would smell it coming off him in waves.

Flaugherty leaned close, and Duke cringed. "I think you're hiding something."

Duke shook his head.

"Oh, but I do."

Duke held his hands out in front of him, palms up, fingers splayed.

Flaugherty slapped them down, and Duke's eyes watered with the sting.

"Not hiding something in your *hands,* dummy." He poked Duke's forehead with one bony finger. "Up here. I think you're hiding something up *here.*"

Duke repeated the shake of his head. *No.*

Flaugherty, perhaps sensing he would find nothing definite on Duke this evening, said smugly: "I still think you're hiding something, Tarkington, and I'll tell you one thing." He leaned closer, almost nose to nose, and Duke could smell the minty aroma of toothpaste and a fainter odor of chocolate. "If I find out—*when* I find out—we're going to find out just how tough a man you are. You got that, mister?"

Duke scowled—doing so only because Flaugherty had backed away—and then he nodded.

Flaugherty looked him up and down once more, the man's features barely perceptible in the shadowy corridor, and without another word he walked back down the hall to his room.

Duke waited until he heard the lock on the man's door click shut before turning and going into his own room.

Once inside, he lay down on his bed and stared up at the ceiling. A lamp glowed from a nightstand to his left, casting an ambient light across the room. He was too tired to change into shorts and tee shirt, his normal bed attire.

The room, like most on Level Four (with the exception of personnel ranked as high as Flaugherty—or Duke's father, for that matter, whose rooms more closely resembled a suite) was small and dorm-like, twice as deep as it was wide, with a single bunk on the left, and a table, lamp, and small desk on the right, flanked by an average-sized wardrobe. The bathroom facilities were midway down the outside corridor, and meals were taken in a centrally located cafeteria. The room was small, yet cozy, filled with books along the back wall, but only a few pictures on the walls. These were unframed, scenic photos cut from magazines, but pleasing enough to Duke's eyes. He'd once had a real photograph, of his father, but the elder Tarkington had ripped it from the wall with a disgusted look on his face. That had happened a few weeks after the 'tongue operation'.

Many of the volumes were copies of pamphlets and books written by some of the compound's staff. Most of them were volumes on various theories brought forward by one scientist or another—and, occasionally, a technician.

A staff member named Janice Fisher was the author of a short book of her own theories and ideas, and some of them were quite amazing. Duke could only guess as to whether or not any work based upon them had been implemented to prove the theories out.

Most of Ms. Fisher's ideas had to do with time and dimensions. (According to her) It had always been assumed that there were only four dimensions, and a few years ago in the mid-90's it had been theorized and arguably proven that there were, in fact, a total of five, even though all weren't necessarily visible. Janice Fisher had expounded a theory in her book—humorously titled: *A Fisher at Sea*—that there were an infinite number of dimensions. Her theory was based on perception, and postulated to the effect that the mind entered different dimensions with little effort, at different times, consistently and often; dreaming was one example, while memory was another. Her primary theory was that each experience, each thought, each second of time, existed in its own dimension. This somehow all tied in with something called quantum physics.

Another of Ms. Fisher's theories had to do with interplanetary space travel, and bending or warping the space-time continuum. A substantial portion of the book was on teleportation, and this idea, while intriguing, had confused Duke enough that he'd flipped through the book to other, more comprehensive theories.

These books, gracing one side of his room like silent tombstones, got him through the gaps of time that existed whenever the library was closed, or he had finished with the latest novel he'd checked out from its ranks.

His eyes grew heavy and he began to drowse. *I'm in another*

dimension, he thought dreamily. *Another realm.*
Yeah, that was cool. Someplace else. How nice.
He dozed.

* * * * *

He was awakened sometime later by a loud thump, interspersed with the shrill of a siren whooping and subsiding, whooping and subsiding.

Fire, was his first thought.

But as he surfaced from the depths of sleep, his mind placed the siren for what it really was. The fire alarm was a steady bell-ringing similar—or so he'd been told—to that which goes off at a real fire department. This alarm indicated a security breach.

Duke thought he knew what had happened; the deactivated satellite had been discovered.

He was thankful he had made it back to his room.

He got up and stepped out into the corridor, which was now bathed in the overhead florescent lights. Half a dozen people stood in the hallway, looking around sheepishly, and others were coming out of their rooms. All of them wore mingled looks of concern and irritation on their tired faces.

Except for Tim Flaugherty. *He* looked wide awake, his eyes darting around the corridor as though searching for something, or someone, and they eventually fell upon Duke—and remained there. "Tarkington!"

The other residents of Level Four—all of whom were not out in the hall—fell silent at once and turned to look at Duke. Some eyes—even after two years—showed pity. Others looked saddened, a few angry.

The alarm continued to whoop.

Duke stood motionless, unable to move.

"Is this your doing?" Flaugherty said and, without waiting for a reply—like Duke could actually voice one—he said: "It is, isn't it?" His voice rose to a yell. *"Come here, boy."*

Duke could imagine that every person eyeing him harbored the same disgust and hatred evident in Flaugherty's voice.

There was no way anyone could know that he'd been the one to tamper with the computers downstairs. The security cameras had all been disengaged temporarily and—

Or had they?

Perhaps a camera on a different circuit had recorded a portion of his progress to and from the Communications Center. Maybe only the cameras in the downstairs hallway had been deactivated, instead of every camera on that level.

Prometheus wouldn't have let that happen. No way. He made sure I was safe.

But he couldn't deny the seed of doubt that had formed in his mind.

He looked at Flaugherty and shook his head hard each way, and a low murmur rose from those in the corridor. Duke recognized Lucas Matthews and Tyler James among them, two whose mealtimes corresponded with Duke's. Lucas also helped Tyler out in the library on occasion and seemed like an okay guy. There were other 'cafeteria faces'—how he categorized people he knew only by name and sight—but he felt nothing at the touch of their gaze. He liked Lucas and Tyler, however, even though he didn't know Lucas that well. Sometimes they told funny jokes at the dinner table.

"I'm talking to *you*, shit-for-brains," Flaugherty said.

At the obvious anger in that voice, Duke's resolve broke and he turned and fled up the corridor, brushing against a few people, who attempted to get out of his way.

"Stop him," Flaugherty squawked, just as the siren stopped. "Somebody grab him." He ran after Duke.

Duke thought he heard a defiant voice say, "Why don't you leave him alone?" but that probably wasn't what they really said.

A voice came over the intercom then, overlaid with duress: "SECURITY BREACH ON SUBSTATION C. EVERY ONE PLEASE VACATE HIS OR HER ROOM AND REMAIN IN THE CORRIDOR ON YOUR LEVEL TO AWAIT FURTHER INSTRUCTIONS." The message was repeated, but Duke didn't hear. Flaugherty had paused to listen to the message, but now he was coming toward him, and Duke was at the end of the corridor, with no place to run.

And then an amazing thing happened.

Just before Flaugherty made it through the crowd of people, he flew forward, off his feet, and landed squarely on his face.

From somewhere among the congestion of people came a snicker.

Before Flaugherty could pull himself up, Duke darted past him has fast as he could, back down the hallway toward the elevators, and—he couldn't believe it—the crowd in the hall parted as he approached them, clearing a path.

He glanced back, and was further amazed and surprised to see that small sea of people merge back together, effectively blocking Flaugherty's passage. Duke caught a glimpse of the man's head bobbing up and down—as though he was jumping up to see—over the crowd.

"Tarkington!" he called shrilly. "Tarkington, you get back here. *Now.*" He bullied his way through the residents of Level Four, shoving them rudely to either side.

Duke reached the elevators and punched the 'down' button. He caught himself grinning and felt hot adrenaline pump through his body, thrumming like a live wire.

The elevator doors slid open on silent tracks.

Flaugherty reached the edge of the crowd, which now murmured excitedly, and *lunged* down the corridor, panting.

Duke hit the button for Substation D, and the doors closed just as Flaugherty skidded into sight in front of them—and then past. Duke noticed that the man was wearing a pair of white socks, and he forced back a grin. The floors here were waxed twice weekly. Duke himself still had on his sneakers.

Flaugherty caught his grin, and a look of pure fury stole over his face.

Just before the doors finished closing, and while Flaugherty was skidding his feet around, trying to regain his traction, Duke took the opportunity to flip him the bird.

And his grin widened.

As the elevator began its descent, there came a muffled thump from outside the door that might have been Flaugherty beating his fist or shoulder against the turgid steel.

Duke breathed a sigh of relief and waited to disembark on Substation D, where there would be a more friendly face.

* * * * *

The elevator doors opened, and the first thing Duke saw was several security personnel running toward him. "Out of the way," one yelled as they approached the elevator, and Duke complied, scooting against the far wall of the corridor.

To the left, the hall led toward the central observation room in the substation—the room in which Prometheus resided.

The security guards had gone right.

Duke dug his digital clearance card from a front pocket of his jeans and hurried toward the sealed door at the end of the hallway. He glanced over his shoulder when he reached the entrance.

There was no one in sight. Apparently, the security force was being concentrated at Communications.

He scanned his card and palm on the computer terminal located outside the room. The steel door slid open with a hiss of released air.

Duke braced himself for the worst as he prepared to enter the chamber. He knew there would be personnel in here, monitoring Prometheus. In light of recent events, he didn't dare try to deactivate the audio and video monitors.

He told himself that he would have to face whatever happened, but at least he was away from Flaugherty…and closest to the only one whom he could trust.

He entered the observation chamber.

* * * * *

The room, as usual, was gloomy, lit by low-wattage light fixtures and the ambient glow of computer screens. Although the effects were familiar, there was still something different about the room, and Duke supposed that was because he hadn't been in here on any days but Saturday in a long while, and his mind was picking up some subtle change unattainable to his eyes.

And there *were* personnel in the room. Two of them, in fact.

Both men were slumped over keyboards in front of computer terminals, one at the bank of equipment on the left, the other on the right.

In the center of the room, sitting on a wood chair behind the hydrabeams, was Prometheus. He grinned when he saw Duke—a triumphant smile that made everything Duke had done worthwhile.

"You did it, Duke. You *did* it."

Although Duke wasn't certain of just what he had done, he couldn't help but smile at the relief on his friend's face. He signed: "You look so happy. Not sure what I did, but I haven't seen you this happy in a long time." Then he looked at the two men slumped over their work stations and raised an eyebrow at Prometheus.

"Sleeping, I suppose."

For some reason Duke doubted that. There was an amused twinkle in Prometheus' eyes. Duke didn't know how, but he felt that Prometheus had somehow *put* the men to sleep.

"Did they catch what I did before it could help you?"

Prometheus laughed, a deep and resonant sound like that of a favorite uncle. "No, Duke. You did very well, and you were just in time, too. Those nitwits will be scrambling around up there trying to repair things for hours yet, I would think."

Duke smiled at his friend, and then his face clouded over. "Flaugherty thinks I've been up to something, that I had something to do with the alarm."

"You *did*," Prometheus said, chuckling gently. "But not to worry, young Tarkington. Tim Flattery (Duke smiled at the joke—he couldn't help it) is busy frying other fish at the moment. Derek has got him busy in communications, reviewing the security videos."

Duke nodded, relieved. He thought about asking how Prometheus knew these things, but thinking is a far as it went. He was accustomed to his friend's unusual insights. It was something Duke couldn't figure out, and which Prometheus would not acknowledge without going into parables and prattlings about the extrasensory and inert powers of which all humans were blindly capable (whatever he meant by that).

"Want to set up the board?"

Duke looked at his friend and then over his shoulder, at the vault-like door. He signed: "Do you think that's a good idea, considering what's happening?"

"Certainly," Prometheus said. He nodded at the two sleeping men. "I think those two are going to be asleep for some time yet, and you won't be missed for at least an hour or more. Of course, if you're too tired, or don't want to…"

Duke signed: "I want to. And if you say it's safe, I believe you."

"Good."

Duke looked again at the two sleeping technicians, then hurried to where he'd stashed the board and chess figures. He moved a chair closer to his friend's cell, and placed the board on the small table he always used. Then he began to set up the game, already concentrating on the task at hand, separating himself from the activity outside, in the rest of the compound.

In his friend's eyes, there was jovial anticipation—and wisdom beyond years.

* * * * *

An hour later, Duke's king was going to be captured. There was no earthly way around it.

"Shit," Duke signed. "I thought I had you this time."

"Never *think* you have something until you absolutely *do*," Prometheus said. And then, perhaps to illustrate his point, he said: "Check mate." He moved his only remaining bishop to knight-four, thereby ending the contest.

"I'm never going to beat you at this, am I?"

"You certainly might," Prometheus said. "In time." He chuckled heartily. "You are getting smarter, more savvy, I'll give you that."

"Yeah, right," Duke signed. "You're trying to psyche me out, aren't you?"

"Absolutely."

They laughed together—Duke in his own way, with his eyes and smile—and then Prometheus looked toward the door, and concern shadowed his chiseled features. "To use one of your terms, my friend: *shit*."

Before Duke could react, the hiss of the airtight door caused him to jerk his head in that direction.

A figure was silhouetted there against the brighter light from the outside corridor.

Flaugherty.

Duke tensed. The chess board sat on the table between he and his friend like a captured fugitive, a secret revealed.

"Well, well, well," Flaugherty said as he stepped from the shadowed hallway into the room. "What have we here? Just *what* have we here?" He was wearing camouflage clothing from head to toe, which was the attire he seemed to favor most. He walked toward them in a casual strut that tried to belie arrogance and power.

Duke was disheartened to see that he was carrying a semi-automatic weapon. His stomach felt twisted, tied in knots. He looked to Prometheus, who was looking at Tim Flaugherty with what appeared to be distaste, disgust, and an intense loathing.

As Flaugherty approached him, Duke drew back in fear, his mind replaying the memory of the night, two years previous, when this man had approached him in much the same manner—stealthy, confident— holding a knife instead of a gun.

"I've been looking for you, Duke," Flaugherty said, and grinned. "You should be in your room."

Duke wanted to defend himself but realized that, even if he'd had a tongue with which to speak, he wouldn't know what to say. Frustration clouded his face like a passing cloud, overshadowing the fear that dominated.

"Well, I'll just take you there myself," Faugherty said. He slung the carbine over one shoulder and rubbed his hands together, the predatory smile still on his face.

Duke cringed back further, now within just a few feet of the hydrabeams.

"Why don't you leave him alone, Tim Flattery? Haven't you done enough damage to this young man? He is hurting nothing by being here—least of all *you*."

Flaugherty's mouth dropped open, and Duke saw something in the man's eyes that he had never seen there before.

"Y-you. You just stay out of it," Flaugherty said, pointing at Prometheus. "He's not supposed to be down here, and you know it. You just stay out of it."

"Or? What are you going to do—lock me up, perhaps torture me?" He threw his head back and laughed, a deep and resonating baritone.

Flaugherty was clearly caught off guard. He was out of his territory here, his 'prey' was not alone, and everything probably wasn't as peachy as he'd thought. "Duke, what happened with the satellites?" He licked his lips, glanced at Prometheus, and then continued. "I know you know something."

Duke shook his head.

"You can deny it, but I know something is going on here, and I intend to find out what it is."

"Leave him alone," Prometheus repeated. "He has not done anything to you. Not once, in his whole life. You have his tongue. Is that not enough?" Now the caged man's eyes were black—and large.

Flaugherty took a step backward. "You—you…"

"Oh, shut up," Prometheus said, and Flaugherty's mouth closed with a snap.

"Duke," Flaugherty said, after a half minute of high-tensioned silence. "Duke, you shouldn't be down here. It—it's dangerous. *He's* dangerous."

"You are the only dangerous one here," Prometheus said, "and we all know it. In fact (his eyes gleamed and held the man's gaze like a vice), why don't you do every one here a favor and use that gun on yourself?"

Now Flaugherty looked repulsed, as if he had bitten something sour, or was about to cry. He began to raise the gun, and then shook his head as though waking from an unpleasant dream. "Shut up. Just *shut up.* Duke is coming with me, and you're staying here, and when Derek hears about this little chess game I caught the two of you playing, I think there's going to be some hydra treatment for somebody." He seemed to regain some of his confidence, almost as fast as he'd lost it. "What do you think about *that?*"

"Do what you think you have to do with me," Prometheus said. "I'm just advising you that you had better not hurt Duke again—ever."

"Or what?"

"I do not think you really want to know the answer to that, my deranged friend. Besides, I think you already know."

Fear crossed Flaugherty's face again like a shadow, then dissipated. "I'm taking Duke with me," he said. "We're going to see Derek, and whatever he decides to do with him is what will happen. Personally, I'm going to advise locking him up downstairs until we find out what he knows about the problem in Communications." He looked at Duke, his eyes now sparkling with a mad light, probably holding thoughts of the possibilities in front of him for extracting information.

"That is your answer for everything, is it not?" Prometheus said. "Just lock them up, torture them if possible. You learn nothing that way."

"It's worked with you, hasn't it?" Flaugherty quipped.

"In your eyes, I suppose so, but you only see what you want, and I am sure you—and Derek Tarkington, as well—have convinced yourselves that you have solved your problems with me."

"No convincing to it. We have."

Prometheus moved dangerously close to the hydrabeams, and once again his eyes were filled with a blackness. "You just remember what I said. You hurt this young man again and you will suffer for it. Remember that. Keep it in mind."

Uncertainty clouded Flaugherty's face, and then he seemed to realize he wasn't the one contained in the cell. "You just shut up, you—you *freak.* Derek will deal with you, so threaten me all you want to. I don't care."

"I beg to differ," Prometheus said. "but, as you wish." He looked at Duke and signed: "Thank you, my friend. Be brave, be patient. You will be well."

Duke nodded.

"What are you doing?" Flaugherty said, alarmed. "What is this?"

Neither man answered.

Duke was jerked around, so that he faced Flaugherty. "Let's go, Tarkington—"

His eyes bulged as he finally noticed the two technicians slumped over their terminals. "What the hell is going on here? Just what the hell have you done?"

"I guess these two gentlemen decided to take a nap," Prometheus said in a conversational tone. "They did not seem to object to Duke's presence here as strenuously as you have. Perhaps you should wake them up and ask *them* what is going on. Or maybe you would like to join them?"

Something in Prometheus' eyes caused Flaugherty to back up two steps, but he still gripped Duke's left arm. "I'm going to find out what is happening here. I'm going to get Derek."

Prometheus did not respond to this. He just looked at Flaugherty until the man had backed all the way to the door.

Flaugherty's eyes darted around the room. He looked from the two technicians to Prometheus, then back again, and then he left the room, Duke in tow.

The door swished shut behind them with a hiss of air.

* * * * *

TWENTY-TWO

The car sped south down Highway 49 at seven miles per hour over the posted speed limit of fifty-five. Ken sat in the back seat, staring out the window, and Chance was asleep in his car seat beside him, sleeping the uncaring sleep of youth. Traffic was sparse as the hour neared three a.m., and darkness still held the night.

They passed a sign announcing the small town of Brookland, and Bobby eased up on the accelerator to keep in line with the receding speed limits. He told Ken that he had gotten a speeding ticket here a few months ago.

A short while later they entered Jonesboro, and then passed through it, the dim lights of Dan Avenue reflecting dully off the macadam.

"Any chance of us running by my house?" Ken said without much hope.

Bobby grunted. "I don't think so."

"That's about what I thought. Where are we going?"

Bobby looked at the road while he talked, and he eased the car through two sharp curves near a *Riceland Foods* plant. "There's a town called Hardy about sixty or seventy miles northwest of here." His eyes moved to the mirror to look at Ken. "You familiar with the Hardy area?"

"Yes."

"Good."

In fact, Ken knew it more than well, and he suspected Bobby already knew that. In the secluded hills beyond Spring River, his father owned a cabin that he used for hunting in the winter and camping in the summer. Ken and Valerie spent several summer nights there each year, but had been up there only rarely since his mother's passing.

Bobby messed with the radio for a few minutes and then shut it off. "Nothing on."

"You should try Z-100," Ken muttered. Some classic rock and roll right now might help pick up his mood.

"What?"

"Nothing. Do you think your partner will catch up to us?"

"Adrian? I would be surprised if he didn't. He's good."

"What if he doesn't?"

Bobby's eyes in the rearview as they passed a street lamp were cold, sharp, but Ken detected worry in them, as well. "Once we get to Hardy, we'll give Adrian two hours, like he said, and if he doesn't show up, then we go on." He looked back at the road.

On to where? Ken thought, but instead asked: "What if those other guys show up instead? What if they find out from your friend where we're going?"

Bobby began rummaging around some of the equipment he had put in the front seat with him during their flight from the house in Paragould. "Look, Adrian would go through the most murderous torture imaginable before he would tell those agents where this child is. And if he *did* finally tell, he would lie. Don't worry about Adrian."

Ken was silent. As he watched Bobby hook a laptop computer to the console with an adapter that plugged into the lighter socket, he thought about what Bobby had said. To think that this guy Adrian—and probably Bobby as well—would go through torture and death to protect his son was incredible. Ken knew Chance was special—he'd seen what he could do first-hand—but before yesterday it had never occurred to him there might be someone else out there who knew, or at least suspected.

There was something else, also. At the house in Paragould, Chance and these two men had seemed comfortable together. The toddler had implied, through his actions, that these guys were okay. For some reason—one that made Ken uneasy, although he didn't know why—he didn't think Chance would have spent most of the night sleeping if he thought the men posed a threat.

Now, here they all were, on the run from government agents. If that wasn't amazing enough, Ken had put he and Chance's lives in the hands of two strangers who appeared devoted to protecting the youngster, even to the point of sacrificing their lives for him. Ken didn't see the connection, and right now he was too overwhelmed to think about it.

Instead, he watched Bobby type in numbers and letters on the laptop. He would look down at the computer, punch a few keys with his right hand, and then look back at the road. The screen cast a ghostly blue light across the front seat. The computer beeped and booped as the screen changed.

After a few minutes, as they passed through Bono (Ken briefly thinking of his father with a nostalgic pang), Bobby said, "We're not being followed, so I think we got a good jump on them. I don't see how they can find us now."

Ken leaned forward, looking over the back seat. "You can tell that by this computer?"

"Not the computer itself," Bobby said. He held up a cellular phone. "I'm linked through this phone and the computer's modem to a satellite system that is relaying the information back into the computer."

"You're kidding."

"Absolutely not," Bobby said.

"Is that safe? I mean, won't the CIA know you're doing that?"

"Eventually, but I'm sub-routing my relays through satellites owned by a major communications company. It will take them longer to pinpoint the location of this signal than it will take us to get where we're going. It's kind of like sneaking in their back door and playing with their toys while they are facing the front of the room. By the time they 'hear' us and turn to see who is making all the noise, all they will see is a closed door, because by then we will be gone."

"Incredible," Ken said.

Bobby seemed to enjoy talking about his knowledge of computers and technology. "Of course, the more we use the laptop, the easier it's going to be for them to extract our location from their own computers. You can bet they are trying to relay through another system as we speak." He was silent for a moment, and then said in a lowered voice, as though thinking out loud: "Unless, of course, they were relying solely on those two agents back at the house. Yeah, they would try that first."

To Ken, all of this sounded like some of the science fiction novels he'd read as a teenager. He looked at the laptop, and thought of something else. "Can you pick up weather satellites on that thing?"

"Piece of cake," Bobby said. "In fact, I could bring in data from any weather satellite in orbit. I've invented a program that can decode almost any encryption known." He straightened up in his seat with unhidden pride. Ken guessed that he rarely got to speak of his talents, and Adrian had probably tired of them long ago.

"So, what's the weather going to be like today?" Ken said.

Bobby pushed the 'end' button on the cell phone and then hit a button on the computer, blanking the screen. "Sorry. We can't take more time than we need on this thing. You can listen for weather reports on the radio. The longer we're connected to a satellite…"

"I get the picture," Ken said. "Forget I asked."

Bobby closed the laptop, but he left the jack plugged into the accessory outlet so the battery would continue to charge. They drove in silence for a while, and Ken tried to sleep, dozing fitfully and wishing he could sleep as contentedly as Chance seemed able to do. The child hadn't woke up one time since they'd left Paragould.

He needs his rest, Ken thought.

Afterall, no matter how intelligent he was, he was physically only a child.

Ken closed his eyes and tried to sleep.

* * * * *

"*Shit,*" Mark Lomax barked as the tire tool slipped off the lug nut and his knuckles scraped against the exposed rim. He shook his hand and stuck the damaged knuckles in his mouth. Under his breath he swore some more. It had been five or six minutes since the stranger had taken off in their vehicle.

"I know how you feel," John Milcheck said. He was holding a makeshift bandage, torn from his shirt, over the graze on his left arm. He felt fortunate that the bullet had only nicked him and wasn't lodged in his chest, throat, or heart. Yet his arm still ached. The second bullet fired from the stranger's gun had not hit either of them. John had mocked a yell of surprise and pain in an effort to fool the shooter, hoping he would quit firing. It had worked, but at a high price: the guy was now in he and Mark's car.

"Go check the house," Lomax told him as he turned back to the tire.

John nodded and went inside, where he drew his gun and quickly checked the place on the off chance that there were others here who hadn't fled. His search yielded nothing, so he put away the gun and surveyed the living room, where there were several computers and phone lines on top of two long tables. John moved the mouse control next to one of the systems and the screen came to life in a blue glow.

He could tell immediately that something was wrong. The icons on the desktop of the screen were smeary smudges and runny numbers and letters. The mouse worked, however, and he tried clicking on an icon to open the program it represented. A jumble of numbers, letters, and symbols filled the screen. Even the *Windows* background was warped.

"Shit," he mumbled.

He tried the computer to his right and got the same results. And again with the third one. He leaned over to look behind one of the PCs and saw a large metal object lying against the side of the desktop case.

Magnets.

The two men, whoever they were—and John was certain Kenneth Malcolm was not among them—had placed powerful magnets in strategic locations behind the computers, which had scrambled the hard drive of each system. There would be no way to retrieve any information.

There was a small two-drawer filing cabinet beneath one of the tables, and John opened both drawers, hoping to find hard copies of some pertinent information. Both drawers were empty.

Damn.

He went into the kitchen. The refrigerator was well stocked and so was the pantry. These men had obviously been living here awhile. The trashcan on the floor next to the icebox had a soiled diaper on top of the usual garbage. He grabbed two cans of soda from the refrigerator and a bottle of aspirin from a cabinet and went back outside, where Lomax was tightening the last two lug nuts on the spare. John tossed him one of the cans.

"This all you found?"

"No. Just the only useful things," John said. "But the kid was here. Diaper in the trash."

"What about hardware? They couldn't have taken everything with them. Surely there must be a computer or two."

"Oh, there is," John said. "Three of them, in fact, but there's also a big magnet next to every one of them. The data is fried, gone."

"No shit?"

"No shit." John took a drink from his can and belched. The cool liquid was like silk to his raw throat. He shook three aspirin into the palm of his hand and dry-swallowed them.

Lomax threw the lug wrench into the trunk of the car and slammed the door. "Well, isn't *that* just great. How the hell are we supposed to follow them now?"

John shrugged his shoulder and took another drink of soda.

"All of our equipment is in our car."

"Yes, it is," John said and belched.

"Shit!"

John walked around to the passenger side and opened the door. "You want to look around some more, or go after him?"

"Neither," Lomax said as he climbed behind the wheel and started the ignition. "What we do now is go to that town back there…"

"Paragould."

"Yeah, Paragould. We go back there and find a damn phone before they get any further from us than they already are."

"Sounds like a plan to me," John said. In the days when he was a P.I. he would have hoped that he could catch up with them men some other time, but in those days he hadn't had access to the CIA's sophisticated technology. He knew he was being lackadaisical, and that he wasn't like that, and…and was he actually sort of glad that Kenneth Malcolm and the youngster had escaped? He thought he just might be. He still had difficulty wrapping his mind around the idea that the child, or his father, was a threat.

"You got any better ideas?"

"No," John said as they backed out of the drive. "But I *did* notice a wireless dealer in Jonesboro yesterday. We're going to need something portable, mobile."

Lomax huffed once and threw the car in drive, spinning gravel and chat. "I've got Calhoun's number memorized, so right now a pay phone will work. The director will know what to do."

John found himself wondering if that were really true.

* * * * *

"PLEASE RETURN TO YOUR QUARTERS. SECURITY SYSTEMS ARE BACK TO NORMAL. I REPEAT, SECURITY SYSTEMS ARE BACK TO NORMAL. PLEASE RETURN TO YOUR QUARTERS. THANK YOU FOR FOLLOWING PROTOCOL, AND FOR YOUR COOPERATION."

Derek Tarkington released the button on the communications, and turned to face his guests. "I apologize for the interruption, gentlemen. We had a temporary satellite malfunction, but it is back online." Actually, it wasn't online yet, but these men didn't need to know that.

"Does that happen often?" one of the men said. He was balding and fat, about fifty years old, and one of the top thirty richest people in America.

"So rarely that I can't remember the last time," Derek said. He smiled, although he was troubled. A satellite malfunction was no way to impress potential investors. Although he had nothing personal at stake here, Derek knew that the need for continued funding for the compound would always exist—it was part of his job to make certain that investors could a) keep their mouths shut, and b) that they would be satisfied with the product being 'pitched'.

He loathed these tours, and only tolerated them because private investment in the projects at this compound outweighed rerouted federal funding by a four-to-one margin.

There was so much going on, and even more was possible.

As long as the funding held out.

"What kind of satellite was that?" the balding man asked as Derek led them out of the room.

"It was just a communications satellite. We have back-up systems, of course," he added.

"Then why the alarm?"

"Most residents are sleeping at this hour," Derek said. "The alarm for a security breach covers a wide array of emergencies. Some minor, some major. This one was very minor, I assure you, but when any type of breach occurs, we don't always know immediately how serious it may be, so we follow the same procedures, as a precaution, until we know."

"Oh," the balding man said.

The three men walked down the corridor, and Derek said. "Now, what would you good gentlemen like to see next—the genetics lab, or the testing facility?"

"I've heard from the other…um, investors that the testing facility is rather intriguing," the balding man said. His partner, who was tall, lanky, and dark-haired, remained silent—as he had throughout the tour, which grated on Derek's nerves—but he nodded his agreement.

The quiet man brought an unbidden image into Derek's mind of his son, Duke, and the silent world he had inflicted upon him. He pushed the image away but it lingered a moment before fading.

"Mr. Tarkington?"

Derek shook his head. "Yes. The testing facility. That would be an ideal look for you, I'm sure. That's where you can see, first hand, some of the amazing results we've had with various projects and field tests."

He led them to the elevators, then snapped his head around when he heard his name shouted.

"Derek! Sir!"

It was Tim Flaugherty, and he was running up the corridor toward him. The man's face was pinched with an odd mixture of tension and relief.

Derek cut his eyes discreetly to his two guests. "What is it, Tim? Something that can wait, I hope."

Flaugherty slowed his pace to a brisk walk.

The balding man and tall silent man looked at each other and fidgeted, perhaps sensing the second abnormality of their early morning tour.

"Excuse me, gentlemen." Derek nodded to the men and walked toward Flaugherty, meeting him at a point about twenty feet from his guests.

"What is it Flaugherty?" he hissed. "Can't you see that I am in the middle of a tour?"

Flaugherty winced at the reprimand. "I'm sorry, sir, but I thought you'd like to know what has been done about the security breach."

"I thought it was taken care of," Derek said, and now anger began to flood his features, although he dammed it as best he could.

"It is," Flaugherty said. "Everything appeared, initially, to be back to normal."

"What do you mean by initially?"

"Well, it appears as though the child has been lost."

"*What?* What happened?"

Derek struggled to keep from shouting, from pulling Flaugherty to him and pummeling him with his fists, his feet. Behind him, the balding man and the tall lanky man had their heads together, whispering animatedly.

So much for Mr. Silent staying that way, Derek thought. *This is all I need right now. We might as well kiss their support good-bye.*

"William Calhoun called," Flaugherty continued, "and he says the child is missing. He wants to do a satellite grid search to locate him."

"So do it," Derek said.

"It's being done now, sir."

Derek's mind raced. How in the hell had they lost the child? It seemed an impossibility in light of the expansive amount of technology being utilized on that project.

Simultaneous with this was the problem of the two guests, who, when Derek checked, still had their heads together. And they *were* a problem now. Although their cooperation would mean millions, Derek knew instinctively that they were discussing withdrawing their oral pledge of support.

He knew this—and was debating on how to handle it—when the balding man harrumphed loudly. "Uh—Mr. Tarkington? My partner and I... that is, *we*...feel that a reconsideration of our support is in order here. We..."

"I understand," Derek interrupted. "It's been one of those rare days where everything just doesn't click the way it should."

"I'm glad you understand. If only—"

"Are you sure I can't talk the two of you into keeping with the original plan?" He smiled winningly at them, although he now knew that any chance of an agreement was gone.

The tall, previous silent man stepped forward a little. His voice was a deep baritone that belied his physical stature. "We're sure, Mr. Tarkington. All of this has caused us much doubt about the security. I assure you that our decision has nothing to do with you, personally, or your splendid attention on our tour of this facility. You *do* understand, yes?"

"Oh absolutely," Derek said, still smiling, as he pulled the *Heckler and Koch* from his shoulder holster. "But you really should have reconsidered." He fired twice, and both men crumpled to the floor like wet sandbags, a hole in the forehead of each. The shots echoed in loud cascades of noise, like painful claps.

Flaugherty looked at Derek with wide eyes.

"They saw too much of the compound for me to let them go without a guarantee of funding." He looked at the bodies with sadness. "And we really could have used their money, Tim. We sure could have."

Flaugherty swallowed, his throat bobbing.

"Remember Toby Myerson last year?" Derek said. "Third richest man in the world."

Flaugherty managed to croak, "Yeah."

"Same thing happened to him, you know."

"But I thought..."

"I know, I know. Most residents believe that Toby accidentally stumbled into that electrical transformer, but the fact is, he saw some of the classified projects—same as these two—and then decided he didn't want in. We proved to certain people that he was here collecting information for the Chinese military, so it was covered up nicely."

"Oh," Flaugherty said in a meek voice.

"Now," Derek said crisply. "You were saying…?"

"Uh—well…I have reason to believe that Duke had something to do with deactivating the communications satellite."

"Duke?"

"Yes. I tried to detain him on Level Four, but he got down to D before I could apprehend him."

"What was he doing on D?"

"That's the good part," Flaugherty said.

In a few short sentences, he told Derek about Duke's chess game with the 'subject', and the ensuing argument.

"Where is he now?"

"I've got him contained in one of the holding cells."

"And you're sure he had something to do with it." It was a statement.

"He was out of his room at the time, and he looked guilty as hell."

Derek thought about this. "I'll go talk to him later. I'll get the truth out of him. One way or the another."

Flaugherty smiled then. "If you need some help…"

Derek stared at him with some contempt. "In fact, I *could* use some help." He pointed at the two bodies. "Clean up this mess. The incinerator."

He turned, stepped over the bodies, and headed toward the elevators, leaving Tim Flaugherty staring at his back.

* * * * *

TWENTY-THREE

The town of Hardy lay sprawled across low mountains along Spring River, which had its origins in Mammoth Springs and wound a course through north central Arkansas. Chance had awakened a few miles back, as though aware that they were nearing their destination, and as they entered the outskirts of town the river was visible on their left in the gray light of impending dawn.

After another half mile they entered Hardy Old Town, the downtown section of the city whose buildings were preserved in an 1800's era that was charming and somehow right for the mountainous region. The town was a comfortable tourist area, and a large portion of its economy was generated by tourists who came through in the summertime, either on their way to Norfork Lake, the Spring River Beach Club, or one of the many campsites along Spring River. Others came just to visit Hardy Old Town, and to browse the numerous stores and antiquarian shops.

Bobby drove through the downtown section at a crawl, in line with the low speed limits. Already, tourists strolled the sidewalks and looked in windows of shops that were not yet open; most of the tourists were older women in sunhats and older men in checkered slacks.

"Are you hungry?" Bobby asked Ken as they exited downtown and some restaurants came into view.

"I could use something," Ken said. He looked at Chance. "How about you, partner. Are you hungry?"

Chance grinned up at him and nodded. Then he pointed to a *McDonalds* sign on the right.

Bobby witnessed all of this through the rearview mirror. "He wants to go to *McDonalds*?"

"I think so."

"Amazing," Bobby muttered as he put on his blinker and turned in to the fast-food restaurant. "We'll go through the drive-thru. We can eat at our rendezvous point while we wait on Adrian."

"How far away is that?" Ken said.

"Another mile, mile and a half at the most. I'm sure you've been there before. It's the scenic overlook up the road."

"Yeah, I've been there," Ken said.

Bobby explained how he and Adrian had discovered the panoramic vista one weekend the previous summer, when they'd felt it safe to leave the Malcolms unmonitored. The two of them had come up for a canoe trip down Spring River, the only respite they'd had during the months they had been keeping up with the CIA's surveillance of Ken and his family.

Bobby ordered breakfast plates for the three of them, then drove around to the pickup window. A young girl attended the cash register, a blonde with too much makeup and dark brown eyes. She winked at Chance as she handed the order to Bobby. "Hiya, big guy."

"Hi there," Chance said. "How are you?"

Bobby and Ken froze, while a puzzled look crossed the girl's face. "He sure does talk well." She looked at Bobby "He yours?"

Before Bobby could answer, Chance spoke again. "That's Uncle Bob." He jerked a thumb toward Ken. "*He's* my daddy." He smiled, showing all five of his teeth.

"Oh," the girl said as she handed Bobby three drinks in a holder, and a large bag containing the food. "Well…"

"Thank you," Bobby said. "Have a nice day."

"Yeah, you too." The girl continued to stare after them as they pulled away.

As Bobby pulled back onto the highway, he looked at Ken through the rearview mirror. "Can you stop him from doing that in public places?"

"That's the first time he's done that in a public place."

"Jeez, that girl looked like the type that might tell the wrong people about him."

"Oh, come on," Ken laughed. "Are all CIA agents this paranoid? She's just a teenager. She's not going to call the police or anything. Lighten up.

Lots of children talk well at a young age."

"Not *that* well. Him talking like that has to seem weird to a total stranger."

"Yeah, well, you need to remember that I've only known for less than two days, and I'm not worried about the girl."

"You're probably right," Bobby said. "It's just kind of...strange to me. I mean, I've always expected him to be more advanced than ordinary children, but to actually hear him speak, you would never guess that he was only fifteen months old."

Ken frowned. "I never told you how old he is. How do you know?"

Bobby grunted as he put his blinker on for a left turn. "Mr. Malcolm—Ken—I know a lot more about your son than you might think." He eyed Ken through the mirror. "Maybe even more than you."

* * * * *

The scenic overlook delivered on its name, and it was here that they ate breakfast.

There was a small road off the highway on the left, near the top of the next mountain out of town. A turnout, skirted by a metal guardrail, braced the left shoulder of this road. Bobby parked the car and shut off the engine. From the confines of the car, facing the overlook, the view was spectacular. It looked as though they were in an airplane flying over a cavernous valley between several mountain ranges.

When they had finished eating, Ken changed Chance's diaper, and the three of them got out and walked to the guardrail. There, they took in the breathtaking vista: from the rail the land sloped away, a cliff covered with green underbrush. The land leveled off at the bottom of the drop, becoming grassy meadows with large trees speckling them in dots and clusters. Far to the right was a campsite for motor homes and campers, which were lined up as neatly as the homes in a sub-division. Winding a course through the middle of everything was Spring River, blue and black and bubbly, looking like a painting from another time. Ken could see a man and a boy fishing along the bank at a sharp bend in the river. The sky was a deep shade of orange and red as the sun crested the horizon. Pale clouds floated in the distance.

"Pretty," Chance said. Ken had set him down, and he was looking at the scenery through a gap in the rails.

Bobby was quiet. He took in the scenery, but also checked out their immediate surroundings. When and if Adrian arrived, he might have company behind him, and Ken figured Bobby wanted to ensure there was more than one escape route.

"How long do we wait here?"

"Two hours," Bobby said. "If Adrian got away, it shouldn't take him that long to get here, but that's the plan."

"We could always go up to my dad's cabin," Ken offered.

"We don't go anywhere until two hours have passed or Adrian shows up, whichever comes first."

Bobby's tone seemed to solicit no response, so Ken kept quiet. He wondered what they would do for two hours. The view from up here was grand, but two hours' worth would be a little much.

A breeze blew around his ankles, kicking up dust.

"Cyclone," Bobby said, and pointed.

Ken tensed at that word, and images from the past seeped through the corners of his mind: *The twister racing across the back pasture, he and his sixteen-year-old brother running as hard as they could toward the storm shelter behind the house, a hundred yards away, both he and Jimmy screaming in fear as they ran. Mom and Dad and Valerie had gone in to town for groceries, because Ken and Valerie had popped in unannounced and Mom was going to cook a big dinner. And of course Ken was bigger, faster, and the twister was on them, it was on them, and Jimmy was slower and only a few yards back, and the twister lifted him up and away, in a screaming blur, and by then Ken had also been screaming. Screaming, yes, but he had still gone into the storm cellar and shut the metal door behind him. He had still done that terrible thing.*

Ken looked where Bobby was pointing, and he saw a dust and pebble cyclone, stirred by a concentrated gust of wind.

But the small cyclone didn't dissipate. It spun and swirled in a neat funnel like a miniature tornado, picking up larger pebbles and rocks. It spun as neatly as a top. As Ken watched, the funnel expanded upward to a height of about four feet, and then shrunk down to only two. Up again, then down. Ken could feel no breeze at all, yet the pebbles and rocks continued to twirl around in the air.

From off to the right, Chance giggled.

"Holy shit," Bobby said. "Is *he* doing that?"

"I don't know," Ken said. "I guess he is."

Chance followed the small cyclone with his eyes, and when he moved his eyes upward the swirling mass of rocks, pebbles and sand grew taller. When he lowered his gaze, they fell proportionately.

"Chance?" Ken said cautiously. He was looking at the child, trying hard not to stare at the twirling cyclone in front of him which, curiously, brought on a heavier anxiety than the apparent fact that his son was its cause.

Chance looked away from the small tornado. When he did the rocks, pebbles, and sand plummeted back to the ground as though being dumped from an open hand.

"Did you *see* that?" Bobby said. "Did you?"

"Of course I did."

"How did he do it?"

"I have no idea." Ken was shaking now, searching for something to hold his mind together, for it felt as though it was being tugged at from two sides, and that sooner or later—probably sooner—it was going to split wide open. He didn't know how much more he could take.

He knew it wasn't only Chance's latest surprise ability that had him shaken; it was the cyclone that the youngster had somehow fabricated, and the memory of his failure to save his brother, which had followed it. In retrospect, Ken realized that the cyclone had upset him more than anything, like a window on his soul. And with it was the inherent and never-ending guilt and shame.

"Does he do stuff like this a lot?" Bobby said. "That was amazing. Can you make him do it again?"

Ken was staring at the rocks and pebbles that now lay in a small pile at his feet—in his mind's eye he could still see the cyclonic swirl of debris—and now he jerked his head up and glared at Bobby. "No, I can't. And I don't want you to ask me that again. Are we clear on that?"

Bobby raised both hand to waist level. "Whoa, man. Look, I'm sorry. I didn't mean anything by it."

Ken shook his head. "I told you, I just found out how intelligent he is a few days ago. Sure, I had noticed a few odd things before, but nothing like this. I'm as flabbergasted as you are, but I haven't had time to even get *used* to it, let alone *train* him to the point where he performs on command. Jesus Christ, mister, you talk as though all of this is an orchestrated, three-ring act."

"Okay," Bobby said, clicking his tongue. "Forget I said anything. I'm sorry."

Ken waved a hand at him, but continued to stare at the small pile of pebbles and rocks. "Maybe you and your partner can fill me in on things when he gets here, like you promised. I have a right to know."

"Of course you do." Bobby looked at his watch. "Adrian should be here before long, and we'll tell you what we know." He paused. "I could tell you some right now, I guess, but I think it would be better if you heard everything at the same time."

"I see," Ken said, though not as crisply as before. He shut off the cyclone in his mind at the same time, right in the middle of an image of Jimmy sailing past, up and away, gone. That's where the memory always ended and guilt sank its teeth into him. "How much longer do we wait?"

Bobby glanced at his watch. "It's almost six. We'll give him his two hours, about eight."

Ken nodded and picked up Chance. Together, the two of them gazed out at the panoramic view.

* * * * *

William Calhoun rose from a fitful sleep and managed to answer the phone on the sixth ring. "Shit," he muttered. There was no wife beneath the sheets to mutter along with him, but that was the only good thing about getting a call this early in the morning. A call this early always meant one thing: trouble.

And the dream hadn't helped.

He had been at the Nevada compound, at night, and sirens were going off. He was in his underclothes, and so he knew he couldn't take control of whatever malfunction was occurring. Instead, he had looked for someone in command, but there was no one. All of the soldiers encamped around the facility that house Project Lone Star were fleeing, and some were dying, with terrible holes gouged through their bodies from what could only be one weapon. The edges of the gaping holes singed and smoked with the crisp smell of burnt flesh. He could make out someone walking toward him at a leisurely pace through the smoke and backlit darkness, but he couldn't identify him or her. He then looked down and saw that he was dressed in full attire. At that point he figured out that he was dreaming. It should have brought relief, but for some reason it didn't. The figure coming toward him brought with it an air of impending doom, and William clasped his hands over his ears as a shrill ringing pierced the night. He squinched his eyes shut because he decided he did not want to see who was in front of him, and he was filled with a dread like he had not known since childhood, when nightmares invoked the all- encompassing fear that could be felt in the teeth and the spine. And still the ringing continued, and he closed his eyes tighter, and that is when he had awakened to the shrill of the phone.

"Yeah," he said into the mouthpiece as he wiped drool off the side of his chin with one pajama sleeve. He listened for a moment, his mind—trained to be alert regardless of the hour, or clarity of nightmares—already soaking up the information and formulating recourse. "You're positive?"

Another pause while he listened to agent Lomax tell about their failure to capture the child, and the subsequent injury to agent Milcheck.

That dark figure—

"I see. Is he hurt bad?"

"No."

—fading—

"Good."

—and gone completely.

Calhoun cradled the phone to his ear and began to dress, thankful that he had lain his clothes out like his mother taught him years ago, in case of a fire in the night, or worse.

This was worse.

"I want you two to stay in the area," he said into the phone. "I'm going to headquarters to start satellite re-con. I'm going to have to activate the trackers, and that's going to take some time, so prepare yourselves. In the meantime, we have to communicate. Go pick up a cell phone as soon as something opens, and call me at the office with the number."

"After that?" Lomax said.

"Keep it turned on."

Calhoun hung up and finished dressing, wondering about the two men Lomax claimed had foiled the capture of the child. They were wild cards for sure—if they even existed at all.

I bet I know who the two men were, he thought, *and their names are Lomax and Milcheck.*

That had to be it. No one working outside his office or the Nevada compound knew anything about the Malcolms and the child they assumed was legally theirs. It was impossible. Yet Lomax had sounded genuinely upset, so Calhoun reasoned that *something* had happened. He just wasn't sure what. And to give the two agents credit, it was difficult to fabricate a bullet wound. He would risk even greater exposure to the project by involving more agents, but that was beginning to look like his next step. He already had a contingency on standby. Always better to be prepared. He would coordinate the moves of Lomax and Milcheck himself, until those resources could be dispatched. He sighed. It looked like it was going to be a long day.

But that was okay.

He was ready to do whatever it took to capture the child. This was the type of work he enjoyed—not standing behind a desk and passing out assignments. There were people in the government who didn't realize the importance and possibilities of Project Lone Star—President Clayton chief among them, of course—but Calhoun understood everything all too well.

An image from the dissipated dream flickered across his mind; a soldier with a hole the size of a basketball hoop burnt through his midsection, and behind him a figure Calhoun could not bear to see.

He grabbed his keys and left for headquarters at Langley.

* * * * *

Bobby opened the front passenger door and sat on the seat, smoking a cigarette, while Ken and Chance played with the stuffed teddy bear Adrian had given the child at the house in Paragould. Shortly after eight o'clock, Bobby rose and said: "It's time. It doesn't look as though Adrian is going to make it."

There was forced optimism in his voice, and Ken detected loss and disappointment there, as well. In addition to being a team, the two had most likely been friends.

"Think he got away from those goons? Ken said.

Bobby seemed to consider this. "I think that if he *didn't* get away from them, he sure as hell didn't tell them where we were going. They wouldn't be able to *torture* that out of him. But there are several possibilities. Adrian could have gotten away—we hope—and the two agents are following him. In which case, it would explain why he's late. He would never come here without shaking his tail. *Or* he might have gotten lost. We've only been up here the one time."

"And what's the other possibility?" Ken said, because it was one he knew Bobby didn't want to contemplate.

Bobby sighed and said it: "Adrian might be dead. That's the other scenario, in a nutshell."

"What then?"

"In that case we had better leave, and in a hurry. The director of the CIA can activate the trackers with a phone call, and that's probably his next move. If those guys caught up with Adrian, and even if they *didn't* kill him, the agency will treat this like an inside job."

"Trackers?"

"Yes," Bobby said and looked toward the highway. "We'd better go now." He keyed the ignition.

Ken put Chance in his car seat and buckled him in. Then he said to Bobby, who was backing out of the cul-de-sac. "Uh, do you mind filling me in on these…trackers?"

"Later," Bobby said. "We've got company. *Shit.*"

Ken looked and saw a dark sedan coming up the small road at high speed. "That looks like the car those guys showed up in this morning."

"It is," Bobby said. He tromped the gas pedal and the car lunged forward. The sedan flashed its headlights at them as they passed. Bobby kept his foot on the gas and his eyes straight ahead.

"*Wait*," Ken said. "I think that's your friend."

Bobby slowed the vehicle some, watching his rearview as he did. The other car would have to be turned around before it could mount a pursuit. "Are you sure?"

"I'm pretty sure," Ken said, "and I only saw one person, not two."

"Okay," Bobby said calmly, and gripped the steering wheel hard enough that his knuckles turned white. He stopped the car and waited, watching his rearview as the sedan turned around and moved toward them.

It moved at a slower speed this time, and stopped about twenty feet from the rear of the car. The door on the driver's side opened and a head peeked out.

"Bobby? Bobby, it's me," Adrian O'Donnell said as he stepped into full view.

Bobby's body slumped. "Thank God."

Adrian walked up to the window.

"What happened, man?" Bobby asked him.

Instead of answering, Adrian looked at Ken and nodded at Chance. "He okay?"

"Yeah," Ken said. "He's fine. But I'm not. What's going on?"

Bobby said to Adrian: "I see you got their car. Did you kill them? You didn't, did you?"

"Of course not," Adrian said. He glanced at Ken. "We'll tell you everything, but we need to do it somewhere other than here."

Ken thought about telling them that he and Chance weren't going anywhere until he found out what he wanted to know, but decided that it probably wouldn't do any good. Besides, there was an urgency to Adrian's voice that made Ken uneasy. They had already been here over two hours, and for some reason the place no longer felt safe.

"How far are they behind you?" Bobby said.

Adrian shrugged. "There was gun play at the house and they blew out a tire on Mr. Malcolm's car. I managed to get in theirs and sneak away." He grinned. "I guess they had to change a flat. I took a roundabout route here, and I took a little time to check out the equipment in their vehicle, see what could be salvaged for our own use."

"Cool," Bobby said.

Cool? Ken thought. *These guys are actually ex-agents of the CIA?*

"Follow me back up the hill here," Adrian said. "I want to ditch this car."

A few minutes later Adrian was moving some items from that car into the trunk. As they pulled out onto the highway, Bobby said, "Which way, Ken?"

"Right," Ken said. "Back in to Hardy and take the first highway on the right."

"Where are we going?" Adrian said.

"Ken said his father has a cabin up in the hills a few miles from here. It might be safe for a while."

"Maybe," Adrian said, and then his voice grew somber. "Bobby, you know what's going to happen now, don't you?"

"Yeah, I know. Trackers."

"How long do you think we have before activation?"

Bobby seemed to mentally calculate. "I would guess anywhere from two to four hours."

"Not long, then."

"No."

"Excuse me," Ken said, "but will you guys please tell me what the hell trackers are, and what you mean when you say we only have two to four hours?"

"We'll talk about it on the way to this cabin of yours."

"Good." Ken looked down at his son, realizing how quiet he had been since he'd caused the pebbles and rocks to spin and dance, but Chance only stared ahead, as if lost in his own world.

Ten minutes later they crossed the river. It sparkled beneath them.

* * * * *

TWENTY-FOUR

The holding cell was small, but not uncomfortable.

Ten feet by eight feet, with a soft mattress on the single cot, a sink, and a private toilet stall that wasn't out in the open like prison facilities in novels. There was never any intention for *real* prisoners to be held here at the compound—at least not any of the residents. But someone got drunk and unruly on occasion and had to be held in one of the six cells until they'd had time to sleep it off. The cellblock was quiet.

Duke lay on the mattress, hands laced together behind his head, thinking. He was not fearful at the prospect of seeing his father. Flaugherty had told him, as he'd locked the cell and put the key in his pocket, that he was going to get the elder Tarkington. "We'll just let *him* get the truth out of you," he had said. Duke said nothing, but had stared at Tim Flaugherty with open hatred, something he had been surprised to feel. It was hard for Duke to hate anyone.

And that included his father.

Despite what Tim Flaugherty seemed to think Duke was not going to cower in fear at the mention of his father's name. He would never again give the man *that* pleasure. And, although he was a little nervous, he had enough self-awareness to know that the nervousness came not from the anticipation of facing his father, but because of the simple fact that he was locked up in this cell. The cell was comfortable enough, sure, but it was still all he could do to keep claustrophobia at bay.

He was thinking about two things to accomplish this.

The first was memories of a time, several years before the evisceration of his tongue, when he had looked up to his father as his idol. He had been thirteen then, and was just beginning to comprehend who his father really was, and how important a job he had here at the compound. Derek had never thrown ungodly amounts of attention his way—although Duke had distant blurry memories, as a toddler, of kissing his father good night, and feeling the man's rough cheeks against his lips, and the secure feeling that one sensation gave him. Duke had spent as much time as he could with the man, although most of it consisted of mealtimes and, occasionally, an evening in the same room, the whole family—Duke, his father, and his long-lost mother—reading quietly in front of a simulated crackling fire.

That had been the year his mother had passed on, and was also the last year in which Duke had felt the warmth of security in his father's presence. Derek had become a more distant man following the death of Meg Tarkington. Duke had, through the years into adulthood, blamed himself for his father's withdrawal in to his work and the subsequent detachment from his only family.

Between the time of this subtle separation and the night he lost his tongue, Duke took solace through books and music and, in his friend on Substation D.

And Prometheus was, of course, the other avenue his thoughts ventured down this morning, as he sat waiting for the supposed interrogation by his father, and tried to ward off claustrophobia.

There was something Duke had not thought of recently; something else that Prometheus had said in the note that had been found in *Cold Fire*. The reason he hadn't thought about it was not lost on him, regardless of how stupid and slow people thought he was: he had been wound so tight with concentration and anxiety in accomplishing the satellite deactivation—and the subsequent flight from Flaugherty during the alarm—that he had forgotten about what else had been written on the note.

He had tucked it into his pocket after punching in the codes on the security systems, and it remained out of mind until after he had been brought here and locked up. He had discovered the crumpled piece of paper after Flaugherty left and had quickly read it again, mindful that Flaugherty or his father might enter the cellblock at any moment.

The note had been detailed on instructions about the satellite, but it had been vague on another subject: the child.

If all goes well, the child will be safe, and I will be with him at last. I hope you understand, and that you will help. That was the portion of the note that bothered Duke, now that he had time to think about it.

He knew the child had his origins at this compound, and that Prometheus was its father, and that he missed his son. That last was amazing to Duke. How must it feel to be wanted so fiercely by your father? He had often entertained silent wishes that *he* was Prometheus' son. It was a private fantasy, of course, but it helped get him through many grueling work days, fetching things for this person, going after something for that one, getting funny looks from some, and behind-hands snickers from others.

To be the son of Prometheus would be so cool.

What did the child look like? How did Prometheus keep a link of communication with him? How come the child was not here with its father? Duke *did* know the answer to that one. Prometheus had told him about it during one of their Saturday chess matches.

Prometheus had fathered the child artificially, and when the surrogate mother was on her way to the compound, there had been an accident—by design, he had said (whose design? Duke didn't know)—and then there had been a reporter. The reporter had gotten news of the accident to his paper before being captured by security forces from the compound, and when word got out the administrations of both the compound and the government in Washington wanted to cover up what had happened. The child was supposed to live here in the compound, to be poked, prodded, and studied, same as Prometheus had been for years. Prometheus had not wanted that. He said he would rather chance his son being monitored from a distance than to be put through what the people here had in mind for him.

Prometheus told Duke that members of the compound's security team had killed the reporter. Duke believed it. This had occurred only six months or so after he'd lost his tongue.

There was still so much that Duke *didn't* know about the child, but Prometheus had told him once that one day soon he would know everything, and all of his questions would be answered.

Prometheus had also told him something else, as well, and in light of what the note in his pocket said, it made him uneasy: *You are not alone here, Duke,* his friend had said in the note. *You are not alone.*

Duke thought he understood the last line of the note better than he did anything else; Prometheus was planning some kind of escape (*I hope you understand, and that you will help*). He *had* helped him out. He was sure to pay a price for doing so, but he had foreseen that certainty with little, if any, concern. He would do even more for his friend if given the chance. What Prometheus wanted him to understand was that, before long, Duke *would* be alone here, for he, Prometheus, would be gone.

That was the hardest thing to contemplate. By helping his friend tonight—by association contributing to his plan of escape—he had at the same time helped cause the *loss* of his friend. When Prometheus escaped, who would be here for him? Who would take time to learn sign language—Tyler James was the only other person who was passingly familiar with it—or have the patience to wait while Duke scribbled his voice onto a pad of paper?

Yet he would do it all over again, despite the risks to himself, if it helped his friend achieve what he wanted. He would keep the note—especially the last lines (*Your Friend Always*)—to remember Prometheus by.

But what if you're wrong? he asked himself. *Maybe he's not planning to escape at all. Maybe he's going to get killed trying to escape, and that's why he said what he did.*

No.

Duke didn't believe that. *Couldn't.*

Prometheus was a big believer in the extrasensory capabilities of the mind, and Duke felt he had touched some of that power with this idea. He couldn't shake the conviction that he was going to lose his friend.

First, though, he was going to have to endure his father, and whatever might happen after. That was okay with Duke. That was fine. In spite of what the man had done to him—what he might do more of, but worse—he was still his father.

And Duke missed him.

* * * * *

Although it seemed much longer to his reminiscing mind, only thirty minutes passed after Flaugherty left before Duke heard the outer door to the cellblock clank open. Footsteps echoed off the floor and bounced against the cool cement walls.

Duke tensed some, but he remained calm. What happened would happen, and there wasn't much he could do about it…other than lie. If he admitted to causing the satellite malfunction, he had no doubt he would be hurt much worse than when they had taken his tongue. He thought it possible that he might be killed. As the footsteps drew closer, he sat up on the cot, facing the front of the cell.

Derek Tarkington stopped in front of the cell, and looked at him. "Well, Duke, what have you done this time?"

Duke shook his head back and forth, pointing at himself.

"Nothing, huh? I guess that's about what I expected you to…say." Derek's right hand stole to a front pocket, where he jingled keys and coins. He appeared to be at a loss for what to say next, and this uncharacteristic act drew Duke's attention.

Derek was dressed in the usual camouflage attire, complete with black combat boots and belt, but his face looked tired. Duke knew from the look that there were more important things on his father's mind.

Yet Derek was a man who could shift his focus as easily as the wind changed direction and speed. Duke knew that, as well.

"I want to ask you something, Duke. Okay?" Derek's voice was— surprisingly—gentle.

Duke nodded slowly.

"Do you know anything about the incident we had this morning with the communications satellite?"

As difficult as it was, Duke looked his father in the eye and shook his head slowly.

"About what I figured," Derek said.

Duke made a gesture for something to write with, and on. He looked at his father, his eyebrows raised.

"That won't be necessary, Duke. I don't know why Flaugherty thinks you're involved with this incident, but he does. He says you were out of your room right before the security alarms sounded."

Duke pantomimed getting a drink of water.

"He didn't mention that."

Duke repeated the gesture—feeling dim hope surface—and pointed at himself. Then he locked eyes with his father.

Derek's dark eyes seemed to glow in the low lighting. "Want to know something funny, Duke?"

Duke tried to smile, but couldn't. He only looked at his father.

"I believe you *were* just out of your room, getting a drink of water."

Duke tried not to show relief, which might be taken as a sign that he was lying.

"Do you know *why* I believe that's all you were doing? Huh?" He leaned forward, until his head rested against two of the bars.

Something in his father's voice had changed—just like that—and it wasn't in a good way. Duke was again on edge. He shook his head: *no*.

"I'll tell you why, then. Because you are too *stupid* to have any knowledge of a complicated piece of equipment like a satellite." He smiled, and to Duke it was shark-like. "Flaugherty should have known that before he ever decided to chase you down to Substation D. In fact, had he thought about that simple fact, he never would have pursued you in the first place." The elder Tarkington then said, almost to himself: "Perhaps he had other reasons for chasing you." He tapped a finger on his chin.

Duke remained still and silent, although there was an acute sinking feeling in his stomach that was like the elevators when they rose too fast.

"But," Derek continued, "the fact remains that he *did* follow you, regardless of his initial intentions, and he claims he found you in a rather interesting place, doing some very interesting things." He stared at Duke, his eyes demanding nothing less than the truth. "Is this correct?"

Duke was at a loss. To tell the truth would mean certain punishment—for himself *and* Prometheus, most likely—and to lie would be dangerous simply because all his father had to do was look at the security tapes of him entering the lab where Prometheus was held.

With no other choice, he looked at the floor and nodded.

When he found the courage to look up again, his father's eyes were hard.

"This bothers me, Duke, it certainly does." He laced his hands behind his back and began to pace back and forth in front of the small cell. "And do you know why?"

Without waiting for a reply, or even looking at Duke, he continued, "I know that *you* don't know anything about the sophisticated equipment in use at this facility, but going through my mind is one other question: How much does our special and secret friend know?"

Duke grew edgy as his father's voice rose and his pacing increased.

"How much does your *chess playing* buddy know about computers?" He chuckled, a mad, creepy sound. "*That's* a stupid question. *Very* stupid. He knows quite a bit, I guess, but there is only one problem with what happened this afternoon. And that problem is this: our *friend* is imprisoned very efficiently. He could not physically lay his hands on a computer—or anything else—if he wanted to. *But*," he added, and quit pacing to stare again at Duke. "What if your friend down the hall has a special friend of his own? A friend like Duke Tarkington. A buddy with hands to do the work, but no mouth to overload his asshole and let slip to someone what is going on?

"Do you suppose that could be an accurate scenario of the situation? Do you think that I might have seen through both yours *and* Flaugherty's bullshit to get right to the meat of the matter? Hmm?"

Duke was stunned. His father was much more intelligent than he had ever given him credit for, and Duke had thought of him as the highest intellect. How had he figured things out so quickly?

He probably read it all in your eyes, he told himself, and on the heels of that came a miserable realization: he had failed his friend. He could only hope that nothing terrible happened to Prometheus, now that Derek was aware of everything. He thought: *if anything happens, let it happen only to me. Please.*

Duke was looking at his angry father when he thought this, and perhaps Derek could read *that* thought in the eyes of his son, as well, because his face softened some and he said: "Okay, Duke, maybe that scenario is a little outlandish, but *something* happened to one of our chief communications satellites, and I have to know what caused the problem. Some vital work on an important project was screwed up because of it, and I'm the guy who is going to have to answer for it if anything goes wrong. Do you understand that much?"

Duke nodded eagerly, sensing the possibility of a lighter punishment.

"I'm not certain of what happened, and I don't know for sure if it's had any adverse effects on other things. I guess I will find out when the satellite comes back online and I see the data and any damage that might have occurred. But I can't, for the life of me, convince myself that you and the subject are together in some sort of conspiracy. I've never seen the two of you do anything but play chess and...and talk."

Duke's mouth dropped open. He couldn't help it.

"That's right, son. I know about you and the subject. Not much gets by me here." He waved a hand. "Oh, I'm aware that you deactivate the monitors on Saturdays for brief periods of time—they're pretty simple, really—but there are backup video monitors of which you know nothing. No audio backup, but that's no concern, really. As long as I can *see* what's going on, I don't have to hear it." He paused, as if swallowing something bitter. "And I understand your need for friendship. Life in this compound is not easy—downright difficult at times—and I'm aware of how people treat you."

He looked at Duke, and this time his eyes were soft, compassionate, although Duke had often wondered if his father had an ounce of compassion left in him. "Your friendship with the subject is fine, and it can continue. I just need your word that what happened tonight with the satellite was in no way a by-product of that friendship." He paused. "Was it?"

Again, Duke made a gesture for something to write on, and this time Derek reached into a breast pocket and withdrew a pen and a small notepad. He passed them to Duke through the bars.

Duke reached for the items, part of him certain that it was a trick, and that his father would withdraw the pen and pad at the last second. He steeled himself for that, but took the proffered items without the anticipated cruelty. He took them to his small cot, sat down, and began to write.

When he was done, he tore off the sheet and returned it, the pad, and the pen to his father, who took it, looking into Duke's eyes the whole time (perhaps looking for a trick of his own, or only a simple reluctance to read what his son had written).

He read the note to himself:

> I would never do anything to jeopardize
> your work here, Dad. Never. Thank you for
> allowing me to remain friends with the Subject.
>   Duke

Below the handwritten message were three more words:

> I love you

Derek wadded the paper into a ball and looked into the cell. Duke could not clearly see which emotions were at conflict on his father's face, but he thought—or perhaps it was only wishful thinking—he saw both guilt and relief written there.

The elder Tarkington's voice hardened and seemed forced, when he said: "I guess you know I'm going to have to hold you here until we can get all of this cleared up. I need to speak with Flaugherty again before deciding what to do with you."

Duke was relieved that another angry outburst was not forthcoming. He hitched in a big breath and nodded.

"Okay," his father said. He turned to leave, then looked back one last time. "I hope you're being honest with me here, Duke. I really do."

Duke nodded again.

Derek stared at him for another minute, as if in quiet contemplation, before he left. His boots echoed down the short hallway. Then the outer door clicked shut and the cellblock was once again cloaked in silence. Duke lay down on his bunk and tried to sleep.

* * * * *

TWENTY-FIVE

John and Mark were having breakfast at *Barnhill's Country Buffet*, in Jonesboro. The sun peeked over the horizon, bathing the restaurant in mellow slats of fire. They were waiting for *Wireless World* to open, so they could pick up a cellular phone. The sign in front of the establishment had said they opened at nine o'clock on Sundays.

"We shouldn't be eating right now," John said. "You know that, don't you?"

Lomax poured gravy over a crumbled biscuit and sprinkled salt and pepper on the mixture. "I can handle it. The last time they activated the trackers, I was in the pool room at headquarters with half a dozen comrades. I was the only one who didn't lose his dinner."

"You weren't nauseated?"

"Sure, I was nauseous, but I kept it under control. I think I can do it again."

"But what if you can't?" John looked around the room. Although most of the patrons had their heads tucked behind either the *Jonesboro Sun* or the *Jonesboro Journal,* the place was still better than half full, and if Lomax were to get sick—hell, if *either* of them were—it would not go unnoticed. Nor would it be pretty, considering the amount of food they were consuming.

"You don't seem too worried about yourself," Lomax said around a mouthful of biscuit and gravy. "So, don't worry about me. I appreciate it, but I think I know my body better than you do."

John looked down at his own plate, on which sat a mound of eggs, sausage links, hash browns, and French toast strips, and thought: *What the hell am I thinking?* Although he knew Lomax was probably cranky due to lack of sleep and the fact that Malcolm and the child had gotten away, John had no excuse for the lax in his thinking. He'd had a nice nap in the car once the aspirin had begun their work on his arm. He could remember all too well the only time since he'd been in the CIA's employ that the director's office had activated the trackers.

It had happened less than a year ago. An agent by the name of Walter Pippin had retired from the agency with full honors a few months before, and when it was later discovered that he was trading intelligence secrets with a foreign agent, the man had fled. He was good at shaking immediate pursuers, but Walter had apparently either forgotten about the trackers, or didn't believe they would work where he had gone to ground. Yet they had. FBI agents had picked him up in an old mine shaft in the mountains of Pennsylvania, nearly three hundred feet below ground level.

When the trackers were activated, John had been leaving a small café on the outskirts of Virginia, a toothpick in his mouth and his car keys in his hand, and he had lost his entire meal to the asphalt parking lot. He'd dry-heaved for nearly five minutes after that—until the trackers were deactivated—and then once more when he got home, when the agency had to activate them again to reestablish Pippin's location. At the time, John didn't know the reason for his sudden nausea, but he had never returned to the same café again, although it was his favorite.

He looked at his food and decided that he didn't want to go through that again. Especially not here in this peaceful restaurant, where most of the patrons had probably come for a good meal and talk with friends before Sunday morning church services commenced. He grimaced and pushed his plate forward, wiping his hands on a linen napkin.

"That's about enough for me."

Lomax looked up from his plate, where he was trying to fork a sausage link that rolled around the vacated side of the plate where the biscuit and gravy had been. "John, I think we've got time to eat. Calhoun said it would be a while until activation."

"I realize that. I just can't chance it, though. I would rather wait until after to eat."

"Suit yourself," Lomax said. He finally managed to spear the sausage and he bit into it, chewing with enthusiasm. "You know, no one makes sausage like the south. The commercials are right." That said, he washed the link down with a swig of milk and then stabbed another. This time he succeeded on the first try.

John nursed his coffee and looked out a window at the birth of the morning on Caraway Road, where traffic was light. He had to have his coffee in the mornings, regardless, and he figured that if he *did* get sick at least it wouldn't be as messy as what Lomax would have to contend with.

He tried to take his mind off the trackers and think instead about the rest of the day ahead of them; first, breakfast and the cellular phone, and then the wait.

* * * * *

"The trackers were introduced four years ago by the Central Intelligence Agency as a means of keeping up with agents in the field in emergency situations," Bobby told Ken.

The highway rolled out in front of them in hills and valleys, and then a right turn took them past the Spring River Beach Club, where the lodges and pools would be full of Beach Club members before the stroke of noon. "They were also put into use in case an agent went rogue and decided to sell information to other sources."

"Other sources."

"Other countries," Adrian said from the back seat. "It's not uncommon for an ex-government agent, or a retired agent, to go bad. And not only in the CIA, either. The lure of easy money, and all that."

"Yeah, just look at us," Bobby laughed. "Always looking for that extra retirement dollar."

Adrian jabbed him on the shoulder. "Right, moron."

"So, how do these trackers work?" Ken said, ignoring their friendly banter.

Bobby seemed to be the most technology-oriented of the two, and it was he who answered. "The trackers are tracking-devices that were injected into all agents of the Central Intelligence Agency roughly four years ago. None of the agents knew until later that these things were being implanted inside of them. Most of us assumed we were being administered another series of vaccinations. Traveling to multiple countries is common for a field agent, and the risk of disease and infection are high without immunization."

Ken said, "You mean these trackers are so small that they were injected into you through a *needle?*"

"Yes," Bobby said. "A rather *large* needle, if I remember correctly."

"Wow."

"Anyway, these things are like little homing devices once they're activated. They emit a signal that is easily picked up by satellites, pinpointing the location of every person with one of these trackers inside them. There had been talk that they would inject these in all military personnel at some point. I don't know if the program ever got that far, but it very well could have by now."

"How do they know to whom each signal belongs?" Ken said as he directed Bobby to make a turn to the right, down a steep incline toward the river, which sparkled like a silver snake on their left. "Seems like that would be next to impossible."

"That's the kicker," Bobby said as he braked the car down the hill. "Each tracker contains vital information about its carrier, but the primary piece of information it carries is *who* its carrier is. Sort of like a molecular barcode. When they activate the trackers, they are going to know that Adrian and I are the two who foiled their attempt to abduct the child in Paragould. They will know that by simple deduction, based on our proximity to the area. They know who is working the case, and it won't take them long to see we are not only not on that list, but that we are also ex-agents. And not *just* ex-agents."

"Yeah," Adrian said from the back seat, "we're deserters, which is considered even worse. And they are going to know our exact location."

Ken shuddered. If what they were saying was true, there was no way to escape. The CIA, or government, or whomever, would find them. If they activated these trackers, that was.

When they activate them. He said when, not if.

Right.

A one-lane cement bridge spanned the width of the river, and they drove across slowly, in silence, each man admiring the view on either side of him, where water gurgled and churned in the sunshine like tangled jewels.

Suddenly a thought occurred to Ken: "Wait a minute. If these things are inside your body, why not just have them removed?"

"Not that simple," Adrian said. "There is no way to locate these things. Micro and Nano-technology has advanced in the past five years. We're talking infinitesimal here. They could be anywhere at all inside the body, and they are in constant motion. Yet they are engineered where they can't be excreted through normal bodily outlets like sweat, feces, urine, or breath."

"That sounds impossible," Ken said.

"Maybe, but it's true."

Ken was silent for a moment as he thought about the implications of these trackers. The road curved gently up an incline and the river was behind them, shining like a length of plastic. "So what you guys are saying, basically, is that we're screwed."

"No..."

"They activate these things, locate us by satellite, and then send in the troops to, what? Capture us? Kill us? Sounds simple enough."

"Ken—"

"I knew I should have kept going when you guys stopped me the other night. I *knew* it."

"Ken," Adrian said.

"What?" Ken said, resignation in his voice.

"Why *did* you pull over for us?"

"Because I—"

Why had he? Now *there* was a good question. He had been shaken by the amazing abilities his son had displayed, and now he was in further disarray over the subsequent events in Paragould. His mind had blocked out the reason he was here at all; Bobby and Adrian had saved his life. They had swept he and his son away from a couple of government agents that had meant them nothing but harm and, so far, they were all still alive. Yet if he wanted to tell the truth here—and why not?—the *real* reason he had pulled over for Adrian and Bobby was very simple: Chance had told him that it was okay.

He could thank his toddler son for saving his life with perhaps even more conviction than he could thank these two men.

Ken mumbled a response.

"Excuse me?" Adrian said.

"I said, Chance told me it was okay. That you two were okay."

Adrian leaned back in his seat and looked at Bobby in the rearview. The two men locked eyes for a moment, perhaps realizing this whole thing might be a lot larger than what they had thought.

Bobby looked back at the road. Up ahead, on the right, another road met this one at a small junction. "Should I go straight or turn?"

"Turn," Ken said.

This road would turn to gravel after a few hundred yards, and Ken looked at the familiar scenery around him; open vistas and meadows on either side of the road, and up ahead a thick forest of trees, as the mountain inclined steeply. He had spent many a summer day in these hills, with a variety of landscapes to explore; the river first, then the grassy meadows on its banks. Last of all the tree-sloped hills in which the cabin was hidden.

As the car rumbled over the gravel terrain, Ken saw that Chance had fallen asleep. He was still, in spite of everything else, a little boy who needed his rest.

"So, how do you guys figure into this CIA business, and how do you know so much about my son?"

"Ken," Adrian said. "Chance is adopted."

"I know that. But he is still—"

"No, he isn't. You need to divorce yourself from the notion that he is your son."

"What?" Ken fumed. He wanted to hit the man.

"When you hear everything, you'll understand," Adrian said. "You'll see that little Chance is very special, more so than even *we* thought, and hopefully you will want to share him with the world."

"With the—?"

"With the whole world," Bobby echoed.

Ken let out a big breath. What they were saying just confused him further. "Maybe you could explain it to me," he said.

Adrian began, while Bobby drove slowly along the gravel. "It all started several decades ago with—!"

The car swerved hard to the right, nearly hitting a tree before Bobby could correct it, and before either man could tell Ken anything else, both of them were violently sick. Bobby stopped the car, but it still wasn't quick enough for Adrian. He vomited in the back floorboard and immediately the car was filled with the sour smell of whatever he'd eaten for breakfast.

"Damn," Bobby said. His head had smarted against the steering wheel, despite the use of his seatbelt.

The near-collision with the tree woke Chance, who blinked up at Ken. "What happened?"

Ken put a protective are around him—no matter *what* these two men said, he *was* his son—and said: "I'm not sure yet, but it's all right, buddy."

"But what's wrong with them?"

Adrian and Bobby were each leaning out their doors, retching violently. Ken tried to block out the sounds of sickness, but couldn't.

Finally, Adrian pulled himself back inside, wiping his chin with the back of one hand, and closed his door. "Damn, that was quick."

"What was?"

"The trackers," Bobby said as he leaned back inside the car and closed the door. "A side-effect of activation is violent nausea."

Understanding dawned on Ken's face. "So what you're saying is that, right now, they know where we are?"

"Probably not just yet," Adrian said. "It will take some time for the data from each tracker to be collected, and then someone has to look at that data to determine each person's location. Someone has to look at a computer screen, anyway."

"And that someone is probably standing ready, waiting to do so," Bobby added. "They know we've got the child, and they didn't activate these damn things without personnel at the ready, to tell the director what he needs to know."

"So, how much time *do* we have?" Ken said. "Should we even be going up to my dad's place at all?"

Bobby said: "It will be harder for them to find us in these hills than it would be in town, or in a city the size of Paragould or Jonesboro. It will take them longer. But you can be certain that they *will* find us."

"How much further is it to your father's cabin?"

"Another two miles or so."

"Then I suggest that we go there, set up some of the equipment we lifted from those agents, and try to tap into the satellite the CIA is using to collect data from the trackers. If Adrian's tracker and mine can be deactivated, it will be through their system, and with their equipment I might be able to do it. I just need a look at the hardware. If our beacons disappear from the grid, they might think they were mistakes. And even if they already have data from our trackers, by making them disappear we can at least stop their satellite from pinpointing our exact location."

"But they'll still come here, won't they?" Ken said.

"Yes, but they will have to activate repeatedly to keep up with us, because they will anticipate us being on the move. They may wind up at the bridge back there, and not know where to go from there. That's one possibility."

"Another one," Adrian said, "is that they will blanket the surrounding area once they are here, which means that they might find us anyway. But even that will buy us valuable time while Bobby attempts to thwart their computers."

"Are there any more possibilities?" Ken said. He hugged Chance closer to him, and the child appeared to take some comfort in the gesture. He leaned his head against Ken's shoulder and closed his eyes.

"Yes," Bobby said as he pulled back onto the road. "One is that I can totally eradicate their data, or at least jumble it up enough so that they won't be certain that a blanket sweep of the area will turn us up."

"And the other?"

"The other—and the one I hope doesn't happen, if it hasn't already—is that those two agents are already close to the Hardy area. Data from the trackers could be relayed to them before we can get the computers and other equipment set up at your father's place."

"I don't like that one," Ken said. "We would be sitting ducks."

"Exactly," Adrian said. "How much further?"

"Turn left up here," Ken said.

Bobby turned the car onto a narrow gravel road that wound through thickening trees. Only a few other cabins and homes dotted the lane. Otherwise, the area was nothing but wooded hills.

"At least they will have problems getting in here with a helicopter, if they resort to that," Adrian said.

"Thank goodness for small favors," Bobby muttered. "But with any luck, we'll have time to scramble them up before it gets to that."

"Here on the left," Ken said. He looked at Chance. "We're almost to Pa Pa's cabin, partner."

"There it is," Bobby said, and slowed the vehicle.

There was a vehicle in the circular gravel driveway at the front of the cabin.

"Shit," Adrian said.

"*Stop*," Ken said, his stomach dropping upon seeing the car.

Then Bobby abruptly jerked the car to a stop as he and Adrian were, once again, violently sick.

* * * * *

The personnel at *Wireless World* on South Caraway were friendly and efficient, providing John Milcheck and Mark Lomax with top-of-the-line service and equipment. The woman who waited on them was a brunette with a nice figure, and a nicer smile that John caught Lomax staring at more than once. She outfitted them with two cellular camera phones, car and electrical outlet adapters, and wireless headsets.

The phones could be activated from inside the store, she said, with a phone call. All she needed was some basic information.

Mark gave her his CIA identification, and seemed to take pleasure at the impressed look on the woman's face. "Out catching bad guys?" she said in a soft southern accent that, later, Lomax would confess to John he could fall in love with.

It took about fifteen minutes for her to run the required credit check on Lomax, and then she packaged everything up for them.

"This phone is fully charged," she told them. "The other one you can probably charge from your vehicle. I'm sorry that we only have one fully-charged battery, but we sell most phones as they come packaged, and virtually all of them have to be charged before use." She shrugged her shoulders. "Best I can do, I'm afraid, but I hope the one will help you out for now."

"This will be fine," Lomax told her, digging a credit card from his wallet and placing it on the counter. "One working phone will benefit us tremendously right now."

"Good." She rang it up, had him sign the receipt, then gave him a copy. "You guys have a nice day, and good luck."

"Thank you, ma'am," John said. Lomax only stared at her, starry-eyed.

On their way to the door, John turned around. "Pardon me, ma'am."

"Yes?" The woman smiled, displaying a perfect row of white teeth that made her lips appear impossibly red.

"Could we have your phone number?"

The woman's blush almost matched her lips. "Why…I…"

John laughed. "Not *your* number, ma'am. The business number."

"Oh," she said, and John thought he heard light disappointment in her voice.

"But your home number would be okay, also," Lomax said, grinning like a fool.

John glared hard at Mark, and then told her. "Just the business phone, please."

"Would a business card do?"

"Absolutely," John said.

She pulled one from a stack on the counter and handed it to him. "We would be delighted to hear from you again." She bent below the counter briefly and came up with another card, which she handed to Lomax. "Here's one for you, sir."

"Thanks," Lomax muttered. "Plain old Mark will do."

"You'll get a call sometime this morning," John told her, "but it will come from headquarters in Virginia, instead of from our new phones."

"Oh? How exciting." She smiled.

"Yes. It's only procedure, so don't worry too much. Whoever calls will probably direct you to destroy any receipts or other evidence that we've been here. My advice is to kindly do what they say."

"Whoa," she said. "You guys *must* be on important business."

"That's true," John said.

"Is there anything else?"

"Just one more thing," John said gently, trying his best not to frighten the woman. "They will in all likelihood ask you to sort of…forget the two of us were ever here. Understand?"

"I—I think so."

"All that means," Lomax blurted out, "is that you shouldn't tell any of your friends or co-workers that two CIA agents were here." He smiled at her—bashfully, John thought. "It doesn't mean you actually have to *forget* us."

The woman gave Lomax a warm smile. "Probably no chance of that happening." Now *she* had a glassy tint to her eyes.

Good grief, John thought.

He grabbed Lomax by one arm. "Let's go, partner, gotta move." He led Mark to the front of the store.

As they left the building, Lomax looked back. "Thanks again…", he looked at the back of the business card, where she had scribbled her name and phone number in a neat, slanting script. "Rita."

"You're quite welcome," she said, still smiling, and then the door closed and the two agents were on the sidewalk.

"What was all that about?" John asked him playfully. "You look lovestruck or something."

"Yeah?"

John shook his head. He knew how Lomax was feeling. He had, after all, felt and acted much the same way when he'd first met Lily. "Turn that thing on and give the director a call, Mark, before he gets anxious."

"Yeah, okay," Lomax said. He seemed to regain his professional composure, but John noticed that he still held the business card tightly in one hand. "Maybe the satellite is back online now, and they'll have the Malcolm's location."

"Well, we can hope," John said. But wasn't he also hoping that they *didn't* know? He thought he might be. He still could not, in his mind, tie the Malcolm child and violence together.

The sun glinted off the windshield of Kenneth Malcolm's car as the two men climbed in, John on the driver's side.

He started the car, put it in reverse, and then both men were suddenly sick, doubled over with the force of the nausea.

For John, it felt like a giant burp after he'd had too much of anything to drink—whether it be water, milk, or liquor—and some inevitably came back up. That is what happened this time. A small amount of coffee trickled out of his mouth, onto the front of his shirt.

Lomax was not so lucky; not with the big breakfast he'd eaten less than an hour earlier. The whole meal ended up in his lap, and on the floorboard between his feet, exiting his strained mouth at what looked like—to John—roughly the speed of sound.

When the cramps had passed, both men were breathing hard. They rolled down the windows for ventilation.

"The trackers," Lomax said between hitching breaths. "They'll locate those two men for sure, now. They have to be inside men, former agents, something. Let's go."

"Want to clean up a little first?"

As if on cue, the woman named Rita ran out of *Wireless World* with two towels in hand (John was at a loss as to where she might have gotten them—probably the restroom). "Oh, my. Are you guys okay? Oh, *my*." She ran to the passenger side and handed the towels to Mark through the window, turning her head away from the mess.

"Do you need some help? There's a restroom at the back of the store."

"That's okay," Lomax told her as he wiped his mouth with one towel and tossed the other to John. "We're in a hurry, but thanks. If it's okay…"

"You can keep them," she said. "Glad to help."

"We appreciate it," John said, wiping his own face and shirt, and then throwing the towel down between Lomax's feet, to help with the mess there. "We really do."

Lomax waved a hand at her as John backed the car out of the parking space. The agent had already turned the phone on and was going through the display menu. "Thanks again, Rita."

When he had pointed the car toward the road, John noticed that she was beaming at Lomax, and despite what had just happened, he saw that Mark still managed to return the smile. Then they called Virginia.

TWENTY-SIX

"Stay down," Darrel Malcolm said. "I'm backing up."
"What is it? What's wrong?"
"I don't know, but stay low."
"Okay."

He reversed out of the driveway, spinning gravel, although he didn't mean to. He didn't want the men in the other vehicle to think he was fleeing, even if that *was* what he was doing.

Surprisingly, the other car pulled into the driveway to his cabin as soon as he backed out of it. Although Darrel expected doors to start flying open and men to begin pursuing them—probably waving guns and hollering for them to 'halt'—that isn't what happened. As he backed down the road in the opposite direction from which the strange vehicle had arrived, he realized that a pursuit was not eminent. So far, at least.

"Shit," he said.
"What?" Voice alarmed.
"Nothing," Darrel said, trying to keep one eye on the vehicle and one on the rearview mirror. "There's a strange vehicle pulled into my driveway, official looking, but they aren't following us."

An audible breath of relief.

He backed into the closest turnout—a few hundred yards from his own—and then he sped down the gravel road toward the intersection where this road met another that led toward the river, checking his rearview approximately every two seconds. When he reached the intersection and turned left, he looked down from the mirror. "You can get up now."

From her cramped spot on the dusty passenger-side floorboard, Valerie Malcolm struggled up onto the seat.

"What kind of trouble is he in?" she said.

A clouded look crossed Darrel's face. That was a question for which he and Valerie had been searching for an answer since she had knocked on his door two nights ago. But that wasn't the reason he felt a sick, sinking sensation in his stomach; one of the three men in that car—if he had counted correctly—had looked familiar, and he could have sworn he'd caught a glimpse of another head, barely poking up above the back seat. A *small* head.

"I don't know what Ken's done," he said, "but whatever it is, I'm glad you came to my house instead of staying home waiting for him."

Valerie's only reply to this was an uneasy look, and Darrel couldn't blame her for that. He felt uneasy himself.

* * * * *

She had gone to Darrel Malcolm's house night before last for the simple reason that she didn't know where else to go. Her parents hadn't been home.

Ken and Chance had only been gone a few minutes when she had decided two things. The first was that something strange was going on, and the second was that, regardless of poor decisions Ken might have made in the past, she was going to do as he'd told her before he walked out the door.

Despite how outlandish Ken's patter had been—how senseless and strange it had seemed—his eyes had been nervous and afraid. Something was wrong.

It had only taken her a few moments to realize that he was running from something.

But what?

She packed a few clothes and personal items before making the short drive to her parents' house. She began to hurry, harboring a vague, uneasy feeling that she must, and that time was running out. Trusting her instincts—she was raised to believe that 'instinct' and 'inner voice' were synonymous—she left the house, locking up behind her, and did not feel any better until she'd merged off Woodsprings Road onto the 63 Bypass.

Then, of course, her parents hadn't been home. Valerie had gone as far as removing the spare key from beneath the big rock in the flower bed (where it had been since she was a teenager on her first date with a curfew later than ten o'clock, when her parents usually went to bed), and checked inside the house.

Nobody home. But that uneasy feeling remained, like a stubborn grease stain.

Not sure what to do, she had almost returned home.

Almost.

It was close. After sitting in her parents' driveway for a few minutes, her uneasiness growing, she decided to go to Darrel's house, despite the late hour.

It turned out to be the right decision, after all, though she didn't know it then. All she had known two nights ago was that something was wrong—terribly wrong. She just didn't know what.

Darrel Malcolm's house was dark and silent when she arrived, as she knew it would be. It was after eleven, and the whole neighborhood appeared to be tucked in for the night. Darrel answered the door after her third round of knocks, his white hair raised in tussled corkscrews, his eyes heavy with drowsiness, but alert.

"Valerie?" he said, then looked over her shoulders. "What's wrong? Where's Ken and Chance?"

"I don't know," Valerie said, turning around to glance quickly down the street in both directions. "Can I come in?"

Darrel backed up. "Sure. Sure." And now his face was clouded with worry.

Valerie went inside, where a single lamp illuminated a corner of the living room in a soft yellow light. She plopped down on the beige sofa. "I don't know," she repeated. She told Darrel what had happened at the house, what Ken had told her to do, and how she felt unsafe, as though running out of time. What surfaced in her mind as she talked was Ken's animated conversation with Chance on the back patio. After some consideration she told Darrel about that, as well.

Darrel hesitated before saying: "You don't think his behavior has anything to do with Jimmy, do you?"

Valerie shook her head. She had already thought about the incident that had revolved around Ken and his younger brother. She was even more familiar with the state of mind in which it had immersed her husband; the occasional bouts of depression, the periodic insomnia, the overwhelming feelings of guilt that no amount of comfort or encouragement could curtail. This was different, yet she wasn't sure just *how* it was different.

"It's more like…well…almost like someone is after him, like he's running from something."

"Or someone?" Darrel said.

"Yeah, like that. But I can't figure out for the life of me who it could be. He has no enemies. None that I know of, at least."

Darrel nodded his agreement. "Kenny's one of the good guys."

Valerie smiled in spite of herself. "Yeah, I guess he is."

"How about some coffee?" Darrel said. "It's all ready to go in there. All I have to do is flip a switch."

"Coffee would be nice."

"Okay." And he left to make it.

While he was gone, Valerie reflected that Ken *was* a good guy: sweet, gentle, kind, the man would do anything to make sure his family and friends were happy. She could think of no one, including Ken's co-workers at the bank—who were competitive, yes, but not violently so—who might 'have it in' for him.

Darrel returned in less than a minute. "It'll be ready in a jiffy."

"Thank you," Valerie said.

He sat in the worn armchair next to the sofa and rubbed his eyes. "I don't like this. It isn't like Ken to take off like this. And taking the baby with him…"

"I know," Valerie said. "If he was in some sort of trouble, or even if, God forbid, someone *was* after him, he wouldn't leave me by myself. He would have taken me with him. He's *very* protective. I don't think he would have left me in any danger." She paused a moment, and then said, "He didn't want me to stay at the house, that's for sure. Like it wasn't safe there, or something."

"Excuse me," Darrel said. He got up and went into the kitchen. Valerie could hear the minute click of coffee cups. When he returned he handed her a steaming mug.

"Thank you."

He sat back down, sipped his coffee, and said: "Do you still feel uncomfortable, as though you're running out of time?"

"Yes," Valerie said immediately, "but not as strongly as before. I don't know what to do. That's the worst part. And…I guess that's why I came here."

"And I'm glad you did," Darrel said. He took a long sip of coffee. "I've got an idea. Might not be brilliant, but…"

"What is it?"

"Well, I was planning on going up to the cabin in the morning, take me a long weekend, and read this new book I bought earlier today." He reached over and picked up a hard bound book from the end table between them. Valerie had not noticed the book lying there. The title on the front was *A Parapsychologist's Handbook to the Greater Supernatural Realm.*

Normally, Valerie would have frowned at the book. Now, curiously, looking at it caused an inner chill. She knew of Darrel's eccentric—to her, at least—belief in all things paranormal, and Ken had told her that the 'afterlife' was at the center of most of Darrel's beliefs. He occasionally told Ken of speaking with his long-lost wife, or of receiving psychic flashes from her. Ken hated that his father talked about his mother in this manner. Valerie knew that. She also knew Ken loved his father too much to ever say anything derogatory about it. "Let him grieve for her however makes him comfortable" is what he told Valerie on an occasion when the topic had come up.

"Do you think the cabin is safe?" Valerie said. She and Ken had borrowed the house in Hardy for several weeks a year over the course of their marriage, and Valerie loved it. She knew its remoteness was what Darrel was probably thinking of now.

"I can't think of a safer place," Darrel said. "We should go up there in the morning—"

"The *morning?*" Alarm in her voice.

Darrel raised a hand. "Hear me out, hear me out." He sipped his coffee. "Whoever Ken is running from, always assuming he is—which I think we have to—they are likely focused on *him*. I'm at a loss as to why he took Chance with him, but I don't believe they'll think to look for *you,* let alone in the small town of Bono. We should be safe here for a while."

"I can't figure why he took Chance, either," Valerie said.

"I think tonight we should gather what we'll need," Darrel continued. "You'll have to wear some of my old clothes if you need a change. I don't want to go back to your house on our way out."

"I've already packed a few things," Valerie said. The significance of what they were doing crept into her mind like a thief.

"After that, we should grab a few hours of sleep and leave early in the morning," Darrel said. He seemed to want to say something more, but

237

instead quietly took the last few sips of his coffee.

Valerie gave him a curious look: "What's your *real* reason for wanting to go up there, Darrel?"

The elder Malcolm set his empty cup on the end table. The book was still in his lap. "There are two reasons, really," he said, raising the book off his lap. "The first one is this." He thumbed the pages and they flapped with a muffled library sound.

"That…book?" Valerie was unable to keep a slight amount of distaste out of her voice.

"Not this particular book," Darrel said, as though sensing her discomfort, "but the paranormal in general. Some people might describe what I'm feeling as a hunch, or intuition, but I believe those emotions and feelings are psychic in nature, and that we all possess those, and other, paranormal powers. Most are just lying dormant, retained that way by society and the strict taboos, and religions, placed on anything it doesn't fully understand…or doesn't *want* to understand."

Valerie had to refrain from speaking what she felt. It would hurt Darrel if she told him that she thought all that 'paranormal' crap was just a bunch of hogwash, fit for the type of person who either couldn't—or didn't *want* to, to use his words—deal with reality on its own terms. If he had been a complete stranger she might have said as much, but Darrel was, all things aside, Ken's father. She thought she might understand—a little—his interest in such subjects, even though she believed he was being misled by whomever wrote and promoted such nonsense. Besides that, it wasn't like he was trying to convert her to his beliefs. He was only telling her why they should go to his cabin in Hardy: he was trying to *help* her, and she would gratefully let him. "What's the second reason?" she said.

Darrel leaned forward in his chair, eyes intense. "It's crossed my mind that Ken also might have thought of the cabin as a safe place to go, to get away from whoever is after him."

Valerie's mouth dropped open. She hadn't thought of that, and she told Darrel as much. It made sense, and she felt better about the situation than she had since leaving the house two hours ago. The thought that they might go up there and simply find Ken and Chance already there brought hope to her like a bright dawn. And yet, why hadn't Ken just called her, let her know he was okay, if not where he was going? Her cell phone was in her purse. Of course, knowing Ken, his was probably dead.

"Let's go with your plan, then."

"Okay," Darrel said, and together the two of them gathered items they would need—mostly food; his cabin had most other conveniences of home—and then settled in for a few hours of sleep.

Valerie slept on the sofa, under an afghan that Ken's mother had made years ago, and although she felt a little better about her missing husband and child, it took a long time for sleep to claim her.

* * * * *

They reached the turnoff of the paved road that led to the river, and Darrel said: "Still not following us."

He and Valerie had arrived at the cabin yesterday morning, hoping they would find Ken and Chance, but had been disappointed to find only an empty house, with no sign that they had been there. Since then, they had waited patiently for something to happen.

Nothing had, until today.

They had been leaving to go into town for more groceries when the vehicle pulled into the driveway.

"What do we do now?" Valerie said.

"I'm going to take us the long way around, up the mountain, and come down in front of the cabin, where we can get a better view of the place."

"Maybe we should just go into town and call the police." Her cell phone had died, and she had not remembered to pack the charger.

"That might not be a good idea."

"Why not?"

Darrel sighed and looked at her. "I'm pretty sure I saw Ken and Chance in that car."

* * * * *

TWENTY-SEVEN

The jet made a smooth landing and decelerated, its engines screaming with reverse thrust as it slowed to taxiing speed. Above Memphis International Airport, small gray clouds scudded across an early morning sky like summertime invaders.

The jumbo jet was owned by the Secret Service, and was used as one of three back-up planes to Air Force One, although the President was not onboard. Nor did the current White House resident have any knowledge that the plane was being used for the large operation being assembled by the CIA.

The Memphis Airport Authority had been given orders to have the plane directed away from the commercial flight terminals, to an outer edge of the facility, where three large National Guard trucks with canvas backs were waiting to pick up the flight's passengers. The CIA had also requisitioned two Guard trucks to carry equipment from Memphis' largest armory. The trucks and equipment had been dispatched and left at the airport, attended by a handful of weekend guardsmen, who had been informed that a large-scale drill would be taking place across the state line in Arkansas.

When the plane came to a stop and the passengers began disembarking onto the tarmac, the five guardsmen were relieved of duty and instructed to return to their weekend base. Over a hundred men dressed in full camouflage replaced them, and these men boarded the three trucks with quick efficiency. Although these personnel appeared to be Army soldiers, they were actually field agents hand-picked by Calhoun. They consisted of agents from the CIA, the Department of Defense, and the National Security Agency, and were being directed in a coordinated effort by the director, from Virginia.

President Ronnie Clayton currently knew nothing of the deployment, and orders were that any agent letting information leak back to him, or to his office, would be dealt with harshly. Hand-picked agents normally worked best in this regard, and this group had worked together before, and they could be trusted.

As was customary, all pertinent city officials in Memphis and the surrounding areas had been advised that maneuvers and drills would be conducted in the vicinity. Such exercises took place regularly in these, and other, areas on Sunday mornings, so it was a safe assumption that no alarm would be raised.

The small caravan had orders to proceed across the state line, into Arkansas, and to keep all lines of communication open, pending further orders. The city of Jonesboro was the rendezvous point in the event that particular city was reached before new orders—which were anticipated sometime during the next hour—arrived.

Most agents in the hastily assembled operation knew only that the mission was classified Top Secret, and a matter of national security, and that more information would be forthcoming. However, several agents and operatives knew the nature of the operation, or at least a portion thereof. Those 'in the know' were not thrilled with the mission's objective—capturing a fifteen-month-old child and terminating his father and anyone else with him—but all of them believed that the work must be important in some regard to the security of the country.

The small convoy of Army vehicles left the airport and began the eighty-mile trip to Jonesboro, Arkansas.

* * * * *

William Calhoun stood behind his desk at CIA headquarters, pacing back and forth as he talked with Mark Lomax who, along with agent Milcheck, had finally found a cellular phone. A device sitting atop the director's desk scrambled the incoming transmission, but because Lomax and Milcheck had lost their vehicle it was a crapshoot as to who might pick up what Calhoun told the agents. Therefore, he would have to be discreet and indirect in what he said on the half-open line.

What he felt like doing now—as he listened to agent Lomax apologize for not finding a cellular phone business that opened earlier than nine o'clock on a Sunday morning—was screaming. He was that frustrated.

Things were going well at the moment, but the hard truth was that they weren't progressing anywhere near perfect.

"I'll call you when the cat has cleared the fence," he said into the phone. "Stay put until then." He hung up the phone.

We didn't have enough time, he told himself, but it didn't help much. Under the circumstances, and in spite of the short time frame, he had handled things rather well. He knew that, but it still brought no comfort.

Damn that Clayton, he thought, and to make it unanimous, that train of thought—ta da!—brought no relief, either.

The trackers had been activated ten minutes ago, and the data he needed still hadn't shown up yet, although the locations of each carrier was being netted from the satellite transmission, just down the hall in DCAM. Calhoun had already made two trips down there, but had become frustrated at his perception of the lack of urgency and effort in the Data Collection and Management wing. "It's Sunday," one of the operatives there had told him a few minutes ago. "We're doing the best we can, but we are severely understaffed today."

Calhoun couldn't argue with that fact. His whole body trembled. He picked up a painted-rock paperweight and threw it across the room, where it promptly gouged a hole in the wallpaper. Plaster puffed up in a cloud from the sheet rock.

He couldn't, with any conviction, blame Lomax and Milcheck for the screw-up that had occurred. After all, he had sent both men to Arkansas knowing full well that Kenneth Malcolm had somehow found the listening devices in his home, and that the situation would undoubtedly be more dangerous than he had let on. Especially to agent Milcheck. He had put John in front as top agent on this leg of Project Lone Star without fully briefing the man, and for the life of him he couldn't believe he had made a mistake of that magnitude. In his younger days, he believed that an agent—any agent—should know exactly what he was getting into when receiving an assignment from headquarters.

He was troubled, in hindsight, that he had gone against his training, procedure, and his instincts.

Maybe it's time to call it in. Retire. Take it easy the rest of my life.

Right. He was only fooling himself with *that* nonsense—and to his credit he knew it. There were no activities even half-exciting, or as full of action, as the position he currently held. And nothing as worthy over which he commanded such control.

Which brought on another possibility; one he didn't like to think about, but which might be as close to the truth of the matter as anything he had contemplated during the past few days. Perhaps he, after all this time, was feeling guilty about Project Lone Star, and its prime—what? Prisoner? All things aside that's exactly what Lone Star was. Or Prometheus, as some at the Nevada compound called him. Who knew the guy's real name? Calhoun wondered if anyone had ever taken the time to actually ask him.

He shivered, then reached for the intercom button on his desk. "Anything yet?"

"Should be about five minutes more, sir. We just about got it."

"Great!" he said with false enthusiasm and released the button.

He rubbed his hands together. They were cold.

The other factor to consider in all of this—especially in light of his approaching retirement, which really was not that much farther in the future—was a couple of old standbys called 'going out in style', and 'winning the big battle'. In this business, morals often had to be cast aside. He had done his share, that was for sure, and there was no accountability involved—not from Uncle Sam's standpoint.

He tried to remember if he had *ever* let morals get in the way of what he deemed best for his country...and could not think of anything.

Is it like that, then?

He paced some more, looked at his watch.

He knew what the next step should be, although he was loath to do it. But he would. That, he also knew. The next step was calling up Derek Tarkington at the Nevada compound, getting their heads together, and coordinating the remainder of this fool's game from the place it began. It was time to bring the child home, to where he should have been kept from the beginning. Time to see what potential existed in the child.

And whether or not it could be duplicated. There was much potential there, but Calhoun believed the child had to be in the right hands.

The intercom buzzed and he pushed the button. "Yes?"

"We have a complete recovery of the data, sir."

"And?"

"We believe we know where the child is."

"Well, don't just sit there. Bring the results to me!"

In less than a minute, a young lady from DCAM knocked and entered the office. There was a small stack of printed material in her hands, which were trembling. She handed him the report and pointed with a pencil to a map of northeast Arkansas, which was on top of the pile. "These two marks are agents Milcheck and Lomax, and these two…" she moved her pencil west and slightly north. "these two marks belong to two agents who defected from the agency a year ago."

"O'Donnell and Templeton," Calhoun said.

"Yes, sir,"

"Good work," he said. "Milcheck and Lomax are close enough to begin looking for them. The convoy out of Memphis International should be arriving in Jonesboro any minute now. Get with Peter in dispatch and have him lead them to this area." He pointed at the two marks that represented the locations of O'Donnell and Templeton. It looked as though they had been marked on a river, in the northern part of the state.

He picked up the private line with the scrambling device attached, checked his watch, and placed a call to the compound in Nevada. Then he placed one to his secretary, so she could plan a trip for him to that desert complex.

* * * * *

Adrian O'Donnell and Bobby Templeton dry-heaved until nothing was left but grunts and strains, while Ken held Chance (he'd taken him out of his car seat) and looked toward his father's cabin. Clouds flittered across the sun's path, causing a play of light and shadow that, coupled with the surrounding trees, was almost stroboscopic.

"I don't believe it."

"What?" Adrian said, his face pale and waxy.

"That's my father's car. He doesn't drive the old Buick much anymore, but that's it. He must be here." Ken's relief was a facsimile of the relief visible on the other men's faces.

"At least it doesn't belong to our pursuers," Bobby Templeton said. He put the car in gear and drove the rest of the way to the cabin, approaching the tan Buick, which suddenly backed up onto the gravel road, spraying rocks.

"That's your father?" Adrian said.

Ken couldn't see because of the sun's reflection off the car's windshield. "It's got to be him."

Adrian said. "Do you think he'll mind if we use his cabin to set up this equipment? And we need to do it, fast."

"He won't care," Ken said as he and Chance got out of the car. "I'll talk to him when he comes back. He sure seemed in a hurry."

Adrian asked Ken in a low voice. "Does your father know about—?" He pointed to Chance.

"No,"

"Well then, at least he wasn't running from us. Are you *sure* he's not going to mind us being here, using his place?"

"I'm sure. Let me handle it. You just start unloading whatever it is you've got to unload."

"Okay." Adrian trotted over to the car, where Bobby was rooting through the trunk.

Ken unlocked the front door with the spare key his father kept hidden in the flowerbed. That done, he walked over and stood by Chance. He wished Valerie was here with him. He should have tried to call her before coming all the way up here.

When have you had time to even think, let alone call Valerie? Which was true. Valerie was probably home—which wasn't exactly the safest place to be, Ken supposed—but he had tried to get Bobby to go there early this morning, and the man had refused.

"Want to get the door for me, please?" Bobby said as he strolled by. His arms were full of equipment, and as he went inside he was careful not to trip over Chance.

Adrian brought the rest of the equipment, and Ken heard Bobby tell him, "We're not going to have much time."

"Okay," Ken said to himself. He held Chance's hand and looked at the empty road, thinking about Valerie, and about his father.

He wondered if he would live to see either of them again.

*****

TWENTY-EIGHT

Duke woke in a sweat, biting back a silent scream.

The low-wattage bulb in the cell cast an eerie glow over the room, which was at first unfamiliar to him. After a few minutes he had his bearings and he sat up on the moist bunk, breathing heavy and struggling to rid his mind of the slow-fading images.

It was the same dream that had often recurred over the past two years, and it painted a chilling picture of a dark reality: he had overheard his father and a small group of technicians and physicists conferring privately about a classified project. They were meeting in a small conference room, the door closed. Earlier in the day, one of the technicians had tasked Duke with retrieving three volumes for him from the library. Duke had forgotten the chore all through the morning. When he *did* remember, he had hurried to the library to get the books, certain that he was in big trouble for forgetting them. Full of dread, he had gone to the technician's lab, but the tech—a short, stocky man named Ted Raker—had not been there, nor in any of the outer offices.

Then Duke heard the voices, muffled by the closed door at the end of the room, and he had walked up to it, prepared to knock, apologize heavily, and give the man his books. But what he had heard as he approached the door caused him to stop: "Regina can't possibly give birth to sixteen babies, no matter how much you've been able to enlarge her womb." Duke didn't recognize the voice, but the voice that responded was his father's: "Sam, these are the only offspring we will ever see from this project, and you know it. To abort now would mean the end of the whole thing."

"What if we aborted all but one or two of the fetuses?"

"That's too risky. Each fetus is attached to the other, you know that." His father again. "We carry on as planned. When they are developed enough to survive outside the womb, we operate for removal and terminate Miss Hayward."

"But—"

"Is that understood?"

Duke had been appalled. Regina Hayward was a nice woman who lived on Level Four and worked in the cafeteria downstairs. She also helped educate the younger children in the compound—had, in fact, been one of Duke's tutors over the years. He had not seen Regina Hayward in several months, but that was not abnormal; he had completed his schooling and had moved on to other things.

With trembling hands, Duke opened the door to the conference room. His eyes darted among the men present, including his father. Then he yelled at them: "You *can't* kill Miss Hayward, you just *can't.*"

His father had looked at him, and said with a pronounced sadness: "Duke."

That one word evoked so much terror and fear that Duke turned and ran, out of the offices, down the corridor, screaming at the top of his lungs: *"Miss Hayward! They're going to kill Miss Hayward. Help! She's going to have sixteen babies and they're going to kill her. Help! Someone help!"*

Then Tim Flaugherty had stepped out of a lab, probably to see what all the racket was. "Duke? Duke, what's wrong?"

Babbling, Duke had repeated what he had heard. But before he finished his father was running down the corridor toward him, his face an angry mask. "Hold that boy, Flaugherty," he hollered. *"Hold him!"*

Then Duke was being pulled, dragged, and tugged into the lab from which Flaugherty had exited. "Hold the little shit still," his father told Flaugherty. "Hold him *now,* or I swear I'll end you."

And, of course, Flaugherty had held Duke down on one of the lab tables, and Duke had looked, wide-eyed, as his father pulled the big knife from the sheath on his belt and moved the blade toward his face. "I don't need squealers who put their ears where they shouldn't," Derek Tarkington told him, "and I'm going to make sure you can never squeal again. If you do, so help me God, I'll kill *you.* Then a different look had passed over his father's face—Duke often wondered if it was only so the man could keep a clear conscious—and he handed the knife to

Flaugherty. "Here, I'll hold him."

Next came the excruciating pain as his mouth was pried open and the blade inserted, too deeply at first, ending the use of his vocal cords. Then the strange feeling that the lower half of his face was just *gone*, and finally the coppery blood, threatening to choke him, to drown him.

And he would always awaken at that point, almost paralyzed with terror.

The dream was always so vivid. So lucid.

Sometimes he would awaken with one hand crammed into his mouth, feeling for the piece of flesh which was no longer there. For the first year after, he had cried bitterly after each dream.

Since he had become friends with Prometheus, however, the bitterness was no longer a side effect of the recurring dream-memories. With his friend's help and encouragement, Duke had learned to accept—and to live with—his handicap. But the dream still frequented his sleep on occasion, especially when he was under an unusual amount of stress or depression, a normal side-effect of living a lifestyle mostly underground.

He looked at his watch—a cartoon character whose arms counted the hours and minutes, and added further to the general perception that he was dumb or half-retarded, or both—and saw that it was nearly eight o'clock in the morning. Sunday, then.

The air was cool. His shirt clung to him like a wet towel and he shivered. He wondered how long he would be kept here.

And then a voice came into his head; clear, soft...and familiar.

Prometheus!

Duke didn't know how his friend could talk to him this way, when he was imprisoned in the room at the other end of Substation D, but it was definitely his voice—and it was very clear.

This had happened before, almost eighteen months ago, when Duke had still been struggling with the loss of his voice. He had been in his room, face-down on his bed, crying hot tears of loss and self-pity—loss for his father, and self-pity for himself and his painful inability to speak—when his new friend's voice had entered his head: *"You are strong, Duke. You can overcome this. You* will *overcome this. This, and much more. I will help you, my friend. I will help you..."*

He had raised his head, expecting to see Prometheus standing next to the bed, or perhaps sitting beside him.

There had been no one there, of course, and the voice didn't come again, but Duke was filled with profound feelings of peace and hope...and with wonder that he'd heard the voice at all.

He had mentioned it to Prometheus the following Saturday morning during their chess game, forming his question on a pad of paper. Prometheus had only smiled at him, his strange eyes gleaming. "Some mysteries are really not mysteries at all, Duke. Especially when you know in your heart—as you do—what, or why, something has transpired." A light chuckle, and then: "Oh, and by the way, my friend—checkmate."

Duke had felt nothing but hazy confusion about those words at the time—his mind relegating itself to the task of trying to figure out how he had, once again, been defeated at the wonderful board game—but since then he had discovered the true meaning behind them. He had been a happier person ever since that sunless Saturday morning; a feeling which had made him feel as though he was outside the compound basking in yellow warmth.

The voice which entered his head now was there and gone in a matter of seconds, but it still brought ensuing feelings of warmth and hope, and made him forget about the terrible dream. It caused him, instead, to wonder about the words themselves.

"Today, Duke. Everything. Today."

And then, four last words: *"Thank you, my friend."*

Although he had been fighting claustrophobia and fear of what his father might do, Duke now felt relaxed and at peace. He lay back on his small bunk, looked at the ceiling, and began to wait.

He did not know for what he was waiting but he knew that, whatever it might be, it was going to be something good.

It could be nothing *but* good.

* * * * *

"I want the Communications Center prepared immediately," Derek barked. He had just gotten off the private phone line with William Calhoun. The CIA director was preparing to make a... trip...to the compound, with the intention of working with Derek and his team, to handle the situation in northern Arkansas.

And it *was* a crisis—Derek saw that now.

He wasn't thrilled at the prospect of working so closely—at *his* facility—with Calhoun, but the man had briefed him on everything that happened last night and this morning, and Derek saw right away that every aspect of the situation had developed the way it had because of the satellite malfunction. And that belonged to him.

All he had been able to say to Calhoun, in light of this realization, was the one thing he and the director had *ever* agreed on: that the child should have never been allowed to be a part of civilian life; that he should have been kept at the compound at all costs.

Yet what was done, was done (he knew that, as well). What happened from here on out would be risky—and Calhoun sending men from so many agencies to Arkansas to assist in the capture was *very* risky, indeed (another point of disagreement)—but at least President Clayton's nose wouldn't be stuck in the middle of things, and Derek would have *some* input and control over events. In light of the screw-up with his satellite system, that was probably more than he could have hoped for.

Flaugherty knocked and entered the office, looking nervous and uncomfortable. "I spoke with Ted Raker by radio, sir. Communications will be ready in less than an hour."

"The equipment?"

"All available PC's and flat-panels will be set up shortly, along with your back-up monitor for the…um…trackers."

"Good," Derek said. "I don't want Calhoun even *thinking* that we aren't prepared to handle this situation. Because we *are,* and I'll be damned if I give up *any* portion of Project Lone Star again." He seemed to consider something. "And I don't like that bastard using the PTP for travel, even if it *is* an emergency. He knows that damn thing is still not one hundred percent safe."

"Yes, sir."

"It's bad enough that we lost Lone Star's child to the likes of the CIA in the first place, but it's even worse to think that it was all because of the bureaucratic bullshit this facility is supposed to be shielded from."

"Sir?" Flaugherty said.

"What?"

"Uh—well, I was wondering…what do you plan to do about Duke? The satellite malfunction?"

Derek turned on Flaugherty, cat-quick. "Why do you worry so much about Duke?" he spat. "Do you harbor some perverse pleasure that is only satisfied by teasing and torturing my son?"

Flaugherty's faced paled. "Sir, I didn't mean—"

"I know exactly what you meant, so just shut your mouth for a minute." Derek rubbed his chin with one hand. Then he cocked his head quizzically. "Tim, do you have any idea how important Project Lone Star is, or how imperative it is for us to capture that child? Do you have any *inkling* what this project is all about?"

Flaugherty kept quiet and shuffled his feet.

"You have been involved with this project for years. *Years*. But it's apparent that you don't get it. You comprehend *nothing* about Lone Star by your actions. You are intelligent, trustworthy, and loyal, yes, but for some reason you have your priorities all mixed up. Why is that? Huh?"

Flaugherty, visibly shaken, opened his mouth to speak, closed it, then finally managed to talk. "Sir…uh, I have always taken pride in my work here, and in having my priorities lined up in the correct order. Um—by asking you about the situation with your, uh, son…I had no intention of lessening the high priority demanded of me by Project Lone Star. I only meant—"

"Situation?" Derek interjected. "So, now there's a situation with Duke? That boy is *locked up*, Flaugherty. I see no immediate crisis, *or* situation, in that. And as for him being locked up, might I ask you *why*? What *exactly*, did that boy do to the satellite, and more importantly, *how* did he do it?" He looked Tim Flaugherty up and down with some distaste. "Have you totally lost your mind?"

"Sir, I don't understand. I just—"

"Do you actually think that Duke is smart enough to crack a satellite surveillance computer for which only two men know the security codes?"

"Well, I'm not certain that he *couldn't*, sir. I only know that my gut feeling is that he somehow managed to do just that."

Derek said: "You and I are the only two personnel in this whole facility who have those codes. Did *you* give him the codes?"

A look of shocked horror spread over Flaugherty's face. "Absolutely *not*."

"Well, I didn't, either, so where did the boy get them? Hmm?"

Flaugherty fidgeted some more. The ticking of the clock on the wall above Derek's desk was the only sound for several seconds as the men stared at each other. Finally, Flaugherty dropped his gaze and looked at his hands. "Derek, I apologize for sounding out of place here, but I think a more thorough investigation of Duke should be carried out." He held up a hand when Derek started to speak. "Please, sir. If you would allow me to finish."

Derek nodded. "Go ahead."

"When the security breach with the satellite happened, Duke was in the corridor outside his room. I know I've told you that much, but something else occurred to me earlier this morning, something that I hadn't considered."

"And what might that be?" Derek said, his interest piqued despite his earlier rantings.

"The codes for that system," Flaugherty said.

"Go on."

"There is no way—in *my* mind, anyway—that Duke Tarkington could commit to memory a numeric code of that length, *and* know to hit the 'enter' key after the correct sequences of numbers. 'Enter' has to be keyed three times, each time after a different sequence of numbers, for the codes to even work."

"Shit," Derek said. He didn't like what he was hearing. Not one bit.

"A person might be able to commit the numbers in the code to memory—*might*—but unless he knows after which numbers to key the 'enter' button, the code itself is useless. And then there's the fact that the same system was set up by a clock timer to come back online, by the same person who did it—with a totally different code. And you and I, sir, are the only two in possession of *those* codes, as well." Flaugherty looked at Derek, not triumphantly, but with a confidence he lacked moments ago.

Derek was silent for a short period, thinking, and then he said. "I think what you're getting at, Tim, is that Duke had to have the information written down somewhere, and if he did…"

"I never *checked* him," Flaugherty blurted out. "That's what I'm saying, sir. I never so much as checked a single stitch of his clothing, his shoes—nothing."

Derek looked at his watch. It was a little past nine-thirty. "Since we have a few minutes before Calhoun arrives, why don't we do this? You go to the holding cell, check Duke's pockets, shoes, wherever you think you have to look. I don't believe you'll turn up anything, but you were right to suggest it. If the boy did it, then it's the only way he could have pulled it off."

"I'll take care of it right now." Flaugherty turned to leave.

"Tim?"

He turned around. "Sir?"

"Two things. If you *do* find the codes on him, I want you to bring him directly here. No detours, return immediately to this office."

"Yes, sir. And the other?"

Derek's eyes hardened. "If you *do* bring him back with you...the codes had better not be in your handwriting."

Flaugherty swallowed, his throat bobbing. "Yes, sir." He left, pulling the door closed behind him.

Derek walked across the room and began to glean the printouts on his desk. They contained data from the recently activated trackers, and had been sent here from Calhoun's office. Derek looked through them while he waited for the arrival of the CIA director, and for the return of Tim Flaugherty.

He began to wonder if Flaugherty would return alone, or with his son in tow.

Derek surprised himself by hoping for the former.

* * * * *

The outer door to the cellblock clanked against the wall as if thrown open, startling Duke out of his pleasant thoughts. He sat up, rubbed his eyes. Footsteps, quick and heavy, came toward his small cell, and he couldn't stop fear from stealing over him like a silent mist. His father must have had a change of heart, and had decided to punish him. What else could it be?

But it wasn't his father. When the person strode into view, Duke saw with a sinking feeling in his stomach that it was Tim Flaugherty.

Worse yet, Flaugherty was grinning, a curiously triumphant smile that stretched impossibly far across his long face.

"Hello, Duke," he said, and Duke saw a secret knowledge in the man's eyes, the meaning of which he could not even guess.

Flaugherty reached into a pants pocket, fished around, and pulled out a key. Duke didn't believe the man had come down here to let him out. He wished he could ask what the man wanted.

Flaugherty wiggled the key into the slot in the door, and when he glanced up Duke raised his eyebrows in a question.

"I forgot something when I brought you here last night."

Duke pulled in a big breath and nodded, then watched as Flaugherty swung the door open and stepped into the cell, seeming to tower over him, although the man was only four inches taller. The door clicked shut behind him, and he took two steps, until he was only inches from Duke.

"Empty your pockets, Duke," he said. "Back first, then the ones in front."

Duke looked up at the man, and sudden understanding filled him. It was the note that Flaugherty was after. The note from Prometheus, which also contained the security codes for the satellite system, proof of Duke's part in the sabotage. His heart sank. He had put the folded not in his left-front pocket. With a trembling hand, he reached back and pulled his wallet from one hip pocket, his comb and ink pen from the other. He held these items out for Flaugherty's inspection.

"That all back there?"

Duke nodded.

"Let's just make sure, then." Flaugherty grabbed Duke, spun him around, and patted his hip pockets with the palm of one hand. Then he poked a finger into each, sweeping the material and coming up empty. After going through the wallet, he tossed it onto the bunk with the comb and pen.

"Okay, now the front."

This is it, Duke thought. *This is it.*

He emptied his right pocket first. It was empty except for a small ball of lint, but Flaugherty swept it with a couple of fingers, anyway.

"One more, Duke," Flaugherty said in a voice which, this time, *did* sound triumphant. The shark-like grin was back also, white and savage.

Duke moved his left hand toward the pocket...then pushed forward as hard as he could, pushing with his feet, hoping to slam the larger man into the bars of the cell.

Flaugherty grunted, but stiffened when Duke connected with him, as though he had been anticipating something like this all along. Duke felt something heavy—like a large rock—strike his abdomen, and pent-up air rushed from his mouth with a *pah!* sound.

The man drew back his closed fist. Duke flinched backward, his face lined with pain, his lungs deflated and unable to draw air. "Shall we do it again?" Flaugherty said, breathing in quick bursts that could probably be attributed more to rage or anger than to physical exertion.

Duke was finally able to draw some air into his scorched lungs, then a little more, until he was able to gag like a normal man. But he also looked up and shook his head.

"Good, then," Flaugherty said, lowering his fist. "Now. The left pocket, please. If you don't empty it, *right now*, then we're going to have us some major problems here, and I am *not* in the mood for any more problems out of you. Do you understand me?"

Trying to breath normal again, trying equally as hard to ignore the ball of fire in his midsection, Duke nodded and stood up as straight as possible. He couldn't believe it had turned out like this. Flaugherty would give the note to his father, who would read it and understand right away that Prometheus was involved, and that he planned to be with his son soon—that he planned to escape.

Duke had failed him this time for sure. Why hadn't he just torn the stupid thing into pieces and flushed them down the toilet or something?

Trembling with both fear and pain, Duke delved his hand into his left-front pocket and pulled out the only item there—the folded note from his friend.

Before he got it all the way out, Flaugherty snatched it. "Stay right there," he said, backing toward the door.

Duke could only watch as the man read the note to himself, moving his lips.

When he finished, he glared at Duke with eyes that looked fiery with hatred. "Just what in the hell is *this?*" He crumpled the paper into a ball and threw it at Duke, who ducked. The wad of paper landed at his feet.

Duke looked up. Flaugherty had reached through the bars and was opening the cell door with his key. It clicked open and he walked out of the cell and closed the door as though in a hurry. He started to walk away, huffed once with what could only be disgust or frustration, then came back to the cell. "You just think you're *so-o-o* smart, don't you?"

Duke was perplexed. He looked down. The note was still at his feet, and he bent to retrieve it. He smoothed the creases of the wad of paper, then read it while Flaugherty glared at him through the bars, as though he were the one imprisoned behind them.

> When you're looking for something that you are certain is there, might I humbly suggest that you look…elsewhere? Have a nice day!

Duke read the note again, trying hard to hide the disbelief he felt. Also trying hard not to crack a smile. He looked at Flaugherty, who pointed a finger at him as he walked backward, away from the cell and toward the outer door. "This isn't over, you stupid egghead. I don't know what you're trying to do here, but this is *not* over."

He stormed out and the cell block door clanged shut behind him.

Duke looked at the note again, relieved and mystified, and discovered that he wanted to know the same thing Tim Flaugherty did: *What is going on here?*

He sat back on his bunk, holding the note in his hands, trying to convince himself it said what it did—that it was real. After a moment, he began to smile.

Then he re-read the note and began to laugh.

* * * * *

TWENTY-NINE

Darrel Malcolm's cabin sat in a wooded clearing forty yards off the gravel road, on a rocky piece of land that sloped downhill toward the back of the property, which was marked by a natural valley in the side of the small mountain. The surrounding woods pressed close to each side of the cleared part of the lot on which the house sat, except for the front, where trees had been cleared in a larger swath to accommodate the driveway and create a rocky front yard.

The cabin resembled a house more than it did a cabin; it was not made from logs cleared from the land, but was instead built like any other home, with wood purchased at a lumberyard. The light brown siding was not packed together with mud and dirt, and the deck—which was attached to the rear of the house and ran the entire length—was made of four by sixes, two by fours, and four by fours, and not raw timber. Yet the place *looked* like a cabin, and Ken's family had always called it that.

Inside, Bobby had finished setting up the equipment. Ken had moved the small kitchen table into the living room, where there was more room in which to work. A stone fireplace and vaulted ceiling provided a cozy feeling of comfort. Sliding glass doors leading out to the deck permitted ample light into the room, while providing a location from which to watch the rear half of the property. Adrian stood at these doors, scanning the lot and surrounding woods.

"How much longer, Bobby?" he said.

Bobby was using one of the laptop computers, deftly tapping the keys. A phone line ran from a nearby wall into an external modem on the right side of the machine. "Hard to tell right now. I have to go through the agency's system first, but I think I can access the right satellite. We really lucked out by taking their car and getting this equipment."

"You're going to have to hurry."

"I know." Bobby went back to work.

On the sofa behind this makeshift workstation, Ken rubbed his hands together and Chance sat beside him, holding his teddy bear and looking toward the sliding glass doors where Adrian kept watch.

"Can you guys tell me some more about all this? About Chance?"

Both men turned around, but it was Adrian who answered. "I guess we can," he said. "I'll tell you what I can while Bobby works on buying us some more time." He came over and sat beside Chance.

"I've told you about the accident, right?"

"Yes," Ken said. "and the reporter, and President Clayton." His laugh was nervous and light. "I'm still having a hard time believing just that much."

"I understand, but it *is* true. Chance's natural father resides at a secret government compound in Nevada, under the code name Lone Star. Bobby and I worked for the CIA, but we were moved to that agency only after the accident with Chance's birth mother. We initially lived and worked at this desert compound.

"The man in charge there is a man named Derek Tarkington. He has lived at the compound his entire life, and he gained control of the facility after his father died. Derek was greatly opposed to the adoption process the president was pushing, and he wanted to place some of his own men within the ranks of the CIA. That agency was indirectly involved in the project early on, and it was much better equipped to handle a covert surveillance of Lone Star's offspring. Work at the compound had to continue in spite of everything else."

"What kind of work?" Ken said.

"Experiments mostly, and tests. New technological advances, innovations in weaponry, gene splicing, DNA and genetic studies—you name it. And everything accomplished there—everything *still* being done—had its beginnings with Chance's father. Everything is a result of Lone Star."

"You can say that again," Bobby said without turning away from his work.

"So how come you two left the CIA? I know you wanted to monitor my son, but wasn't that already being done?"

"Yes, it was," Adrian said. "but it was being done for the wrong reasons, and both Bobby and I knew it. This child," he looked at Chance and smiled. "This child cannot be forced to live his entire life at the compound, subjected to the rigorous tests and obscenities that his father has had to endure—"

"My father only wanted to help," Chance said, setting the teddy bear down. "He has helped already, and he *still* wants to help, but…"

"But they are slowly killing him, right?" Adrian supplied, and Chance nodded.

"We know that, Chance, and that's why we're here. Bobby, myself, a few others, we all know that." He looked up at Ken. "and we have to stop it. We have to protect this child, and we have to expose Lone Star, and everything he represents, to the world."

"I don't understand," Ken said.

"Everything in our planet's recent history has led up to this," Adrian said. "and it's time everyone knew."

Chance smiled then and looked at Adrian O'Donnell. "Yes," he said. "Today."

Ken looked at his son, not knowing what to say.

"*Got it*," Bobby yelled out. He leaned back and ran a trembling hand through his hair. "I *got* that sucker!"

"Are we clear, then?" Adrian said.

"Just about. I've accessed the satellite used to activate the trackers. Now I'm going to confuse it by giving false coordinates for every tracker in existence. I should have a grid on here shortly marking each device."

"Good deal," Adrian said. "Just do it before they activate them again."

The laptop beeped. "Here we are," Bobby said. "Let's see…wait a minute." He tapped the keys rapidly. "Oh, no…oh, shit."

"What?" Ken said, alarmed. He and Adrian rose from the sofa at the same time to look at Bobby's computer. "What is it?"

Bobby pointed at the screen, where a map of the middle third of the United States was displayed on a black background, with green boundary lines. Red spots dotted the map in various places. "The red dots represent the locations of agents carrying the trackers. I'm going to zoom in another twenty-five percent over the top half of the state."

"Good lord," Adrian said. "Is this thing right?"

"I'm afraid so." Bobby backed away from the screen so they all could see, as the screen finished displaying the enlarged image.

Chance toddled over, and Ken bent and picked him up without taking his eyes from the screen. He held the child close, hoping to comfort him, and then realized that he had also done it to comfort himself. "Oh, boy," he whispered.

On the screen, in an area of the map depicting northern and northeastern Arkansas, in the vicinity of Jonesboro, was a thick cluster of red dots.

"How many, can you tell?" Adrian said.

Bobby sighed. "At least fifty, probably more."

"Damn!"

"See these two dots here?" Bobby pointed west and north. "That's us. And these two here," he trailed his finger down and slightly east, about midway between Hardy and Jonesboro. "These two are probably the agents who found us at the house last night."

"So they're close," Ken said.

"Very close," Bobby said, "but that's not the worst thing."

"What could possibly be worse than this?"

"It's been thirty minutes or more since the trackers were last activated. I can change our coordinates, but we were only fifty yards or so from the cabin when these locations were entered into the databases at the CIA. They will already have this location pinpointed, and they will check it out no matter where I place our coordinates."

"Then we're screwed?" Adrian said.

"Probably," Bobby said, resignation in his voice. Then he said something which made them all look at the screen and wonder: "If they activate the trackers again, how much closer will this cluster of red dots be to Hardy? To our location here?"

* * * * *

John and Mark entered Hardy a little after eleven o'clock. Traffic in the downtown area was heavy, moving at a slow crawl. Tufts of gray clouds were at war with blue patches of sky and sunshine.

"Can't these people move any faster?" Lomax said from the passenger seat.

"The speed limit is fifteen," John said, "and I don't know about you, but I'm not in a hurry to rush into this thing before our backup gets here."

"We're not *going* to rush in," Lomax said. "Calhoun said to wait at that beach club place and keep our eyes open. Nothing dangerous in that. I just want to get there."

"And that's where the data from the trackers showed them to be?"

"Yeah, almost right on the water. But that could change when they call us back with information from the second activation."

"Which I hope was the last one," John muttered. They had been at a small rest area just west of the town of Black Rock, using the bathroom facilities, when the trackers had been activated for the second time. John had cramped painfully with the dry heaves, but Lomax had apparently saved some of his breakfast, because he lost the rest—though not as much as before—to one of the porcelain sinks.

"They'll probably have to utilize the trackers at least once more," Lomax said, "but hopefully no more than that." He chuckled. "Oh, man. As bad as that made me feel, think about all those agents and soldiers on their way from Memphis International. Calhoun said it was a hundred men in three trucks. I bet *that* was a scene."

"I thought he told you there were only thirty CIA agents?" John said. "Every man wouldn't get sick, would they?"

"No, but I bet some did after the affected agents did. Being in a confined space like that..."

"I get the picture," John said. "Thanks for the image. Now if you don't mind tell me which way to go up here."

They exited Hardy Old Town and when the road curved to the right, John saw another highway on the left, across from a *McDonalds* restaurant.

Lomax consulted the map that lay across his knees. "We go left here and a couple miles after that we should hit Spring River Beach Club, on the right."

"Good." John slowed, turned left, and in a few minutes slowed again when he saw signs for the beach club.

The road wound past cabins, swimming pools, and other recreational areas, and John drove slowly, mindful of the abundance of pedestrians and children, all of whom were involved in outdoor activities.

A steep incline brought them to the crest of a hill. The river sparkled on their right. "Turn here," Lomax said, folding the map and tucking it between his seat and the console.

John maneuvered the car down a steep hill, then across a one-lane cement bridge which spanned the river. A few men and young boys stood on the narrow, rail-less structure, fishing poles in hand, casting lines into the swift water. "Beautiful," John said.

"Let's just get across this thing without hitting anybody or driving off the side," Lomax said.

There was a playground and a parking area to the left immediately across the bridge, and he pulled the car in and parked where they could see both the bridge and the road leading down to it. "This good enough?"

"Should be," Lomax said. "I think this is the area they were in when the trackers were activated."

"Then we should be close."

"I know we are," Lomax said. "I can feel it, can't you?"

John could feel *something*, but he wasn't sure it was merely a close proximity to Kenneth Malcolm and his son. Instead, he was bothered by a nagging feeling that something immense was going to happen—and soon; something far larger and more important than this crazy assignment about which he still knew so little. "I don't know what I feel," he told Lomax, "but I *do* know that I'm going to get out and stretch my legs."

They got out of the car, Lomax carrying his cellular phone, and walked over to one of several picnic tables. A few children frolicked in the water, and at the river's edge, watched over by adults either in the water with them or sitting in lawn chairs and on picnic benches.

"So," John said as the two men sat down. "Are you going to call this cellphone queen…this Rita?" He smiled so Mark would know he meant it to be nothing more than the light joke it was.

"You know," Lomax said, "I actually might. Once all of this is over, anyway." He smiled boyishly, and John once again glimpsed an honorable man beneath the smile. "She *was* pretty, wasn't she?"

"Can't argue with you there," John said.

Lomax picked up a rock and threw it into the river, away from the children. "What about you? I noticed your ring. Married?"

"No," John said. "I just…she died."

"Oh. Sorry."

"It's okay. It was a long time ago."

Not that long ago, his mind protested. And that was true. But how could he tell his partner that Lily was dead because he—John—had killed her husband? Garret Burgess had been smarter than either he or Lily had credited him. He had vowed that Lily belonged to him, and no other, and had made related arrangements in the event he died before her: *if she ever fell in love and married someone else, the contract would be carried out two months after her wedding, when Garret judged she would be at her most happiest.* John might have pulled the trigger on Garret Burgess, but Garret—and by association, John—had pulled the trigger on Lily. From the grave, he had done that.

John shook his head. This wasn't the place for that kind of thinking.

"I hope we hear something soon," Mark said as he threw another rock into the water.

John looked out at the rolling water and the steep wooded hills on either side. "We will," he said in a low voice. "Something…"

The river churned and chuckled soothingly, in a voice all its own, but John only heard the memories of Lily's panicked cries…and his own screams.

Would his mind ever quit?

* * * * *

THIRTY

The Particle Transmission Portal was at a nearby Air Force base in eastern Nevada. It's lone arriving passenger boarded a waiting helicopter and from there was flown to the edge of a nearby desert, at the base of a small mountain range. The wind from the rotors slung dust and sand in swirling gusts. The pilot slowed the rotation of the rotors and then opened a side door, letting in a burst of heated air.

William Calhoun, carrying only a briefcase, exited the craft, head ducked low, and ran toward the desert-camouflaged jeep parked twenty yards away. He threw his briefcase on the back seat and climbed in.

"Any problems on the trip, Director?" Derek Tarkington said, holding out a hand.

Calhoun shook it absently. "Other than it taking too long, no."

Tarkington laughed and put the jeep in gear. Behind them, the helicopter departed with a chopping roar.

"I didn't expect you to come out yourself," Calhoun said.

"I was going to send an associate, but to tell the truth I haven't been out in a few weeks and I thought the sunshine and fresh air might do me some good."

"I see," Calhoun said, looking at Derek's pale skin and wondering how anyone could live the way he did. "Is everything ready?"

"We are always prepared here, Director." Derek's grin was broad, showing most of his teeth. "If I could, I will also add that it looks as though our missing child is holed up in the same area he was earlier. I hardly think all those agents and soldiers you sent—"

"Always assuming the child is still *with* those two flunkies," Calhoun interjected.

"Of course," Derek said. They neared the mountain, where a bay door opened for their arrival. "But I think we both know he is. O'Donnell and Templeton will not let the child out of their sight, now that they have him."

"What makes you so sure of that?"

Derek looked at him with hard eyes. "Would *you*, if you were them?"

"I suppose not," Calhoun said in a lower voice.

"All I'm saying, Director, is that the deployment of so many personnel seems a little high-risk."

Calhoun huffed. "Considering the irony of your satellite malfunctioning at the precise moment the child disappeared, I think I made the right call. We can't take even the slightest chance with this crisis. O'Donnell and Templeton are not stupid. You know that as well as anyone. And we *must* capture the child so we can—"

"Bring him back here," Derek interjected. "where he belongs."

"At least we agree on that," Calhoun said. "And how is Lone Star?"

"Same as usual. A highly intelligent and capable subject about whom we can't really complain, given his nature." He looked across at Calhoun. "I think we're wearing him down, though. Burning him out."

"Why do you think that?"

"Something about him is…different. I can't really put my finger on it. His usefulness to us may be nearing its end, hard as that is to imagine. Perhaps the difference I see in him is merely his awareness of that possibility. Hmm?"

Calhoun stared at him, speechless. This man was crazier than he had always thought.

They entered the compound and the mountain swallowed them.

* * * * *

The Communications Center on Substation C was a hive of activity, with technicians at every monitor and others buzzing from station to station, carrying clipboards and recording incoming data on charts and hand-held computers.

Derek swept an arm in front of him as they entered the room. "Suitable enough, I would hope?"

Calhoun didn't answer, but instead walked over to the nearest monitor, which showed red dots on a map of the state of Arkansas. "How long has it been since activation?" he asked the curly haired man sitting in front of the terminal.

The man looked up and recognition lit his eyes. "Just over two hours, sir."

Calhoun pointed at the two dots near Spring River. "Any chance that these two have changed position in that time?"

"Not really, sir," the technician said. "Satellite reconnaissance shows only one conventional route off that mountain, and that it through a small resort. Which is most likely the way they went in."

Calhoun turned back to Derek. "Can we keep that road watched?"

"It's being done already."

"And agents Milcheck and Lomax?"

"Agent Lomax phoned your office a short time ago, and the call was forwarded here. He and agent Milcheck are already at this Spring River, on the only road going onto the mountain. I also contacted your other deployment of agents, who were waiting in the city of Jonesboro, and directed them to that location. They should be arriving there within a half-hour or so."

"Good." Calhoun looked around the room, trying to think of anything else of which he might need to be made aware. "I suppose all there is to do then is to wait until the backup arrives. Then we'll have them converge onto the mountain in a wide sweep." He looked at Derek and forced a small smile. "I think we'll have them by early afternoon."

* * * * *

Derek left Calhoun in Communications and went back to his office. For now, the director was doing no harm. Every task being done had been ordered by Derek, and would remain so. If Calhoun suggested or decided something that disagreed with Derek, he would take whatever action was necessary to convince the director his way was right.

He traced a finger along the outline of the handgun holstered beneath his field jacket. It was the same weapon he had used to shoot the two potential investors.

Calhoun was getting on up there in years, close to retirement age for sure. Derek thought: *And if he shows me by his actions that an early retirement might be in his best interests, I will gladly see that he gets it.*

Derek Tarkington grinned.

* * * * *

Around noon of that day, the muffled click of an opening door brought Duke out of a light sleep which was void of any bad dreams. His mind was groggy but he was still able to assume, from the moment he woke, that Flaugherty had come to extract revenge for the strange note. He could picture the man—clear as day, in his mind—strolling up to the cell, pointing a gun through the bars, and pulling the trigger until every bullet was expended. They would find Duke crumpled in the cell, blood spilled around him in a thickening pool.

He heard footsteps whisper up the short hall to the cell; soft, cautious.

Before he could decide what to make of the sound—before his mind could even convince him that it was indeed Flaugherty approaching—a man stepped into view in front of the door.

"Hello, Duke." A low, soft-timbered voice.

Duke squinted in confusion. *Tyler?*

It was Tyler James. The librarian moved to the side as another young man stepped forward, smiling. "Hey, Duke."

Lucas Matthews, who sat at Duke's table at mealtimes—along with Tyler—was twenty, with blond curls topping a freckled face that belied his age and made him look younger. He raised a finger to him mouth—"sh-h-h"—and looked back the way they had come.

Duke signed: "What are you guys doing here? Flaugherty might be back any time."

Tyler smiled at Duke. "Tim is going to be busy for a while. He kind of had a little accident in his quarters. Busted water line."

"Yeah," Lucas chimed in. "Son-of-a-bitch flooded the place. Water everywhere, all over his shag carpets."

Duke giggled, a sound that was like a hoarse whisper. "No kidding?" he signed.

"True story," Tyler said, "but that's not the best part."

"It's not?" Duke thought it was pretty funny.

"No, the best part is that we've come to get you out of here."

"What? How did you know I was here?" Duke signed.

Tyler relayed the question to Lucas, who said: "Remember the other night, when Flaugherty was chasing you around upstairs?"

Duke nodded. Actually, he didn't think he would ever forget.

"Remember when he tripped and fell?"

Again, Duke nodded. That had been the only reason he'd managed to get away at the time.

"That was *me*," Lucas said. "I just stuck out my foot and, wham, down he went, right on his ugly face." He laughed softly. "Man, that was the coolest thing I've ever seen."

Tyler was smiling, but his face was nevertheless serious. "We need your help, Duke. *Prometheus* needs your help. He needs help from all of us."

"Prometheus? But—"

"Did you think you were his only friend here?" Tyler said.

Duke thought again of the voice that had entered his head all those months ago, when he'd been lying on his bed, crying: *You are not alone here, Duke. You are not alone.*

He shivered. "How did you know?"

"Duke," Tyler said patiently. "Remember the other night, in the library? You found a note in the book you were reading. A note from Prometheus."

"Yes. But I was reading the book before you started your shift. It had to have already been in there."

"It was," Tyler said. "I put it in there the day before. It was a Koontz book, *Cold Fire*."

"But I didn't know I was going to read it until I pulled it off the shelf."

"No, but *he* knew, Duke. Do you see? *He* knew."

Duke could only look at the two men, his mind vapor-locked.

Tyler reached into his pocket and pulled out a key. He inserted it into the lock and looked at Duke. "With that note, with what you did to the satellite, we helped his son." He turned the key and swung open the cell door.

"But it wasn't enough," Lucas added. "He says the child is in trouble again, and that he must escape this time in order to help him. Today."

Today, Duke. Everything. Today.

"Help us?" Tyler said, holding the cell door open.

Duke nodded eagerly.

"Then let's be quick about it."

Duke closed the cell door behind him, and the three of them walked toward the door, the corridor, and Prometheus.

"The first thing we need to do," Tyler said, "is find a way around the hydrabeams. Lucas thinks he knows how it can be done…"

THIRTY-ONE

The computer screen still showed the black and green map interspersed with red dots, but no one sat in front of it. A radio was turned low in one of the back bedrooms where Chance Malcolm lay sleeping. Ken had fed and changed him, and Chance had corked a thumb in his mouth and went promptly to sleep. Ken, Bobby, and Adrian were outside on the deck, sitting in lawn chairs and drinking from cans of beer Ken had found in the refrigerator.

Tired of running, seeing reluctantly that there didn't seem to be any other options, they had relegated themselves to waiting for whatever would come next. Adrian had used up all his ammunition at the house in Paragould, so his empty handgun was useless to them.

Because Darrel Malcolm used the cabin while he hunted up here in the winters, Ken hoped that they would find a gun or two in the closet of his father's bedroom. He *had* found one: a small twenty-two caliber rifle that Darrel used for taking shots at squirrels or black-birds from the deck. Now the gun lay on the table in front of them, holding all of two rounds. It was better than nothing at all.

"So, let's hear it," Ken said. "Even if there isn't much time left, I want to know everything."

Adrian cleared his throat. "We don't know *everything*, Ken, but we know enough. All I ask is that you don't let skepticism get in the way of the truth. Hear us out, and then take it all however you want." He jerked a thumb over his shoulder. But remember who is asleep in there. That's also important.

"Fair enough," Ken said. He emptied his beer and pulled another from the six-pack that sat on the round picnic table. He looked through the trees at the sky, where thinning clouds gave way to a ceiling of deep, exotic blue. His hands trembled. The atmosphere should have been relaxing, but wasn't.

Even though Ken had asked, pleaded with, and hounded Adrian and Bobby to let him know what was going on, he realized with something like grief that what they said would in all likelihood change things; little Chance would no longer be the innocent child—how could he be?—with whom he and Valerie had fallen in love. Ken's feelings for his son had already gone through subtle changes, and he trembled not from fear of change, but from fear that those changes might diminish the love and pride he felt for Chance.

Adrian, perhaps sensing Ken's mental reservations, said: "Are you *sure* you want to do this now?"

"Oh, yeah," Ken said, waving a hand and producing a shaky laugh, "go ahead. If something happens before I find out…"

Adrian smiled. "Okay. Chance's father is called different things by the staff at the Nevada compound," he began. "Prometheus, the Subject, and Lone Star, which to me is the most apt name. Project Lone Star is the actual classification for his captivity and study, and it all began in Roswell, New Mexico. Are you familiar with that story?"

Ken sat his beer down carefully and looked at the two men, a slight sinking sensation in his stomach. "I've heard things about that on television programs—*and from my father*, he didn't add—A UFO crash and an alleged government cover up? Something like that?"

"Right," Adrian said. "An unidentified flying object was supposed to have crashed there in 1947. There were many witnesses who saw unusual things in the sky that afternoon and evening, and several who actually saw the field of debris where the crash occurred. The sheriff in that area, a man by the name of George Wilcox, was contacted by a man named Mac Brazel, who had seen the debris field and had even taken some of it home and stored it in a shed. Wilcox suggested that Brazel contact the military base located near the site, and he was then excluded from the investigation by the government, and later sworn to secrecy about the story. It was a controversial occurrence at the time, to say the least, and several reports about it being a crashed UFO actually made a few newspapers before the government stepped in and got the word out through the papers and radio that the object had been nothing more than a downed weather balloon.

"There is a faction in society that has believed ever since then that the cover-up had something to hide. There were witnesses who claimed there were also three beings laying among the debris in that field; one of them dead, one injured, and the other alive. The injured being supposedly died enroute to a hangar on the military base, where the government allegedly took everything from the crash site. They had done this, partly, to curb public panic. The country had just come out of World War Two, and if the public knew our airspace was being uncontrollably invaded, there might be wide-spread panic, riots...you get the picture."

Ken nodded and picked up his beer. "You keep saying 'supposedly', and 'allegedly'. Is that what you really mean?"

"That's how the reports are viewed by most of society, even today," Bobby answered for him.

"Right," Adrian said, "but there is no 'allegedly' to most of it. What I'm going to tell you now is the absolute truth."

"Okay." *And do I actually want to hear it?*

It only took a second for Ken to come to the reluctant conclusion that he did. He *did* want to hear the truth. In spite of the scars it might inflict upon his family. He had been in the dark on this thing long enough.

Adrian took a sip of beer, took an even bigger breath, and began: "The crash *did* happen. Let's get that out of the way first. And there *were* humanoid beings. One of them *was* alive and unhurt, and that was Prometheus—Chance's father.

"He was housed at different military installations while the compound was under construction, and communication with him was established early. He learned our language in a matter of hours, and already knew most everything else about the human race."

"How?" Ken said.

"His race had been here a long time, conducting their own observations and studies."

"How did you find out about all this?"

"Bobby and I were born and raised in that Nevada compound, and when we saw this being for the first time, we became interested in him. We accessed archives and reports that dated all the way back to the late forties. A knowledgeable person can access anything stored on a computer, and Bobby is that kind of guy. I was his eyes, watching for security and administration personnel while he dug information out of the system."

"And it still took us years to gather enough data to see the whole picture and fit everything together," Bobby added.

"Exactly," Adrian said. "It wasn't accomplished overnight, but it *was* accomplished. And we weren't the only ones in the compound who realized the full impact of what was being done there. In fact, there are still others there who do."

"Why the name Prometheus?" Ken asked. He wasn't completely sure he believed the story so far, but it was the only question that came into his mind. "Isn't that Greek?"

"Yes," Bobby said. "Prometheus was a mythological god who gave fire to man. In that sense the name is fitting, I guess."

"And he is the best-kept secret the world has ever known," Adrian added. "Or *not* known, if you'd prefer. Held captive by the very government he has helped over the years.

"You see, once they were able to communicate with this being, the government was able to extract information from him. They did this through the development and use of devices called hydrabeams, which they use to keep Lone Star captive."

"Wait a minute," Ken said. "You're going to lose me if you start using words like that."

"Okay," Adrian said. He took a sip of beer and continued. "Hydrabeams are made from a mixture of hydrogen and a foreign molecular substance derived from the weapons system that was aboard the alien craft, and retrieved from the debris field. I'm not exactly sure how it works, but the hydrabeams are very painful to Lone Star, although you or I could bathe in the stuff.

"What is sad about the government's use of these hydrabeams is that Lone Star was—and has always been—*willing* to give them the information and technology they wanted. Because his race came here, is *still* here, for that very purpose. To advance our primitive society to the point where we can go beyond the confines of our religions and myths on earth and become a real member of the neighborhood that is the universe. But the human mind is limited by its self-imposed boundaries. What if Lone Star wanted to leave? What if the Russians discovered him and his race's advanced technology and knowledge? What if *he* went to *them*?

"Pain is a reality to anyone it is inflicted upon. Humans—especially the governments of the world—know that better than anyone. Pain is the one thing common to any race, no matter how far advanced that race may be. And the technology of this race…it's amazing, really."

"When you walk through your home you never think about where all the nice gadgets come from; things that make your life easier, or simple. The television set, the computer, the DVD player, the intricate complexity of optical fibers behind the phone system, or the cable or satellite connected to the TV set. When you *do* think about them you just consider them as nice, handy things to have. You take them for granted."

"Wait," Ken said. "These things were all invented by people, not aliens. Even I know that."

"Of course they were," Bobby said. "But without this one being to spark these ideas and allow creativity to foster in the minds of men, *and* to help with some of the basic details, most of these things wouldn't have come about for years. Or perhaps decades."

"But the most important thing behind Lone Star," Adrian continued, "is something the government—or at least the people in charge at the compound—cannot comprehend, because all they understand is what is practical for their own use. Not what will benefit the entire race. But there is a faction who *does* see, and who *has* taken steps toward that end."

"What do you mean?" Ken said. While he wanted to disbelieve most of this, he was taking Adrian's advice and thinking about Chance. It was becoming more difficult, in light of what he had recently experienced with his son, to be skeptical about something this fantastic. "What end are you talking about?"

"Why, cohabitation, of course," Adrian said. "Lone Star's name may be deceiving in that regard. His name fits him because he was the only humanoid that survived the crash at Roswell. Prometheus fits him equally well because of the technology and knowledge he has given our race, both directly and indirectly. But it fits better with a form of technology that was painfully extracted from him by our government. One that forever changed the world and our perception of it: the technology used to mass-produce nuclear weapons.

"We already possessed atomic capabilities at that time in the late forties, but the Hiroshima and Nagasaki bombs were about as far as anyone could take that technology. Lone Star knew the physics of nuclear power, however, and gave it only reluctantly. Now the proliferation of nuclear warheads on the planet make it a certainty that the next world war will mean the end of the human race, and of the planet as we know it."

Adrian paused and took a drink. The sky was almost totally blue now. The tension they all felt from waiting for whatever was coming was lessened, at least, by the story Adrian was telling. It was all Ken could do to digest the information as quickly as he heard it. Their pursuers might have been eons, light years, away.

"I know for a fact," Adrian emphasized, "that Lone Star wished he had let them kill him, instead of giving up information that enhanced that technology."

There was nothing Ken could say to that.

"Anyway, to get back on the subject," Adrian said. "Cohabitation. It has long been the desire of Lone Star, and of his race, to live as one with humans, here on earth. That would be the first step of man-kind's leap forward, to the stars and rest of the universe. Without their help, and without *our* cooperation, it will take decades, perhaps centuries, for the human race to reach that point.

"There has been some progress made to that effect, but it has taken a long time. Perhaps too long. Lone Star's race has made themselves known on an increasingly frequent basis, for one thing. Before Roswell, there weren't a whole lot of UFO sightings. There were some, mind you. But from that point on—and especially after people became convinced the government *did* know something—the door was opened wider. More and more movies have been made depicting cohabitation, numerous documentaries on the subject of aliens and UFO's have been made and broadcast around the world, and thousands of books have been written on the subject. And fueling this boom in interest and belief is our own government, who remains—at least publicly—the most skeptical of all skeptics. They don't spread this propaganda of their own volition; the more they dispute the existence of extraterrestrials, the more Lone Star's race allow themselves to be seen, which in turn fuels the imagination and creativity of the people involved. The word eventually gets out through various art mediums, and the public slowly begins to get used to the idea of life existing beyond our own solar system. They become desensitized."

"Which is," Bobby added, "what this race wants."

"Exactly," Adrian said. "and the primary reason for the government's denials for this points toward the fact that they don't want cohabitation to happen, because if it *did* they wouldn't be able to retain the tight control and influence they have over our culture, our religions, our economies. It's nice to fantasize that it might happen anyway—and believe me, I've thought about that a *lot*—but the reality is that it would probably not happen in this generation, or even the next."

"And that, my friend," Adrian said, looking at Ken, "is where Chance comes into play." He smiled. "No pun intended."

Ken leaned forward.

"Hold on a sec," Bobby said and stood. "I just want to run in and check the computer."

"Okay."

Bobby got up and went inside. A few minutes later he returned. "No change, but I feel like something is going to happen pretty soon. They haven't activated the trackers again, thank goodness, but I still wanted to look."

"Guess we'll just have to keep waiting," Adrian said.

And then both he and Bobby doubled over, expelling the beer they had drunk.

"Damn!" Ken said. "Are you guys all right?"

Adrian nodded, and Bobby held up one hand.

Then, from inside the house, came Chance's cries, loud and almost hysterical, screaming over and over: "Daddy! Daddy! *Dadde-e-e-e!*"

All three men jumped up and ran into the house, Adrian and Bobby holding their stomachs and grimacing, but their faces filled with apprehension.

Chance was standing in the living room, in front of one of the laptops. When he saw Ken, he pointed. "Look." Then he began to cry, like an ordinary child who has been frightened by something too terrible to see.

Ken scooped him up and hugged him close. "It's all right, buddy, it's all right."

But it wasn't

He looked at the computer screen.

The cluster of red dots had moved, and were so thick on the map around Spring River that it was hard to tell Bobby's and Adrian's markers from the rest.

* * * * *

THIRTY-TWO

John and Mark were met by Calhoun's deployment of agents and soldiers shortly after noon. Five Army vehicles crawled down the winding hill to the river, where they crossed the cement bridge like hungry, giant termites. Onlookers (most of the parents were corralling their children and moving to their vehicles) stared open-mouthed at the procession, and those fishing from the bridge were invited to vacate the structure by personnel who jumped off the trucks, two on either side. These men had carbines slung across their shoulders and handguns in their belts, and their faces were blank, dispassionate, like that of hardened rocks.

The trucks pulled to either side of the road after crossing the bridge but a small jeep, carrying one man, sped on up the road into the foothills. A man jumped down from the cab of the first truck, and he met John and Mark as they were walking toward him.

"Agents Milcheck and Lomax?"

"You got it," John said. He stuck out a hand and the man gave it a brisk shake.

"I'm Anderson, CIA, St. Louis office."

"I've heard a lot about you," John said. And he had. Timothy Anderson's name was legendary among CIA agents. Fifty-five years old with a head full of sandy blond hair and a face that looked carved from stone, he had carried out—if you believed what you heard—more operations and assignments in the agency's history than the director himself. His militant approach to any situation, no matter how small, brought him great respect among his peers and instilled fear among his subordinates. John wondered secretly what Anderson would think if he knew that Lomax's supposed adventures would rival his own.

There was a dark stain down the front of Anderson's camouflaged shirt, and a paleness to his face. "The trackers will be activated in exactly—he consulted his watch—three minutes, if you'd like to prepare yourselves."

John and Lomax both groaned. "Ah, shit," Mark said.

"Any movement off this mountain?" Anderson asked, all business.

"We haven't spotted Kenneth Malcolm, or the child," John said.

"Or the other two," Lomax chipped in.

"O'Donnell and Templeton," Anderson said, his lips pressed flat. "I advised against letting those two remain alive."

John and Mark were silent as they contemplated those words.

"After activation," Anderson continued, "we should have the child's location and we will conduct a wide sweep up the mountain, under my command." He looked at the two men. "I've sent a scout ahead of us, and he'll come down the higher part of the mountain, toward us. Any problems with that?"

"No, of course not," John said, and saw Anderson wince.

"No, *sir*," Lomax said, and Anderson's face relaxed.

Then his face immediately crinkled in a grimace as he, and every other agent or soldier in the vicinity—around forty in all—were hit with violent stomach cramps.

When they had passed, Anderson hollered at someone in the second truck, which had a satellite mounted on its roof. "Advise me when the data is updated."

"Yes, sir," came the reply.

Anderson wiped his mouth with a handkerchief that, from its dingy look, had been recruited for the same type of work earlier in the day. An agent from one of the trucks handed him a large rolled up paper. "Satellite map of the area, sir," Anderson took the map and then looked at John and Mark. "Let's go over this map, men, and plot a course to the child."

John shuffled his feet. Going through his mind was the memory of holding Kenneth Malcolm's small son, and sensing nothing at all unusual about him. He had appeared to be an ordinary, sweet child. He couldn't get that memory to leave his mind. It hung around like the lingering trace of a pleasant and not-quite-remembered dream.

They walked over to the picnic table that John and Mark had sat on while they waited. The remaining regiments had exited the convoy of trucks and were either standing around waiting orders or pacing back and forth. A few had removed articles of clothing and were at the river's edge, attempting to hand-wash the soiled materials, and casting uneasy glances at the mountain. Anderson unrolled the map, placed river rocks on the corners to hold it in place, and the three men bent over it.

A few minutes later the agent from the communications truck came running over. "Sir, we have their location." The agent put a finger on the spread map. "Here."

John felt a sinking in his stomach, and it was not a feeling that could be attributed to the trackers. This one came from an intense sense that something was not right here—was in fact *wrong*.

Something was going to happen—he felt that with every fiber in his body—but something was also wrong.

He wished he knew what it was.

* * * * *

Darrel pulled his battered station wagon off the gravel road onto a narrow dirt trail overgrown with weeds and thistle. He looked at Valerie, whose face was drawn tight in thought. The sunlight filtering through the swaying trees caused a mask of light and shadow to spar across her pale skin.

"This ought to be a good place to park," he said. "It's far enough away from the house."

Valerie blinked and seemed to come back to herself. "What do we do now?" Her voice cracking, she said, "Oh, Darrel, what are we going to do? My *baby* is in danger. I know it."

"It's okay," Darrel said in a voice meant to be soothing. "Everything is going to be all right." He didn't know if those futile words would calm her—wasn't even sure if he believed them himself—but he had to try. For both of them.

They got out of the car, closing the doors as quietly as possible. Darrel took it as a good sign that she didn't need to be advised to move with caution and stealth. He spoke in a low voice: "We'll move through the trees here." He pointed past her to the thick woods. "The cabin is on a straight line that way."

"What then?" she said.

"We'll get as close as we can and watch the house, see what's happening."

"What if they've already left?"

"I don't think they have." And he *didn't* think that. Darrel thought that, if anything, Ken and Chance, and whoever was with them, were still there. He thought he would be able to hear a motor leaving his cabin from here.

"How are we going to get close enough to see anything?" Valerie said.

The trees across the road from the cabin were sparsely scattered, not close together like these. They would not provide as much cover.

"I've got a pair of field glasses in the back of the wagon," Darrel said, "along with a few other things that might come in handy. These woods thin out about a quarter mile in, but we'll only go as far as the edge of the tree line, and we'll try to stay low."

Valerie's face relaxed. A little. As Darrel walked behind the wagon and raised the back hatch, she said, "What we really need is a gun."

Darrel rooted around and then stood up, holding something for her inspection. "Will this one do?"

"Where...?"

"I haven't unloaded my hunting gear since deer season ended back in the winter. Forgot all about it. Old age, I guess," he said and chuckled. The gun he held was an old shotgun, the stock chipped and faded. "It's just a single-shot twelve-gauge, but it's better than nothing."

"Ammo?" Valerie said.

Darrel bent and retrieved a box of shells, opened it. "Only five in here."

"Is that all?"

He lowered the hatch until is snicked shut. "We'll have to use them wisely, I guess, but at least we have them. I hope we don't need them."

She nodded, her lips tight. "I'll follow you."

They moved off into the woods.

* * * * *

The going was slow at first, with brush and brambles scraping their legs and arms. Valerie had an image of the woods trying to stop them; to even, perhaps, kill them if necessary. She knew it was a silly notion, of course, but it persisted until the undergrowth thinned out a couple hundred yards in. Then she fancied that at any moment the trees would move in even closer than they already were—that they would form a wall around her and Darrel, blocking their passage.

She watched Darrel's back as she followed him. Despite the moderate temperature, there were sweat stains seeping through the back of his shirt. She felt her own nervous perspiration on her brow and beneath her clothing.

After a while, Darrel shifted the gun to his right hand and raised the binoculars, which hung on a strap around his neck. He looked, lowered the glasses and shook his head, and moved on. The buzz of cicadas and other insects was low, and it would have been soothing at any other time. Instead, the noises frayed at the edges of Valerie's nerves, making her aware of how alone they were out here.

Darrel stopped after another hundred yards or so. The trees ahead of them were a lot thinner, and she caught a glimpse of something downhill towards her left.

The cabin.

Darrel raised the binoculars. After a moment he handed them to her. "Recognize the car?" he whispered.

"No," she said, "but it's the same one we saw earlier, isn't it?"

"Yeah, that's it, and it's empty."

"What do you think they're doing in there?" Through the field glasses, she could make out the entire front of the cabin except for three places where trees blocked her field of vision. She could only see two windows—a small one to the bathroom and one to a bedroom to the far right of the house—but closed blinds prevented her from peering inside.

"I don't know what they're doing," Darrel said, "but it looks…quiet."

"Yes, it does," she said. "I want to get closer."

Darrel whispered and pointed. "See that tall oak up ahead to the left?"

Valerie nodded as she handed back the binoculars.

"It's wide enough to conceal us. We'll also have a better view of the house." After a pause he added. "It's also as close as I feel safe going."

"Okay."

The tree was about twenty yards closer and from it they could see the entire front of the cabin. Darrel brought the glasses up. "I can see someone moving around through the kitchen window."

Valerie thrummed with anticipation. "Who is it?"

"Can't tell. There's also someone out on the deck. I can see the sliding glass doors. Barely."

"What now?" she said.

"Wait, I guess. Watch. Until we know more, it's about all we *can* do."

*****

Forty minutes later Darrel stood and stretched. Valerie was sitting at the base of the tree, looking through the binoculars. "See anything new?" he asked her.

"No. They're all still out on the deck at the table. And I *still* don't see Chance." This worried and irritated her more than the endless wait.

"Are they still drinking beer?" Darrel asked as he sat back down. He lay the shotgun on the ground in front of him, barrel pointed forward.

Valerie sighed. "Yes, they are. Drinking and talking. I just can't figure it."

"Must be allies instead of enemies," Darrel said, giving voice to the suspicions he'd had when he saw Ken and the two men open their first beer out on the deck.

A motor droned in the distance off to their left, then slowly faded. It was only the second one they had heard since leaving the station wagon. A twig snapped in the woods somewhere behind them. Insects buzzed and chirruped in a soft droning pitch.

Valerie grew impatient. "If those two guys are friendly, I think we should go on down there. If they haven't hurt Ken or Chance then it must be safe. *They* must be safe."

After a moment Darrel said, "You're right. We're not getting much done just sitting here. Let's go."

He was reaching down to pick up the shotgun when something clicked behind them and a voice said: "It's got a silencer on it, so be real still and quiet and maybe I won't have to use it."

*****

Duke, Tyler, and Lucas were huddled in a small room on Substation D, next to the room where Prometheus was held. They had their ears as close as possible to the air vent in one wall, listening. The room was used for storage, its tight quarters too small to be of any practical use otherwise, and boxes of files and miscellaneous office equipment took up most of the available space.

Through the air vent, they could hear loud voices from an argument being conducted below them, in the Communications Center.

"I don't care what it takes, I want that child captured, *today.*"

Duke didn't recognize the man's voice, but he recognized the voice of the man who responded as belonging to his father.

"And I don't care what you want."

"Oh, you don't, huh?"

"No. You should understand that you are here to compliment this operation, not facilitate it yourself. The child *will* be captured today, Director, but understand that it will be because of decisions made by the *two* of us. Not just you."

"Do you realize how important this is?"

"Of course I do. I know more than you do yourself what's at stake here, because if *you* had any inkling, you would have *never* involved so many agents."

Duke moved away from the vent and looked at Tyler and Lucas. "Who is he?" he signed. "The one talking to my father."

Tyler, who knew the silent language, said: "That's William Calhoun, the director of the CIA." His eyes darted around the room, then to the door and back. "Something big is about to happen."

"What is it?" Duke said with his hands.

"I don't know, but what we've got to do—what we have to do for Prometheus—is probably the most important part of it."

Instead of asking further questions, Duke once again leaned closer to the vent. Tyler and Lucas followed suit.

Faint, yet clearly, they heard Derek Tarkington say: "I know how to get them off that mountain without using *any* of your troops."

"Oh? And just how do you propose to do that?" Tense. Sarcastic.

Duke envisioned his father's face cloaked by a dark, cloudy smile, even before he heard the same darkness in the voice that answered the director's question.

"I happen to have the one thing the child's adoptive father would do anything for—including giving up the child to us peacefully—and without any over-the-top maneuvers that might cause civilians, or worse the media, to take a closer look at what you have going in Arkansas."

"And just what is it that you have that will allow you to do this?"

"Kenneth Malcolm's wife."

"His *wife?*"

"That's right. His wife." Now Duke could hear the smile on his father's face. "Valerie Malcolm is being held at the sight in Arkansas, by Anderson and his men. My ace in the hole, if you will."

"That's pretty risky," the director said, and then sighed. "Risky, but nevertheless clever."

"I believe in preparing for any eventuality, Director, even though capturing her was an unexpected surprise."

"Well, the least you could have done is advised me of your situation with Mrs. Malcolm. *That* would have saved a lot of manpower and time, had I known."

"I assure you, William, that it only happened minutes ago."

Duke moved away from the vent. He had heard enough. He looked at Tyler and signed: "Whatever you have in mind, we have to do it now. They have the child cornered."

"So it seems," Tyler said. He turned to Lucas. "We go now. Duke is right. We don't have much time."

Lucas nodded. "Follow me." He walked quickly to the door and Duke and Tyler followed him, all three being as quiet as possible.

The hallway lay in shadows, like always, and the three young men made little noise as they made their way to the room where their friend was held. There was a bad moment when a doorway opened down the corridor, but the man who walked out went right, in the opposite direction, and never glanced back once toward the three shadowed figures.

Duke slid his card into the console to the right of the door. The escaping air as the chamber opened sounded like the fiery hiss of a dragon.

Lucas and Tyler stood to either side of the door, waiting, and when Duke nodded the three of them lunged inside. The door hissed shut behind them.

* * * * *

THIRTY-THREE

"Don't shoot," Darrel said. "We're not going anywhere." He eyed the shotgun at his feet. Concealing leaves covered enough of the weapon so that, apparently, the man behind them had not yet seen it.

Valerie was shaking, her hands raised above her head like a criminal on a television show who has just been busted by the police. "Please," she said. "I just want my baby."

"Your baby? Are you…Valerie Malcolm?"

"How did you…?"

"Never mind. Just get up," the voice said, then chuckled. "Anderson's not going to believe this."

Darrel glanced behind him and saw a tall man in Army fatigues, square chinned and wearing sunglasses. His face seemed dispassionate and the pistol he held in one hand was equipped with a silencer, just like he had warned.

Darrel tensed as Valerie rose to her feet. He was scared as hell, pumped up with adrenaline, and his nerves were strung wire, but he wanted to act somehow—to *do* something. The man reached for Valerie with his free hand, and as if watching himself from outside his body, Darrel grabbed the shotgun, rose, and swung the barrel at the man, all in one quick move.

The man grunted in surprise and—Darrel hoped—pain as the barrel caught him on the forearm. The gun dropped from his hand with a muffled plop and Darrel stared at it for a second, unable to believe what he had just done.

The man let go of Valerie to grab his hurt arm.

"Run, Val," Darrel breathed. *"Run."* Then he took his own advice and ran, hoping that she was behind him.

He heard her squeal, and when he looked back he saw that the man had grabbed her again and was even now stooping to pick up his gun.

Darrel decided he had no choice but to run. He hated to abandon Valerie, but he couldn't help her if he turned back. To do so would mean the end for both of them.

He had to get help, and he thought he just might know where to find some.

As he zigzagged around the thinning trees, he kept expecting to hear the discharge of the man's gun, and to be cut down by a hail of bullets. Then he remembered that he wouldn't be able to hear it if the man *did* shoot at him.

Tense and frightened, he ran on.

Toward his cabin.

* * * * *

The beer cans, both empty and full ones, were left on the deck, forgotten. Everyone was inside. Ken had managed to calm Chance, but the child's chest still hitched occasionally.

He and Chance were on the sofa and Adrian was pacing behind Bobby, whose fingers raced over the keys of the laptop. Every fifteen seconds or so Bobby would tap a key and mutter, "shit", or "damn." Ken's unease grew.

Adrian had suggested that the best—and only—thing they could do was to stay put in the house near the computers. Bobby and Ken had agreed, Ken reluctantly so. His first instinct was to run, but he saw the logic in staying put. And it helped when he remembered what Bobby had said about he and Adrian's 'mission' in all of this: they would protect Chance with their own lives, if it came to that.

That makes three of us, Ken thought. *And better odds. And it probably will come to that.*

"Can you divert our tracking signals?" Adrian asked Bobby.

"That's what I'm trying to do." Bobby's voice was laced with frustration. "One minute I think I have it, and the next minute the screen will flash up an 'access denied' message."

"What's causing it?"

"I'm not sure, but the only thing I can think of is that they have an operator monitoring the system manually, looking for my attempts to breach their systems."

"That's protocol in emergencies, isn't it?"

"Yes, it is. So I guess they think this qualifies," Bobby muttered.

Adrian managed a grin and put a hand on Bobby's shoulder. "They know you're involved, and they are aware of what you can do with a computer. Keep trying."

"I will."

Adrian sat down next to Ken and looked at Chance, whose eyes were alert and—Ken noticed—full of that fierce intelligence he'd seen when Chance had discovered the listening devices in their house. "What do you know, big guy?" Adrian said.

"We're in trouble," Chance said simply.

Adrian sighed. "Yeah, I guess we might be, at that. Any ideas?"

"No," Chance said. "I'm scared."

Such a simple statement, naked and true, Ken thought. He hugged him tight. "I'm scared too, buddy, but everything will be okay. I won't let anything happen to you."

"Neither will I," Adrian said. "We'll think of something, don't worry." Ken sensed that Adrian was uneasy about something, but he didn't know if the man was only uncomfortable talking to Chance or if he was trying—but was unable—to believe the words he'd just spoken. The man had, after all, just resorted to asking a fifteen-month-old if he had any ideas.

Chance nodded and lay his head on Ken's chest.

"*Damn,*" Bobby said. "Oh man, they are close."

Ken and Adrian both got up and stood behind him. On the screen, Ken could see the mass of red dots. He knew the two belonging to Adrian and Bobby were most likely on the outer edge of the cluster, but knowing that did nothing to help the situation.

And then he had an idea: simple, yet risky, it was still better—in his mind—than anything they had come up with so far.

"I've got an idea," he said.

Bobby turned around and said to Adrian: "This is no use. I give up."

Adrian ignored him and looked at Ken. "What is it?"

"Well, if they are able to track you and Bobby with these trackers, then it's obvious how we can keep them from finding Chance."

"Oh no," Adrian said, apparently sensing what Ken was getting at. "We stay with you and Chance."

"Why? *Why*? If we separate, I can get Chance away from these people and the four of us can meet up later, or…"

"And just where would you go?" Bobby cut in. He looked at Ken with a bland frankness.

"Anywhere you two aren't," Ken said angrily. "I don't recall being…chased…like this until we met up with the two of you. I knew *something* was wrong, but things haven't gotten much better since then, let me tell you."

"Okay, I get it," Adrian said. "But just hear me out for a minute, can you do that?"

Ken shrugged.

"The signals from the last tracker activation may no longer be accurate," Adrian said. "What if all these agents"—he pointed at the screen—"are right now hiding among the trees outside? What if we're already surrounded?"

"I don't think that's likely," Ken said. "They haven't had *that* much time. Have they?"

"But are you willing to risk walking out of here and getting hit by sniper fire as soon as they can get a clear shot?" Adrian's gaze was piercing. "They will take the child after they shoot you, Ken. It's that simple. And *then* where will you be? How can you possibly help your son if you're dead?"

Ken's shoulders slumped. Those words struck him like a physical blow. He said, "That's a big 'if'. Personally, I don't think they are that close yet, but you're right about one thing. I can't risk it."

Just then there was a thump from outside the door to the kitchen, followed by three loud knocks.

Ken swallowed hard, held Chance tighter, and looked at Adrian and Bobby. Adrian held a finger to his mouth—"shhh"—and picked up the .22 caliber rifle. He motioned for everyone to move into the hallway, away from the windows.

The pounds at the door came again: louder, frantic.

A thick dread wormed its way through Ken's stomach as he watched Adrian creep to the door, the gun cocked and held out in front of him.

* * * * *

"I knew you would come. I knew you would not fail me."

Duke looked through the hydrabeams at his friend. "I guess there will be no more chess games, huh?" he signed.

Prometheus leaned his head back and laughed loud and deep. "Oh, Duke. Did you not get my message today?"

Duke looked to either side of him at Lucas and Tyler, but from the looks on their faces he knew they were just as confused. The two technicians on duty were 'asleep' at their terminals.

"Message?"

Prometheus tapped a finger on his elongated forehead. "The one up *here*, Duke." He held Duke with his eyes.

Today. Everything. Today.

Duke smiled as understanding dawned.

"Of course there will be more chess," Prometheus said. "You mustn't think such thoughts, Duke. Remember, optimism colors everything in a clearer and brighter light, while pessimism distorts the truth and veils the eyes."

Duke nodded, his cheeks blushing.

Lucas and Tyler still looked confused, but Lucas seemed struck with wonder, as well. Duke raised an eyebrow and Tyler said in a low voice, "Lucas has never seen Prometheus in his native form."

Duke, smiling, turned and patted Lucas on the shoulder. Then he gave him a thumbs-up to let him know it was okay.

Duke himself had seen Prometheus as he truly looked on many occasions, without the morphed features of a regular human being: pleasantly lined face, dark eyes, accented by a scruff of black close-cropped hair. His native features were less appealing, unless—like Duke—one could put aside the outer appearance of this being and see—*know*—what he was made up of inside, where it truly counted.

Prometheus' height was short, about five foot four, his body small and gray beneath the dark blue coveralls he wore. His hands were humanoid, with five digits, although each finger had an extra joint, making his hand somewhat longer. His face was long: narrow at the chin and widening to the bald forehead, beneath which were two large almond-shaped eyes. Duke knew his friend's features were nearly identical to how the outside world generally perceived 'aliens'. The main difference was his height, which was taller than the usual depictions of 'grays'. Books and movies were plentiful inside the compound, and it was because of this that he was surprised at Lucas' reaction to their mutual friend.

"Hello, Lucas, Tyler," Prometheus said, nodding at each of them in turn. "I'm glad all of you are here. We haven't much time now."

"What should we do first?" Duke signed.

"I have an idea," Lucas said hesitantly, "but I don't know how good it is."

Prometheus smiled. "Your idea is a good one, Lucas. And since there are three of you, it might just work." Prometheus paused, his eyes like two dark, fathomless pools. "In fact, it's our only chance. I *must* escape. And quickly."

Duke looked at Lucas and signed: "What's your plan?"

"What's your plan," Tyler interpreted.

Lucas looked at Prometheus, who nodded, then he said: "The hydrabeams. I don't know how to shut them off, but maybe we can…divert them."

Before Duke could ask him to clarify what he'd just said, Lucas pointed to the perimeter of Prometheus' quarters. The brownish-orange liquid flowed from holes in the ceiling to identical receptacles in the floor. Each hydrabeam was spaced eight inches apart. Lucas' plan was for each of them—Duke, Tyler, and himself—to interrupt the flow on three consecutive bars. This could be accomplished by using three pieces of flat material placed in the middle of each flow, near the ceiling. The hydra substance could then be directed away from the perimeter, onto the floor, so that Prometheus could simply walk out of his quarters.

The three men set quickly to work while Prometheus watched, occasionally offering advice—such as "use a screwdriver on those filing cabinets."

Duke located a flat screwdriver in a drawer of the desk occupied by a slumped technician, and in a matter of minutes each man held a metal piece from the file cabinet.

They were ready.

Duke looked at Prometheus' quarters, which had housed the alien for as long as Duke could remember, and probably a lot longer. The furnishings spoke of long use. Although the quarters were large, the small worn table and chair set near a narrow bed and long bookshelf emitted a semblance of coziness and comfort. A small sink, faucet, and toilet—along with an enclosed shower stall—set apart from everything else was the only indication of the room being a cell.

"Good luck, my friends," Prometheus said, standing back. As Duke watched, he morphed into his familiar human features. It happened in less than two blinks of an eye—alien one moment, human the next.

Lucas appeared taken aback by the sudden transformation, but seemed to recuperate quickly, as he was familiar with the human form. He held up his piece of metal. "I'm ready."

The three of them positioned themselves near the center of the cell and held their metal pieces at the ready.

"Remember to angle the flows as far away from the center as possible," Lucas said. "On my count of three."

Duke and Tyler nodded.

"One," Lucas said. "Two...*three!*"

Each man, their piece of metal raised high, slid them under three flows at the same time, as high up as they could reach. There was a slight chug and moan from the equipment in the next room that moderated the hydrabeams. The in-flows into the floor receptacles were diminished and then eliminated.

Duke, Tyler and Lucas strained under the unexpected force of the hydrabeams, at first getting some of the warm liquid on them, which had a curious odor like burnt wood and vinegar. As they watched, the liquid ran down the makeshift funnels and spilled out onto the floor.

Duke sensed, more than saw, Prometheus glide by him through the clear area they were making. He *did*, however, see his friend jump stridently over the pooling mess on the floor and land safely on the other side.

"Now!" Prometheus said as he scampered to the far side of the room.

The three of them let the pieces of filing cabinet clank to the floor, and then jumped aside without getting spattered much by the slimy substance.

The laboring motors in the next room leveled off as the streams of hydra poured into the floor receptacles.

Prometheus looked in to his former quarters. "All the years I've dwelled in there. All that time. I always thought I would end in that place, as well." He looked around at Duke, Tyler and Lucas. "Because of you—and for my son—I am free."

"Almost, anyway," Duke signed.

"Thank you," Prometheus said. "Each of you. Thank you."

"Don't thank us too quickly," Tyler said. "We've still got to get you out of the compound."

"Of course," Prometheus said. "And what shall we utilize for that bit of fun? The PTP?"

Duke's brow furrowed in confusion, but apparently Lucas knew to what Prometheus referred. "That would be the best and quickest way," Lucas said, "but the PTP is outside the compound, at another site."

Duke spread his hands and raised his eyebrows.

"Yeah," Lucas said. "Particle Transmission Portal. A sort of... teleportation machine, just like in the science fiction novels in the library." He described it to Duke, who smiled after a moment and nodded.

"Like the one in my father's office?"

This time, after Tyler interpreted, it was Lucas who looked confused. "In your father's *office?*"

"Yes, I'm fairly sure, anyway," Duke signed.

"That's our next step, then," Prometheus said, already moving toward the door. Duke wondered how many times over the years and decades his friend had imagined walking out that door, to freedom.

As the four of them left the chamber and sealed it shut behind them, Lucas protested, "But there has to be a PTP wherever we're going, doesn't there?"

"Yes," Prometheus said. "But I will take care of that, and if I can't...well, perhaps it has already been taken care of."

Duke saw some sparkle in his friend's eyes. *He knows something we don't,* he thought. *And he probably already knows what is going to happen next.* He was amused to find himself comforted by the thought.

The four of them moved down the hall, toward the elevators.

* * * * *

Ken peeked around the corner as Adrian neared the door, the gun in front of him. The pounding had stopped and another sound replaced it. It was the sound of a key being slid home into a lock. A second later the doorknob began to turn. Adrian raised the gun to eye level, aiming it at the door.

"Hold it," Ken said. "Hold it. I know who it is. Put down the gun."

Of *course* Ken knew who it was. He had earlier taken the key to the cabin from beneath the rock out front, and only one other person possessed another—his father.

Before he could tell Adrian as much, the door opened and Darrel Malcolm poked his head inside. "Hello? Don't shoot. My name is Darrel Malcolm. I'm Ken's father."

Ken heard Adrian's exhalation of breath and was thankful the man hadn't been would tight enough to shoot through the door. Adrian lowered the weapon as Darrel came into the kitchen, closing the door behind him.

"Dad?" Ken said. "What are you doing here?"

Darrel looked dumbstruck for a moment, and Ken could see that he was wanting to smile, but couldn't. And then Chance came running out from the hallway. "Pa Pa!"

Darrel knelt and scooped Chance into his arms. "Hey, big fella." He hugged the youngster and looked at Ken. "These two men. They're friends?"

"Yeah," Ken said. "I guess they are." He quickly introduced Adrian and Bobby, then turned back to his father. "What's wrong? Why are you here?"

As Darrel told them about he and Valerie's deductions about the situation, and of their subsequent stake out and Valerie's capture, Ken's heart sank. He tried to tell himself that Valerie wasn't as good as dead, but his heart would not listen. It ached and wrenched at him like a rotted tooth. He slumped down onto the sofa. "Valerie," he said, his voice shaky and weak.

Adrian came and sat beside him. "Don't worry too much yet, Ken. Your father didn't hear any shots, and I don't believe that agent would just up and shoot her—not when he was probably looking for you and Chance in the first place."

"Agent?" Darrel said. "The man was in Army fatigues."

"Doesn't matter," Bobby said. "You can bet he was an agent." He pointed to the laptop. "See all those dots? They are each a government agent."

"My God," Darrel said. "And they want *Chance?* Why? We knew *something* was going on, someone after you or something, but we couldn't figure out what. But...*Chance?*"

Ken waved a hand at his father. "It's a long story, Dad, and if what you say is true then we have no time to fill you in."

"You got that right," Adrian said. "They will be on us in no time."

"Yeah," Bobby said with a trace of sadness in his voice. He stroked his light beard with one shaking hand. "What we need is a miracle."

That brought back the feeling in Ken that something was about to happen; something other than a shootout with a bunch of government agents. He couldn't put his finger on what his hunch was, or why he even had it. He only felt that—for this brief moment, at least—he almost *could* believe in miracles. He had to, for Valerie's sake, for he felt that it would likely take one for him to hold her—alive—in his arms again.

"I think we need to—" Adrian began.

And that is when they heard motors coming up the road from both directions, and a moment later the road and driveway in front of the cabin was filled with Army-issue jeeps and trucks.

* * * * *

THIRTY-FOUR

John looked at Mark Lomax with ill-concealed contempt. Lomax was holding an AK-47 in his hands with what looked like a skittish excitement. The two of them were in the back of one of the Army trucks with agent Anderson and a few other men. Anderson had a radio in one hand and was conversing with Calhoun. John could hear the director's muffled voice through the tiny speaker.

"We have the PTP aboard with us now," Anderson spoke into the radio. "Transmit when ready, sir."

"Roger," came the reply.

In a low voice John leaned over and asked Lomax, "What's going on?"

"Huh?" Lomax grunted, apparently pulled away from whatever war fantasy was playing in his head. Perhaps he was thinking how, after today, he would have one more heroic story for his endless arsenal.

"What are they talking about?" John jerked a thumb toward Anderson, whose back was to them.

"I don't know."

John looked toward the front of the truck, at the odd machine positioned there. It was a small mechanism, except for a tall rectangular frame in the center that resembled a doorway. The computerized motor to the right looked out of place next to this metal structure, but John could see that it was connected to it by a small bunch of cables and wires. More high-tech government gadgets, he supposed.

Earlier, while looking over the area maps with Lomax and Anderson, John had witnessed the return of the single jeep belonging to an advanced scout. He had been stunned to see the scout had returned with a passenger, and that it was Valerie Malcolm. *Oh shit,* he had thought.

What is going on here? What is so important about that child?

Shortly after that, Anderson had organized the large group of agents to follow his truck up the mountain. John had since overheard him telling someone—over the radio—that Mrs. Malcolm was cooperative enough to tell him where her husband and son had holed up. John didn't like to think about how they might have gone about extracting that information from her.

The truck he and Lomax were in was the lead on the excursion into the hills, but the jeep had pulled out ahead of them, with Mrs. Malcolm still residing in the front passenger seat. Two other agents had also climbed aboard the open-topped vehicle. Presumably, John thought, to make sure that she didn't try anything funny.

The only consolation in all of this was that at least the trackers would not have to be activated again. His stomach felt turned inside out, sprung.

He began to wonder again what might happen once they reached their destination. He and Lomax, along with every other agent involved, had been ordered by Anderson to shoot, on sight, Kenneth Malcolm and whoever might be with him. They were to spare the child at all costs.

John wondered if Anderson had had the tenacity to bark these orders within earshot of Valerie Malcolm (he hoped not), and was preparing to ask Mark's opinion about it when the vehicle began to slow, and the strange machine at the front of the truck began to hum.

What happened next was something that simultaneously startled John, filled him with awe, and embraced him in the cold grip of fear.

* * * * *

The elevator came to a stop on Level C, and the door opened onto a corridor that was dark and silent save for the fading click of heels to the right.

"Wonder who that was?" Lucas said as he, Duke, Tyler, and Prometheus poked their heads out of the elevator and peered each way down the hall.

Tyler shrugged, but Duke only shook his head.

"It doesn't matter," Prometheus said. "We must hurry."

The hollow echo of the boots filled Duke with unease and fear. He imagined that those footsteps belonged to Flaugherty; that the man had discovered the empty cell and was out on the prowl, angry, and searching for his escapee. Duke knew he shouldn't preoccupy his mind with such thoughts, and it was only after an inner struggle that he managed to push them aside and concentrate on leading his friends to his father's office.

The office was in a hallway that ran perpendicular to this corridor. Duke was hesitant about going in the same direction as whoever was just ahead of them, but knew they had no choice. Lucas and Prometheus had both said that they needed to get to one of these particle transmission portals as quickly as possible, to they *had* to go this way.

Still.

"Are you sure your father has a PTP in his office?" Lucas said skeptically. It was only the third time he had asked this of Duke.

Duke nodded vigorously.

"He's not lying," Prometheus said. "If Duke says there is a portal in Derek Tarkington's office, I believe him. I don't think he would lie about it."

"I don't, either," Tyler said.

"Well, I don't either, necessarily," Lucas said, a little defensively. "I just find it hard to believe that Derek has been able to keep the location of a PTP from becoming common knowledge within the compound."

"He *is* the boss man," Tyler pointed out.

"Regardless," Prometheus said. "We have to get to that portal. Now, listen."

Duke strained his ears but could hear nothing. At least, not at first. But as they came to the T-junction of the corridor he heard faint voices. There was better lighting in this hallway, and the four of them did not dare more than a look either way down its length, staying back in the shadows.

A moment later Duke stepped into the hallway and turned right. Prometheus was behind him, followed by Tyler and then Lucas. With a sinking in his stomach, Duke realized they were going down the same hallway—to the same room, in fact—where a crude surgery had been performed on his tongue and vocal cords in another time. He began to shake. He couldn't help it. The trembling ceased as a gentle hand ran light fingers across his lower back: Prometheus.

"Easy, my friend," he said in a low voice. "This trip is only as frightening as you make it. When a thing has to be done—when it *has* to be— the only choice you have is to do it. Letting fear clog your thinking complicates things. Focus. Like a game of chess. Focus."

Prometheus' words and touch had a calming effect on Duke. His breathing slowed to a steady rhythm and his mind suddenly cleared—completely. It was as if his head were filled with brilliant light. He continued to lead his friends toward his father's office, but at the same time seemed to witness all of their moves as if through a television screen. Every thought was filled with clarity. He led them boldly down the hall to the closed door, and there stopped.

From behind the door came animated voices, and Duke recognized them as those of his father, and the man whom Lucas had said was the director of the CIA. He peeked through the small glass window and saw them across the room, in front of a recessed closet that was now open. This was where he had seen the strange machine his friends called a PTP. Duke hadn't known what it was, but he had known by Lucas' description that it was this machine Prometheus needed. Duke and his friends listened to the voices, which were almost as clear as they had been through the air vents next to Communications.

"The portal is charged and ready," Duke heard his father speak into a radio. Then the other man took the radio when it was handed to him and said, "We're ready on this end." The reply came through the radio in a ghostly crackle: "We have the PTP aboard with us now. Transmit when ready, sir." And the reply: "Roger."

Duke looked at Prometheus, who raised a finger to his mouth and shook his head. "Wait," Prometheus whispered. The four of them crowded around the window and watched.

They watched Derek Tarkington and William Calhoun—their backs to the front of the office—walk briskly to the machine with the tall rectangular frame...and then disappear through that door. For brief seconds the air inside the frame shimmered like a static-filled wave of rising heat from the outside desert, and then the office was empty. Both men were gone.

Duke's eyes were large and round when he looked at Prometheus and signed: "Where did they go?"

Prometheus looked determined and angry at the same time. And Duke thought he also spotted a light fear on his friend's face. "They are going after my son," he said. "We must hurry."

Lucas pushed opened the door and they went inside. The sparsely furnished office held a faint pine scent of disinfectant and a stronger metallic smell, similar to that made by an electric train transformer. Across the room, the doorway hummed, and the four men stared at it.

Each seemed hesitant about what they now knew had to be done. Behind them, the door clicked shut.

Prometheus walked closer to the portal and the others followed.

"I'm scared," Tyler said.

"Me, too," Duke signed.

"You have good reason to be," Prometheus told them. "When we follow those men, we arrive where they are, and so we must be prepared to fight. If any of you wants to stay here, I understand. Feel free. I thank you for bringing me this far from my cell, and so close to my child, but it would not be fair of me to expose you to more danger than is necessary."

"I'm going with you," Duke signed.

"So am I," said Tyler, who turned to Lucas. "You want to stay here or go with us?"

Lucas looked startled at the prospect of remaining at the compound alone. "I'm going with you," he said. "No way am I staying here."

Behind them, the door to the office banged open. "I don't believe anyone is going *anywhere*," Tim Flaugherty said as he stood in the open doorway.

In his hands was a large gun, and on his face a wide grin.

To Duke that grin looked comic but predatory.

"I told you this wasn't over, Duke," Flaugherty said, "and by god, I wasn't joking." He advanced toward the four men with the gun raised and the grin still floating on the lower half of his face like the loony smile of a circus clown.

* * * * *

As John watched, the doorway at the front of the truck bed shimmered and rippled, and hummed even louder than before. The truck came to a halt. He heard Lomax mutter, "What the hell?" Then, in a matter of seconds, two men materialized in the doorway and stumbled forward.

Agent Anderson caught the first man, a pale-skinned man in camouflage whom John did not recognize, and moved him away from the doorway. The second man who stumbled out was William Calhoun.

John rubbed his eyes with one hand, not quite able to believe what he had just witnessed. But when he looked again, both men were still there, and they moved with Anderson to the back of the truck, where steps were being unfolded, by another agent, to the ground outside.

298

Neither man looked back at the machine.

John noticed that even Lomax looked perplexed, and he had thought it impossible for the man to react like that to anything.

"Let's go, men," Anderson shouted at them as he jumped from the bed of the truck, avoiding the stairs.

John, Lomax, and the other few agents aboard got up and exited the truck.

The air outside was bright and redolent with the smell of oak and pinesap. The small house they had stopped in front of looked well-kept and comfortable among the trees.

At least it *would* have been. Armed agents now surrounded the front of the house, a few running forward to flank each side, moving through the trees at the outer perimeters.

Anderson had retrieved a bullhorn from the cab of the truck and John saw him hand it to the man who had arrived with Calhoun. It was clear that Anderson was relinquishing control.

The man raised the bullhorn to his lips.

Oh boy, John thought. *Here we go. Oh, shit.*

* * * * *

THIRTY-FIVE

Ken and Chance were in the hallway, where Adrian had ordered them to stay. Darrel sat on the floor beside them. Adrian and Bobby were in the kitchen, taking surreptitious peeks out the two windows, Adrian holding the .22 rifle. After a few minutes the two of them joined Ken, Chance, and Darrel in the hallway.

Well, I guess we're pretty much surrounded," Adrian said, some resignation in his voice. "They aren't going to take him easily, though." He looked at Chance and smiled. The youngster returned it with one of his own.

Sunlight streamed into the living room through the sliding glass doors that led to the back deck and Ken looked at it, thinking about all the times he and Valerie had been to this place, how many times they had sat on the deck in an afternoon patch of sunshine and enjoyed hamburgers and potato salad, their favorite 'cook out' food. It was hard to believe that government agents, who were prepared to kill everyone in the house in order to capture Chance, surrounded this same place that was filled with so many good memories. It shouldn't be happening. Not here.

"Tarkington's out there," Adrian said, and Bobby nodded.

"Who's that?" Ken said.

Adrian shook his head. "Doesn't matter. He's the big cheese at the compound. I guess that should tell you all you need to know about him."

"I suppose," Ken said. He returned his attention to that patch of sunlight on the deck; a bright spot on an otherwise dismal setting. If they could only...

He jerked suddenly as the idea that had been playing at the edges of his mind took a clear form. *Of course,* he thought. *Why didn't I think of it before?*

It might not even be possible, he countered himself, *let alone work.*

That was true, he guessed. He also knew that whether or not it was possible all depended on his young son, who had thus far remained as calm as anyone in the room.

He leaned forward and spoke to him in a low voice.

Chance said something to him, and then they both smiled. "It just might work," Ken said, and Chance nodded.

"What might?" Adrian said, looking over his shoulder from his position at the front of the hallway.

"We have an idea," Ken said, and he began to tell Adrian, Bobby, and his father what he and Chance had discussed.

* * * * *

"I want all of you to move away from that door," Flaugherty said. He motioned to his right with the gun. "*Do* it."

"Tim, Tim, Tim," Prometheus said in a sad voice. "You will never learn, will you?"

"You shut up, you...freak," Flaugherty spit. "You just want to shut right up before I put a bullet in one of your buddies here."

"Why not shoot *me*?" Prometheus said.

"Yeah, right. Do you think I'm stupid? No. What's going to happen here is that *you're* going peacefully back to your quarters, and *Duke* is coming with me." Flaugherty looked at Lucas and Tyler. "As for you two, you get the hell out of here and I'll deal with you later." He motioned with the gun to the door behind him. "*Go*. Get out of here."

"Do it," Prometheus told them in a low voice. "And thank you, my friends."

Lucas and Tyler looked uncertain.

"I'll be fine," Prometheus said. "Now go, before he changes his mind and does something stupid."

The two men ran toward the door.

Grinning again, Flaugherty turned and fired his gun twice. The impacts spun Lucas and Tyler around like rag dolls. Their faces rippled in pain as they dropped to the floor.

Flaugherty laughed and turned to Duke and Prometheus. "I decided not to wait for later to take care of them. It's probably better anyway, because most likely they would have come back with guns, or something to brain me with." He laughed again.

Duke stared at Lucas and Tyler, each lying in a spreading pool of blood. Then he looked at his friend.

Prometheus was staring hard at Flaugherty. His eyes were black with rage, something that looked strange and out of place on that kind face. "You stupid, stupid man," he said in a venomous voice.

"You shut up," Flaugherty said casually, "or I'll shoot your chess-playing buddy here next."

"I do not think you will," Prometheus said. "That would be too simple, and not nearly as much fun. Isn't that about right?"

Flaugherty's face clouded for a moment and then the grin reappeared, but looking diminished, and not as full or as confident as before. "I don't know what you're talking about," he said. "All I know is that Duke here has got some explaining to do about a satellite control system that went offline earlier, and that's all I want from him. After that, I'll let his father decide what to do with him. All I need right now is a confession."

"Do you think Duke could do something like that?" Prometheus said. "Are you really as stupid as I suspect you are?"

Flaugherty's face clouded again. "You want to watch the way you talk to me, freak. Far as I know, a bullet will kill you as easily as hydra."

"Perhaps," Prometheus said, "Or—perhaps not. Why don't you find out...stupid man?"

Duke was frightened at the fury in Tim Flaugherty's eyes, but at the same time he wanted to burst out laughing at the way Prometheus was talking to him. Wasn't he worried that he might shoot them as he had Lucas and Tyler? Duke *still* found it hard to believe that those two men were dying on the floor in puddles of drying blood. In fact—

In fact, it looked as though Lucas Matthews *wasn't* dead. He stirred and sat up, rubbing the side of his butt and grimacing. Duke tried hard not to stare at him. Flaugherty might catch him and turn around, and if he did that...well, Duke didn't want to think about what might happen then.

"If you call me stupid one more time, freak, then we're going to *see* how well you handle bullets."

"Sure we will," Prometheus said pleasantly. He paused a moment while staring into Flaugherty's eyes. Duke knew it was coming even before his friend said it, and he grimaced.

Prometheus looked at Flaugherty and finally finished his sentence: "Stupid man."

"All right," Flaugherty said. "All right, that does it." He raised the gun. "Here it comes, freak."

Duke ducked, but Prometheus stood still, hands clasped behind his back as though he were a Pullman waiting in front of an elevator.

And then he smiled.

Flaugherty hesitated, and must have registered the flickering movement of Prometheus' eyes as he looked over his left shoulder. He spun around fast, but he wasn't quick enough. Lucas Matthews struck him between the neck and shoulder before he could turn completely, and Flaugherty fell to his knees with a grunt. The gun discharged into the ceiling and then clattered to the floor as he reached up to grab his neck.

Lucas limped to the gun, picked it up, and turned it on Flaugherty. "Get up," he said.

Prometheus ran straight to Tyler the second Flaugherty dropped the gun, and he knelt beside him, feeling all over the front of the silent man, apparently looking for the bullet wound.

Duke ran after him. He hated to think that Tyler might be dead, but the man wasn't moving. He had been an excellent librarian and, Duke realized now, a good friend as well. Duke wished he had known him better. He also wished he had known that Prometheus was a mutual friend. Maybe then their time spent together in the library would have passed better.

"I shot you," Flaugherty said to Lucas. "You should be dead."

"Yeah, you shot me, all right. Right in the ass. I guess your aim was off."

Flaugherty, still on his knees with his arms raised, said: "No way. No *way* did I miss you that badly."

"I guess you did," Lucas said.

Then Prometheus startled them all by saying, "Well, stupid man, you missed Tyler here completely. I can find no wound at all. In fact, I think he fainted."

"What?" Flaugherty said.

"I'm afraid so," Prometheus said, and even as he spoke Tyler James began to stir. Then he sat up.

"What happened?"

Duke watched all of this, fascinated. He could still see a small puddle of blood where Tyler had been laying, but as far as bullet wounds went, he couldn't see where the injury might have occurred.

"This is bullshit," Flaugherty said. "I hit both of you dead on. I know it."

"Apparently you didn't," Prometheus said. His voice was teasing. "I wish we could stay around and discuss it, Tim, I really do." He looked at Tyler and Lucas. "Will you stay here with him? I really do not want to risk all of us going…or him following us."

They nodded. "Sure," Lucas said. He was grimacing, but he held the gun steady enough on Flaugherty.

Prometheus turned to Duke. "Perhaps you would like to stay here, as well?"

Duke shook his head.

"I did not think so. Okay, let us go then." He moved toward the machine in the closet, and Duke followed close behind him.

Duke turned around and signed to Tyler: "Will you two be all right?"

"We'll be okay," Tyler said. "We've got a special place for 'ol Flattery here, now that you're no longer locked up there."

"Wait a minute, wait," Flaugherty babbled. "You can't lock me up. Derek will find out, he'll get both of you for this, he'll—"

That was all he got out, because Lucas brought the butt of the gun up and connected squarely with Flaugherty's chin. He slumped to the floor, unconscious.

Duke smiled at Lucas. "That was excellent," he signed.

Lucas returned the smile. "Good luck, guys."

"And to you, as well, Lucas," Prometheus said. Then he turned, took Duke by the hand, and the two walked through the rippling doorway and disappeared.

* * * * *

"SURRENDER THE CHILD NOW," Derek Tarkington hollered through the electric bullhorn. "WE KNOW YOU'RE IN THERE, O'DONNELL, TEMPLETON. YOU ARE SURROUNDED."

There was no reply, and after thirty seconds he raised the bullhorn again.

"THIS IS YOUR LAST WARNING. I REPEAT, THIS IS YOUR LAST WARNING. COME OUT NOW, OR WE'LL HAVE TO FORCE YOU OUT."

After another minute there was still no reply. The house looked silent and, Derek thought, empty.

But of course, that couldn't be. He himself had seen someone at a front window just minutes ago.

"Do you think they're armed?" he asked Calhoun, who was beside him behind the hood of the truck.

"We have to assume they are," Calhoun said.

Derek nodded. "Okay," He turned to the agents in the jeep. "Bring her over here."

He watched as two men tugged and pulled at Valerie Malcolm, until they had her out of the vehicle. They brought her to the truck, each of them holding her by one arm. Then Derek raised the bullhorn again: "WE HAVE YOUR WIFE, MR. MALCOLM. SURRENDER THE CHILD, AND WE WILL SPARE HER." He paused a moment to let that sink in. "YOU HAVE ONE MINUTE. THEN WE ARE COMING IN."

Derek turned to Calhoun. "Which agents do you want to send in?"

Calhoun nodded to two men who were crouched behind a nearby tree, one looking nervous, the other anxious. "Milcheck and Lomax over there."

"Milcheck! Lomax!" he called. "Get over here."

The two men ran over in a low crouch, Lomax carrying an AK-47 and Milcheck toting a handgun. "Sir!" Lomax said. Milcheck merely nodded. He was the one who looked nervous.

Derek said: "In one minute you two will go in through the front door and bring out the child. If you have to shoot the others, do it, but make *damn* sure you bring that child out alive. Tell them that Mrs. Malcolm here gets a bullet if they do not cooperate."

"Yes, sir!" Lomax snapped.

"Yes, sir," Milcheck muttered.

Derek looked at him. "Are you going to be able to handle this?"

"Of course...sir," Milcheck said.

"Good," he said. He looked at his watch. "Please move to the front entrance and wait for my signal."

The two men ran to the house and positioned themselves on either side of the door.

"YOU NOW HAVE THIRTY SECONDS!" Derek yelled through the bullhorn.

Again, there was no reply. Thirty seconds later Derek gave the signal, and the agents advanced through the door.

*****

THIRTY-SIX

The door gave in with a splintering crunch. One good kick from Lomax's foot did the trick. Guns held out in front of them, he and John entered the cabin.

Before going in, John had wondered what to expect on the inside. He still held—only to himself, of course—that there was something not right with this operation, and that the Malcolm's child was as ordinary as they come. He'd held him once, for goodness' sake. An ordinary baby if he'd ever seen one, except…except he knew better, didn't he? If the child was normal there would be no need of the government's involvement, and of the firepower assembled outside. Still, he hated like hell to take the same position as Lomax and the others did—that the child was dangerous, a serious threat. He just could not imagine it. And though he didn't know what to expect when he and Lomax entered the house, he certainly did not expect what they found.

The place was empty, deserted.

There was a small work station of sorts set up in the living room; a laptop and modem, a printer, a couple of cellular phones. John recognized the equipment as that which had belonged to he and Mark. That was it. After a quick check of all the rooms and bathroom—including closets—it was apparent no one was here.

"This is ridiculous," Lomax said. "Where are they?"

"Not here."

"Bullshit. I saw someone moving around in here, didn't you?"

John had to admit he had. At least he *thought* he had. "Maybe we really didn't see anyone," he said. "It could have been a glare on the windows. You know, the leaves on the trees moving."

"No," Lomax said. "They were in here. I know it. Let's check out back."

John followed him to the sliding doors, which were open. They walked out onto the deck, which ran the length of the house and had rails and lattice work all the way around. Most of the deck was shady, but it was clear that it, too, was deserted.

Lomax walked over to the railing and looked over the side, which was steep. There was an agent to the left, among some trees, and Lomax shrugged his shoulders at him. "There's no one here!" he hollered. "Tell Calhoun that the house is all clear!" The man nodded, then left his position and ran up the hill, toward the driveway.

Lomax went back inside, but John lingered a moment in the sunshine outside the door. It was odd, but for some reason he felt as if he were being watched. It was possible, he guessed. There *were* other agents around the house, concealed behind various trees. But he didn't think the feeling came from any of them. Instead, it was more like a presence. He felt as though something was surrounding him, in fact.

A chill made him shudder. The silence around the house was almost eerie. Even the agents in front of the place were quiet. John supposed they were all letting the bad news sink in that the place was empty. Yet, the feeling still persisted: someone…*something* was watching him.

Then Lomax popped his head through the sliding doors. "Get ready. Calhoun has just called headquarters. They're going to activate the trackers again. See where they went."

"Oh, great," John said. "That's just what I need."

Lomax left, and John was turning to follow him when his stomach cramped. He cried out in pain…and his cry echoed eerily in the silence. It seemed to come from directly behind him, as well as from his mouth.

He turned around slowly and looked down.

His eyes widened.

There were two small puddles of vomit on the wood deck. As he watched, a few small dollops fell out of the air and landed on top of one messy puddle. He looked up, thinking that whichever agents had done it might be located on the roof of the house. But no one was up there. He backed up and looked. The roof was bare except for a scattering of dry leaves and twigs.

"Stay right where you are," a voice said from near the door.

"What?" John said. "Lomax?"

"No. Not Lomax," the voice said, and then John heard something that curdled his blood, because he couldn't see where it had come from: it was the playful giggle of a very small person—a child, in fact.

He turned around, trying to look in all directions at once.

Nothing.

No one was there.

He looked down. The two puddles were still on the deck, although a lot of each had run through the spaces between boards. He could even hear the stuff dripping onto the ground beneath the decking.

What the hell?

The giggle came again, from behind him, and he turned. Nothing.

And then someone…appeared…on the deck. Just like that—snap—and he was there. John had time to notice that he bore a passing resemblance to the actor Nicolas Cage, and then he did what came natural to him at that point: he turned and fled through the sliding doors, back into the house.

* * * * *

Lomax was just outside the front door, conferring with Derek, Calhoun, and Anderson. John almost ran into them before he could stop, breathing hard and shaking uncontrollably.

"What the hell's wrong with you?" Lomax said, and then he looked over John's shoulder, into the house, and said softly. "Impossible."

John, Derek, and the director all turned and followed Mark's gaze.

Walking across the living room were ex-agents Adrian O'Donnell and Bobby Templeton, O'Donnell holding a rifle out in front of him. And behind them was Kenneth Malcolm, holding the child, and an older man whom they didn't know.

* * * * *

In the hallway, Ken had asked Chance about his ability to turn invisible. He had witnessed this phenomenon in the early spring, when he thought the baby had disappeared from his playpen behind their home in Jonesboro, although he hadn't at the time known it for what it really was. Two days ago, Chance had *told* him that he could become invisible.

The patch of sunlight near the door in the living room, and on a portion of the deck, had reminded Ken of his son's ability, and he had then asked Chance another question: "If you hold onto something... some*one*...when you are invisible, will that object, or person, *also* disappear?" Chance's answer had been a simple one, and had confirmed what Ken suspected, and what Adrian and Bobby had said to him at the airport that day that seemed so long ago. *If you want a normal child, keep him out of the sun.*

"As long as we are in the sunlight," Chance had said in his small voice. "As long as I am, at least."

Then Ken told Adrian, Bobby, and Darrel his idea. Bobby thought it might work, but Darrel had a confused look on his round face, although he went along willingly enough. He had not seen Chance the way Ken had the past couple of days.

They had simply linked hands, the five of them, and walked into the sunlight near the door, Chance leading them, and as soon as he reached the sunlight that slanted in to the room, he disappeared. They all had. When Tarkington had started with the bullhorn, they had eased through the open door and outside, onto the deck.

Ken thought that becoming invisible would be a strange, if not terrible, feeling. But he had been surprised: although he could no longer see the others, or himself, he could nevertheless feel Chance and Adrian's hands. If he didn't look down, he found he could walk just fine.

And everything had gone okay for a while, even though one of the agents—who Ken recognized as the man who'd come to his house with car problems one dark night—seemed to sense their presence on the deck. At one point the man had almost brushed up against him.

Then they had activated the damn trackers again, and when the agent heard Adrian and Bobby's retching he had turned around and spotted the telltale signs on the deck. Adrian had then broken the link, pulled the gun down by the strap off his shoulder, and advanced toward the man.

But it wasn't fast enough, and the man had run through the house like he'd seen a ghost. Chance's giggles had not helped things, of course, but in a way it *was* funny. It was.

After the agent exited through the front door in the kitchen, Adrian whispered for everyone to go inside and release the link. "We're going to have to get out of this the hard way," he had said, a smile like a grimace on his face.

And now here they were, Ken, his father, and Chance, following Adrian and Bobby to the door.

Ken saw the surprised looks on the agents outside as those men noticed them walking across the living room. "We sure could use that miracle you were wishing for about now," he muttered to Bobby.

"I'm *still* wishing," Bobby said ruefully. "Just stay behind us."

Walking at a steady pace, the five of them reached the front door and went outside.

* * * * *

Ken caught a glimpse of Valerie as they emerged from the cabin.

She was up on the driveway, in front of a jeep, being retained by two blank-faced men in camouflage.

"Valerie!" Ken yelled. She hollered in return when she saw him and Chance. "Let her go," Ken told the man in front of him.

"Not just yet," said one of the men. "I'm William Calhoun, director of the CIA. Mr. Malcolm, I would like to make this as easy as I can. Look around you."

Ken did. Although Adrian had a gun pointed at the men in the front yard, he could see that there were at least twenty other guns pointed in their direction from behind trees and an assortment of Army vehicles. His shoulders wanted to slump but he forced them up straight. An odd sort of anger had stolen over him when exiting the house, and he didn't want to give these men the impression that he was defeated. One look at Valerie had melted most of the anger away. Now he just wanted her back safely. Just her and Chance and his father, and everyone else could go to hell and back for all he cared.

He looked squarely at Calhoun: "I don't care if you're the President of the United States. I want those men to let go of my wife, right now."

The man standing next to Calhoun spoke up then. "Mr. Malcolm? Derek Tarkington. Let's cut the crap here. We have something *you* want, and you have something *we* want. It looks like a simple trade to me. What do you say?" He spread his hands—which held no weapon—in front of him.

"I say that *you're* the one spreading the crap here," Ken said, his voice laced with scorn, and the anger returning like a combustible fuel. "This is my son here. *My* son, through a legal adoption. And even if I *did* turn him over to you, and you turned over my wife, you would just have these men shoot us down like dogs once you had Chance. *All* of us." He paused a moment while he looked around, and then glared again at the man. "You wanted to cut through the crap? I believe I just did."

"You said it right, Ken," Adrian said. "That's exactly what will happen."

Derek looked at the ex-agent. "Adrian," he said. "Bobby. I'm sorry to see that you two got mixed up in all of this. It makes me really sad."

"You're sorry, all right," Bobby said in a low voice.

"What was that?" Derek said.

Bobby looked hard at the man. "I said go to hell."

Derek smiled and turned back to Ken. "What will it be, Mr. Malcolm? Hmm? The child, or your wife?" He nodded to one of the men holding Valerie. The agent on her right pulled a handgun out of a holster and put it to her head. Ken heard her whimper.

"Well?" Derek said. "If you *don't* give us the child, we will shoot your wife, then the four of you, and we will take the child anyway." He smiled. "Hand him over right now, and we'll do the same with your wife. Then, perhaps, you will both live through this." He turned to Bobby and Adrian. "You two. Put that gun down and move away from this man."

"Screw you," Adrian said plainly.

"Do it now, or Mrs. Malcolm gets it. I promise you that, and you know I mean what I say."

Reluctantly, Adrian threw the weapon down and he and Bobby moved away from Ken, Darrel and Chance.

Derek nodded again at some agents, and four of them immediately trained their weapons on Adrian and Bobby.

"Now, Mr. Malcolm," Derek said. "Shall we make this a little more interesting? Hand over that child, or your wife *and* two of your close friends die. What do you say?"

Ken stared hard at the man. He was scared silly, but there wasn't much he could do. It all came down to this, he guessed, and in the end it wouldn't matter, anyway. This man was just playing here—Ken could see it in his eyes. He would have his men slaughter all of them, he and Valerie included. "Screw you," he said, echoing Adrian's sentiments. "Screw *all* of you."

There was a palpable silence around the yard as that statement sank in. A few men shuffled, as though uneasy.

Derek's smile faded. He looked at Ken, who could see nothing but madness swirling there. "Okay, hero," Derek said. "Okay." He turned to Calhoun. "We go with Plan B, I guess. Better than nothing, hmm? Pick your agent."

Calhoun looked around. "Milcheck! Get over here!"

Ken watched as the nervous-looking agent came over, his gun held down at his side. "Sir?"

Calhoun looked flustered, but resigned, and he nodded toward Derek, who said in an offhand way. "Agent Milcheck, please shoot this child for me, and then shoot his...father. When that is finished, we will take care of the rest. I'm tired of fooling with this man. Besides," he said, turning to address Calhoun, we have the procedure down now, and we can always make more children like him."

Derek moved to the side, his eyes never leaving Ken's.

"Hurry, please, agent Milcheck.

* * * * *

THIRTY-SEVEN

Ken swallowed, his throat parched and dry. He held Chance close to him and it seemed, for a moment, as if the two of them were the only people here, set apart from everyone and everything, including Valerie. He vaguely recognized the feeling as an acceptance of sorts; this was how it was going to end, then. Okay. He would accept that. But what could he do in the precious little time he had left? What could he do *with* the time?

He'd had a close friend at work a few years ago who had been diagnosed with pancreatic cancer—a virtual death sentence. The guy had found out after it was too late for any treatment that might postpone the inevitable. He had died only a few months later, in great pain that was dimmed only by large amounts of morphine, which kept him incoherent and asleep most of the time. Ken had—on occasion—mentally put himself in his friend's shoes during those last two months and the one following, and he would wonder what it might possibly be like knowing you were close to your end. Most importantly, what he would do with the remaining time allotted him. Each time he would wind up at the same scenario; he would spend as much of it as possible with his wife, let her know how much he loved her—*be* with her.

Now he had his wife *and* Chance—a family. But he had much less time than his unfortunate friend had been blessed with.

And he realized it *had* been a blessing. Time always was.

He held Chance tight.

He looked for his wife among the men and vehicles, found her.

"I love you, Valerie!" he yelled. "I'll always love you!"

He heard her sobs and thought his heart would burst.

He leaned down and whispered in his son's ear: "And I love you, too, buddy. I've loved you since the day we adopted you."

A tear ran from his cheek and dropped onto Chance's upturned face. "I love you, too, Daddy," he said in a small voice. Then he leaned closer to Ken and whispered: "Don't worry. It's going to be okay."

Ken nodded, and then kissed his son. As though in slow motion, the agent in front of Ken raised his gun and pointed it and him and Chester. Ken saw something in the man's eyes that might have been compassion or, perhaps, an inner torture the likes of which Ken could not comprehend.

Then the agent's mouth flattened in a grimace of determination.

Here it comes, Ken thought.

He closed his eyes, hugged his son close, and waited for it to happen.

* * * * *

John held the gun at his side as he stood in front of Kenneth Malcolm. The hand holding it began to shake, but he fought it as best he could. He was completely horrified at what he had been commanded to do. The only alternative would be to put the gun to his own head and pull the trigger, because he knew if he failed to obey this order, he himself would be shot, and some other agent would be forced to stand here and shoot this child and his father. That other agent would probably be Lomax, and John was beginning to like the man a little. Enough so, that he would not want this same task put on Mark.

He felt three dozen sets of eyes upon him, and a cold sweat broke on his brow. Tarkington's words still echoed inside his head: *"Hurry, please, agent Milcheck."*

John thought of Lily, and how he had killed her husband. He had done so while the man was begging him not to, and he had done it without knowing that Garret Burgess had already made the diabolic arrangements for Lily's own death. He had since regretted having done that. Many times over he had regretted it, and not only because it had gotten Lily killed. Aside from that, Garret Burgess had been guilty only of spousal abuse, and while that was bad, the law did not administer the death penalty to those who were guilty of such an atrocity.

Now, he was being told to take an innocent life—he had been ordered to take *two*. He had not witnessed anything by Mr. Malcolm *or* his son that would warrant the death of either. It wasn't fair that he should have to do this. He had killed a couple of times since the Burgess affair, but each had been in self-defense on some assignment or another.

But this...

This was a *child*. How could he do it? He had been ordered to murder a human being—and he knew he would do it, that he would *have* to—but it wasn't the least bit fair.

John raised the gun and pointed it at Mr. Malcolm. He had been ordered to shoot the child first, but Mr. Malcolm was holding the boy close and was half-turned away from John, whispering to the child. One shot from the .44 caliber gun would effectively kill them both.

Then Kenneth Malcolm looked around, as though searching for someone. Probably his wife. He had already cried out to her in a heart-wrenching voice. Then he turned, looked at John, and closed his eyes.

He was waiting, John saw. Waiting for the bullet to slam into him.

That decided John. The man would have to wait no longer. He applied pressure on the trigger.

The yard was silent, all eyes on John.

And he turned and shot Derek Tarkington, point blank, in the head. Then he turned the gun on William Calhoun.

After that, things happened quickly.

* * * * *

The report from the single gunshot echoed across the mountain, and was punctuated by the mail sack thud of Derek's body hitting the ground.

Calhoun looked down the barrel of the gun. "John. What are you doing?"

The agent was breathing hard, his hand shaking, but not enough to cause the big gun to waver away from Calhoun's face. "I don't know why you want the child so bad," John said, "because you haven't told me everything there is to know about this...project of yours. But I will *not* shoot an unarmed child, *or* his father. Now, you call these men off and clear them out of here or you join your partner there, on the ground."

"John," Calhoun said in almost as sad a tone as Derek had used with Adrian and Bobby. "You don't understand what you're doing here, what you've done."

"I understand plenty," John said. "Now, call them off."

Calhoun looked over past John at a cluster of agents, who appeared taken aback by these new developments. "The plan has not changed!" he yelled. "Fire at will, men, starting with the child." He turned and looked at Milcheck. "Go ahead, John. You can't bargain with me on this, so go on and shoot if you...oh my *God!*"

Calhoun was looking over John's shoulder, so he was the first to see Lone Star as he exited the back of the covered truck.

The agents who were scattered around the yard had raised their weapons to carry out Calhoun's command when they caught the director's horrified gaze and turned to look themselves.

Prometheus, in his native form, walked slowly toward the house. A soft glow surrounded him, as though he were wrapped in a yellow florescent cloak. Duke Tarkington followed close behind him, trying to look everywhere at once, but looking mostly at the slumped figure lying on the ground.

"Someone shoot him!" Calhoun yelled as he backed toward the house. "For God's sake, *shoot* him!"

Agent Anderson, he of the St. Louis office and the militant demeanor, strode up beside Calhoun and pointed his gun at Prometheus. A brilliant white beam of light flashed from somewhere around Lone Star's head and hit the agent squarely in the chest. The wound was mortal, and huge. Through it, Calhoun could see Lone Star advancing, and at his peripherals he was aware of a big commotion as agents hollered and began to run. There was also a sharp burst of gunfire, and Calhoun caught a glimpse of O'Donnell and Templeton slumping to the ground.

It was the dream he'd had two nights ago come to life, except in the dream it had been dark, the sun blotted out by a surreal darkness, and bolts of liquid fire had been streaking everywhere from a gigantic weapon: Lone Star

Calhoun wanted to do what most of his agents were now doing—running—but he found he couldn't. He could only watch as Lone Star advanced toward him, enveloped in that eerie glow.

* * * * *

At the first sight of the being emerging from the back of the truck, Darrel was filled with a mixture of surprise, fear, and joy. There was no question, in his mind, that he was looking at an alien, and that is what caused the thrill through his body. He had believed in aliens for so many years, at the expense of his integrity (as perceived by everyone he knew, including his own son—who would have never said so out loud, Darrel knew), and it was almost like elation that his beliefs were validated at this moment.

The fear came from watching his son and grandchild on the brink of death at the hands of the agent who had turned and shot his commanding officer. But it hadn't ended there. The other man's command for his agents to fire at will seemed to Darrel like the true end. For real, this time.

When several agents raised their weapons, Darrel threw himself at Ken and Chance, knocking them to the ground. He waited for the piercing sting of the bullets he was sure would riddle his body at any moment. He was okay with that. He felt an odd sort of joy, of satisfaction, of doing something noble at the moment of his death. Protecting those he loved was noble enough for him.

But the bullets never came, and Darrel looked up.

The being was advancing slowly across the yard. A burst of shots rang out, and Darrel saw Adrian O'Donnell and Bobby Templeton collapse in a heap against the house. Some of the men had apparently hung around long enough to carry out their final orders.

Then Ken and Chance were squirming beneath him.

"Let us up, Dad," Ken said. "Let us up."

Darrel got up, and as soon as he did Chance broke loose from Ken and ran toward Adrian and Bobby. Darrel saw an agent near the right side of the house raise his gun and train it on the child as he ran. Darrel could do nothing but watch.

Then a beam of light struck the agent in the chest and nearly tore off his upper body. Other nearby agents threw down their weapons and bolted into the trees.

And a few moments later something stranger happened: it began to grow dark, as though the day was moving rapidly toward dusk.

* * * * *

Valerie struggled against the two men who held her, and when the agent shot the man who had commanded him to kill Ken and Chance she struggled harder still, but to no avail.

It wasn't until the strange being emerged from the truck that their grips loosened, and she was able to break free with a quick jerk. She ran toward the house and saw a tangled pile of bodies near the door where

Ken, Chance, and Darrel had been standing. "No!" she screamed. "Oh, God, *no!*" She started toward them, and stopped when a sharp bolt of light zipped past her and hit a man who had his gun raised and pointed at Chance—who wasn't dead after all. The man was turned into a grizzly mess that she barely registered.

Then Chance was bent over one of the men, who was slowly sitting up and rubbing the front of his neck. There were so many people running around, so many yells and screams, that she sensed she was crossing a battlefield to get to her husband and son, instead of a shallow front yard.

As she moved again toward the house, she saw that Ken and Darrel were once more on their feet, and that Chance was leaning over the other downed man. He looked like a miniature doctor checking for a pulse. That's the image that came to mind, anyway, and she ran toward him. But before she could reach him, she was intercepted, and strong arms embraced her.

And it was Ken. "Valerie, Val. Oh, thank God, are you all right?" His hands roamed over her face and head, searching for nonexistent injuries, and in spite of all the chaos around her she had never left so much relief. Together she and Ken ran to Chance and scooped him up. They planted kisses all over his face.

She looked down and saw the second man struggling to his feet. His eyes looked dazed, and he rubbed a bright red spot on his chest—blood, Valerie saw—with one shaking hand.

"You okay, Bobby?" Ken said.

"Gone," the man said. "Gone."

"What's he talking about?" Valerie said.

"You're still here, Bobby, you're alive," Ken told him.

"Gone," Bobby said again.

Then Valerie and Ken turned around as Chance said: "Father." And the child pointed to the alien being as the sky abruptly darkened.

* * * * *

"Stay with me," Prometheus had told Duke after they had emerged through the portal and into the back of the Army truck. "And wherever I go, stay just behind me. Do you understand?"

Duke had nodded.

Prometheus had then held one of Duke's hands. "Your father must die today, Duke. I know you may not understand that, and that you still hold something for him deep inside your heart."

Duke had only stared at him, his eyes large and scared.

"But always know this," Prometheus said. "What you hold for your father inside you is something you will always have, and it is more than he ever was, or ever will be. Do you know what I mean by that?"

Again Duke nodded, and a tear spilled down his cheek. "I understand," he signed.

Prometheus looked at him with those strange almond-shaped eyes. He looked for what seemed a long time. "Remember the day at the compound, when I told you that you would overcome everything? I was not speaking only of the loss of your voice, but everything you had yet to endure...including *this* moment. And everything you've *still* yet to endure. Do you remember?"

Duke nodded again. If he'd *had* a tongue he wasn't sure he would, at this moment, be capable of speech.

"I meant that, as well," Prometheus said. "My time here is not long now, Duke. I am sick. I never told you before, but I only tell you now because it will take the last of my strength and power to do what must be done here. And if I must walk the Final Path today, I would take my last journey on this earth with the one person who has been my one, *true* friend. That is you, Duke." He paused then, and there was a moment of comfortable silence between them that sealed their friendship even more than had the Saturday morning chess games.

"I will save my child," Prometheus said with conviction, "and whether I live or not will be of no consequence. He will be enough. He will show the world...he will show everyone."

And those were the last words Prometheus ever spoke to Duke. A few moments later he was moving down the steps at the rear of the truck, and Duke walked that last journey with him, just like Prometheus—*his* one, true friend—had asked him to do.

* * * * *

John dropped the gun he was pointing at Calhoun as he watched the small being approach. He registered the director's orders to shoot the strange creature, but little else. As the being drew close in front of the director, John found himself standing inside the luminescent glow surrounding the alien (*yes, an alien,* he thought, *like in all the movies*).

John was captured by that soft glow, cloaked in it…and he suddenly understood everything.

*****

The glow surrounding Lone Star was soft and radiant, and it stopped within six inches of Calhoun, although the director noticed that it had engulfed agent Milcheck.

"William Calhoun," Lone Star said, and the director found he could not answer; could not, even, meet that dark gaze.

"You are a powerful man," Lone Star said, "but one who does not understand what that power can do, nor the consequences of its misuse."

"How…?" Calhoun tried. "How…?"

"Not important. What *is* important is that I need you. To be more precise, my *son* needs you. In the days and weeks ahead, he will need you to help start what he is meant to accomplish during his time here."

"I don't…I can't…" Calhoun shook his head as though shaking a thought from his mind. He looked at Lone Star. "You…you must be eliminated. You must be…"

"It is okay, William. I will show you. I will help you to see."

Prometheus, Lone Star, the Subject—whatever name given to him anywhere—moved forward, and the light enveloped the director. Calhoun's eyelashes fluttered and his eyes rolled up to the whites. His body shook, but subtly, like soft ripples on a pond.

He opened his eyes…and he saw.

*****

THIRTY-EIGHT

"Father," a small voice repeated. "Father!"

Prometheus smiled as Chance ran across the yard. Valerie tried to grab the child, but Ken restrained her gently. "Don't, Val," he said. "Let him go."

As they watched, Chance wrapped his small arms around his father's waist and was engulfed in the yellow glow.

Adrian and Bobby stumbled over. Bobby seemed to have gained back most of his equilibrium.

"Why did you think you were dead?" Ken asked him.

"What do you mean?"

"Well, you kept saying, 'gone', over and over."

Bobby smiled. "I was talking about the wound on my chest. Where one of those guys shot me."

"And the one in my neck," Adrian said. "It's gone as well, Ken. Don't you *see?* Chance did this to us. Chance *healed* us."

"Oh my God," Valerie said softly. "You're serious, aren't you?"

"Of course we are," Adrian said. "And look up there." He pointed through the trees, to the darkened sky.

And the sky wasn't an early dusk at all. It had darkened with the approach of three large ships, all of which hovered silently over the property and surrounding woods, and all of which held the complete attention of every other person in the yard. Every agent who was still present—there were a few—stood looking up, their necks craned back, their eyes and mouths wide.

"Oh my God," Valerie said again.

Ken pulled her close to him, hugged her tight. "That's where

Chance's real father came from." He pointed. "Up there, with them."

"I don't understand all of this," Valerie said in a trembling voice. "Oh, Ken, what's going on?"

"Shh," he said. "it's okay, honey. I'll tell you everything I know later, and I have a feeling that Chance will take care of the rest. *Look!*" he said and pointed at the ships.

Bright beams of light streamed from the bottom of all three ships. They were not angry bursts like those that had somehow been produced by Chance's father. Instead, they resembled searchlights. And they indeed appeared to be searching, for when one of them landed on an agent it stopped, and then winked out, taking the agent with it.

All Ken could see was the gray, circular bottoms of the massive ships, and the lights. They didn't need to see more to know what they were. The beams of light probed the surrounding woods, stopped when they found what they were in search of, and then winked out, one by one.

Chance came running back to Ken and Valerie as more beams came down from directly overhead and trained on each of them, and on the agents left in the yard. Valerie scooped him up, and Ken put his arms around them both.

"It's going to be okay, Mommy," Chance said, smiling. "Everything is going to be okay." He turned toward Prometheus and waved. "Good-bye, father." It was brief, and Ken guessed that the two had said their own good-byes out in the yard, while everyone else's attention had been on the ships. He also thought that had probably been the best—and most private—way for both of them.

Prometheus waved back, and to Ken his face was both sad and happy, although it was hard to distinguish through his alien features. What was even sadder was the look on the young man's face who stood behind, and slightly to the left of, Prometheus. The young man was curiously silent, but his body was wracked and shaking with sobs. Ken raised a hand in return and then the others did, as well. Even the three agents left in the yard.

* * * * *

Prometheus, his glow now diminished, turned and waved at Duke *(remember, Duke, always remember)* before the beam of light that was trained on him winked out…and then Prometheus was gone.

The remaining lights blinked out all at once, leaving everyone where they were. No one else was taken.

* * * * *

The small group of people watched as the ships moved silently to the north, gaining speed. As they departed the sun reappeared, sprinkling the yard in dazzling rays of light that were warm and somehow welcoming. The trees rustled in the light breeze.

And in the air around the small group of people was a feeling of blessed relief, a sense of impending change.

And a shared sense of wonder at what the future might hold.

* * * * *

AFTER

Five Years Later

A journey can be either difficult, or easy.

Society's journey into the technological age had been slow, and it had really begun with the Roswell incident in 1947, when a sole captive from an alien race had been forced by the U.S. government to teach certain leaders what he knew. Even though this captive and his race, morally reluctant of any type of retaliatory warfare, would have, in time, given it freely.

In spite of the resultant modern wonders, that journey had been difficult, at the costs of wars, tyranny, hunger, and other atrocities.

The journey that began in the weeks and months following the events at a small cabin in northern Arkansas, was an easier one.

With the last of his strength, an alien being named Prometheus had passed on to humanity his race's most precious gift, and he gave it to three people: John Milcheck, William Calhoun, and to his own son, a child named Chance, who had been born during the aftermath of an accidental nuclear detonation, the most terrible technology ever created by man.

The greatest thing about Prometheus' gift was that it could be passed from one person to another, and that each person who came in contact with this new 'light' of understanding saw that, if humanity were to live peacefully, as one, with their many neighbors in this vast universe, then they would first have to learn to exist that way with each other.

And they also saw that it was, indeed, possible.

In time, even more would be.

* * * * *

It was a new day...a new world.

* * * * *

"Did you remember the candles?"

"I certainly did," Ken said. "I also got this," and he pulled something from behind his back. It was a child's baseball glove. "Don't you think it's time?"

Valerie laughed. "Well-l-l...I guess so."

Ken hugged her close. "I love you, Val."

"And I love you," she said, "but that doesn't mean you get out of any work. Put the silverware on the table for me, will you?"

He sighed in a playful imitation of resignation. "Okay, if I must. But are you sure we have enough?"

"I bought two new sets to match our old one, so I think we'll be okay. I think Mom is glad I'm not borrowing hers, as usual."

Ken tossed her the glove and she caught it deftly. "Wrap this for me and you've got a deal. Even swap. You know how awful I wrap."

"Deal," Valerie said. "I think I have just enough time."

Twenty minutes later the table was set, the food prepared, and the first guests arrived: Adrian O'Donnell and Bobby Templeton.

Bobby's hair had thinned a little more, edging him closer to that fabled state of baldness. Adrian's hair had grayed some, but he still resembled Nicolas Cage. The two of them had just returned from Pakistan, where they were finishing up their work in that country.

"Where is the man of the hour?" Adrian said as he held out two wrapped gifts.

"Taking a nap." Valerie took the packages from him. "Growing boys need their rest." She laughed. "That kid has more energy than three of me. Come on in the kitchen and enjoy these few quiet moments. I've got coffee on."

"Sounds great."

Five minutes later two more guests arrived and everyone moved into the living room with fresh coffee. John Milcheck and William Calhoun were both dressed in charcoal gray suits and red ties. Their initial work in Washington D.C.—with former president Ronnie Clayton and his cabinet—had been completed nearly five years ago. They had then spent a lot of time with each member of the House and Senate, as well as various other government agencies—both legitimate and covert. They were now coordinating their efforts with these leaders, as well as those with the expanded U.N., to take Prometheus' gift to a few remaining Third World countries. Neither man looked as though he had aged much despite what Ken and Valerie thought must be a very demanding job.

Mark and Rita Lomax arrived next, holding hands like new lovers even though they had not been newlyweds for better than four years. As they joined the group in the living room and sat down, each of them pulled out a cellular phone and laid it on an end table, within easy reach. Every person in the room was aware of how much Mark enjoyed civilian life.

Another chime from the doorbell announced Duke Tarkington, Lucas Matthews, and Tyler James, who shook hands all around and handed Valerie a shopping bag filled with wrapped gifts. The three men now ran the Nevada compound and had—with the help of some of its former residents—turned it into one of the world's most famous tourist sites. Its voluminous library was its most popular attraction, the wealth of knowledge there unrivaled.

Valerie's parents arrived next, and when she opened the front door they were out on the steps, arguing.

"I thought *I* was buying the gift, and he thought *he* was, and we ended up getting the same thing," Beatrice Holman said as she entered the foyer. "That's the second time this month that's happened."

Valerie laughed, took their gifts—"I'm sure he'll want two of whatever it is," she told her mother—and they joined the others in the living room.

When the last two people arrived, everyone was just sitting down in the dining room to a magnificent dinner of lobster, shrimp Creole, a spicy Cajun gumbo, and garlic toast.

Ken looked up and smiled, and everyone turned as the two new arrivals entered the room. "Can't you make it *anywhere* on time, Dad?"

Darrel Malcolm smiled, his cheeks slightly blushed. "Oh, hell, son. You know how excited I get when I go sight-seeing with my buddy here."

All eyes turned to Chance, who stood, smiling, next to Darrel.

Chance was almost seven now. His hair had turned from the fine blonde it had been when he was a toddler, to a sandy brown that accented his large brown eyes. His smile was as sweet as it had ever been. "Hello, everyone," he said. Then he looked around the table and asked Valerie: "Mom, where's—?"

"Mommy," a small voice said from the doorway behind Darrel and Chance. "Is it time yet?"

"*There* he is," Chance said. He ruffled the youngster's hair. "Are you awake, Ethan?"

Ken and Valerie's son grinned at Chance, and the smile was just as wide as Chance's had been at that age—and just as charming. "Yes, Chancers. I'm awake. Is it my birthday yet?"

"It sure is," Valerie said, coming around the table and scooping him up. She hugged him. "I've got a nice plate of your favorite food waiting, all of our friends are here, and there's a big birthday cake with three candles for after. And there's ice cream, and lots of presents for you, too. Sound okay?"

"Yeah!" Ethan said with an exuberance only a child can truly know. "That sounds *good!*"

Everyone laughed then, and that, too, felt good.

* * * * *

The dishes were dried and put away, the company gone, and the house was quiet except for an occasional thump on the ceiling. Darrel had stayed on for a while and he and Chance were upstairs playing with Ethan. Ken figured his father was also undoubtedly having a discussion with Chance about where the two of them might travel next—which solar system, if Ken knew his father.

He and Valerie went outside onto the back patio, beneath an open sky filled with stars that sparkled like white gemstones. He reached for her hand and held it. They breathed deeply of the clean, refreshing air, and found it as sweet as life.

For life *was* sweet, and the air *was* clean.

The world around them had changed.

It had changed so much.

Automobiles, oil companies, and other pollutants were already rare, and would soon no longer be a necessity at all. Nor would war, or even the threat of war. It was becoming a world led by a new type of government, a new Order; one based not on politics, but on individuals, and families. And on neighbors. A world where no cancer spoiled living cells, no disease rotted living tissue. A world where no person starved for food, or for enlightenment.

Ken held his wife's hand. A cool breeze blew against his forehead. He gazed upward.

Soon, he knew, the world would move beyond what he could see…

…to what he, his friends, and his family had already embraced.

*****

Afterword

This story is set in 1996, and reflects the era during which it was first conceived and put down on paper. It went through very few changes between 2000, when the first draft was finished, and 2012, when it was pulled out of the trunk and dusted off for a final rewrite.

Even then, I was very aware that the story could not be updated to reflect current, more modern technologies. If you've read it, you know what I'm talking about; it wouldn't work.

Yet I liked the story as it was, anyway. Afterall, while technology seems to constantly change, people rarely do, and often it's simply because they don't realize they *can*. Technologies are handy, and as plot devices are fun, but in the long run, in *any* era, people are more complicated, more complex, and *much* more interesting.

November, 2023

About the Author

Ivan Tritch lives with his wife, Melissa, in the northern part of Arkansas, where much of this novel is set.